ALSO BY M. G. VASSANJI

The In-Between World of Vikram Lall

The In-Between World
of Vikram Lall

———————

M. G. VASSANJI

ALFRED A. KNOPF NEW YORK 2004

THIS IS A BORZOI BOOK
PUBLISHED BY ALFRED A. KNOPF

Copyright © 2003 by M. G. Vassanji

All rights reserved under International and Pan-American Copyright
Conventions. Published in the United States by Alfred A. Knopf, a
division of Random House, Inc., New York. Distributed by
Random House, Inc., New York.

www.aaknopf.com

Originally published in Canada by Doubleday Canada, Toronto, in 2003.

Knopf, Borzoi Books, and the colophon are registered trademarks of
Random House, Inc.

ISBN 1-4000-4216-X

Manufactured in the United States of America
First United States Edition

For my father—
always vivid
whose absence inspired

———————————

"Who is the third who walks always beside you?"

T. S. Eliot, *The Waste Land*

"Neti, neti." (Not this, not that.)

Brihadaranyaka Upanishad

"Po pote niendapo anifuata."
(Wherever I go he follows me.)

Swahili riddle; answer: shadow

———————————

The In-Between World of Vikram Lall

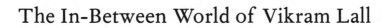

MY NAME IS VIKRAM LALL. I have the distinction of having been numbered one of Africa's most corrupt men, a cheat of monstrous and reptilian cunning. To me has been attributed the emptying of a large part of my troubled country's treasury in recent years. I head my country's List of Shame. These and other descriptions actually flatter my intelligence, if not my moral sensibility. But I do not intend here to defend myself or even seek redemption through confession; I simply crave to tell my story. In this clement retreat to which I have withdrawn myself, away from the torrid current temper of my country, I find myself with all the time and seclusion I may ever need for my purpose. I have even come upon a small revelation—and as I proceed daily to recall and reflect, and lay out on the page, it is with an increasing conviction of its truth, that if more of us told our stories to each other, where I come from, we would be a far happier and less nervous people.

I am quite an ordinary man, as you will discover, and moderate almost to a fault. How I came upon my career and my distinction is a surprise even to me. But my times were exceptional and they would leave no one unscathed.

PART I

———————

The Year of Our Loves and Friendships

ONE

———————

Njoroge who was also called William loved my sister Deepa; I was infatuated with another whose name I cannot utter yet, whose brother was another William; we called him Bill. We had all become playmates recently. It was 1953, the coronation year of our new monarch who looked upon us from afar, a cold England of pastel, watery shades, and I was eight years old.

I call forth for you here my beginning, the world of my childhood, in that fateful year of our friendships. It was a world of innocence and play, under a guileless constant sun; as well, of barbarous cruelty and terror lurking in darkest night; a colonial world of repressive, undignified subjecthood, as also of seductive order and security—so that long afterwards we would be tempted to wonder if we did not hurry forth too fast straight into the morass that is now our malformed freedom.

Imagine an outdoor mall, the type we still call a shopping centre there, a plain stubby strip of shops on open land, with unpaved parking in front. It was accessible from a side road that left the highway, less than a mile away, at the railway station. Far out in the distance, the farthest that you could see through the haze over the flat yellow plains, rose the steep green slopes of the great Rift Valley, down which both the railway and the highway descended to reach us at the floor. Behind us lay most of the rest of Nakuru, the principal town of our province.

My family ran a provision store at this Valley Shopping Centre, which was ten minutes' walk from the Asian development where we lived. We sold Ovaltine and Milo and Waterbury's Compound and Horlicks—how they roll past memory's roadblocks, these trademarks of a childhood—and macaroni and marmalade, cheeses and olives, and other such items that the Europeans and the rich Indians who emulated them were used to. Beside us was a small bakery-café run by a Greek woman, Mrs. Arnauti, for the Europeans—as all the whites were called—who trundled down from their farms in their dust-draped vans and pickups to stop by for tea or coffee and colourful iced cakes and neat white sandwiches. Next to it was Alidina Greengrocers. On Saturday mornings, with the schools closed, my sister and I went down to the shop with our parents. Sun-drenched Saturdays is how I think of those days, what memory's trapped for me: days of play. Though it could get cold at times, and in the morning the ground might be covered in frost. At the other end of the mall from us, Lakshmi Sweets was always bustling at midmorning, Indian families having stopped over in their cars for bhajias, samosas, dhokras, bhel-puri, and tea, which they consumed noisily and with gusto. By comparison our end was sedate, orderly: a few vehicles parked, a few rickety white tables outside Arnauti's occupied by Europeans on a good day. My father and mother always ordered tea and snacks from Lakshmi, and my sister and I could go to Arnauti's, where we were allowed a corner table outside, though not our black friend Njoroge, who with quite a straight face, head in the air and hands in his pockets, would proudly wander off.

After hastily consuming sticky Swiss rolls and doughy cheese or spinach pies, Deepa and I ran out to play. There were two handcarts outside the shop for pulling loads, one of them had its handle broken and no one usually minded when we took it out to give each other rides. Deepa, who was seven, ran along beside Njoroge and me, and habitually, in domineering big-brother fashion, I refused her a place in our conveyance, became annoyed at her for running after us, a girl in her two long pigtails and Punjabi pyjama and long shirt. She cried, and every time she did that

Njoroge would give her a ride, obligingly push the cart for her all around the parking lot, and I believed they had more fun together than he had with me. That was why I thought he was in love with my sister. Every time I said that, Mother would have a fit, but she never objected to our playing with our friend.

One morning just before noon a green Ford pickup drove up and parked outside our store; from it emerged a tall and slim white woman, with brown curls to her shoulders and trousers that seemed rather broad at the hips. She had a long and ruddy face with a pointed chin. She paused to scrutinize the shops in the mall and, I thought, stared severely for a moment at me and my companions, before bending to say something to the two children who were in the passenger seat. The door opened on the other side and out tumbled a boy of my age and a young girl who could have been six; from the back jumped out with some flair an African servant— well dressed in expensive hand-me-downs, as the more favoured servants of the Europeans usually were, much to the envy of other servants. This one sported a brown woollen vest and a tweed jacket. The woman escorted her two children to Arnauti's, where they sat at a table outside and in loud voices ordered from the waiter who had come running out to attend, and then she went over to my father's shop. Soon our own barefoot servant hurried out to hand the European woman's servant a bottle of Coke.

When she had finished her shopping, her servant was called and he carried her two cartons of purchases to the back of the pickup. Then Mrs. Bruce, as was her name, returned to Arnauti's patio and joined a table with two other women and a man. Her two children came out, where Njoroge, Deepa, and I, upon seeing them, now somewhat self-consciously continued our preoccupations with each other and our cart. The boy and girl stood quite still, outside the guardrail, staring at us.

Do you want a ride? I asked the boy suddenly.

Without a word he came and sat in the cart and we pushed him away at top speed with hoots and growls to simulate various engine sounds. When we stopped, after a distance, having gathered up a cloud of dust across the parking lot, the boy got out and dusted himself off as his sister whined, Now me, Willie, it's my turn now.

He paid her no attention but shook Njoroge's and my hands solemnly, saying, William—call me Bill, and pleased to meet you.

We shook hands wordlessly, then I pointed to my friend and said hesitantly: Njoroge.

That day Deepa and I stopped calling Njoroge by his English name. And I believe he also stopped using it for himself.

Now he in his turn pointed at me and said: Vic—Vikram.

Well then—jolly good, Bill said. Let's give those two girls a ride—

He wore shorts of grey wool, with a rather fine blue checked shirt. His hair, like that of his sister, was a light brown. And both wore black shoes and white socks. The girl was in red overalls, and two ribbons of a like colour tied her hair in clumps at the back. We drove the two girls with speed right up to the line of shops, as they hung on, clutching for dear life, screaming with joy.

The boy and girl came every alternate week like clockwork, and we awaited them with anticipation, for they represented something out of the ordinary and exotic, and Bill was always imaginative and original in his play and Njoroge and I learned much from him. Sometimes we were a Spitfire raining bullets on enemies, other times a racing car, or an Empire Airways plane, or the *Titanic* or the *QE2*, or the SS *Bombay*, the boat that regularly plied the ocean between Bombay and Mombasa.

They had rather refined accents, their language sharp and crystalline and musical, beside which ours seemed a crude approximation, for we had learned it in school and knew it to be the language of power and distinction but could never speak it their way. Their clothes were smart; their mannerisms so relaxed. But these barriers of class and prestige were not so inviolable or cruel at our level, and we did become friends. Mrs. Bruce would drop them off at our shop first thing before going off for her other chores on the main street, and return an hour or so later.

Njoroge and Deepa continued to have that closeness, their bond of protector and dependent; I deferred to Bill, because he was a little older, and also because he simply was a leader in our midst.

And the girl?—her name was Annie, and I came to think I was in love with her, and she with me. Ours was a natural pairing. We found each other like magnets, and we could watch the world together with laughter in our eyes.

And so when flight captain William Bruce went bang-banging in his Spitfire, shooting down Germans or Japs or Eyeties as he self-propelled with his feet, and went tumbling over, the handcart dragging him ignominiously in the dust like a fallen charioteer, who should catch my eye than Annie, wrinkling her nose a few times in an expression of bemusement and glee, which I returned with a wide grin, before we rushed to Bill's rescue and clucked appropriately at the grazed knees. And when the fisherman Njoroge, at Bill's instigation, took Deepa out in his boat, Bill serenading with a mock guitar, Annie had slipped her arm casually in mine and we stood behind watching. So many such moments I could recall, gentle as dewdrops, transient and illusory like sunbeams; charming as a butterfly's dance round a flower.

Much of my life has been a recalling of her; my Annie. Each remembered moment, each fresh thought like a bead in a rosary. How old would she be now? I've asked myself countless times, and provided an answer. Now she would be in her early fifties. What would she look like, what would her life have been like, would we have kept up that friendship? Would she still sing? Who could have guessed her fate, that darling of a privileged family, that bundle brimming with life and future and charm? . . . I go on and on.

My sister Deepa has always considered this proclivity of mine something of a sickness; Njoroge thought likewise, but showed some understanding of it. I do not deny the affliction. I never imposed it on those around me, I carried it like a private ache of no consequence to anyone but myself. Only lately have I admitted the obvious, that I let it deform me, freeze the essential core in me, so that for a large part of my adult life I remained detached from almost everything around me, explaining away this coldness as the result of a stoic, even mystical temperament.

She had freckles on her arms, and a few—exactly three, as I imagine it—on one side of her nose. And sometimes when she wore a dress her knickers might show, at which my sister would blink her eyelashes or look away in an almost unconscious response that I couldn't help noticing. She was a burden to Bill, who either ignored her pleas or paid extravagant attention to her. She brought her dolls over sometimes, when Deepa and she would disappear, before tiring eventually and emerging to play with us boys. Once the servant, Kihika, had to walk around with Annie's teddy bear in his hands so it could watch her play. This was evidently the aftermath of a recent tantrum. She, driven around in the cart by the rest of us, looking happily at my face, the tears now dry on hers; Kihika keeping pace, in his vest and tweeds, a tender smile on his face. It is a scene carved vividly in the brain, because it would return so often to tease and to torment.

One bright afternoon Mrs. Bruce stayed away an unusually long time, and my parents wondered whether someone should be sent to look for her. Lunch hour was passing, Alidina Greengrocers and Arnauti's Café were already shuttered, Lakshmi Sweets was lifeless. Finally she arrived, two hours late, just when in a corner of the parking lot Bill, acting the part of a Special Branch inspector, toting a toy pistol he had brought along that morning, was administering a loyalty oath to the "uncovered" and "repenting" Mau Mau terrorist Njoroge, assisted by his faithful sergeant Vic and watched by an amused Kihika and the two girls. Bill's other, outstretched hand proffered a chocolate as prize for the renunciation.

I shall be loyal to the Queen of all of the British Empire, Njoroge was mumbling, . . . and the dominions . . . I renounce the Mau Mau and the oath I have taken . . . if I give help to the terrorists may I die . . .

Mrs. Bruce had come out of the pickup and was walking toward us; suddenly she let out a terrifying shriek: Willie! Stop it at once! At once!

She had come to a trembling halt a few yards away; she uttered something inaudible and raised a hand to her forehead, closed her eyes. Kihika hurried over to steady her: Polé, mama, they got tired waiting, it's only a game. Ni muchezo.

She went with him to our shop, she sat down and accepted a glass of cold water. Tears were running down her face.

I am sorry, Mrs. Bruce, said Papa. We all know him and will pray for him in his sorrow . . .

All of us children had gathered around in the shop and stood watching.

The cause of Mrs. Bruce's grief was a piece of news she had received during her visit to the shops downtown, news that my parents had also apparently received in the meantime. Just over an hour ago, Mr. Innes, the manager of the chemists Innes and McGeorge, upon returning home from work, had discovered his wife and daughter hacked to death by the Mau Mau.

That was the closest that the killings had come to us.

————————

Out in the distance, across the waters of Lake Ontario, the dim glow is the city of Rochester, I've been told, where Deepa now resides. The waves of this vast lake before us, under the midsummer night sky, produce a steady murmur, invoking for me the immensity of time and space, mocking the trivial rhythms of an ordinary human life and its perishable concerns. Yet that life is all we have and is perhaps more than we think it is, for we continue in each other, as the arrival of my young visitor reminds me.

One of the cats suddenly nuzzles strongly against my leg, then just as abruptly ceases, vanishing somewhere; I think it's the black one, Zambo, for whom this is the most but essential intimacy he'll allow.

Oh, he's gone, I mutter sheepishly, having reached out too late to stroke the cat.

There he goes, says Joseph, with a nod toward my back.

My young visitor has a surprisingly deep voice; his tall thin body with long black face rises like a silhouette before me in the dark. I'm still not sure why he agreed to come, what can he find here to interest and to keep him? He will start university in September, in Toronto. Meanwhile we are to be each other's soulmates, as per instructions from Deepa, who has sent him to me to cool off. He had become involved in student activism back home in Kenya, a tempting and hazardous preoccupation, so I understand

Deepa's concern for him. You are his family there, Vic, said Deepa over the phone, drum some practical advice into him. Be his anchor when he needs you.

I'll try, Sis, I replied. A young man like that wants to do his own bidding, he is not going to heed the cautionary advice of some middle-aged Asian man. Especially someone like me. I am the notoriously corrupt, the evil Vic Lall, remember?

Don't give yourself airs, she said. Besides, he'll do you good.

Which balances the equation, I surmise. Joseph has his instructions too. When he arrived yesterday, when I picked him up at the train station in Korrenburg, he was respectful but reserved. We have yet to break that reserve, behind which may hide all his suspicion and distrust of me. What does he know, think of me?

He has been away from home a month now, and from what I understand, he left just in time to escape the clutches of the police following a large riot. He must hide a lot of anger too, at his world.

I remember the day he was born, Joseph, twenty-three years ago, a tiny wrinkled baby in the arms of his mother Mary, not quite black but, surprisingly to me, brown. I had gone to visit his mother in hospital, with my own six-year-old son in tow. The two of us stood together in rapt admiration. The years of the Mau Mau disturbances were long over; what were once termed terrorists were now called freedom fighters, and in the seventies, in Nairobi, we had daring robberies to occupy our minds, and political assassinations. Once in a while a former freedom fighter would emerge from the forests, or publish a memoir, aided by a foreign scholar. The happy scene in the hospital room that afternoon, though, belied a painful reality, for the boy's father, my friend Njoroge, was not there.

That is the bond between us, Joseph and me, I realize, whatever else he may think about me. I knew his father.

TWO

My father fussed over Mrs. Bruce, that afternoon of the attack on the Inneses, and was unwilling to let her go home alone, insisting that he call Mr. Bruce to take her away. She protested it was not necessary, evidently annoyed at the attention he pressed upon her, which he didn't seem to see, rather abjectly ingratiating himself further. I simply *cannot*, Mrs. Bruce, let you go. There are terrorists about, and a European lady alone on the road with her two children . . . She had been seated on the stuffed chair across from his desk and given a glass of water; he himself had come around and stood before her, effectively blocking the aisle leading out from the store. Crates of tinned and bottled eatables stood piled waist-high on either side of him. Finally, after a few of my mother's veiled remarks and annoyed signals, Papa relented, and Mrs. Bruce walked away stiffly to her vehicle with her two children close beside her, Kihika following faithfully behind. When they had gone, Mother scolded Papa, Why do you have to be so craven in front of her, they don't care one cent for us. To which he said, Our children play with her children. Came the reply, So what, are they doing us a favour? Why didn't you offer to drive her home, then?

That last remark was unusually sarcastic; he looked at her, surprised, but didn't say a word.

Mother did not like Mrs. Bruce; she would look peevishly from behind the sanctuary of our shop window whenever the white woman came and dropped off her kids and servant and drove away to finish other business in town. But Mother was from India and not as intimidated by the angrez-log (as she called the Europeans) as Papa was; and her younger brother, our Mahesh Uncle, was an outspoken local radical whom, although he made her nervous by his ways, she also quite admired. Still, it did surprise me that my mother would feel so hostile toward the mother of our two European playmates.

We have been Africans for three generations, not counting my own children. Family legend has it that one of the rails on the railway line just outside the Nakuru station has engraved upon it my paternal grandfather's name, Anand Lal Peshawari, in Punjabi script—and many another rail of the line has inscribed upon it the name and birthplace of an Indian labourer. I don't know if such rails ever existed, with Punjabi signatures upon them, but myth is more powerful than factual evidence, and in its way surely far truer. We always believed in the story, in our home. Our particular rail, according to my dada, was the one laid just before the signal box, outside the station. He had used acid and a nib of steel wire to etch his name. There was many a time during a visit to the station when we would stare in the direction of that rail, if not directly at it, in that very significant knowledge central to our existence.

The railway running from Mombasa to Kampala, proud "Permanent Way" of the British and "Gateway to the African Jewel," was our claim to the land. Mile upon mile, rail next to thirty-foot rail, fishplate to follow fishplate, it had been laid by my grandfather and his fellow Punjabi labourers—Juma Molabux, Ungan Singh, Muzzafar Khan, Shyam Sunder Lal, Roshan, Tony—the cast of characters in his tales was endless and of biblical variety—recruited from an assortment of towns in northwest India and brought to an alien, beautiful, and wild country at the dawn of the twentieth century. Our people had sweated on it, had died on it: they had been carried away in their weary sleep or even wide awake by man-eating lions of magical ferocity and cunning, crushed under avalanches of blasted rock, speared and macheted as proxies of the whites by angry Kamba, Kikuyu, and Nandi warriors, infected with malaria, sleeping sickness, elephantiasis, cholera; bitten by jiggers, scorpions, snakes, and chameleons; and wounded in vicious fights with each other. They had taken the line strenuously and persistently six hundred miles from the Swahili coast, up through desert, bush, and grassland into the lush fertile highlands of the Kikuyu, then through forest down the Rift Valley and back up to a height of eight thousand feet, before bringing it to descend gently and finally to the great lake Victoria-Nyanza that was the heart of what became beloved Africa.

Anand Lal, my dada, stayed on in the new colony after his indentureship, picked Nakuru as the spot where he would live. A small thin man: rough chin and thin moustache, white lungi and loose shirt, and a fluffy white turban on the head. Thus he is captured, staring wondrously out of a photo, with three other Punjabi coolies and the legendary Colonel Patterson on a railway inspection trolley outside Machakos. It was 1897. I imagine him six years later, at the end of his second contract, seated atop a small pyramid of steel sleepers at the Nakuru railway yard, with a companion or two perhaps, chewing on a blade of grass or lunching on daal and rice from the canteen. The last key had been driven home on the railway, at Lake Victoria by an English lady, and he and a few others had been brought back here to complete work on the station. I see him contemplating the vast flat grassy plains of the Rift Valley, the pointed Mount Longonot, its sides grey with volcanic ash, rising up like the nipple on the breast of some reclining African god, the two escarpments in the distance, along whose steep slopes they had lain the railway in the direst of wet muddy conditions, the shimmering Lake Nakuru, its blue surface painted over by the white and pink of a million flamingos . . . I see this turbaned young Indian who would be my dada saying to himself, This valley has a beauty to surpass even the god Shivji's Kashmir, and the cool weather in May is so akin to the winters of Peshawar . . .

What makes a man leave the land of his birth, the home of those childhood memories that will haunt him till his deathbed? I received a warning telephone call late one morning, left home that night with my heart in my mouth; but for Indians abroad in Africa, it has been said that it was poverty at home that pushed them across the ocean. That may be true, but surely there's that wanderlust first, that itch in the sole, that hankering in the soul that puffs out the sails for a journey into the totally unknown?

For many years I did not know the exact circumstances that made my grandfather want to leave his home and cross the black water—as the exiling oceans were called in his homeland. Those circumstances had to do, as I came to find out, with a quarrel he had with his elder married brother soon after the death of their father, who had been the only shopkeeper and moneylender in his village. And so the prospect of going home, after his indentureship, even with a bit of money of his own now, must not have seemed so very compelling.

He found a job in Nakuru's railway machine shop, married a Punjabi girl living with her relations in Nairobi, received a decent dowry, and soon after opened a grocery store in Nakuru's only and burgeoning street at the time. The town had become a business centre for many of the sons and daughters of England's landed class who had come to settle and farm in the sunny and temperate clime of the Rift Valley.

Dadaji! Dadaji!—we would happily shout, Deepa and I and our several cousins, and scamper up to him for our candies, immediately after the Sunday family meal in my parents' home, when all the other adults had retired for their naps wherever they could. Seated on the armchair which was his siesta place, Dadaji would bring out a paper bag and hold it up and hand out to each of us, in turn, one choice sweet, always beginning with Deepa, the youngest, her mouth wide open like a puppy's. These presents were slight, compared with the chocolates we received from our parents, but the ritual was a delight; at times we felt that it was we who were the indulgent ones. Little could we even begin to imagine what his life had been like, what his thoughts were now. Sitting at his feet, we would often be treated to his stories. The lion stories were always the favourite, because they were scarier and so much more immediate and realistic than the Indian tales of

Lakshman and Rama and Sita speaking with monkeys and devils in the enchanted forests of a distant land.

So we are sitting round a fire like this, he would say, drawing us into a circle, each of us representing a coolie friend, and he would place his large white handkerchief on the nearest child's head to represent a turban. Eh listen, you! So we are sitting round a fire like this, the six of us, Ungan Singh there, and there Birbal Singh, and Muzzafar and Chhotu and myself . . . and Malik. Ungan, saying Aha!, plays his hand, thus, and we lean forward to look—a baadshah, a king of clubs. Wah! says Birbal, you had it all along, and Muzzafar turns to Chhotu and says, Eh Lala Chhotu, if you had kept your ace! But there is no Chhotu! While we have been all admiring Ungan's king there in the middle like it was a bridegroom, Chhotu—the littlest coolie among us—has disappeared! And on the ground, leading to the bushes, is a trail left by his body—the poor fellow's feet—and a few, eka-do drops of blood. We start shouting and running about—here, there, here again, and the askaris and Nicholson Sahab arrive with their rifles . . . Poor Chhotu, only his head was found—hanging from a tree branch, beside a baobab fruit! With his turban on!

Tell us more, tell us more, Dadaji!

But Dadaji was beginning to forget the details by the time we were around. Sometimes it was the skull that was found, beside a river, with Chhotu's turban beside it, all unwound. But of one thing he was certain, as he would sometimes say emphatically to our parents: those lions of Tsavo were the ghosts of dead men. Anyone eaten by a lion would himself come back to eat his fellows—otherwise, how did the lions time their attacks so perfectly?

It was a strange prospect, friends coming back to eat you. Then perhaps the lions didn't mean ill after all? Dadaji had no answer to that. Another thing he was certain about was that the lions all had hypnotizing powers.

For every mile of railway track laid, four Indians died, our radical Mahesh Uncle would remind us when he was around.

. . .

India was always fantasyland to me. To this day, I have never visited my dada's birthplace. It was the place where that strange man with the narrow pointed face, bald head, and granny glasses, Gandhiji, had lived and died, and where the man with the white cap, Nehru, now ruled, and where the impossibly four-armed and pink-faced gods of my mother's statuettes and Lakshmi Sweets' annual calendar pictures had fought their battles and killed devils, and where Sir Edmund Hillary and Sherpa Tensing had that year conquered Everest. It was Vrndavan where the butter thief Nandlal Krishna presided, where Dadi was born and the goddess Dayamati had presided. My mother had a dresser on which she kept her statuettes of Rama and Durga and Hanuman and of course Ganesh, and at times of stress she went and stood in entreaty before them. Our daily preservation, especially in those nervous times, was due to their faithful intercession, she had no doubt about that. Even now, even here in this Canadian wilderness, I cannot help but say my namaskars, or salaams, to the icons I carry faithfully with me, not quite understanding what they mean to me. But I am convinced they represent some elemental force of nature, some qualities of it, like gravitation and the electric force and all other entities conjured up for us by scientists from our mundane existence. But I digress.

My father—proudly Kenyan, hopelessly (as I now think) colonial— went to India once, and brought back my mother.

He found everything in India dirty and poor, and for the most part he had a miserable time of it. Even to see the Taj Mahal you had to walk over gutters and push through a street fight, he would say. Beggars and touts everywhere; men standing around openly picking at their crotches. Even a taxi! he would exclaim. Even a taxi! You hail one, you want to feel posh and escape all the scum around you, you open the door and what happens? You step into a lump of fresh shit! It was one of his favourite stories, he would get graphic, and Deepa and I would roll with laughter. Mother would simply smile and say, There he goes again, with his taxi-shit story. It was 1944, the year he went, and the streets were in turmoil with strikes and demonstrations in aid of India's freedom. While walking along a street in Peshawar once, Papa chanced to see a girl on a bicycle—evidently returning from college, her books clasped to the carrier behind her. She had one long pigtail almost down to her waist and she wore an embroidered cap. There was something in the face she made, when she had to halt and wait for a handcart full of smelly onion sacks to go past, that caught his fancy. It was like discovering a single, solitary rose blooming on the grimy sidewalk— he would go on, coming to the part designed to please my mother. Here were tongawallahs screaming at each other, the babagadi of half-rotten onions, an open kiosk selling tea and puris next to a gutter, everyone bare-foot or in chappals and wearing dirty clothes, and this girl comes by on her cycle wearing a crisp pink and white shalwar-kameez, with glistening black hair, full pink cheeks, and flashing black eyes! Impulsively, he began hum-ming a film song and followed the girl in a rickshaw until she reached home. The next day, waiting for her at the same place and time as he'd first seen her, he saw her and again followed her in a rickshaw. He then asked a boy, who had observed him staring after her as she went through the gates of her house, Tell me, what college does she attend? The boy gave a wink and told him, and so the following afternoon my father waited for the girl outside the college gates. Before he could muster the courage to speak to her, she said to him, Ay budhu, you oaf why do you follow me? You must be a stranger in these parts, don't you know my father is a police inspector? He'll have the pleasure of having both your legs broken for you. Never-theless, she let him escort her home. She was enchanted by his foreign ac-cent and awkwardly Indian ways. After a few days my father made an appointment with her father at police headquarters and did the unorthodox thing of proposing to marry his daughter Sheila.

Inspector Verma—my father would say, running forefinger and thumb above his lips to indicate his father-in-law's military moustache—did not speak a word for a full ten minutes, staring at a report in front of him, on his desk. His midmorning cup of tea came and he proceeded to drink it, he nibbled a Marie biscuit. My father had of course introduced himself in some detail. Finally Inspector Verma raised his head and eyed the brash young man who was by now utterly discomfited. He grilled him about his background, made sure my father realized that his antecedents in India amounted to nothing, being village banias at most, and that his father had demeaned himself further as a labourer. When Papa was completely deflated, Inspector Verma told him to send his relations with a formal proposal.

Inspector Verma was a widower, and also somewhat unusual; he worked for the British, and in his duties to maintain law and order he often had to arrest Congresswallahs agitating for independence, one of whom was his own son Mahesh, or send laathi charges against street demonstrators. Gandhi was in jail, there were sporadic riots between Hindus and Muslims. The civilizing order of the day, to the stern inspector, seemed to be on the wane, and the country was on the verge of falling apart. So he agreed to let his lovestruck daughter get away to a part of the world—be it in Africa—where the Empire still held firm, English values and manners still ruled the day.

My father returned to Kenya with my mother in late 1944. I was born the following year. In 1948, after the partition of India, in which Peshawar became part of Pakistan, my mother's kid brother Mahesh—one of the millions of refugees now—followed her to the colony. My father and his brothers called him "communist," because of his radical ideas, the term having a special ring to it in those days, meaning worthless intellectual ranter. My father actually tolerated him and could hold a conversation with him, but his brothers detested Mahesh Uncle. He was broad-shouldered and muscular, with a black untrimmed beard and wild glaring eyes behind his black-framed glasses. He was argumentative and sometimes ill-tempered, and he had a degree in English. And just to irk the settlers and the colonial Indians, on occasional days, such as India's national day, he paraded Nakuru's main streets in khadi, the pyjama and long shirt combination of homespun cotton that had been the symbol of Indian protest, the uniform of those who had fought for India's independence. It had the desired effect in this British colony, in the heart of white settlerdom, where they still believed in the fifties that the sun would never set on their empire.

My mother and her brother had a very special closeness. Many times I came upon them sitting together on the sofa in silence, he having turned toward her, eyes lowered, his hands in his lap in respectful repose. A few times I saw her in that silent communion freely wiping tears from her eyes. She was very fair, her pink cheeks now fuller than when my father had first laid eyes on her, her hair still long and black and thick, her pride and (on washing days) her cross. They had lost their mother and been brought up by a taciturn, high-minded father unable to show his softer nature, especially to his son, and this had not been easy for them. With the independence and partition of India they had lost their homeland. That weighed heavily on all our family, but especially on those two, the freshest arrivals from there. By some perverse twist of fate, Peshawar, our ancestral home, had become an alien, hostile place; it was in Pakistan.

Mr. Innes, whose wife and daughter were slaughtered that Saturday, was a big, gruff, red-haired and -whiskered bully of a man, who always refused to serve Mahesh Uncle at Innes and McGeorge. Hey you, son of a coolie—he would bark briskly and harshly as soon as my uncle pushed through the glass doors. Out! Go back to cowland, Bengalee bastard! Undaunted by the insult, Mahesh Uncle would return on another day, always ostensibly intending to buy a tube of Colgate, which he could have bought for half the price from an Indian merchant, and which he didn't use anyway, patriot that he was, preferring the traditional charcoal concoction that went by the name of Monkey Brand. My Punjabi mother, though, was offended specifically by the description "Bengalee" applied to her brother: But you are not dark-skinned, how *dare* he call you a Bengali!

When our new friends the Bruce children entered our lives, Mahesh Uncle was no longer living with us. He had come as a teacher to the Indian school in Nakuru, but his indiscretions soon lost him the job. Finally Dadaji, through some contact, found him the post of manager of the Resham Singh Sawmill near Njoro, some twenty miles away.

As Mrs. Bruce drove off from our parking lot that day of the Innes murders, she almost ran over Mahesh Uncle, who had to jump aside. He often came to spend weekends with us, a mill lorry dropping him off on Saturday and picking him up on Sunday. He had gone to our home and missed us, then walked up to the store. He too had heard of the gruesome incident.

They'll never learn, Mahesh Uncle said, looking in the direction of the pickup which had just barely avoided hitting him. Arrogant bastards, even as the forest fighters pick them off one by one . . . and they say they don't understand why they are hated.

Must you now go and support those heinous murderers, my father muttered in irritation. Mahesh Uncle did not reply but looked away to meet my mother's smile of greeting.

The dog had been hacked on the head with a panga, though he was still breathing when found, lying on his side on the back stoop. The front door was unlocked but shut; the back door hung wide open. One servant had the day off, the other had disappeared. Laundry was hanging out for drying. The lunch awaiting Henry Innes when he came upon the scene of carnage was macaroni casserole, with fruit and custard for dessert. Mrs. Innes, forty years old, was discovered in the sitting room where she had died from her wounds, one of them a blow to the neck. She was Kenya-born, and her husband had come to the country some ten years earlier. Their eleven-year-old girl, Maggie, was in her shorts when the attack occurred; she had run up to her bedroom in terror, where she was followed and met her end.

For the remainder of that day, right into the late evening when in Nakuru's residential areas doors were fastened and alarms checked, the talk at home and over the phone and with neighbours was about nothing else but the Innes murders. The following day's Sunday papers brought all the details and important opinions. There was a boxed message from the Governor of Kenya, Sir Evelyn Baring, on the front page and a quote from Mrs. Innes's father in England. There were calls for the Governor to resign for not being firm on terrorists. Special Branch officers were photographed in the wooded area outside the Innes house. Clara Innes, it was reported, had been an indefatigable community worker, a tireless dogsbody at the RSPCA and the annual flower show.

The Mau Mau are devils, I said, echoing my mother. Her term was "daityas" from mythology. Krishna had slain many daityas, even as a child.

Rama had slain the ten-headed Ravana, and Mau Mau were like that wily daitya, changing shapes at will in the forest, impossible to defeat.

Njoroge and I were sitting in the backyard, having finished with our toy spear, bow and arrow, and gun. All were gifts, made for us from wood and string by Njoroge's grandfather Mwangi. We always took strict turns on who was to be Indian and who cowboy, who cop and who robber. We never played Mau Mau and Special Branch. It was one of those times when, after involved play and play-acting, we sat beside each other and felt close. Perhaps our play provoked questions about our lives that we then felt the need to share but simply couldn't. I do recall that his being different, in features, in status, was not far from my consciousness. I was also aware that he was more from Africa than I was. He was African, I was Asian. His black skin was matte, his woolly hair impossibly alien. I was smaller, with pointed elvish ears, my skin annoyingly "medium," as I described it then, neither one (white) nor the other (black).

Yes, said Njoroge, in response to my observation, they are brave devils.

Brave, sure, brave—I said, not to be outdone in bravado—a daylight attack too, and the Europeans carry guns!

It was close to the time of our Sunday family lunch at home, and all my uncles, aunties, and cousins had already gathered, with our dada and dadi. Smells of hot ghee and spices filled the air in the backyards, ginger and garlic and chicken from one house, saffron and onion from another, fresh phulki chappatis and daal from yet another. Lilting melodies and sad lyrics from Saigal, Hemant Kumar, and Talat filled the air, courtesy of KBC's Hindustani service on the shortwave. One song, a favourite among kids, went,

O darling little children, what do you hold in your fists?
In our fists (sing the beggar children in chorus) *we hold our fates!*

Soon the songs would give way to the one o'clock news delivered in depressingly funereal tones. Whatever the news, it always sounded tragic.

African music played in some of the servant houses. In one song, in Swahili, the singer lamented being sent to Bulawayo to the diamond mines.

Deepa came running out from our house and hurriedly sat down beside us, on her haunches.

Mrs. Innes was brave, wasn't she? Deepa must have heard a snatch of our conversation, probably from the French window above our heads.

She died, Njoroge said.

I don't want to die, Deepa said. I don't want to be a hundred.

In her mind, at that time, to die meant to reach exactly a hundred years.

Njoroge's grandfather Mwangi called him from their flat, a neighbour's servant quarter, and our friend stood up to go. Deepa took a few steps to follow him, then stopped. He turned, smiled, and waved briefly.

Out in the distance, on the spit of land needling the giant lake, Joseph's gone fishing with two young friends he has found, a girl of ten and a boy of eight from the neighbourhood. If he catches anything large enough he'll bring it back for the barbecue. Sometimes he shows off to his young friends a few deft moves of soccer, and other kids from the few houses nearby come scampering down to join in the play. It is the boy who reminds me of Annie—the innocence with which he runs his hand up and down Joseph's arm, for instance, to feel the black skin, is so reminiscent of my friend from long ago. It has occurred to me—how can it not?—that my picture of my past could well have, like the stories of my grandfather, acquired the patina of nostalgia, become idealized. But then, I have to convince myself, perhaps a greater and conscious discipline and the practice of writing mitigate that danger. I do carry my album of photos with me and my acquired newspaper cuttings and other assorted material, and there is always Deepa to check facts with. Still, what can ultimately withstand the cruel treachery of time, even as one tries to undermine it?

Joseph too has an obsession with the past, that of his people, the Kikuyu. Many peoples in East Africa resisted the European colonization, but they had early on been subdued by the superiority of rifles against arrows and spears. It was the Kikuyu, at least a large section of the tribe, who organized a systematic guerrilla war that struck large terror among the settlers. And it was the Kikuyu who paid the harsh price of British countermeasures and settler rage.

We may need their methods, Joseph says to me once, with a sparkle in his eyes and all the earnestness of his age, speaking of the Mau Mau. Even these days, right now, my people are being oppressed, they are being driven from their homes and butchered. But we will fight back—with guns, not machetes!

He is referring to the recent occurrences of ethnic violence back home, in which the victims have been the Kikuyu of the Nakuru region, whose ancestors were immigrants from across the Aberdares. The youth of his people, he assures me, are now ready to take on their enemies. But the government, as I well know, itself implicated in condoning the ethnic violence, has always been nervous and vigilant about new breeds of militants inspired by those heroes of the past.

Violence and civil war lead nowhere, Joseph, I tell him. Nobody wins. We all lose.

I don't think I sound convincing. We exchange looks, and turn away from each other to face the lake lying still in the dark.

THREE

Sunday silence, a ripened equatorial afternoon sated and senseless in the heat, and suddenly an abrupt whine and growl of trucks, and a thunder of many army boots ominous outside, proceeding at a pace in the gullies between the buildings; a halt and a prolonged shuffle sounding like the rains. A woman's rising query quickly chokes into a brief but painful scream. And then gruff, hectoring African voices call out, pitching venom and terror and rude, electrifying authority, right there, behind the houses, in the backyards.

Kikuyu!
  Out, you hyenas!
  Hands in the air!
  Tokeni nje! Sasa hivi!
  All Africans, come out!
  And-if-any-of-you-fancies-hiding-away-inside, surely he is my meat . . . and I will eat his brains and wear his skin.

. . .

The last taunt muttered by the sinister Corporal Boniface, a jowly Idi Amin of a man, Grimm giant known to all.

And a theme emergent: a command or two uttered in high-pitched English accents, followed by the murmur of two like voices chatting casually.

Here they come again for the poor Kikuyu, Dada muttered from his armchair, opening his eyes but otherwise not stirring, just as Mother and Papa came hurrying out of their room. Mother looked flushed and soft, deliciously dishevelled, as she always did when she took a nap in the afternoon; she was still arranging her kameez, and I went to stand close to her.

A police raid, looks like, she said irritably. What Mau Mau can they expect to find here in this location?

The police regularly raided the Indian residential areas, expecting to find Mau Mau hiding among the servants.

It's good they are vigilant, na, Papa replied.

Mahesh Uncle, who had earlier gone to my room to rest, was already out the back door and audible. My parents headed that way, followed by me, and Grandfather reluctantly got up on his feet also to go witness the clamorous proceedings outside. Dadi had gone to the Molabux household three doors down, to visit her friend Sakina-dadi, as she always did after the Sunday family meal.

She must be asleep, Mother answered when Papa inquired about Deepa. Let her be.

Outside, in our backyard, Njoroge stood wide-eyed, looking lost and nervous, a hare petrified before the hounds, praying for the earth to swallow him up right there under his feet, or my family to somehow do something for him.

Hide somewhere quickly, child, Mahesh Uncle admonished just as a European police inspector started coming toward us, in the company of an askari.

The Asian development in which we lived consisted of four rectangular buildings on either side of a small street, each with two adjoining homes and servant quarters at the back. The large French windows in the fronts of these homes and facing the street must have seemed modern and fashionably suburban once, but in the current fearful climate were a nerve-wracking security risk; our windows were heavily draped at night, the casements always checked and securely fastened. In the daytime, however, our street, lined with tall fern trees with swaying branches that rustled noisily in the wind, looked beautifully innocuous, contentedly residential. It turned off from the larger road which began at the railway station and alongside which, not far from us, was the shopping centre where my family had its business and Deepa and Njoroge and I went to play on Saturdays. Ours was the fourth home from this intersection, on the right side. There was a champeli tree in our garden, and bougainvillea bushes climbing at the hedge; the roses under the windows were evidence of an enthusiasm caught from the flower displays at the annual Nakuru Show, where the European ladies showed off their gardening skills.

Dada and Dadi lived in an apartment downtown, in the main street of Nakuru; Omprakash Uncle, my father's older brother, lived in the same building as my grandparents and ran a hardware store; my father's younger brother Mohan was a bookkeeper at the Farmers' Association and lived in one of the houses across our street. My father had two sisters, both of whom had been married out of town.

That Sunday during the family lunch my uncles and father, all the adult males except Dada, had begun another of those quarrels, episodes involving far too much talk and erupting in shouts and abuses, which always began by startling us children and ended up amusing us.

There they go again—Dadi cried out shrilly, turning to all the women present, especially Mother. *Politics,* why do they discuss *politics,* what problems have they solved for the world with all their *politics?* Dada said nothing, looked both pained and peeved; he would suffer this one out, as he had done all the other ones. As usual, Mahesh Uncle, haughty, opinionated, and far more educated than the rest, wound up as the butt of his brothers-in-laws' jibes. He had spoken in support of African rule in Kenya, an idea extreme and idiotic to my father and his brothers. I remember him finally, big and burly as he was, pushing himself out of his chair, ready with raised fists to have it out with puny Om Uncle, and the slightly larger Mohan Uncle standing up ready to defend his brother, while my father looked up at the ceiling in mock helplessness and my mother screamed, Stop it, I tell you!

He dared call me a monkey, Mahesh Uncle spluttered, to which Mother replied, Why do you have to get into arguments with ignorant folk who know nothing? Om and Mohan Uncles stormed out of the house with their families.

They'll come around, Dada said to my mother, and looked at her brother Mahesh with some distaste. Mahesh Uncle went to wash his hands and retired to my room, which he used as his base when he was around. Dadi said she was going to look in on Sakina-dadi. Dada retired to his armchair and, as on every Sunday, gave the children sweets, but this time there were only two of us, and so having given us double shares he leaned back and closed his eyes.

Not long afterwards the police raid on our area began.

There were two English officers in khaki drill, large tan holsters slapping at their belts. The African askaris were about twenty in number, in their khaki shorts and blue sweaters, some carrying rifles, and they proceeded to round up all the servants from their quarters. Out, out, out, toka nje! Any oaths given here, any Mau Mau hiding here? The Mau Mau recruited collaborators by ritually having them swear an oath in secret, and the police were perpetually on the search for those who had taken the oath and especially for those who had administered it. In a frenzy of angry, impatient activity, the suspects—for all black men were suspect—were pushed and jostled, slapped for replying, kicked in the behind for tardiness. I watched the gardener, Njoroge's grandfather Mwangi, pick himself up from the ground with a wince. He was a short, stout man with a strongly lined face and some grey in his hair, a dignified man who always moved and spoke with deliberation. How could these men and women we knew, who spoke softly and served us so gently, who held our hands and looked after us when we were left in their care, be the dreaded Mau Mau? How could Mzee Mwangi, with the worry lines on his forehead and holes in his ears and a front tooth missing, be one of those killers who stalked the nights? He had made the toy weapons Njoroge and I played with, the pistol in particular carved and grooved smoothly and applied with black bicycle paint. He would sometimes call Deepa over and silently put in her hair a white and pink champeli flower plucked from our tree. I wanted to call out to them and say, Polé sana, I am your friend, I trust you all.

A patronizing attitude—how could I have helped it, risen above that? An Indian boy in shorts and a bush shirt, in socks and shoes, hair oiled and combed, secure in the bosom of a doting family, with a magnanimous thought for the pathetic servants—"boys," as they were called, however old they were—rounded up and demeaned in front of him. I would like to defend myself against that charge, give a finer shade of meaning, a context, to my relationship with the Africans around me. I wish I could explain to Joseph, a descendant of those people, that that world was not of my devising. But I fear I already sound too earnest.

That was a sad day in my life.

Out with your karatasi, your tax receipts! Show your work permits, or you have explaining to do before you go back to Kikuyuland. Hiti! Fisi! Hyenas! Chop-chop!

Two men who had foolishly made a dash for it when the police arrived had been chased and captured and now, thoroughly dishevelled, were shoved brutally by Corporal Boniface into the ragged line of Africans awaiting inspection.

The entire population of our four blocks of flats was now outside, it seemed, at the back stoops or in the yards, eyes fixed on the policemen; only Njoroge was nowhere in sight, as if the earth had swallowed him up. Where had he gone and hidden himself? He was always afraid of being caught and sent away. Suppose he was discovered now? Askaris were searching the interiors of the servant quarters, emerging now and again with whatever they found suggestive of possible Mau Mau ritual to show to their superiors. An ebony walking stick, a banana leaf, a newspaper with a picture of Jomo Kenyatta on the front, a sheepskin-covered Bible, a bicycle pump, a half-eaten joint of beef in a porcelain bowl. A drunk was dragged out and pushed into the line, given a couple of slaps. No Njoroge, yet. Beside me, Mahesh Uncle was muttering a stream of invectives in Punjabi— badmash salé . . . kaminé . . . neech . . . kambakht log . . . bastards—and my mother told him a few times to control himself.

One of the two English officers was coming by the houses with an askari, chatting up the Asian residents, peeping discreetly inside their homes. He was a man of compact build, with fine features under his peaked cap, and held a swagger stick behind his back. He looked friendly yet menacing, and beamed a smile as he approached us.

How are you, kem-ché, namaskar, salaam—you can never be too careful with the terrorists, this is for the safety of you and yours. Remember, even the most trusted boy can turn against you with a panga (makes a chopping gesture with a hand) if he has taken the Mau Mau oath, so you must report anything suspicious. Don't hire Kikuyu. Safeguard your guns, get proper training in shooting, even the women, yes, you too, madam, and you, sir, have you installed your alarm . . .

Yes, sir, Lieutenant Soames, Papa said, you can never be too careful. Of course I have taken shooting lessons, I do the Home Guard patrols in this area, and it's a good thing you're keeping an eye on the blacks . . .

The man was at the back window of the house, peeping inside with curiosity as Mother drew a sharp breath, and he spoke softly, How are you, little girl, missing out on all the excitement, are we? What's your name?

She was asleep, explained Mother anxiously. My daughter—Deepa. She must have woken up just now.

Just then an uproar began outside the third house from ours, as Corporal Boniface and the second European officer staggered from the back door, pushing out someone who, though dark as an African, was known to most people in Nakuru as Saeed Molabux, nicknamed Madrassi and the son of a pre-eminent Nakuru family. He was thrown violently on the ground. He shouted something defiantly at the officer, the herded crowd of servants stirred into a collective murmur. Provoked, the officer, the corporal, and other askaris converged on Saeed, raining rifle butts and kicks on his back as his body curled up on the ground like a worm and he tried to shield his head with his raised elbows. Behind, at the doorway of the house, his mother Sakina-dadi, my dadi, and his sister Amina were all shouting incomprehensibly.

A furious Mahesh Uncle, Saeed's friend, charged forward bull-like, shouting, He's Juma Molabux's son, don't you know that? Stop or I'm calling his lawyer Mr. Kapila in Nairobi, *right now*!

Wisely, my uncle halted halfway, before reaching the policemen, and a glaring match ensued.

The beatings stopped, and a bloody-faced Saeed stood up, saying, Yes, I'll call my lawyer—

The lieutenant at our doorstep, who had just finished greeting Deepa, said in his gentle manner, It's the Emergency, they only mistook him for a bloody—pardon me, ma'am—Kyuke hiding away inside. You can't be too careful, can you.

Touching his hand to his cap in a salute, he strolled away, reserving a sharp look for Mahesh Uncle as he passed him.

What will happen to my silly brother? Mother whispered helplessly. To her surprise, Papa told her, In this case, he stood up for his friend.

They took away four of the servants for questioning, including the two who had tried to escape. They confiscated a few goats and chickens, a radio, and some other items, including the banana leaf and the newspaper. Bastards, Mahesh Uncle was still muttering, bloody kaburu bastards, even as the police officers turned to cast a final eye upon the scene. Saeed had been supported to his house by a servant and his sister.

And from our house emerged Njoroge, hesitant, frightened.

Where did you hide, Njoroge? asked Mother.

Under my bed, said Deepa, gaily tripping out behind him.

That girl is going to be the death of me!

No, she has done you proud, Mahesh Uncle replied, picking up Deepa, and I felt proud and yet jealous. Yes, she had been brave, she would always be the brave one.

I watched Njoroge's back, his tall bony shape, as he slowly made his way to his grandfather's single room, entered its dark interior, leaving the door wide open. Mwangi was one of the men taken away for questioning.

When on the following Saturday Mrs. Bruce came to drop off Bill and Annie and to order the groceries she would take with her later, she asked Papa if he had a bottle of whisky she could borrow or buy from him. Papa said, Of course. I could hardly refuse, she looked so desperate, he explained to Mother. It's not that they are lacking water, she retorted; let her drink water for a change. When Mrs. Bruce returned, Papa had a new bottle of Johnny Walker waiting for her. Our friends' mother left in very high spirits, ruffling Deepa's hair on her way out. That gesture pleased Mother.

Juma Molabux, the only wine merchant in town, in retaliation for his family's humiliation by the police, had announced that his stock of whisky had been destroyed by accident. The District Commissioner sent the police to check, in case there was whisky around and Molabux was in breach of hoarding laws, but they found that the three cases of whisky which had been in stock had indeed crashed down from a height, breaking all the bottles. And so the Europeans had to send for their whisky from Nairobi or go without; since many of them had credit terms with Molabux & Sons, and were not doing so well in that year of drought, they went without. Except, that weekend, the Bruces.

Saeed Molabux was kept in hospital for two days of observation. He received an apology from the District Commissioner and from the Commissioner of Police, who assured him that the officers in charge of the raid had been duly reprimanded. The police had been irresponsible, an editorial of the Nairobi paper said, this was hardly the time for the Europeans to antagonize another community, when the world's eyes were upon Kenya.

The Masai and Kikuyu peoples have traditionally been rivals, if not enemies, though there has been a tendency to deny this in recent times, in the interest of national harmony or political correctness. The Masai were herders of cattle in the vast plains of the Rift Valley, and the Kikuyu farmed the highlands and kept cattle and goats and sheep under the benevolent gaze of Ngai, the God on Mount Kenya. Occasionally, the Masai and the Kikuyu came into conflict. Governments, the British in the past and the more recent ones now, have found it expedient to exploit this rivalry, as my young visitor Joseph is only too ready to attest.

And so there was some irony in Lieutenant Soames calling Saeed a Kyuke, the Europeans' hate-filled term for the Kikuyu. For Sakina-dadi, Saeed's mother and Dadi's closest friend, was a full-blooded Masai. Such dark, exotic knowledge, portal to a forest of imaginings about the adult world, was obviously not deemed suitable for my sister and me, being brought up as Punjabi Hindus to the best of my mother's abilities. But after that violent police visit, the secret couldn't stay hidden for long.

Sakina-dadi, as I had known her, like any Punjabi woman wore a shalwar-kameez and dupatta, spoke Punjabi fluently and perfectly, at least to my young ears, and cooked formidable kheer, karhi, and dahi-wada. And when she cooked goat, Papa went off quietly to partake of it—Mother staring anxiously after him, having instructed him not to overdo it—for we did not cook meat in our home.

One day at breakfast Mother said, referring to Saeed's beating by the police, Imagine mistaking a Masai for Kikuyu! Immediately realizing she shouldn't have made that comment in front of the children, with a guilty look toward me she put an admonishing hand to her mouth and just as quickly removed it. Half Masai, Papa couldn't help interjecting before he too realized his error.

Is he, is he really a *Masai*? I asked excitedly.

Then why doesn't he have a spear, Papa? Deepa asked.

Next you will ask why doesn't he go around wearing only a red shawl with his bum showing, Papa replied. Budhu! He only *looks* like a Masai—doesn't he?

But the secret door had been opened. One day, Dadi exclaimed, to something Deepa said about Saeed's Masai looks, But his mother was such a beautiful Masai girl! There was a stunned silence, and then Dadi said quietly, Yes, Sakina-dadi was a Masai girl when Juma-dada married her long ago.

It was so obvious afterwards: Sakina-dadi was distinct. She was taller than my dadi, skinnier and long-legged; her face was round and her eyes large. She was dark, though in a way some Indians were. I never saw her hair, it was always covered by the dupatta. And there was a reserve about her, for instance when I went to her house to call my dadi; I don't recall her ever touching me. I have often wondered why.

Juma Molabux, at the end of his indentureship with the railway, chose to settle in Kijabe, where he opened a store to sell blankets, beads, and copper wire to the Masai. Kijabe was also on the railway line, a thriving town full of Indians at the top of the escarpment and directly overlooking the Rift Valley. Masai women and girls would come to Juma's shop, looking vigorous and free and happy, decked out in their latest fashions for this trip to the market. In his loneliness he must have found the maidens unbearably exciting, dressed so scantily compared with Indian women. They laughed at him, but not unkindly. One day a large Masai man, who called himself Jerom, came to Juma and said, You are staring at my women. You like them. You must marry one of them.

The Indian was flabbergasted. The Masai roared with laughter, called a companion over from the doorway, then turned to Juma.

What's the matter, you don't feel the urge to lie down beside a woman?

The companion said, more insultingly, with the appropriate gesture, You don't have that thing to shove into a woman?

Arm in arm, the men swaggered out. Their red cloaks, pulled over the tops of their bodies, with nothing else underneath, showed off portions of their smooth buttocks as proudly as their supple limbs; their long hair was plaited and dyed red, their pierced earlobes dangled low to their cheeks. Were they serious, or laughing at him? And if they were serious? As if he would marry a primitive Masai who put sheep fat in her hair and red earth on her body and drank cow's blood!

Jerom returned the next day. Well? Have you decided? With him was a maiden who had caught Juma's fancy several times—tall, smooth, and round-faced; she was beautiful, wearing discs of coloured beads round her neck, circlets of steel wire round her calves, and apparently nothing under her robe. She looked shy. Meeting her eye, Juma Molabux made his decision, based upon his soul-searching of the previous, sleepless night. He was lonely, he had no family in the country and not much status, and he badly wanted a woman. Cohabiting with, or even marrying, an African woman was not entirely unheard of among Indians. And nothing in his upbringing forbade marrying someone from another community, or race, provided—

I will marry her, but I must make her a Muslim.

This would grant him even a place in heaven, he had concluded the previous night.

You must pay me a cow, the prospective father-in-law said, already with more authority.

I don't have a cow, Juma countered, looking at the girl, his blood now surging with desire. I don't have that much money, I am a worker. But when I have earned enough I will pay you.

Done, Jerom said, and crushed Juma's hand inside his.

Was she truly beautiful? Mother asked Dada, who had opened up finally about his friend's story one cozy family evening.

Dadaji gave a thin smile but said not a word.

Papa spoke up, oblivious to his mother's presence: Bauji, tusi vi kadii tempt hoye hoge, na . . . all those tall, lithesome Masai girls—

Dada's ears turned red. Deepa looked at me, my eyes searched Mother's for some reason that I did not understand.

Biji was not any less beautiful, Mother put in, referring to Dadi.

True, true, said Papa, I was only pulling the old man's leg!

The marriage terms agreed on, Juma Molabux went to Nakuru and fetched his friend and fellow Peshawaree, my grandfather, to act as his escort, and the two of them drove a bullock cart from Kijabe to the Masai manyatta down on the plains beside Mount Longonot for the marriage ceremony. They stayed with the Masai for two days and took away the new bride. Her groom had brought her a shalwar-kameez and dupatta, which she wore shyly but proudly. She wore leather chappals. And she did not have several discs of many-coloured beads round her neck, but rather a plain gold chain and pendant, a gift from my dada and dadi. There was no sheep's fat on her hair. Her people had laughed when they saw her thus, bedecked as a stranger, sitting on the cart, but they had also cheered. And they told the groom and his escort to sing, as they took her away, and the two men sang happy verses from the Punjabi story of Heer and Ranjha. Juma Molabux took his wife to live in Nakuru, where they could rely on the support of their friends, my dada and dadi.

What was the marriage ceremony like? Papa asked.

Dada said, The medicine man sprinkled the couple with water, they had to wear leaves and walk around, and then they went to spend the night in a hut.

Wah, said Papa with a sigh.

You sound regretful you didn't marry a Masai, Mother reprimanded.

He put his arm around her, gave her a squeeze. You are my Masai woman, na.

One of those heartwarming moments between them, when Mahesh Uncle was not around.

But she speaks Punjabi! Deepa said.

Better than me, said Papa.

Ha sahi achi to bolti hai, Dadi said.

Dadi explained how, in Nakuru, she had taught Punjabi ways to the Masai girl.

———————

My young visitor stays up late sometimes, turned on to the Internet, through which he keeps abreast of developments in Kenya. He has become a member, I learn, of a chat group called MuKenya, styling themselves Sons of Mau Mau. Some of the rhetoric of the group is bitter and inciteful, but perhaps that's all it is: rhetoric. And perhaps Joseph's distance from the turmoil back home, in these calmer surroundings, will help him to think of more constructive responses. His current passion certainly puts a barrier between us.

The town closest to where we are is Korrenburg, an hour's walk away, ten minutes by car. We sometimes walk there. The library has the usual thrillers and a surprisingly good collection of historical volumes on the African colonies of the Empire. There is an Agatha Christie society and a reading club. It is the kind of small, quiet town where Dame Agatha might well have sent Miss Marple to spend a few days with a married niece and solve a mystery. In fact, the local Christie club organizes regular events, including mystery getaways and fashion shows in which members appear dressed as Christie characters. The librarian here, to my surprise, turned out to be an Indian, a Ms. Chatterjee. The three of us had a lunch of fish and chips together.

According to Ms. Chatterjee, Korrenburg was founded more than two hundred years ago by seven Loyalist families from the United States. It was called Georgetown and later renamed to commemorate the marriage of one of the daughters of King George IV to a Bavarian prince. Korrenburg boasts many cultural activities, some impressive architecture, its own town crier, and a marina. You will like it, says the librarian.

FOUR

———————————

Vikram?
   Yes.
   What was that?
   What?
   That *sound*—did you hear it? (She whispers.)
   There's nothing.
   Do you think they could come for us?
   No, of course not. Go to sleep.

It was the nights that curdled the blood, that made palpable the terror that permeated our world like a mysterious ether. The faint yet persistent chir-chir-chir of crickets or the rhythmic croak-croak of frogs when it rained, the whine of the solitary vehicle on the road, seemed only to deepen the hour, enhance the menacing ominousness lurking in the dark outside. The Mau Mau owned this darkness, which cloaked them into invisibility; then suddenly they materialized, a gang of twenty or forty seeking entry into a marked house, throwing poisoned meat to the guard dogs, hacking a watchman to death . . . or a single murderer looking down upon you as you lay in bed.

Such were the stories we had heard about them. The Mau Mau are your enemies, they will kill and maim your family and children, they perform bestial rites and orgies under the cover of night in the homes of their sworn supporters, one of whom could well be your Kikuyu servant in his room. A pamphlet was distributed by the government. It was in Swahili and illustrated with pictures of purported Mau Mau doings. Two of them seared my young mind then, have become forever unforgettable. In one, a naked African child of about four lay curled on the ground, in a posture of sleep; the neck abruptly drooped down, and at its back, the only disfiguration on the smooth body, a black inky smudge with thick bristly protrusions like crawling worms. It took a few days of brooding over and compulsive staring at the picture in secret, eventually through a stamp collector's magnifying glass, for the realization to catch hold that those were not worms on the back of the child's head but broken ends of skin, bone, and muscle, all the exposed tissues of a neck hacked by a panga. In the other picture, a girl of about six, also naked, lay bent over a log; there were short panga slash marks on her calves; there was no head on the body, it lay about a foot away. The panga had cut away part of an ear, this I remember too.

Report Mau Mau activity in your area, the pamphlet exhorted. If you suspect that someone has taken the Mau Mau oath, or if you yourself are approached to take it, talk to the police. Call 999.

After Mahesh Uncle took up his job in the Resham Singh Sawmill near Njoro, Deepa was given his room to sleep in. Still afraid of the dark, she often slipped into my bed, her warm body close to mine, and she would start her fretful querying: Vikram?

Once a week, on Tuesdays, our father would go out on a patrol of our area of Nakuru in the night. He had volunteered for this Home Guard duty rather brashly, as Mother always made it a point to remind him, telling him there were enough younger men who were willing to do the job. He would go with one other person and the duty lasted from ten p.m. till one a.m. Before he left, as he stood at the door, Mother made sure he wore his thick sweater under the windbreaker and had his police whistle in his pocket. She put a flask of coffee and a box of savouries in his hands, and she would hear out his long string of reminders—to keep an occasional eye on the lighted backyard, to keep within rapid access of the alarm switch and the gun by their bedside, when to use the telephone and always to be brief whether calling out or answering, to pay heed if neighbourhood dogs started barking, how to listen for the reassuring sounds of the two Dorobo watchmen who did the rounds of our development every night armed with bows and arrows . . . and what to do just in case . . . no point in hiding the kids, they should all stay together. If he didn't stop, she would interrupt him and put in her plea: Now listen, don't be foolish and step out of the car, did you hear? Yes, yes, don't worry, he would say, which hardly convinced her. One night, while going around some house to inspect the servant quarters, as he was required to do occasionally, he had been brought to the ground by two Alsatian guard dogs. The consequences, if the residents had been tardy in their response or too quick with their guns, could have been dire for him. Finally it would be time to leave. If it was his partner's turn to drive, the car would arrive outside and toot its horn briefly. Adjusting his khaki cloth hat, of which he was rather conscious, with a reassuring glance at his official white armband that said "H.G.," and saying, "Accha, mein jaunga," Papa would take leave, and Mother would secure all the bolts and locks on the door and turn around to face us, white as a sheet. She would hurry to the table which held the statues of all the important gods and whisper brief prayers. It was her puja day and she would already have been to the temple earlier.

Morning came refreshingly, vigorously, with the cocoricoo of a cock, brilliant sunlight smiling through the windows, the radio tuned to Hindustani service, servants chatting outside in Kikuyu, Luo, Nandi, or Swahili, tea paraphernalia clattering in the house, the smell of woodsmoke and hot toast and parantha and butter, and we were all alive and the world was wonderful.

Mwangi, Njoroge's grandfather, was released two days after being taken away during the police raid. Deepa and I were sent by our mother to take some bananas and chappatis for him to welcome him home. We did not bring curry, because he did not like our curries, preferring his own spinach or bean stews without spices but with a lot of salt. One of the three other men who had been taken with him had been sent to a detention camp. He had been sporting a "Jomo" beard, I had heard, and was one of the two who had tried to escape when the raid began. In my experience, Africans often disappeared, having gone "back home" or been taken into detention or sent to jail for not paying tax or rent or for getting into a brawl.

After we had made our presentation, Deepa ran off to play somewhere. Njoroge was not around. I stayed back and watched Mwangi as he sat crouched outside the doorway of his quarters and proceeded to eat. His knees were grazed and dusty, from going down on them while gardening, and his fingertips were coarse, the nails black-edged. He probably found ugali, a meal made from maize flour, more filling, but chappati was a delicacy for him, and he ate it carefully, cutting each one into quarters, and then into smaller pieces, which he used to scoop up the vegetable and sauce.

What did they do to you at the police station, Muzee? I asked, when he was finished and had put aside his plate.

He smiled, took a long draught of water, emptied the glass. He said, They asked and asked.

What, Muzee? What did they ask?

Am I Mau Mau? I said no.

And then?

They asked me again, as if they had not heard the first time.

And that Corporal Boniface, that fat one who calls himself the lion, did he ask, too?

Eeh, yes, he too asked, that one. The dog barks loudest in the presence of its master—always know that.

Grinning mischievously at my befuddlement, he stood up to go. I watched him amble toward the front side of the houses, where he usually worked and liked to be found. He was employed jointly by the families on our side of the street. People brought him all sorts of cuttings and seeds to plant and tend to in their patches, though in this year of drought keeping everyone happy about their plants was not easy. He cut the grass and trimmed the hedges. He swept the ground. And he acted as the daytime watchman. For rest he would sit on a front step of a house or under a tree. He was unique among our workers, for no one was rude or shouted orders to him as they did to the others. But there were some complaints that he was slow and that there wasn't enough work for him. I hated the thought that he might have to leave us. He had worked for a European family in Thompson's Falls before coming to us, when they left the country. He had been hired and brought to Nakuru by one of the Asian families, who had also helped Njoroge get enrolled in the local Shamsi school.

That was about six months earlier, when I came upon an African boy sitting in our backyard on a stone, shooting pebbles. It was Njoroge.

Ay, I said, don't you know this is our house?

He looked up, then quietly took a few steps and stood in the no man's land between our area and the neighbour's in the next building, and watched me. I knew he was not a servant, a "boy," because he was in a school uniform, khaki and white. Inspired by his game, I went inside and brought out my set of marbles and started shooting and showing off.

Deepa came running out to join, and as usual started an argument, and as recourse to winning it she casually asked Njoroge, Didn't you see my shot just graze that marble—a little? No, he said, and smiled with sympathy at her disappointed face.

It's his turn now, anyway, not yours, she told me with a provoking look and put the shooting marble in Njoroge's hand.

He was a bony chap, a good three inches taller than I and a year older. His shorts were too big and needed a tight belt to hold them up. For several days after that first meeting, we played with only the most perfunctory words exchanged between the two of us; it was as if we needed each other, yet couldn't bring forth our private selves, our real natures. It was Deepa, when she would join us, who broke the barrier and brought light and laughter to our play.

His father, Njoroge told us, had gone away to study in Uganda; of his mother he said nothing.

My mother, I think, felt a kinship for him as a child without a mother, and she would sometimes stop him and ask him questions, this being the usual way of conversing with others' children. What did you eat today, William, what did Grandfather cook? (She couldn't decide between using his English and Kikuyu names.) Was it enough? How was school? She had already once grilled him about himself: how old he was, who his teachers were, where his village was. This last was an obvious question to her, as an Indian from India. Then she asked where his mother and father were. Yes, nampenda, he had told her, I love my mother, and my own mother smiled, very satisfied.

Once she told him, I too lost my mother when I was young, William. And he gave her a long stare full of awe.

We don't have heroes, I grumbled to Mother once.

She glared at me, then looked offended. What do you mean, we don't have heroes? Think of Shree Rama, who was so gentle—

I mean *heroes*!

He slew the ten-headed Ravana! That's a hero! And Bhim of the Pandavas took on a whole army alone in the great battle of Mahabharata—

Not *those* kinds of heroes, Ma! Not gods!

What kind, then? What better heroes than gods?

Bill as Field Marshal Montgomery riding high on his tank (a box atop our cart) searching for the lurking enemy (Vic and Njoroge) behind a sandpile in Tunisia (the dusty, unpaved parking area of the shopping centre). And when subaltern Lall lay wounded in a hospital bed (ours but to do or die, at Bill's bidding), who should come to tend him with gentle hands and worried face but our own Florence Nightingale, Annie, the Lady of the Coke-bottle lamp, saying, Tut-tut, Vikram Lall, you didn't take the medicine! And when I was Davy Crockett—a more likely hero than any of my mother's godly nominations—Njoroge had to play the Indian (Bill refusing because he was not a native) and Deepa was his squaw with her tea set.

But Njoroge's hero, he said, was Moses.

Moses sent plague on the pharaoh and destroyed his crop and animals, he sent the angel of death in the dark of the night to kill the Egyptians' eldest sons, until finally the pharaoh gave up and Moses took his people to freedom.

But Jesus hurt no one and he still won, said Annie. Only he himself had to die, as Vicar Robinson said.

I don't recall our ever enacting a Moses scene.

In the privacy of our backyard, eating scalding-hot pakodas straight from the kadai, courtesy of Mother, Njoroge told me significantly: Jomo is Moses.

Jomo? He is a man?

I had thought Jomo was a kind of beard, an African goatee.

Njoroge nodded. Jomo was the one who was in jail in Kapenguria; when he came out he would take his people to freedom; all the lands of the Kikuyu—he made a sweeping gesture—would be returned to them, all the cattle and sheep would come home to graze. All the white people would go home to England.

A different kind of Moses, then. He would not take his people anywhere, just send the others away.

Even Bill and Annie?

He didn't reply.

And the Mau Mau—are they his angels?

He shrugged.

I stared at him in wonder. Why did I know so little of the world? What cattle would come home with Jomo? And would the Asians go home to India? I didn't want to go to India, to the tumult and the dust and where you stepped into shit even in a posh taxi, as Papa described it. Not even to the enchanted forests of Rama and Sita, as Mother would have it. I knew of no world outside my Nakuru, this home, this backyard, the shopping centre, the school; this town beside the lake of flamingos, under the mysterious Menengai Crater where we sometimes went on family picnics, passing the European area on the other side of the tracks.

All our heroes did wonderful things, but Njoroge's Jomo-Moses was different. He was alive! He was in prison! And he had powers.

There was a depth to my friend that I could not reach, could never fathom even when we became close. Just as there was a mystery and depth to Bill and his Englishness. Why was my own life so simple? Why did it seem so irrelevant? In that fateful year of our friendship, when we played together I couldn't help feeling that both Bill and Njoroge were genuine, in their very different ways; only I, who stood in the middle, Vikram Lall, cherished son of an Indian grocer, sounded false to myself, rang hollow like a bad penny.

It goes without saying, though, that with Annie I was entirely myself, at ease and happy.

Deepa came over and dropped, from the basket she had improvised by lifting up the front of her dress at the hem, some more steaming pakodas in the plate between Njoroge and me, and then ran off to play on the swing, throwing curious looks at us as we talked and ate.

You must swear not to tell anybody, Njoroge said, about Jomo. He is our secret.

I swore, by an oath that he called Number One, not to tell anyone.

But I did *ask* my mother later, Who is Jomo? She gave me a sharp look and shuddered. He is Ravana himself, the leader of the Mau Mau, she said, but he is in prison.

Who is Jomo, Mahesh Uncle? I asked when my uncle next visited from the sawmill. And he too gave me a sharp look.

Jomo Kenyatta, he said. He is the leader of the Africans, and he wants the lands of the Kikuyu returned to them.

Is he Moses?

Another sharp look, then Mahesh Uncle nodded. Yes, he is like Moses, in some ways. But say, who's been telling you this?

I kept quiet.

He must have thought there was at least some hope for me, if not for his brothers-in-law. He could become extremely tender at such moments, as he became then, saying, while adjusting his black-framed glasses, Now run along, child, go and play, hunh. You're a bright chap.

This Jomo, I figured, would very well have to leave Mahesh Uncle alone; and if so, my family and I were safe.

Mahesh Uncle's bluster and angry outbursts, I sensed even as a boy, only camouflaged his emotional vulnerability. I was extremely fond of him, always felt defensive of him when he was put down, usually in his absence by my father's brothers, as an idler and a failure. His life harboured an essential sadness that resulted from displacement following India's partition. Mother wanted dearly for him to marry. She made discreet inquiries in Nakuru and Nairobi. But his reputation was known, no one wanted a communist for a son-in-law. But the hope remained in our family that he would mellow and sooner or later find a bride and settle down properly.

Mahesh Uncle's vocal support of the Kenyan freedom struggle, as he insisted on calling it, made my family rather nervous.

We fought for the independence of India, dammit, he would say. The Africans are doing just the same!

But Gandhiji's way was nonviolence and . . . and . . . negotiation, Mother told him once, Gandhiji didn't tell us to go and butcher the British!

The British are not being butchered in Kenya—they are exaggerating only to gather world support for their oppression.

Tell that to Mr. Innes, Papa put in. Tell that to the man whose wife and child were cut to pieces.

The one who calls me a Bengali. Don't you see, sometimes people have to *fight* for their freedom! All peoples have done it one time or another. So Gandhiji's way was nonviolence, even that is debatable, but Netaji Bose's way wasn't—

Subhas Chandra Bose, Mother uttered with distaste. *He* was a Bengali.

There was silence.

To Papa these Indian references were quite alien. Even though he took pride in Gandhi's renown in Europe and America, he couldn't help also voicing the opinion that the mahatma had been a crafty and definitely an embarrassing-looking Gujarati banya, who in the manner of his wily people had simply fooled the gullible. Of Subhas Chandra Bose, leader of an Indian army that helped the Japanese to fight the British in the Second World War, my father had simply not heard.

It was a moment of triumph for Papa when my uncle had agreed, several months earlier, to take up the position of manager of the Resham Singh Sawmill. My mother was in tears when her brother left. What will he do there, alone in the jungle?

He'll be *safe* in the jungle, Papa told her, and muttered, If he doesn't decide to go and join the Mau Mau himself . . . He could be sent to jail, with his attitude, he could be sent to detention like that Makhan Singh fellow . . . He could even get himself *hanged*!

Tauba! Don't say that!

Don't worry, Papa said, going to her on the sofa, sitting beside her. He put his arm around her and squeezed her. We'll look after your brother. And he is not that far, he will keep visiting us.

My father adored my mother. I loved Mahesh Uncle, but I knew that my mother would have loved my father much more if my uncle had not been around.

I recall a scene in our living room.

Do you remember—

What?

He shook his head, smiling, then looked away.

No, tell me, Mahesh, come on.

Mother and her kid brother, together in our living room, on a Saturday afternoon (Papa pottering about somewhere), discussing their childhood in Peshawar in pre-Partition India. They were seated on opposite sofas, her face flushed with pleasure, concern, tenderness. She always wore shalwar-kameez, and today the top was white with red flowers, the pyjama all red, crisply starched. At that moment, not attendant upon my father or the household, or upon Deepa and me, all the needs and demands that took up much of her life, she was a girl once again, radiant and free. How we treasure those youthful years of our lives, what happiness hers must have meant to her.

I would climb on your back and you would take me around, Mahesh began.

On all fours like a horse—hut-hut-hut-chalo!

From room to room and even to the neighbour's—you must have scraped your knees from that ordeal.

She smiled, said: And you held on to me by my pigtail.

They were silent for a while. Then she murmured: How I remember that house, each and every corner in it, every crack on the wall, I can take you to the spot where the ceiling leaked during monsoon, where the floor was broken under the dining table, the chip on the seventh step—

And I can take you through the streets of Peshawar blindfolded—the halwai where we bought jelebi, the police station where Father locked me up, the dhaba where the Congress youth would meet for strategy. I can name for you all the attendants who served at that dhaba. We'll never see those streets again. All that madness, cutting up a country in two—that's the British for you: divide and rule.

But we asked for Partition.

Who?

The Hindus and Muslims.

Not all of them. Just the rich and privileged, misleading the others.

They were silent again. Mother looked up toward the rooms where Papa had gone a few minutes ago, in case he needed her. Then she said, Do you remember when Ma died?

He looked vacantly at her, nodded. Father took me to the pyre when he lighted the fire. Her soul has flown away, he said, it's only the empty body. She'll come back in a new body. I rather preferred the old body. How would I recognize the new one, I used to ask him.

I remember, she said. I had to be with you even as I knew she was in pain and dying, and her sisters had gathered around . . .

After a pause, my mother looked at him and said quickly, Mahesh Bhaiya, why didn't you make up with him—poor Father—

He was the one who cast me out! He arrested me, his own son, he put me in prison!

Not you alone, and that was his *job*.

Fine job. Working for the British. And there was that other thing too, in 1946, after the world war.

That was also his job.

He was a traitor.

Don't *say* that, Mahesh! It was his job, his duty. He was a police inspector. If he had not kept the law—

If who had not kept the law? Papa said, walking in, having just had a wash, smelling of hair oil. He pulled me gently by the ear from where I sat, at the door, looking outside at the road, and said, My spy will tell me, won't you?

Meanwhile Mother pretended the tears were not glistening in her eyes and gave us all a smile.

Grandfather Verma a traitor! Mahesh Uncle in jail! Now *that* was food for the imagination . . . but that life was far away in India and in the past. *My* life was so ordinary!

There was a framed photo of Grandfather Verma, from the chest up, on one of the walls in the house. He seemed to be in some kind of uniform, police I assumed; he had a large forehead and a thin moustache, and there was a trace of a smile on his lips. He looked rather like the police superintendents of the Indian movies of the fifties and sixties, someone who could have been the movie idol Dev Anand's superior officer. He sent us cards for Diwali and New Year, with little notes that began, How are you, my little ones? And we in turn wrote short letters to him guided by Mother. After that overheard partial revelation from Mahesh Uncle, I looked upon the photo of Grandfather Verma with some respect. He was my past and there was a mystery about him, which I would find out as I grew up, when the time came for me to know.

I remember another ritual of my father's. It was a frightening one, performed once or twice a month, late on a Sunday night. Very suddenly, a little after nine o'clock just as the news ended, as if at a whim he would go over to the front door, pull aside the drape on it, and stare outside for a minute or so. By this time Mother would be extremely nervous. Slowly

Papa would undo one of the locks. Then, purposefully he went to his and Mother's bedroom and brought out his revolver, a rather large and ugly, dull black thing inside a brown holster, and a small cardboard box of ammunition. He also had with him a yellow piece of paper, a pamphlet on which he placed the gun and ammo on the dining table. He would pick up the gun and, facing away from us all, hold it up in his hand. Then he would walk to the door, open it wide into the dark night. He would take a step outside.

Hé Rabba! Mother would exclaim, holding us close to her. Don't shoot into someone's house!

I won't, I'm aiming to the side. I have to check it, na . . .

Don't shoot at anybody!

As if I would. And who would be out at this time? I'm aiming high, anyway.

We would hear a loud report that went tearing into the silence of the night, and then another one, even as the first one still echoed somewhere far away. He would come in, blowing the smoke off the gun, catching our frightened eyes and looking a little sheepish. The gun has to be checked, you see, he would explain, placing it on the table, on the yellow pamphlet. With the weapon now inert in front of us, Deepa and I taking sneaky, quick reaches to feel its grey metallic heft, Mother brought glasses of milk for us all.

We all knew the pamphlet well, another government warning. This one had a drawing of a devilish black man with large eyes and open mouth, leaping out of the yellow page, under the caption: The Mau Mau want your gun! There were instructions on safeguarding the weapon. Do not leave it in the car when you step out for shopping, one of them said. Papa always kept it locked in the drawer of his bedside table and took it out, it seemed, only for this practice ritual.

Muzee, why do the Mau Mau kill little children? I once asked Mwangi.

I don't know why I asked him this. Perhaps because he had a gravity about him, and an honesty, and he was an African and a Kikuyu.

They are evil and mad, those who kill children, he told me firmly.

I have never understood the full implication of those words. Mwangi often confounded me.

────────────────

There is a nip in the night air outside, a reminder that autumn waits around the corner. If you look hard during the day, you might even spot a telltale traitor yellow leaf among the green foliage. The night is moonless, thickly dark, rendered more so by the shadows of the trees and hedges; the stars above, though, look cheerful as diamonds, if I permit myself a nursery-rhyme image. The luminous hour-marks of my watch shine no less brightly. It is close to eleven. I step back inside this lakeside house, a hallmark of lonely luxury—and so extremely desolate compared with the bustling, peopled household of my childhood—to await Deepa's phone call. In the sunken living room, Joseph watches television, with a bag of chips and a can of soda. Before he arrived I wisely had a satellite dish installed. He likes to watch soccer—football, we used to call it—and a Kenyan player recently drafted into one of the English teams thrills him no end. Perhaps here, in the first world, he can be corrupted away from his brash and dangerous idealism, I tell myself—but then hard on the heels of that thought comes the quick and cynical reminder: corruption has been my recent forte, hasn't it.

The hour turns and the phone rings. Joseph looks up as I pick it up at the kitchen table. Deepa wants to know how the two of us are getting along here, in our Canadian retreat. We are doing fine, I reply, and how is she? Her son Shyam, she tells me, might shift to Washington, D.C.—he is a resident epidemiologist in Rochester—and she will then have to decide what to do. Her worry, though, is Joseph.

Vikram?

Yes.

Look after him, please, Bhaiya.

He's all right. Don't worry.

Keep talking to him. Make him understand that his education is the only important thing, it is not to be sacrificed for anything silly like politics—

I'll try, Deepa. I can only tell him what he allows me to say to him.

Vikram?

Yes.

He's like my son.

I know that. I'll do the best I can.

Rakhi day is coming, Bhaiya, I'll send you something.

I'll look forward to it, Sister.

FIVE

There are wonderful moments sometimes—a splash of colour, the sweet taste of icy kulfi on a Sunday afternoon, the feel of hot steam on the face and arms from a gasping locomotive—that stand out purely in themselves, sparkles of childhood memory scattered loosely in the consciousness. They need not tell a story, yet moments lead from one to another in this tapestry that is one's life; and so we feel bound, unhappy adults, to look past and around those glimmer points in our desperate search for nuance and completeness, for coherence and meaning.

Be that as it may, the following is one delightful moment that often twinkles before my mind's eye.

One afternoon after school I was sitting at the dining table, hunched over homework, when suddenly a commotion erupted outside. There was the sound of drumming and chanting and servants running in the alleyways, heading toward the front. I raced to the sitting room; the door was wide open and I ran through it, and came upon a most amazing spectacle in progress.

About twenty Masai youths were performing a traditional war dance outside the Molabux residence, three doors down from ours. A crowd had rapidly gathered on both sides of our street, to watch and marvel and comment—such happy idleness never before having been witnessed by me in our area. The dancers—tall and supple, the skin dark brown, the long hair plaited, combed back, and dyed red, multicoloured beads at the neck, the wrists, the arms, the pierced earlobes stuffed with more decoration, the red wool shawls only partially covering the torsos and waists—were arrayed in a line. They swayed to and fro and thumped the ground with their feet, to the rhythm of song and drum. Every now and then, suddenly and all together, they sprung high into the air, their bodies erect, their spears glinting, their teeth flashing in friendly smiles. Splashes of red and dark brown and white leapt up at the blue sky out of the dust. A small gang of Masai women of assorted ages provided the treble accompaniment from under a tree in what seemed a rather dispassionate manner compared with the vigorous and joyful displays of their men.

All this while Sakina Molabux, the dark, wizened matriarch of her house, stood motionless at her doorway, watching the performance intently, as if it were for her benefit. As indeed it was. Her husband Juma Molabux stood quietly beside her.

After a while, some of the Kikuyu and the Luo among the spectators joined in, with their own dances but not as expertly, and the performance soon wound down. There followed a solemn shaking of hands by the towering Masai with whoever stepped forward. They did this in three stages, first the normal clasping of hands, then a rotation of the hands so the two thumbs met and embraced, and then a twist back to the hand clasp before release. Two police Land Rovers had appeared on the street but were not intrusive. From somewhere, two men on stilts came tottering up, with white-painted faces and ostrich feathers around their heads. Coca-Cola was served to the performers, brought out from the back of the Molabux house in two crates.

It turned out that the Masai were in town to rehearse for festivities being organized by the government. Coronation Day was almost upon us, and Empire Day would soon follow.

But that afternoon as I watched these tall red-clothed men in amazement and clapped my hands to cheer them and mingled with the crowd to do the weird handshake and drew in their strange odour just for the heck of it, I was still too young to understand the full import of their performance outside our house. Since then I have wondered about it, about Sakina-dadi standing at her doorway taking it in. She was a full Masai whose wedding to Juma Molabux my own dadaji had gone to witness. In what manner would the drumbeat, the dance, have brought back her youth? Did she ever yearn for the simplicity and open life of the grasslands? Or, like the wife she was expected to be, had she easily given up thinking of that past, relishing her privileged urban status and her wealth? Did she ever stop worshipping the God Ngai of her childhood, did the spirits of the trees and the forests and the grasslands haunt her? The sour note of that moment came when Saeed Molabux angrily stormed past his mother and father and drove off noisily in his car. He obviously didn't think much of his Masai heritage. I would learn that Saeed had an elder brother who had disappeared, had in fact gone back to his maternal origins to become a Masai moran, and had that afternoon, following rehearsal at the football ground, brought his friends to perform for his mother.

As the Masai dispersed, walking in the middle of the street in bunches, one of them, a somewhat middle-aged man clutching his bottle of Coca-Cola in one hand and his staff in the other, came toward our house. He wore sandals and had a very slight, almost a shade, of a beard on his chin, and he had a wry little smile on his face. He stood a few feet outside our door and a worried-looking Mother came out. The man bowed to her and asked after her family; she replied politely and anxiously. The man asked after my grandfather Anand Lal, to whom he sent good wishes, and then he strolled off, still with that wry and perhaps even thoughtful smile on his face. My parents, and my grandfather when he came the next time, could make nothing of this incident. But it has often made me wonder about Dadaji.

We used to laugh at the Masai as kids. We thought of them as dark exotic savages left behind in the Stone Age, with their spears and gourds and half-naked bodies; when one saw them on a street they were to be avoided, for they smelled so. Yet we were also in awe of them, we did not make open fun of them, for they were warriors, they hunted lions with those spears, didn't they. There was a belief among Indian traders that the Masai could not count; yes, they couldn't, some of them, not in Swahili, which was alien, and not in the foreign units of feet and inches, years and months, shillings and cents. And it was not only the Indians who disparaged the Masai. Country bus drivers were known not to stop for them, or when they did, to move all the other passengers up front so these red warriors with their odour could sit at the back by themselves.

Because of my dada and dadi's close connection to the Molabuxes, I have often seen an affinity between myself and the Masai. I have even fantasized that Dada perhaps sought comfort with a woman of that people, perhaps she had his child and I have cousins in some of the manyattas of the plains. There is no proof anything like this ever happened—and my fantasy has partly to do with desperate need to belong to the land I was born in—but it's not impossible either. The Indian railway workers were not known for their abstinence; reports of their British overseers, quoted in histories of the railway, attest amply to that. Perhaps that man who came over and spoke to my mother was a connection to the past; he has never been explained. But my grandfather among his family was the picture of calm reserve and propriety, with no hint whatever that he had once been young and without care; the only time I saw that reserve crack was in the presence of his old friend Juma Molabux, when the two went on their walks together. In fact, it did not simply crack then, it burst apart like the shell of an overripe nut to reveal a softer, more nuanced inside.

On Sunday at noon, when Dada and Dadi arrived for the weekly family get-together, a servant would sometimes come from the Molabuxes with a message for Dada, Would the muzee like to go for a walk later with the other muzee, Juma? Dada usually said yes, and so after the siesta, at about four, the two men met by the road. Dadaji liked to take me along, and I was encouraged to go, it being implicit that this was just in case something untoward happened and a fleet-footed messenger were needed. We were sent off from the house with much fanfare. The sight of two old cronies more than seventy years old going out for a walk together, with a grandson to accompany them, was enough to warm the hearts of all. Even the servants would smile and well-wish, with admiring comments like, He who takes the road truly finds the elephant's tusk, meaning that these two muzees had come from afar and had finally acquired large families and well-being as their just rewards. I cannot imagine them, always unassuming, dressed simply in white drill pants and plain jackets, ever being the target of attacks. They were both compact in build, Juma-dada somewhat stouter and rounder in the face. I would walk beside them patiently, dutifully, and when not called away by some boyish diversion like climbing upon a rock or throwing a stone at a lizard or vainly chasing a passing car, I watched and listened, enthralled. I did not know of any relationship like these two old men's, their utter familiarity with each other, their constant chatter followed by a long silence except for the sound of their short breaths and the taps of their walking sticks, and then the sudden effortless resumption of their conversation, as if an engine had simply been allowed to idle awhile and was now back in gear. Their arms would occasionally brush against each other, as they spoke of Chhotu and Motu and Ungan and Ghalib (who had regaled them with poetry around a fire on many a night) and of Buleh Shah (who had the voice of a nightingale), and of such-and-such who had settled in Eldoret, and another who had recently lost his wife in Eastleigh, and so on. I remember Juma-dada chortling one time, and—to my shock—my grandfather breaking into a brief giggle, and then after a short exchange Juma-dada, with a look toward me, saying, But he's too small.

During another of these walks the two men suddenly stopped in their tracks and extended their arms toward each other, as if enacting the beginning of an Indian wrestling match or a fight. Then pointing out my anxious face to each other, they laughed and walked on.

My grandfather as I had known him at home was simply Dadaji, father of my father, a kindly old man with close-cropped white hair who had been born in faraway India in a faraway time, who had a certain past from which he pulled out partly recalled and perhaps exaggerated stories on Sundays when the mood struck him, the dada who after giving the children candies took a nap in the armchair in our sitting room. His mouth would hang partly open, he snored. But on these strolls with Juma-dada another person came out from inside him like a genie. I wished I could understand all that they said. But they spoke in a fluid Punjabi too quick for my ears, and the words and phrases I grasped were often alien to me.

A short walk away, our street met the perpendicular road, which led first to the shopping centre and then to the Nairobi highway, where it met the railway station. The yellow building of the station, visible in the distance, beckoned like a magnet and every few times the old men succumbed and turned toward it, heedless of the reminders from their families not to go that far, it was quiet that way and not entirely safe on a Sunday. Having decided to walk to the end, they picked up a discernible spring in their step, a purposiveness to their manner; the talk became less, the breathing heavier though steady. We would walk past the car park and up the station steps and through the gate to the platform, check the time by the station clock— presumed unimpeachable—walk up and down, examine the arrivals and departures notices on the blackboard, cross the pedestrian overpass to the other side. The all-important Nairobi–Kisumu and Nairobi–Kampala trains always stopped at Nakuru late at night, and not many people were around on a late Sunday afternoon.

One day the two men, over an argument about the laying of a rail, stepped down from the platform onto the tracks to take a closer look. First, Grandfather clambered down the ladder, which the two of them had dragged over from somewhere, then Juma-dada followed. They stood down there on the rails discussing the quality of the metal sleepers compared with the wooden ones used elsewhere, and if the fish bolts and plates were the original ones they had fastened, when from the Railway Restaurant (Europeans-only), a man came and angrily bawled us out. What are you doing here? Jao, jao, kambakht! Who gave you permission to come inside? Imbeciles! They climbed back up, apologizing profusely—Sorry huzoor—which made the red-faced man even madder, and I thought he would strike one of them. The station master hurried up and also started apologizing profusely to the white man, then added, These two gentlemen, you see, sir, were coolies who worked on the construction of the railway.

The white man, I think, seemed to shrink back. He gave a nod and briskly walked away. Grandfather and his chum looked embarrassed, like normally decent schoolboys who had been caught out of bounds and scolded by the headmaster. They had been severely humiliated, and I was close to tears that someone would talk to my dada that way. The station master went inside the restaurant and brought the old guys a bottle of soda each, which they sipped appreciatively through the straws, and an ice cream for me. The return walk was mostly silent. I did not tell a soul about the incident. But the station still beckoned, now and then, tugging at the men's hearts. That station master, when he was on duty, always felt obliged to bring something for us from the restaurant. His name was Sidhoo. Not surprisingly, he was well known to my grandfather as the son of a former railway coolie.

But when a train happened to be in the station, having been delayed for some reason, the three of us would hasten to greet it with boundless joy. I would run ahead, the two curmudgeons following on their delicate legs. I would prowl up and down the platform examining the rolling stock, the mysterious numbers inscribed on them telling a story I could never guess, the EAR insignia on the crimson-coated locomotive. There would be lots of people about, including curious-looking passengers who had no relations in town, and vendors of all sorts. Grandfather and Juma-dada would stroke the locomotive as though it were a pet elephant, and chat up the engineer, usually a Sardarji with bright turban and fierce moustache. He would look down like a monarch from high above the awesome wheels that were bigger than any man, leaning out to watch up and down the length of his immense conveyance. There would be the shouts of workers and the clanking of hammers and spanners, grunts and huffs as the loco-motive released great clouds of steam that enveloped its admirers. In the cabin with the engineer would be the fireman stoking the fire through its open grate, his face and bare back streaming with sweat, glowing from the heat.

The one who picked me up to bring me inside the cabin one day was called Tembo. He was a Goan, brown as cinnamon, and was called Tembo to mock his extreme thinness. If he ate more ghee he would make engineer, eh, Tembo? the Sardarji engineer teased. Osnu andar aanta deyo, he said to my two companions, with a gesture toward me, Dekhan ta deyo, Let him come inside and see, these days who's interested in trains, it's all aeroplanes for the little guys. And so, as I clambered up, the two old men pushed me along, and Tembo the fireman, teeth gleaming like pearls, pulled me into the cabin.

Young man, began the Sardarji in English as I stood gaping inside. You are inside the injuneer's cabin, from where the whole train is controlled. Kadi esa vekhya hai? The train-brain, ye . . . es, this is the brain of the train. And I am the brain of this brain. Brain-brain—ha-ha!

No, I shook my head, I had not seen anything like this train-brain before. I was in a magical gleaming enclosure of wood and brass, with a dozen little wheels and myriad gauges with quivering black needles that told of the current state of this giant locomotive. It was made in England, as a small brass plate in the centre of the front panel indicated, giving also the name of the company responsible. Sardarji pulled a green knob a couple of times and invited me to look out his window at the puffs of steam emerging from several parts of the engine where the release valves were located. I grinned and waved at bystanders. I pulled the chord and made the train whistle. Everywhere I touched and smudged, the brass or glass or wood was carefully wiped with a rag by sweat-streaming, smiling Tembo.

There was nothing more impressive for me in the world. Bill could go and become a fighter pilot chasing enemies when he grew up, Njoroge could become Moses to his people; I would be an engineer of locomotives, racing the length and breadth of the country, from Mombasa to Nairobi, through Nakuru and all the way to Kisumu or Kampala, and then back again, from Indian Ocean to Lake Victoria on that steady rhythm— a-jeeka-jeeka . . . grunt, grunt . . . a-jeeka-jeeka . . . grunt, grunt . . . a-jeeka-jeeka-jeeka-jeeka-jeeka-jeeka—on the railway line that my grandfather and Juma-dada and Ghalib and Buleh Shah and the other old folk had left their homes in Punjab to build.

As I emerged from the locomotive and waved back at the Sardarji, he blew a short whistle for me. And, mischievously, he released a giant puff of steam that drenched me and all the others watching him in admiration.

That was engine number 5812 of the East African Railways. A 4-8-4 + 4-8-4 Garratt locomotive, as Papa called it when I described it to him, the numbers designating the configuration of its wheels. He too had loved trains and knew about them. Dadaji would take his entire family to the railway station when they were young, and Papa and his brothers too recalled the shrouds of wet steam released by a grinning Sardarji engineer.

Another Sunday afternoon, and again there was a train on the platform, this time eerily filled with hundreds of grim, black faces—Kikuyu men, women, and children, looking out through the windows, silent as ghosts, some with their passes and tax receipts in a metal box worn around their necks with a chain, on their way to their reserved areas, pushed out by the travails of the Emergency. Hoo-ooo, the whistle blew, the Sardarji from his engine seat picked up in his arm the tablet in its tennis racquet–shaped holder—which gave him the go-ahead to enter the next section of track—and the black faces in the third-class windows lurched forward, to where?

To Embu, Nyeri, Karatina, Othaya, all the towns of the Kikuyu reservation. Does the British government think, Dada muttered, that by shunting these people away they will disappear and the problems go away?

In such a way did reminders of the Emergency spring up, suddenly, when least expected—it was as if in the midst of a happy, technicolour family movie some black-and-white footage had slipped in, grim, unhappy, and foreboding.

The taste of kulfi on a Sunday afternoon—sweet and rich as childhood— nothing else will quite capture its texture, its flavour, that perfect frozen blend of green and yellow that melted in your mouth and lingered and lingered. The Sunday that comes to mind was unusual. The family get-together was at Dada and Dadi's so we could go to see the much-publicized annual cricket match between the Nakuru Club and the Asian XI. My grandparents lived in a flat above Bombay Sweets, a small restaurant with tube lights and glass-topped tables and oil-painted grease-glazed walls, whose glorious savouries and sweets—laid out in kaleidoscopic heaps on the counters—were renowned throughout the country, and even beyond, in Uganda, Tanganyika, and Belgian Congo. Across from this eatery was a long and high grey wall, beyond which was the posh, exclusive Nakuru Club. Nonwhites were not permitted in the club, but on special occasions such as this one, an area of the pavilion was set aside for the Asians. The Europeans, dressed smartly in white, the ladies wearing hats, sat in the wide, open, raised veranda of the clubhouse or outside on the grass where tables had been laid out. African waiters moved about wearing long, white kanzus, green sashes across their fronts, and green fezzes. This annual cricket match was always controversial, which made its appeal to the Asian spectators all the greater. This time, even before the toss, it was discovered by the Europeans that one of the Asian players had actually come all the way from Mombasa to assist the local side. He was promptly dismissed. News spread among the Asian crowd that a traitor had betrayed their Spartan side arrayed against a rich club. In response, the Asians objected to a club player who was visiting from Middlesex County in England; the man was said to have emigrated, and the objection was not allowed. Asian youths heckled the decision.

Look, said Mother, watching the Europeans, even when they are taunted they look so composed.

You talk like our father, Mahesh Uncle scolded, and she laughed.

She was very happy and playful that day. She watched the beginning of the match (the Asian side batted first) before going off to Dada and Dadi's to help with arrangements for the family meal. When the match broke for lunch, we all crowded into our grandparents' flat and ate on the floor. After the lunch the males returned to the match. Just before the official tea break, our family met at the restaurant, crowding round two tables, and consumed bhajias, kachori, and bhel puri, with hot tea to scald the tongues already burning with spices (as was customary), and topped that all off with the miraculous kulfi. No water in that kulfi, no colouring, all cream with almonds and pista, saffron and sugar. And, as Papa typically wisecracked, a swipe of salty sweat from the brow of the half-naked, hairy, Brahmin kandhoi-chef.

The cricket match was won by the Nakuru Club, which was saved from defeat by the batting of the man from Middlesex, who scored sixty-odd runs. The Asians left the club with cries of Foul! and We'll show them next year!

S I X

———————

The sun shone gloriously but without a thought for how much the land could bear, and only reluctantly, it seemed, did it go down to retire each night, during which interim no cloud dared come close to bring relief to the earth. And so the drought continued. Daytime heat was unrelenting, the streets and roads were dry, the grass was parched and yellow, the corn and wheat stalks in the farms were limp and red with dust. The weather map of Kenya in the newspaper showed the same feature from Moyale to Nairobi, Lake Victoria to the Indian Ocean, Turkanaland to the border with Tanganyika: an open circle for a cloudless sunny sky. The weather charts we drew in school had gone from cheerful blue and sunny to a mindless white and yellow. The rains would not come. Meanwhile Papa and Om Uncle and all the other traders in town were getting anxious, because their credits to the European farmers kept increasing and their own creditors in Nairobi were on their backs. Indian shops went bankrupt when their European clients could not pay.

But not to worry, said Mr. Bruce as his servant Kihika carried away another box of groceries to the truck. Mrs. Bruce's father, who was a wealthy man, had extended them a loan. And the Farmers' Association's insurance payments were small but regular. And once the rains came, as surely they would . . .

Still, Papa said, if you could kindly make a payment forthcoming soon . . . my creditors won't wait.

Mr. Bruce turned red. All eyes were upon him, including those of the children, who were always in the shop prior to the departure of the Bruces, sipping soft drinks. Slowly he took his cheque book from his breast pocket and briskly wrote out a cheque.

There, Mr. Lall—for the time being.

Mr. Bruce was a big man who always wore a brown suede vest and a matching, worn-out, floppy hat. I would stare in wonder at his gigantic black boots, into which were tucked his pants. He was a gregarious sort. His wife seemed to send him for the groceries whenever the balance on their credit had become embarrassingly high. But this was to Papa's advantage, because he found it easier to ask the husband for payments than the wife.

No money, but they won't give up the most expensive items on their budget, said Mother. That smelly cheese, for instance—I am certain we are losing money on it. And I can't even tell the good part from the rotten part sometimes. I swear that I could have thrown up over it and they would not have told the difference.

Papa looked up, surprised, and she blushed, saying, Have their purchases gone down at all?

Somewhat. The Molabuxes have stopped extending credit on drinks, Papa said musingly.

We should do the same for groceries.

Can you deny them food?

The food they eat, we can't even afford.

But the Bruces had become friendly and familiar to us and Mother's attitude to them had softened. Mrs. Bruce was a gardener, and she had recently given Mother a rose cutting from a variety she was breeding for the annual Nakuru Show later that year. The flower was expected to be orange and she had tentatively called it Borneo Rose, for want of a better name. It was a cross between two South African varieties. Mr. Bruce had suggested My Kenya Beauty, she told Mother, but that was a more likely name for a thoroughbred and hardly something you would call a rose. She herself preferred a name that would commemorate the Queen's coronation.

When Mrs. Bruce brought the rose cutting over to our house, it was Sunday around noon and cooking was in progress full swing throughout the development. The first thing she said as Mother met her on the porch was, What a wonderful smell!

Mother beamed. Everybody's cooking at this hour, she explained. And they are making the best meal of the week. That aroma comes from hot ghee and spices.

It's delicious, observed Mrs. Bruce.

One day you and your family should come and have luncheon with us, Mother told her.

Why, thank you.

Bill and Annie had come with their mother, and all three were in their Sunday best. They came inside and we all sat properly in the sitting room, arrayed in a circle and looking at each other a little nervously. This was the first time any European had come inside our house, and everything in sight of the visitors possessed an extra shine and sparkle that day, from the linoleum on the floor to the plastic flowers in their Indian brass vases and the glass on the framed reproductions of a charging bull elephant and a herd of zebra. As we waited for the servant to bring around the soft drinks and the eatables, Papa and Mrs. Bruce began to discuss the weather. If it didn't rain for another month, Mrs. Bruce said, their well would go dry. Papa said he understood that the flamingos on the lake were fewer this year, and that at the temples and mosques prayers were being offered for rainfall to come soon. Indeed, said Mrs. Bruce, looking surprised. Papa told her he had read that the Americans had developed the technology for making rain, now if that technology were available in places like Kenya . . .

I recall that Annie looked scrubbed and radiant that day, her cheeks were the pink of peaches. She wore a constant, shy smile and had on a polka-dot pinafore and two ribbons in her hair. Mother was so taken by her angelic look that she caressed her cheek and chin in the Indian way and asked her if she took music lessons; she herself had taken a bit of sitar and singing in India—though (she turned to explain to Mrs. Bruce) she had not been able to find an Indian music teacher in Nakuru yet.

To everyone's surprise, Annie responded with a few words sung softly but in a very high voice.

You sing beautifully, Mother exclaimed. What is that? How lovely! What a voice you have!

It's from choir, Mrs. Bruce said, they had choir practice this morning after church.

Oh, can they sing us something?

Yes, give us a show, Papa said. He seemed to hover in a limbo between his boisterous self and the respectful Indian, while also under the watchful eye of Mother.

Can you sing something, darlings? Mrs. Bruce asked her children. Something short?

Annie stood up but Bill declined with a face.

Laudate dominum . . . omnes gentes, she sang in a high, clear voice, completely unselfconscious, her face transformed by concentration. A few lines followed by long amens. Mother stared open-mouthed and in tears.

That was an Annie so different from the one I knew, an Annie I could have known better. Do I now imagine that she looked at me for a sign when she finished the last, long amen?

When we went outside to plant the cutting, Mwangi was called to do the job. He ambled over from the back, barefoot and in shorts, and with a small shovel lovingly spaded out the red earth in the flower bed under our front windows and placed the stem in the hole, which he filled up tightly again. He went to another part of the garden and brought over manured soil and sprinkled it at the site of the new transplant. He stood up and said to Mrs. Bruce, Don't worry, Mama, this will become a beautiful plant. He placed one hand on his chest and briefly bowed his head, one gardener to another. When he had watered the cutting, he brought two champeli flowers and placed one each on Deepa's and Annie's hair, inadvertently dropping from his hand a few grains of sand on their heads. Bill, Njoroge, and I had started kicking around a ball.

It was Papa who named Mrs. Bruce's rose, on Coronation Day.

King George, the thin-faced, quiet-looking monarch, had died early in the previous year and we had a beautiful new queen. She could be seen everywhere, in the photographs at the railway station and in every classroom in school, on the postage stamps, the coins, and the notes. She came on in the cinema before the movie started, riding her horse outside Buckingham Palace, the Union Jack flying fiercely behind her, and we stood up in silent accompaniment to the ode to her nobility and grace, lines that we would never be able to forget. How proud we were to be her subjects then, to belong to the mighty empire. Only Mahesh Uncle scoffed at her stupidity and uselessness, after which an enraged Papa one day called him a "blardy communist," and said, Good thing your Joseph Stalin is now dead!

What made Queen Elizabeth more special was that she had been visiting Kenya when she received news of her father's death and became queen.

The newspaper on Coronation Day carried a full-length picture of her in gown and crown, with the caption: God Bless Our Glorious Queen. In the morning there was a march-past in town, of the police and the army, which included awesome yet smart-looking members of the Lancashire Fusiliers, who had come especially to Kenya to hunt the Mau Mau, and the Boy Scouts and Girl Guides, the Brownies and Cubs. A jubilant public lined the streets wearing badges, waving flags, and throwing confetti at the soldiers.

Later, Papa sat in the living room with his ears glued to the radio, listening to the BBC's live commentary on the ceremonies taking place in London at Westminster Abbey. Papa gave his own running commentary for the benefit of Mother, who was going about her chores and didn't seem much interested. But she would pause to ask him an indulging question now and then, so he would not feel he was talking to the walls, and Deepa did likewise.

Deepa: What's an ampulla?

Papa: Shhh, listen—she's coming, the Queen is coming—eh, Sheila, listen—

BBC: The young Queen looks stunningly beautiful as she approaches the church from the western door in a simple gown yet lacking no elegance, weighing with all the frills and train—

Mother (as she approached): What colour gown?

Papa put a finger to his lips. Mother came and stood behind him, running her fingers through his hair.

Deepa: What's a mitre?

Papa: How would I know? Shush!

BBC: . . . where the procession of archbishops and bishops awaits. . . . O Jerusalem, Jerusalem . . . Sirs, I here present unto you Queen Elizabeth, your undoubted Queen—

Papa: Wah! Undoubted Queen, of all the British Empire . . .

Mother: Yes, the fruit of all her karma . . .

BBC: Madam, is Your Majesty willing to take the Oath? I am willing. . . . Will you solemnly swear to govern . . . the United Kingdom . . . the Union of South Africa . . . Canada . . . and all your Possessions and other Territories . . .

Papa: That's us, you and me . . . Kenya, Uganda, Tanganyika . . . Gold Coast, Nigeria . . . and . . . and Sarawak, and Borneo and Malaya and Hong Kong . . .

Mother: And they call us only possessions—no name even?

Papa: Be quiet, now listen.

BBC (the Queen, in a low voice): I solemnly promise so to do . . . I will. . . . All this I promise to do . . .

Papa wiped a tear from his eyes. This makes you happy to be alive, he said solemnly, looking up to Mother, who stood over him and caressed his hair once again.

When we reach our hundred years, Papa said to Mother, we'll recall this moment proudly . . .

Mahesh Uncle, who was visiting and had come upon the scene, stared through his black-framed glasses, mouth agape, too confounded for words.

BBC: And God save the Queen!

Papa: And God save our Glorious Queen Elizabeth!

It was then that inspiration struck Papa and he came up with a name for Mrs. Bruce's rose: Call it Beautiful Elizabeth for our Queen, he said. And so it was.

It being Tuesday, Papa was on Home Guard duty that night, and as usual he left after giving Mother many reminders and instructions. But this time Mahesh Uncle was around and the situation seemed less worrisome. Papa even told Mahesh Uncle about the location of his gun, just in case. Deepa and I went to our rooms, leaving my mother and her brother in the sitting room to talk in low voices. Later in the evening Deepa would be picked up and taken to my parents' room and Mahesh Uncle would sleep in her bed. Neither I nor Deepa could sleep well when Papa was out at night. At Deepa's insistence the two adults came to sit at the dining table, which was closer to the bedrooms. Their voices were reassuring, their conversation as always intriguing and mysterious, about faraway places and events.

I could have made it in the diplomatic service, Mahesh Uncle said, if only I had stayed in Delhi . . . an assignment in a small country, Bulgaria or Albania . . . or even Kenya . . . What do I have here, managing a sawmill in the jungle, the Mau Mau hovering outside the gates . . .

Why don't you go back to India? I'd miss you, but you can go and make up with Bauji . . . and I could even follow you later with my family.

He grunted. I could never make up with Bauji, not at this moment. And do you think this husband of yours would leave his Queen and her Empire to go to Primitive India, as he calls it?

I could only imagine her smiling at that.

There was a scream outside the house, somewhere; there came the sound of a car door shutting and gruff murmuring out in front. It was dark and chilly where I lay, in bed. I tried to cry out, but my voice refused. Outside, the voices continued, louder, urgent, and brisk; there were footsteps inside the house; and still no word I could utter. I struggled with my bedclothes, to draw them closer around and hide me, and I could hear my heart thumping fiercely, almost choking me. I was aware of the window over my head and that something terrifying could enter through it, even though it was barred. And then with great relief I heard Deepa and Mahesh Uncle outside my door, sounding sweet and familiar, and I slowly climbed out of bed. There came the voice of my father outside, shrill, and other, African voices. Through the back door I followed my uncle and sister and my mother out. Dawn had begun to break.

In front of the house, under the street light, an African man was being restrained by two Indians, one of them Saeed Molabux. The captive was moaning and wailing pathetically like a child, and lurching forward as he struggled to free his arms. When he suddenly raised his head, it was to reveal a gruesome sight. He had no eyes in the sockets.

We saw him walking in the middle of the road, Papa was saying excitedly, he was coming straight toward us, and we thought, My God, we are done for. We braked but he kept coming and crashed right into the bonnet. And nothing else happened—luckily no Mau Mau from the bushes. We came out to have a look at this chap and—he had no eyes!

No eyes, but runny wetness and bloody pulp. Papa had rather thoughtlessly shone his flashlight on the man's face. His mouth gaped open as he emitted his pitiful moans.

But who did this—this ek-dum beastly thing? Mother asked, her eyes wide and tearful.

Some drunken Brits, it seems, out celebrating the coronation, plucked out his eyes with a bayonet or something—

But why hold him like this, Saeed, Mahesh Uncle protested, loudly as usual. Let him be, let him sit at least, where will he run off to?

Saeed and the other Indian reluctantly let go of their man, who shot off like an arrow only to stop abruptly a few yards later in all his blind predicament. And he was gently brought back with the words, Ngoja, utaenda wapi? Where will you go?

He sat down on the ground still moaning, his poor brutalized head in his hands. Mother, he wants water, Deepa said, he's asking for water. Do you want water? she asked the man, and he seemed to nod, but Mother simply said yes and did nothing. Everyone was waiting for the police—they should be coming, they've been called. Probably a lost Mau Mau, what was he doing on the road during curfew? Finally Njoroge went and brought the man a trickle of water in a mug from our miserly garden tap.

A police patrol car followed by a truckload of rough askaris came and took the man away.

All the excitement early in the morning meant that Deepa and I got to miss school. After breakfast, while Papa was rummaging through his things, he noticed that his gun and ammunition box were missing from their place, the drawer beside his bed. Papa was beside himself, he seemed to go berserk, venting rage at the servant Amini, slapping him around, but Amini insistently, plaintively denied stealing the weapon. Bwana, it wasn't I, I never entered the house until Mama let me in at seven o'clock, I swear to you, you are my mother and father, tafadhali Baba, have mercy . . . He was terrified. The house servant is the prime suspect always, he knew that. My father's slaps were friendly pats compared with what the police would do to him, unless the Bwana, my father, supported his testimony. Papa was frightened too. There was a stiff fine for losing a gun, there could be stiffer repercussions. Amini was weeping. Mother looked frantic. Were there Mau Mau among the servants, after all? Amini was a Muslim, from Mombasa; he would not have taken the oath. Still, how was one to tell?

With visible trepidation, his hands shaking, Papa telephoned the police. Predictably he received a sharp telling-off right then for his carelessness. He was instructed to keep Amini in the house and to inform no one else about the theft. The police were on their way.

They came in two trucks and a car—Lieutenant Soames, without the charming smile of before, that terrible predatory giant, Corporal Boniface, another white officer, and all their gruff, angry men. Every servant quarter was turned inside out, the latrines were inspected to their feculent depths by disgusted-looking askaris who put on cloth masks to cover their mouths and noses, as the servants stood outside in a line, their hands on their heads, and were subjected to a loud and rude interrogation. Papa, Mother, and Mahesh Uncle were grilled, our house was partly searched, the backyards and gardens were combed. Finally about ten of the servants were taken away, the main suspect among them, our Amini, with a beseeching look toward Mother.

You should go and vouch for him, Mother said to Papa. Yes you should, Mahesh Uncle added. Why should I?— snarled Papa. To become a collaborator with murderers? Only *he* could have stolen it. Who else would know where to search, who else could go in and come out with the gun in such a short time?

We never saw Amini again. We often wondered what happened to him. He had been a young man, not over twenty, light-skinned and short, who always wore white collarless shirts of drill cotton of the coastal variety. None of us, not even Papa, was really convinced that he was guilty, even though the police said he was half-Kikuyu and a likely suspect. But if Amini didn't steal the gun, who did? Both my parents were troubled by the question. Papa was fined seventy-five pounds for losing the weapon plus ammunition, and received a reprimand even from the *Nakuru Times,* which once again questioned the wisdom of letting the Indians carry guns.

That blinded African was never spoken of again. But he has continued to haunt me from the frightening backdrop of my childhood memories. Although I did not see him this way, I have always imagined him in the middle of a road, against the glare of headlights, a tortured, eyeless Frankenstein in a tweed jacket and trousers too short for him, moving slowly and stiffly in the night, his arms extended to help his steps. What could happen to such a man? Perhaps he became lucky and ended up in the care of an institution for the blind, making mats for the tourist trade to while away his time . . .

Far away, in the dim glow that hangs suspended across the lake and above the earth, must be a light (I tell myself) that comes from Deepa. Her name too evokes light. She is the only one who knows virtually all about my life, with whom I've shared almost every private thought. The reverse is not true; it needn't be, she is a woman.

Who is this librarian I hear about? she asks me when I telephone.

Seema Chatterjee—a Bengali—she is our happy discovery. I was going to tell you about her. She is rather fond of Joseph . . . in a big-sister sort of way. She's good for him, she talks to him. What else has he been telling you?

You are quiet and brood a lot.

Really. And I thought I was quite chatty with him. I talk to him about the past, what I'm writing, and sometimes his presence even jogs my memory a bit. We plan to drive around to look at the towns in this area. It's called Northumberland County.

You could go to Toronto and meet people there.

No, I couldn't handle all the bustle. This is my quiet period, my retreat. But Seema went to Toronto and she brought some kulfi for us.

Any good?

Yes, though not as good as—

Those from Bombay Sweets of Nakuru! I know! For you nothing could surpass the kulfi from there, Bhaiya!

Yes, they were the best. Deepa—do you remember Amini?

She is quiet, draws a breath. Then: Yes, I do . . . It doesn't pay to dwell too much on the past, Bhaiya.

I know. But we must remember, sometimes. Not too much, but a little. They are a part of us, aren't they . . . those we knew?

Yes, brother.

Laudate dominum omnes gentes, Deepa, I want to say to her, can you recall that also, *laudate dominum* . . .

Earlier this week I went into town and purchased a CD of children's choir music, and I have several times now subjected poor Joseph's ears to that song. Perhaps he's already told her about this.

Amen . . . amen . . . amen . . .

SEVEN

Diwali is the day when Lord Rama returned victorious to Ayodhya, an enchanted place in far-off India, having defeated the ten-headed demon Ravana, way south on the island of Lanka. Rama was the pink god on the table in Mother's puja corner, and on the calendar of Lakshmi Sweets, on which he appeared with his wife Sita and the monkey god Hanuman. Lakshmi was the goddess of wealth and was also worshipped during Diwali. The sweet shop was owned by Gujarati banyas, those special disciples of the goddess, according to Papa, who would crawl on hands and knees even for a chavani, a fifty-cent coin. Mother often wished there was a Punjabi sweet shop around, like those at Bengali Market in Delhi. I did not understand how Bengalis could make Punjabi sweets and Gujaratis could not. And besides, Mother did not think much of the dark Bengalis anyway.

But in the couple of weeks before the great day, our house was transformed into a heavenly place reflective of the glorious Ayodhya of ancient India. Smiling Mother appeared in bright saris or shalwar-kameez, taking any opportunity to make halwa or kheer, regaling Papa and the two of us with stories of how Dussehra, the actual day of Rama's victory, was celebrated in her native Peshawar—while in our home in East Africa light shades were draped in colourful streamer paper to become mysterious and magical lanterns, auspicious swastika signs made of sparkles appeared on all bedroom doors, and the gods' corner glimmered and shimmered with lights and glossy crinkled paper in green, gold, and silver. And Papa felt more loved as the Rama of the house, the dutiful son, husband, and father. Thus addressed, he would do the puja with Mother in the mornings, then head for the shop with an orange tilak-mark on his forehead. The Hindustani service of KBC told Rama stories, recited or narrated in a language Deepa and I barely understood, but they gave our mother her cues and she would make the two of us, and sometimes Njoroge, and sometimes a boyish Papa, sit and listen to the adventures of the wondrous and righteous Rama, his dutiful wife Sita and brother Lakshmana, and his resourceful monkey companion and general Hanuman.

Once upon a time in the kingdom of Ayodhya ruled a wise old king called Dasaratha. He had a wonderful son called Rama, brave and honest and respectful, and also a great archer. It was because of his prowess with his bow that he won as his wife the princess Sita, who was the daughter of another wise old king called Janaka—but that is another story. Rama had a half-brother called Bharata, whose mother Kaikeyi was jealous of Rama. Like all mothers she wanted the best for her own son. She desired very much that Bharata, and not the older Rama, should become king after Dasaratha. So she connived that Rama should be sent into exile. Rama left for the forest with his wife Sita. Rama had another half-brother called Lakshmana, who loved him very much and decided to go with him. And Bharata, who was also good, did not sit on the throne after his father, but placed Rama's slippers upon it instead, thus wrecking his jealous mother's evil design.

You know, Papa said, it always amazes me that Rama would not stand up for his rights—explain to his father what the situation was. And was old Dasaratha such a fool as to believe—

That was a different time, Mother strained to explain, it was a more righteous age when duty to a parent was the highest of virtues, and the word of a parent was beyond question! Don't you remember the story of Shravan?

One story to explain another. Why couldn't Rama use his head and save himself?

Absolutely right, Bhaiya, Mahesh Uncle boisterously butted in. I agree with you one hundred percent—such problems abound in religious stories. In fact when Sita returns after her ordeal in the forest, and doubt is cast on her purity—

Mother put her hands to her ears. I don't want to hear that! I know all about your objections!

They both laughed, sharing a secret from a wealth of common memories, and it seemed that Papa for a moment was by himself.

Sita had been kidnapped by the wily Ravana, who assumed the shape of a wounded doe to appeal to her soft woman's heart and entice her to approach, while Rama was out hunting and Lakshmana, who should have looked after his sister-in-law, was distracted. Ravana took Sita to his fortress-isle Lanka, later called Ceylon, from where Rama, Lakshmana, and Hanuman with his troop of monkeys rescued her after an epic battle.

Another thing, Papa said. This business of monkeys building a bridge to Ceylon—

Bhaiya, Mahesh Uncle replied, if you knew about the sheer genius of Indian monkeys—

I've seen them, replied Papa.

Mahesh Uncle went on, I was in Simla once as a cadre for the Congress Party. Gandhiji was visiting and . . . in any case, the monkeys there are the cleverest little fellows you ever saw.

There followed a hilarious tale of the antics of monkeys, to demonstrate to my father that they were smarter than many humans and could very well have built some kind of movable bridge to take Rama to Ceylon to rescue Sita.

The Africans should use monkeys to fight the British, Papa said, perhaps smarting from having been pushed out of the limelight. But, he went on, these African monkeys are not as smart as their Indian cousins.

Mother threw a look at her brother to keep him quiet.

Myth and reality often got mixed up in our lives. In Mother's eyes, the supposed leader of the Mau Mau, Jomo Kenyatta, who had been imprisoned at Kapenguria, with all his wiles was the demon Ravana himself. Sometimes it was the Mau Mau that collectively became Ravana. And I, somewhat evilly perhaps, always wondered if she sometimes saw Rama and Sita as her brother Mahesh and herself, and Africa as the forest of exile. And Papa as the monster Ravana who stole her away? And as wise but erring Dasaratha, my grandfather Verma, whom Mahesh Uncle had called a traitor? But that whole comparison was monstrous and I would be embarrassed by it.

When Rama's exile was the subject of the stories, it was never far from our consciousness that Mother and her brother shared a deep sense of exile from their birthplace, Peshawar, a city they would never be able to see again because it had been lost to Pakistan. And since Peshawar was the ancestral home also of my dada Anand Lal, the rest of our family could somehow share in that exile, though not with the same intensity.

Rajat's Toy Store was selling masks for the festival, depicting the faces of the main heroes and demons of the Ramayana story. And so on a Saturday in the parking lot of our shopping centre, the great battle began for the liberation of Sita and the conquest of Ceylon. I was the only possible Rama. I was Indian, this was my story; I had a name to match, Vikram for victor. Bill, who liked to win battles, backed off. But who would be the monkey king Hanuman, and who the ten-headed demon king Ravana? Bill would have loved to be the mighty, terrifying, and havoc-wreaking demon, with island for fortress and ocean for the moat around it. But Ravana ultimately had to lose, and the fortress had to be set aflame. Furthermore, Deepa and I reminded him, one of Ravana's heads was that of an ass, because the demon had a truly stupid side to him, for why else would he provoke invincible Rama and court disaster? So Njoroge happily became Ravana, a character for whom I have always harboured some sympathy for all the forces allied against him. And Bill had to be the monkey, a role he accepted as a grudging sportsman.

Now who would be Sita the fair bride? If Deepa became Sita, Njoroge would steal her from me, only to be forced to relinquish her in his final humiliation and defeat. Deepa did not care for this conclusion. Besides, she was my sister, as she pointed out to my eternal gratitude, to clinch the matter. Oh was I happy to have fair Annie beside me, my Sita, as hand in hand and beaming with pleasure we traipsed in the jungle of my father's store aisles and among the tea tables of Mrs. Arnauti, and even up to Lakshmi Sweets, where we received burfis. Annie had stuck a rosebud in her hair, Deepa showered bougainvillea upon us as we walked, and Bill-Hanuman behind a monkey mask leaped and bounded and chattered and whooped wholeheartedly all around us. And finally Njoroge with his ten-headed mask, as the demon Ravana who had been lurking in ambush among parked cars, stole my bride and took her to his island of boxes and a potted plant, and Hanuman went to fetch her with sword and sticks. After the last pitched battle, scarecrows were made of Ravana and his cohorts, with appropriate demon masks as heads, which Bill-Hanuman then put to flames with a matchbox, to the cheers of delighted shoppers. But in the end Sita could not be Rama's any more, for when a spiteful public cast doubts on her purity, the earth split open where she stood and took her away. We could not leave out that conclusion and be true to the story, could we? I had to lose my Sita. Deepa knew that ending too well, which was another reason why she would not be Sita. And Mahesh Uncle always reserved his strongest objection for this treatment of Sita, which when he raised it in our home, would prompt Mother to put her hands to her ears in mock protest.

The day of Diwali arrived and that afternoon uncles, aunts, cousins, and grandparents were all crowded noisily in our sitting room for the celebration. Most of us were on the linoleum floor and it was the time for family stories and games. The servant was rolling in a trolley laden with tea stuff, Mother hovering watchfully behind him, when one of my aunts began a filmi song, which she rendered beautifully. It was Sunanda Auntie, the family nightingale. She stopped abruptly in mid-verse and pointed naughtily at Mohan Uncle beside her. He was required to sing, beginning with her last syllable, and the game of anantakadi was thus underway. Everybody's turn came—even Dadaji sang a few lines by the legendary Saigal, there was "Baa, Baa Black Sheep" from one of my cousins, and Mahesh Uncle recited an Urdu ghazal. Anything passed, provided the rule regarding the last syllable was followed. And so in that spirit, when my turn came, following Papa's "It's a Long Way to Tipperaree" what could be better than to show off to the cousins with—

> *He said to the Pharaoh*
> *Let my people go, oh go*
> *said Jomo*
> *Let my people go!*

Rendered with a flourish. There was a momentary pin-drop silence. And then I caught a movement in the periphery of my vision, and sudden as a bolt of lightning a resounding slap landed on my cheek. It was from my father, who had swivelled on his haunches beside me and was leaning over me in rage. My mother had screamed. Exchanging a brief fearful look with Papa, I stood up and ran to Mother, my head pounding and cheek burning, tears barely restrained: completely completely crushed.

Badmaash! Where did you learn that obscene song! Papa shouted, now up and glaring at me as I took shelter in my mother's arms. And she pleaded with him with her eyes.

Someone in school taught him, no doubt, Mahesh Uncle said, with a meaningful look toward me, and I nodded in a hurry.

Who? Papa exploded. He must be reported, jeopardizing people this way—

You don't want to get involved, Bhaiya, Mahesh Uncle said, you don't want to be a target now.

Papa realized the wisdom of that comment and sat down, and I ran to my room to shed my tears freely.

I sat on my bed, staring at the door I had shut behind me. Why did I sing something so obviously offensive to my family? I had learned it and had sworn not to repeat it; in a part of my brain I realized that I had broken my promise so as not to be distanced from my family, not to have any secret separate me from them, because they were my precious everything. It had seemed so innocent, my singing; what did the song have to do with us?

My mother predictably came in after some time, brought tea and held my hand in silence. She looked beautiful that night in an orange and red sari that rustled and gold jewellery that chimed, her face made up, her eyebrows long and shaped, smelling like the sweetest sweetmeat. That is what Sita must have looked like in Ayodhya. My father was proud of her, of her beauty and of the fact that she was from India, a genuine article, even though he often despised that homeland as backward and barbaric.

Mahesh Uncle came in a little later, adjusting his black-framed glasses, and said, Do you want to get your family in trouble? You have no business learning such songs, the police will lock you up, or your father . . . or your friend, whoever he is.

He met my eye, asked: Who taught you that song, Vic? Someone must have taught you. Who was it?

I did not answer, though I knew that he knew it was Njoroge.

He waited awhile then said softly, All right, then. But you be careful, young man. No more saying silly things—is that a promise?

I nodded. We exchanged the three-part Masai handshake, which we sometimes did to seal a pact. I tickled his beard to let him know I was back to my old self.

By the way, Vic, do you mind if I take your old bicycle with me tomorrow, there are some fellows at the sawmill who could use it to run errands. Even I could use it.

I said he was welcome to it.

And the pump, can I take it too?

Sure, I said.

We came out together and Papa greeted me warmly, ruffled my forelocks affectionately, and stroked the back of my neck, as he liked to do. He was a loving father to whom I had given quite a scare. He still had not recovered from his nighttime encounter with the eyeless man and the theft of his gun.

Soon the men started drinking and playing three-card flush, even Mahesh Uncle, who said jovially that he had no intention of being turned into a porcupine, for that was the fate of a man who did not gamble on Diwali night. This was the night Goddess Lakshmi smiled upon you, and it was good to start off the new year with a winning streak. Of course not everybody won, but that seemed beside the point. Mahesh Uncle, for one, was losing, and his face soon wore that characteristic frown. The women played cards by themselves, quiet and more dignified, using pennies only. My mother seemed to be having all the luck.

It was eight in the evening and the back door was open, for a while at least, Mother said, so that good fortune Lakshmi had a chance to come flying into our home. I was playing carom against my cousins, with Deepa as my partner. With her little fingers she was no match for the older among us, and the two of us almost always lost.

Njoroge came and stood at the open door behind us, watching the proceedings in the house.

Psst, he said, beckoning with a hand. I'm playing, I said, I can't come. Come, Njoroge said, beckoned again, and disappeared from view. The game was soon lost and I went outside, saw Njoroge waiting for me beside the back wall of our house.

So, what are you Indians celebrating tonight?

Diwali—

Heh?

When Rama comes victorious to his country, remember—after killing Ravana?

He nodded. He had played Ravana at the shopping centre, after all.

There is a lot of food—you Indians sure eat a lot.

Shall I go and bring some?

No.

Why? There is gulab jamun and—

It gives me diarrhea.

I stared at him. I had never heard that complaint from him before. Perhaps he was feeling bashful because he did not want to seem to beg.

At this moment Deepa walked out with a bowl of the very thing—deep-brown balls in a lake of enticing golden syrup. Give him a bite, I said to my sister. She cut a jamun piece with her spoon and let him taste it. He made a face at first, but then the syrup had its effect and he said, Sure is good. Is there more?

There was a sound at the back of the neighbour's yard. A man was suddenly visible there, short and tubby, wearing a jacket and facing away; behind him came a large man in a greatcoat open at the front; someone else had gone on ahead of them and disappeared in the shadows. It became apparent that a file of Africans was proceeding stealthily toward the fence at the back and disappearing through it. Some of them carried baskets, others walking sticks, one a four-gallon can.

I looked at Njoroge and he stared back, meaningfully, defiantly, as if to tell me he knew things, as if to dare me to tell my elders.

Mother's figure stood framed inside our door and she said, There you are. You're not supposed to be outside at night, the police will take you away. And you, Njoroge-William, what are you doing here—you should be home.

Her eyes, though, lingered thoughtfully in the direction where the file of African men had gone. She had seen something.

Come and light the sparklers, she said to Deepa and me; and then to Njoroge: You too, come in and play.

We all went in and she carefully locked the door. Here, Papa said, you kids—Njoroge, it's late—

Everyone was staring at Njoroge. I will never forget the sight of Nirmala Auntie's horrified expression as she took in my friend's black-black Kikuyu face. It was as if her eyes had lighted on a monster. Is it safe? she whispered to my mother, who replied, He is only Mwangi's grandson.

Sparklers were placed in our hands, and in those of my cousins, and were lighted by the adults, and for a few minutes we forgot everything, all our faces beaming and blinking as we waved our sparkling phuljadis in spiralling circles, round and round, and ran about, until finally we held only the cindery, glowing wires in our hands.

The next morning Mahesh Uncle left for the sawmill, taking with him two young Africans who were brought to him by Mwangi and who needed a ride to Njoro.

I don't know what Mahesh is up to, Papa said irritably, he could get himself and all of us into trouble.

You know he sympathizes with the Africans, Mother said, but that doesn't mean he is doing anything illegal.

But she must have told my father about what she had seen in the backyard the previous night. For that afternoon at around one, just after lunch, police trucks suddenly arrived, and in their usual loud and rough fashion the askaris began rounding up the servants and searching their quarters. Mwangi was again taken away with other servants. Njoroge had run away to hide in the bushes.

———————

Many years later I reminded Njoroge of my aunt Nirmala's reaction when she saw him that Diwali night.

He laughed. She was terrified, he said, but so was I. She was white like a ghost, her eyes big and round and her mouth wide open. I used to be frightened of Asians, if you have to know.

I protested: How could we have seemed frightening?

You were in with the whites, so you had power over us. And you are so alien, more so than the whites. We never know what you think. You are so inscrutable, you Indians.

I thought it was the British who were so inscrutable. And Mahesh Uncle?

The exception. As transparent as . . . as . . .

Cellophane?

We laughed together. Yes, Mahesh Uncle had been special, his emotions ablaze and on full display when we knew him in Nakuru. There was never any doubt what he felt about anything or anybody. But he also had his private moments, some of which he shared with Mother and some of which he didn't; he had his dark secrets.

I had turned thoughtful and distracted, recalling my uncle. Njoroge peered into my face in a mock-curious way and brought me back to earth. Nobody's totally transparent, I know, he said, not me, not you. It depends on what side you look at a person from. But one thing is for certain: You Indians eat all the time. And we laughed again.

That last comment is almost exactly what his son Joseph has repeated on at least two occasions when Seema (Ms. Chatterjee) has been around. She stops by sometimes, when she's finished at the Korrenburg Library, during evenings when she's not at a meeting of the armchair sleuths of the Christie club or volunteering for the local amateur symphony. Then food always becomes a major issue and suddenly there seems to be an abundance of it. She has taken it upon herself to bring or make food for us single men at every opportunity.

One hot evening, outside on the veranda, after a dinner of pilau, pakodas, and grilled fish, while we sip the last drops of our Kingfisher lagers, and the cats nuzzle against our legs, Seema asks, Who owns this house?

It was custom-made not very long ago for an academic couple who divorced soon afterwards. It is shaped like a hut—circular and with a high, vaulted ceiling—but is perhaps twenty times the size of a typical African hut. There are no interior walls on the lower floor, and the wood stove in the centre of the sunken living area should be a wonderful place to sit around when the cold weather arrives. This house has every modern amenity, with three bathrooms and four bedrooms, and Ms. Chatterjee is welcome to stay over when she wants to.

She notices, with a curious look at me, how I do not answer her question while skirting close to it, but she says nothing. We fall quiet. I wonder what Mother would have made of her.

I am aware that my evasiveness regarding her question is due to Joseph's presence; those large, watchful eyes. He is my judge, I cannot help but feel, and quick and harsh too, in the manner of youth. I am, after all, one of those who made uncountable millions while our country slipped further into poverty.

Seema breaks the long silence, serving out the remaining beer.

A lonely and odd threesome we form, with our tortuous histories and migratory roots, in this little small-town haven, when burgeoning Toronto is just two hours away with its India- and Chinatowns and people among whom we would seem only too commonplace. There's a savage war on in the Balkans, and from that perspective my memories are of a time ages and ages away. A humbling thought: the First World War was closer to that time of my childhood during the Emergency than the present time is to it.

EIGHT

_____

Psst!

There was Njoroge at the open back door.

What is it? I asked, from the dining table where I had been confined with strict orders from Mother not to move until I had finished my sums. My glass of sweetened milk and plate of biscuits and almonds were beside me.

He beckoned briskly with one hand, the other in his shorts pocket. Come.

What is it? I gulped down my milk and, a little reluctantly, stepped outside. Homework was serious business with Mother. Only with education will you go anywhere in this world, she would say, advice that Deepa now visits anxiously upon Joseph.

Njoroge was leaning against the back wall of our house.

Hey, Njo, you got no homework?

He did not reply but said instead, very seriously, How do I know you are my friend?

It was my turn for silence. I was too confounded to speak. His grandfather Mwangi was still with the police, and Njoroge ate what others gave him.

Can I have a biscuit? he said.

Grateful at this show of trust, I ran inside and brought out the two re-maining biscuits.

I think you will betray me, he said casually, nibbling at the two biscuits twinned together.

No, I will not, I replied. But my heart sank with guilt even as I made that glib assertion. Hadn't I belted out the Jomo song two days ago in front of my entire family, and didn't Mahesh Uncle know whom I had learned it from?

All those secrets I have told you, you will not tell them to anybody? Not to Bill—

I will not tell him.

Not to Annie?

I will not tell Annie. And Deepa?

He paused to ponder, then said, She is too young. Later, maybe. And not to your parents or your uncle.

I will not tell anybody.

You must swear.

I swear.

You must take an oath.

I will take an oath.

You must come with me and take an oath. It will be a serious oath, a Number Three oath.

Okay. I met him eye to eye, he nodded, and I too gave a nod in solemn confirmation.

He ran off to his house and brought back a polished brown wooden bowl. With it we started off toward the back of the yard, at the very end of which was a wire fence covered with a rough thorny hedge. The bottom part of the hedge in our neighbour's area had been cut away in one place, and the ground there excavated discreetly to make a shallow and narrow tunnel passageway, which was much in use by the servants to take a short cut without being seen. You bent almost double to go through this passage-way, then immediately slid or clambered down into a dry ditch running alongside the houses, then climbed up again to arrive at an empty but wildly growing patch of land. Njoroge took me some distance through the bushes to a place where there was a large tree, some twenty-five feet away from the ditch.

He stopped and we stared at each other for a few moments and caught our breaths. We were both red with dust—our knees and elbows, our shirts. Mugumo tree, he nodded to it; it is the tree of God. I nodded without understanding but was intensely excited. Then suddenly he undid his belt and dropped his shorts. His underwear was a pair of grey cotton shorts, which he also dropped, revealing a curving black penis at which I couldn't help staring in wonder. He gave it a proud pluck, making it jiggle, and then I too dropped my shorts and repeated his motions. We stood staring at our nakedness.

In the shade of the tree stood an arch, which had been constructed of branches and, away from it, closer to the ditch, lay sprawled the grisly remains of a dead animal. Beside the carcass was a stone, red with drained blood. A sickening stench suddenly became noticeable in that chilling air; perhaps the wind had changed. It was drawing toward evening, the sun abating. We saw two men emerge from the spot where we ourselves had come out, glance briefly in our direction, and walk away.

Come, Vic, Njoroge said.

We passed through that arch seven times in turn, going around and returning. Then I followed him toward the stone and the slaughtered animal, a goat or a sheep, its guts spilled out of its side, its head cut off and missing. The smell hit me like a blow, yet I persisted, and we knelt at the red stone, on which strands of brown animal hair were stuck. Njoroge placed his wooden bowl on the stone, then produced a penknife from his pocket, flicked it open. Pressing the sharp point into his skin, hard enough that he gasped, he cut himself in the upper forearm, and blood spurted out from the small gash and dripped slowly into the bowl. The blood still pouring down his elbow, he motioned for my arm, and I felt the sharp pain of the cut, and my blood poured out to mix with his in a shallow pool in the bowl. Using a twig we mixed our blood, taking turns, and he said to me, Now take the oath.

I repeated after him:

I swear allegiance to our leader Jomo Kenyatta, the saviour, and if I disobey him, let me die.

If I worship any other leader than Jomo, who is the prime minister and knight commander of Africa, let me die.

If I am called upon to fight for the freedom of the country and I refuse, let me die.

If I fail to report any enemy of my leader and saviour, let me die.

If I tell the secret of this oath to my parents, let me die.

If I tell the secret of this oath to the police, let me die.

If I tell the secret of this oath to the teachers, let me die.

Seven grave oaths I repeated after him, after each one rubbing my finger into the blood and licking it.

With two fingers we each took a pinch of meat from the rotting carcass in front of us and put it in our mouths.

Finally we daubed our penises red with the blood. We touched it to our eyes. Then, wiping our wounds with leaves, we tied them up with our handkerchiefs, put on our clothes, and went home.

My mother let out a shriek when she saw me dusty and bloody and almost fainting.

I was climbing a tree, I said to her, and there was a nail stuck in it. I refused vehemently to see a doctor, so she washed the cut with antiseptic, then applied a traditional dressing of turmeric preparation and bandaged it. The next morning, miraculously, the wound was on its way to healing.

When she found out that Njoroge too had been wounded by the same nail, she was thoroughly mystified. So if one of you gets cut in the arm, the other has to go and try it too? So what are you, two paagals? One jumps in the lake, the other has to do the same. Like Laurel and Hardy, the pair of you.

Njoroge recovered without medication. Africans are stronger than us, Mother said.

From that time onward I carried a strange secret that implicated me in things I did not fully understand, and yet which I could not share with my family. This secret was a curtain that came between me and my loved ones, and there were times when I would feel intensely sad and guilty. I never told anyone about it, I write of it only now, in the presence of Njoroge's son, who has dug out sweet potatoes from the garden and will roast them on the grill for us to eat.

The Mau Mau oath, as described by the colonial authorities and their informers, required participation in gruesome rituals involving acts of bestiality and even cannibalism. More benign forms of the oathing process have been described by some former Mau Mau and their sympathizers. The truth is complex and elusive. There has no doubt been both exaggeration and suppression in the published accounts. Historical veracity and the confidence to deal with it have not been strong points in our region of the world; the three-piece-suited African leader with a son at Harrow wants no reminder of the primitive processes that were sometimes at work behind the freedom struggle. The grimness of the ceremony undoubtedly gave it its shocking and binding value. Having taken the oath, when called upon to assist the freedom-fighters in any manner they asked, you had no choice but to obey. Of course you might be lucky and not be called upon for your services. But an oath once taken could only be revoked by a counter-oath—of which the government had its version, in which you swore loyalty to Queen Elizabth II.

When we were older, even when we spoke of the past, I never could bring up with my friend the subject of that oath he administered to me. In my inner being, though, I felt—and still do feel—that an offence was done to me. Through friendly coercion I was made to participate in a private, debasing and repugnant ceremony. I swore to things I did not understand, I had to lie to my family, I had even tasted flesh, an act abhorrent to my Hindu upbringing. But I did not hold the experience against Njoroge; it was just one of those boyhood unpleasantries one has to face in school and college. We were only eight and nine years old! But from where had Njoroge obtained his inspiration for the oath? There was a rudimentary similarity between it and those Mau Mau oaths I subsequently read about.

He must have witnessed something at that bloody makeshift altar he took
me to. And Mwangi? It is almost impossible that Mwangi, or any other
Kikuyu who worked in our development, could have avoided taking the
oath. Was the benign-looking, elderly Mwangi, the wise and patient man,
the dignified gardener, anything other than that? I mean, was he secretly
involved with the Mau Mau, in its violence? I could never bring myself to
believe that.

Mwangi returned from police detention intensely sick. He and the others
who had been taken with him were kept outdoors in the cold and rain for
three days while they awaited their turn at interrogation. There were brag-
garts among them, as well as cowering boys who wept. As they sat and
squatted on the ground, several hundred of them behind barbed wire, they
were taunted and beaten and threatened by the police—chief among them
the sinister Corporal Boniface—with all manner of dire consequences if
they did not confess to being Mau Mau. Finally Mwangi was brought into a
hut where sat Lieutenant Soames and an inspector, who remembered him
from previous interrogations. There is a saying in our language, Mwangi
wa Thuku, said the inspector, that bad money always returns. If you have
been bad, confess and you will be forgiven. You will take an oath to the
Queen our Mother and be sent home. You might even be rewarded if you
agree to work with us. But, Bwana Sir, Mwangi had replied doubly respect-
fully, it is you who have brought me here every time. I am a simple gardener at the Indian housing estate, I have not been bad. I am old, as you can
see yourself, I have danced my dance. This old fat doesn't sizzle any more.
We shall see, said the inspector, if it sizzles or not. Mwangi was asked many
questions, as he told Mother, by the inspector, by Lieutenant Soames, and
by that Bonifacio (as he called the corporal). They were relentless and
harsh, listening to them was like trying to give heed to a waterfall. Afterwards he was stood among a long line of suspects as a number of witnesses,
their heads and shoulders covered with sack-masks to hide their identi-
ties, were brought over by the policemen to pick out their oath-givers.
Mwangi's number seemed up when one of these witnesses coughed and

hesitated momentarily in front of him. Subsequent to this, Mwangi was beaten mercilessly until he was almost senseless. He was taken to a hut by Boniface and two others and tortured. As a last resort they dunked his head repeatedly in a bucket of water, for over an hour until he thought he had died again.

How did they torture you . . . inside the hut? Mother asked.

Mama, you don't want to be told.

And then? What happened?

What was there to confess? Mwangi replied rhetorically.

They let him go.

Dr. Sethi had been called to examine the shivering patient and, predictably, pronounced him with malaria and prescribed a strong dose of quinine, and light meals only. Mother and Sakina-dadi had accompanied the doctor, which is how they heard Mwangi's story. He refused to let his body be examined privately, and after the doctor had left, the two women stayed on and instructed the old man how to look after himself. Mwangi did not believe in European medicine. He had his own potions, he said, prepared for him by a mundumugo. Still, the women argued, he should take the quinine also. Hitherto they had been speaking in Swahili, of which Mother's version was quite rudimentary. Now, toward the end of their visit, Sakina-dadi switched to Kikuyu and began a lengthy discussion with Mwangi, asking him in a gossipy manner all about his birthplace and his life, and translating choice bits for my amazed mother.

Sakina speaks Kikuyu so fluently, Mother told Papa later, and then she added thoughtfully: What must it be like to be a Masai and also a Muslim Punjabi . . . Are we really Africans?

Papa, reading a paper: Eh? What are you going on about?

The next time, Mother took me and Deepa along to see Mwangi in his room. He lay in his bed sideways, huddled inside his bedcloth like a child. His eyes were yellow, his hair seemed greyer at the temples than I had ever noticed before, and his deep black face looked as ancient as a mountain. He sat up, still covered by his bedcloth, and to every question from Mother regarding his well-being, he answered a grateful Ahsanté. She had brought a

box of digestive biscuits for him and tea in a Thermos. I have often wondered at this innate kindness in my mother—her spontaneous sympathy
for an old man who was sick; and how she always treated Njoroge as a boy,
like me, and not as the grandson of a "boy," a servant. She was intuitive
and not political, and though she had her prejudices, they were hardly
consistent.

Soon Mwangi was up and about, pruning and weeding and planting,
and when he sat down in the shade for a rest, washing his face with water to
cool down, Deepa, Njoroge, and I would sometimes go and sit with him.

Are you Kikuyu, or son of Kikuyu? Deepa would tease, and Mwangi
would pat her hair and gently tweak her long braid.

This is the story of Njoroge's grandfather Mwangi, as I have learned and
come to tell it to myself:

The craggy white-striped Kirinyaga—called Mount Kenya by the
Europeans—rises high into the mists, overlooking the ridges and forests
of Kikuyu country. In Africa only Kilimanjaro rises higher, in the south,
but Kirinyaga looms more mysterious and imposing, for on it among the
clouds resides the One God, Ngai. Once upon a time, when the world
was yet young and fresh, Ngai created the First Man, called Kikuyu, and
sent him down from the mists to rule over the highland country that would
be called Kikuyuland. Here the First Man built his homestead in the fertile land filled with mugumo trees under which he would place sacrifices for
his God. In due time, Ngai gave his son a wife, Mumbi, who bore nine
daughters. When the girls were grown, there were no men to be their hus-
bands, therefore Ngai told Kikuyu to sacrifice a fat ram under a sacred
grove. This Kikuyu did, after which each of these nine daughters found
standing beside her a handsome man. And then from each of these nine
daughters sprang a clan of the Kikuyu people. One of these clans was An-
gali, into which Mwangi wa Thuku was born. It was the time when the red
foreigners had begun to arrive like a plague on the land and impose their
godless ways upon the Kikuyu. In the area in which Mwangi's father had

his huts and wives and children, there arrived a fat and bearded stranger who came to be called Muruaru, the Sick One, because it was believed that although he looked healthy, it was due to some illness that he had neglected to shave.

Mugeni amiaga mbirira, it has been said; a bad guest shits even in the cemetery. The red-faced Muruaru quickly took control of the area, the Kikuyu's magic having failed against his guns. Muruaru imposed his own ways on the land. He installed a greedy young upstart called Njagi as chief among the Kikuyu, when previously there had been respected elders to lead the people and no one chief. Muruaru demanded taxes and he wanted labourers. Defiance was punished by imprisonment or whipping.

In the year of Mwangi's circumcision, half of his age group—those who had gone through the ceremony with him—disappeared, taken away forcibly to fight in the war of the red foreigners, far away in Tanganyika. He didn't know how old he was then, perhaps seventeen. Of those who went away to that terrible war, fewer than half returned, after many months. They came back—these young men who had never ventured beyond the ridges—sad and old, unwilling to speak of the horrors they had suffered. Some had grown beards like foreigners; some returned missing an arm or leg or eye; some wore bandages on their heads. There were those among the veterans who showed no respect for the elders, got into brawls, abandoned their farms. Mwangi escaped this fate only because his young sister became Njagi's third wife.

When the danger of conscription was over, Mwangi, after much soul-searching, decided to leave the land of his ancestors, to travel west beyond the ridges and over the mountain range Nyandarua to settle somewhere in the plains of the valley where the Masai had used to graze their cattle. The Masai had been pushed away and the red foreigners were farming large stretches of land using ploughs that could do the work of a hundred women in a day. But they were giving land to the Kikuyu immigrants, so Mwangi had heard, to grow crops and make their homes. People of the clan had gone there and returned to tell their stories. Here in the land of the Kikuyu ancestors, the old ways were no more; disputes were no longer settled by the elders. Friends of Chief Njagi became richer and more arrogant. There was no more land to cultivate, for the serikali, the government, had forbidden the clearing of forests. Young men who had gone to the foreigners' towns to work returned with rupees and threw their weight around. The medicines of the foreigners competed with those of the mundumugo. And yet sickness increased. Drunkenness spread. Finally even the God of the Europeans was gaining prominence over the God of the Kikuyu, who had become deaf to their pleas.

Early one morning, while it was still dark, Mwangi and his wife Wanjeri and their son Thuku, who was two years old, departed from their homestead. With them they took a few goats, a goodly amount of rupee coins earned by selling their other animals, gourds of water, a sack of seeds, and their household pots. In his hand Mwangi carried a panga for defence and to cut through the forest where needed. Gradually, as they traversed the ridges, the sun rising every morning behind their backs, majestic white-striped Kirinyaga receded farther and farther in the distant mists, until finally, with one more twist in their path, the home of their God Ngai had disappeared completely behind forests and hills. They knew they were in a foreign land. He could always return to the land of his ancestors, Mwangi told himself, but the thought held little comfort, for he knew that the life of his people had changed so much since his birth that there was no telling what the future might bring.

They had hiked up the slopes of Nyandarua (which the Europeans called the Aberdares), making their nervous way through thickets of tall bamboo and sighing forest, across burbling streams and over squelchy ground, the mountain air thin and misty and damp. At the end of the fourth day they arrived at a clearing at the edge of a great valley. Down below stretched mile upon mile of grassy flatland, dotted by trees and animals. A grey lake lay still as a mirror. Beside it was a large settlement. In the far distance, where the sun was setting, rose the opposite wall of the valley.

The lake was called Naivasha, as was the village. Mwangi had been told he could catch a train from here to take him to a place called Njoro, where he would find land to work on.

Mwangi had never seen a train before. He had never heard so much noise as it made. He had never seen anything go so fast, puffing and panting and shaking the earth, as this beast of iron. Now he knew that the lines on which the trains ran had been built by the labour of men like those brown-skinned bana-kubas, Anand Lal and Molabux and their like, who had come all the way from a far land while still in their youth. It is fate, he said, taking out a box of tobacco, picking out a pinch and stuffing it into one wide nostril. It is fate, heh, which takes the young to distant lands. It is when the mother that is the land says to her children, Go elsewhere to fill your belly. But these Indian wazees have made their fortune, why do they delay going back to their home?

But they don't want to go, it's been a long time, Mother told him. This is their land too now, where their children and grandchildren were born. Isn't that true?

Mwangi said nothing.

Did you ever go back to your home? Mother asked.

I dreamed of going back to the land of Kikuyu, he said.

Did you go?

Silence.

Mwangi settled in Njoro, farther up from Nakuru. He was given a plot of land to grow crops, and in return he and his wife and children, like the other tenants—or squatters, as they were called—had to labour on the estate of their European family: work in the fields, graze the cattle, and provide domestic help.

This way he brought up a son and two daughters. The girls were eventually married off to men who followed the new religion, repudiating the Kikuyu God who had looked after their people since time began. And the fate that he himself had escaped in his youth caught up with his son Thuku, who was conscripted to fight another war of the Europeans and was taken even farther away than those who had fought in the previous war. Thuku returned from this new war silent and restless. Gradually he recovered, but he did not want to settle on a farm. He went to work in Nakuru, where he found a job as a mechanic. Soon he moved to Nairobi. His wife Wangui followed him, leaving their son Njoroge with his grandparents.

And now—what is Thuku doing? Mother asked.

He is in Uganda, isn't he, studying to be a teacher.

Which was a lie.

———————————

Ms. Chatterjee, whose family were refugees from East Bengal, which later became Bangladesh (what a curious coincidence, both our families rendered refugees by the Indian partition), tells us that her father would talk about how he had once seen black human carcasses floating in the Ganges outside Calcutta, during the Second World War. They were presumed to belong to the sick and dying African soldiers tossed out from troop trains in the middle of the night by their British officers. A feast for the crocodiles . . . are there crocodiles in the Ganges? I suppose not; I have not asked her yet. Joseph tells her that his grandfather served in Burma, but he returned from the war and disappeared a few years afterwards.

Joseph claims only vague knowledge of his great-grandfather Mwangi's roots in the Kikuyu heartland. He has been close, however, to his mother's folks, moderately wealthy and established people of the Nyeri township. He is, of course, aware, as is everyone else familiar with the history of the country, that Chief Njagi was one of the first victims of the Mau Mau, gunned down with a pistol in his Bentley while returning from a government function in Nairobi. The chief's grandchildren are currently among the country's elite businessmen and politicians, some of whom I have come to know well.

Tea! From McGinty and Lloyd's! Seema Chatterjee exclaims in her rich melodious voice from the kitchen. Where did you get it from? she asks, coming out to the deck.

I had it sent from London . . . an old habit, I explain, uncomfortably.

How absolutely decadent! she smiles in wicked satisfaction. And are your suits from London too?

I look away, catch Joseph's thoughtful eye belying his soft chuckle.

Kenyan tea is the best in the world, he tells me, throwing down a schoolboy challenge.

Which I take up, unnecessarily, with: Yes, but do you know, the best of our tea can be purchased only overseas, from people like McGinty's.

Immediately I regret my retort, noting his embarrassment.

There is such a chasm between us, which I don't see ever closing. What do I tell Deepa, who has such high hopes for our relationship? How do I explain that this boy can never trust me, with my bitterness of age and experience, my corrupt wealth, my alien Asian ways?

NINE

A postcard came airmail from London:

Dear Vic and Deepa, We're having a wonderful time here! Hope you
have a smashing holiday too. Say "jambo" to old Njo. Kwa heri! See
you soon!

—Bill and Annie

On the reverse side, Piccadilly Circus in full colour, a city scene grander and infinitely more bustling than our own modest and quite somnolent King Street roundabout. Look, said Papa, who was holding up the postcard, the biggest city in the world.

Where's the circus, Papa? I asked him, our self-styled expert on matters English.

Maybe there was a circus there a long time ago, he said, trying to sound confident and unable to hide his uncertainty.

Mother, Deepa, and I were gathered round Papa in the shop, poring with him over every detail of the glorious scene. The black taxis, a red double-bus carrying advertisements on its side, men and women in hats, a red mailbox, a newsagent, all the store and street signs. Papa turned a wistful eye to Mother, who acknowledged with a smile; it was his dearest wish to visit that centre of the universe once in his lifetime. It was his Mecca, his Varanasi, his Jerusalem. A visit there conferred status, moreover: you became one of the select group, the London-returned.

He tacked the postcard on the upright behind his table, where it stayed for more than a year, proud reminder not only of his yearning but also of his European "friends."

Bill and Annie had gone without their parents. To my parents, it was a sign of European irresponsibility that they could send their children on an expensive voyage and yet run up sizeable debts in town. Though Mother remembered graciously that Mrs. Bruce did have a wealthy family in England. But how could she allow herself to send the children by themselves, unescorted, on a voyage that took twenty-four hours, with stopovers in strange places? Suppose someone kidnapped them? Who'd hurt a British child, Papa snapped in reply, they'd have every policeman in the world looking for them. That privilege comes from ruling the world.

The postcard had been written by Bill, who had signed both their names, but then Annie must have insisted on putting down something of her own, for there after his bold writing was the wobbly scrawl "Annie," struggling valiantly up a hill. She would not let him dominate her. It was mid July, a month and a half since they had gone. Six weeks was an eternity to a child in those days. Saturday playtime at our shopping centre became subdued and lacking in adventure. I recall Deepa, Njoroge, and myself sitting on the cement floor of the veranda outside our shop, playing a game of imagining by turns all the exciting things our two friends must be up to in London: riding double-buses and taxis, visiting all those castles and palaces and bridges we had read about, shopping at wonderful stores spilling over with comic books, toffees and chocolates. If you ran out of something to say in this game, you were "out."

That postcard clinched the case for my mother: her children too needed to visit places during their vacation. And so it was resolved in our home that all of us would go to Nairobi and Mombasa for the August holidays.

. . .

The Africans had described it aptly, an iron snake gliding along the bottom of God's bowl that is the Rift Valley. Around us the savannah with its sporadic thorn trees, the herds of zebra that came so close you could almost feed them—and there were a few on the train who threw chappatis at them. To our left, in the east, rose steeply the green and jungly Aberdare Range, or Nyandarua, where a band of Mau Mau fighters, the Land Freedom Army, made their home under the leadership of the dreaded Kimathi and Mathenge. The fighters came down from this range to attack European farms, but it was also down the same paths into the valley that many Kikuyu squatters, including our Mwangi, as Mother sometimes called him, had come many years ago to seek new homes on those farms.

The train from Kisumu had come in late, and so we left at a little before dawn from Nakuru, which was as well because we could see more, though the Kisumu passengers were irate for having to wake up from their rocking slumbers. We reached Naivasha as dawn was breaking beyond the mountains.

How can I describe that feeling of looking out the sliding window above the little washbasin, as the small second-class cabin jostled and bumped along the rails, and taking in deep breaths of that cool, clean air and, simply, with wide hungry eyes absorbing my world. It was to become aware of one's world, *physically,* for the first time, in a manner I had never done before, whose universe had encompassed our housing estate and my school, the shop and my friends, the tree-lined street outside that brought people in and out of our neighbourhood. That scene outside the train window I can conjure up at any time of the day or night; I would see, feel, and experience it in similar ways so frequently in my life; in some essential way it defines me. This was my country—how could it not be? Yes, there was that yearning for England, the land of Annie and Bill and the Queen, and for all the exciting, wonderful possibilities of the larger world out there. But this, all around me, was mine, where I belonged with my heart and soul.

African herdsmen in skin cloaks waved back at us, women with gourds and baskets on their backs would pause to look up and stare. A little later in the morning, a spotter plane, perhaps deviating west from its course while searching for the forest fighters, accompanied us for a distance, swooping down low in figures of eight, to the delight of passengers.

Gilgil, Naivasha, Kijabe, announced by their name boards and altitudes, the raised signal boxes outside the stations, the railway crossings where cars, people, and cattle waited and stared, the station master waving a flag, vendors and coolies scurrying for custom. At every stop Indians got on or off, and there were people who were known to my family. For in each town was an Indian main street, with the same squat shop-houses of brick, with stores similar to those I was familiar with in Nakuru. The Naivasha station master was a family friend and brought along some hot tea and snacks.

I never saw my mother so happy. She would put her head on my father's shoulder, hold a samosa or a cup of tea for him, sing Indian love songs about spring and birds and flowers and rain.

Finally we climbed the slopes of the escarpment, leaving the basin behind, and tall trees surrounded us, the ground was red, and there were little Kikuyu farms abundantly planted with corn, banana, vegetables. In the distance behind us the Rift Valley lay in a haze, stretching all the way north, Papa said, to the Red Sea which Moses had parted.

This is Africa, he said to Mother, all this beauty and vastness, dekha hai esa, tumhare desh mein? Have you seen anything like this in your country? She smiled sweetly. This is where I have married and made my home, she said. And this is my husband's and children's country.

How happy he was that Mahesh Uncle was not with us, and how sad Mahesh Uncle had looked to see us all going away. I imagine that my mother for a moment did lose her lustre, at Papa's reminder of where she was born.

Nairobi is a wonderful place, our relatives assured us, it is halfway to London. Halfway from where? I inquired, and they all laughed with delight. It was four in the afternoon and I had never seen anywhere as busy as the railway station, and after that Delamere Avenue, where a policeman in white uniform and helmet was guiding traffic with white-gloved hands, and then

Government Road with its huge grey mosque and clock tower. My uncle Rakesh, who was actually Papa's cousin, and his wife Shanti had come to pick us up. If only this Mau-Mau Shau-Mau fear goes away, Shanti Auntie said, this is a wonderful city. Rakesh Uncle worked in the Post Office. Part of his job, as I learned later, was to assist in the censoring of letters to and from the Asians; not only did many Indians write in Punjabi or Gujarati or Urdu, Rakesh Uncle explained, they used codes which the British would never understand. Daitya for the Mau Mau, Bhut-lok for the Europeans, Ravana for Jomo Kenyatta. Have you found anything suspicious or caught anyone? Papa asked. No, Uncle said, but some false alarms.

The first trip out is by repute the most memorable. I did not remember previous travels, of which there had supposedly been two, so this was my big journey into the wide world. We were the country cousins: even my parents looked cowed by the savvy and the modern ways of our hosts.

My aunt and uncle had four children, of whom the eldest two were boys close to my age. It was with them and their neighbours that I learned to play cricket the proper way, competitively, and gilli-dandi and naago and a host of other Indian games. We lived in the Eastleigh section of the city, which was filled with Punjabi-speakers, a lot of whom were connected in some manner with the railway. The Eastleigh aerodrome, used by the armed forces, was close by and sometimes very noisy, especially when the Harvard bombers set off on their sorties to the forests of the Aberdares. But even more so than in Nakuru, the dark nights with the chirrup of insects and the occasional bark of a dog were fearful. There was a gun in the house, and my aunt and mother had that look of concern as they saw us off to bed. You could actually speak with people in these streets whose houses had been raided by the Mau Mau, who took away rations and money, and the Asian Home Guard went on foot patrols every night armed with staffs, knives, police whistles, and a coal burner swinging on a chain to keep them warm. On the way from Eastleigh to the other Asian district called Ngara, or to the city centre, you passed the racecourse and then the African residential area of Pumwani, its small yellow houses running into each other, a few small children playing outside and women hanging out clothes, the smell of woodsmoke filling the air. This was believed to have been the hideout of the terrorists until the Emergency police raids cleaned it up. It looked a sad, deserted place, a bedroom community with most of its inhabitants out at work.

Still, it was an exciting, hustling, bustling metropolis to which we had come: *halfway to London* with indoor public garages and drive-in cinema, Woolworths and Nairobi Sports House and other fancy shops, River Road with pakoda-and-chai shops and cheap cobblers, and Indian Bazaar with its smell of spices. Across from Woolworths, which sold comic books and English sweets, and Enid Blyton and Biggles novels, was the New Stanley Hotel; outside it was the famous patio restaurant where dozens of Europeans in smart clothes and hats sat at tables waited upon by liveried African waiters as they surveyed the action on Delamere Avenue. It was here that Grace Kelly and Ava Gardner had stayed to film *Mogambo*, now awaited with great anticipation in Nairobi. But even if the New Stanley and its patio restaurant had not been marked "Europeans Only," we would never have dared put our feet inside. All we did was stand outside in a large group and gawk rather shamelessly through the palm-frond barrier at the edge of the patio.

The Railway Club Fete, on the other hand—Ticket 1 shilling, women and natives 50 cents, children free—was open to everyone but was actually for the benefit of Asians and Africans. The former came in flocks of ten to twenty. A band played marches, a fierce-looking Sikh policeman in scimitar-shaped whiskers walked about pompously, every now and then raising a finger and telling off naughty children, and local schoolboys performed gymnastics in which they formed a human pyramid and dove through hoops of fire. There were some skits, including one about recent arrivals from India, and another rather risky one, about a gang of Mau Mau. In the latter, the fighters went to a European home and were met by the cook, who was dressed in a livery of long white kanzu and red fez. Why do you dress like a woman, the leader of the gang gruffly scolded, don't you have any dignity as an African? If I didn't dress like a woman, how would I be able to help the likes of you? retorted the cook. He lifted up his fez and, lo and behold, on his fuzzy hair a packet of Kit Kat, some matches, and a leg of chicken.

At another show, the world's strongest man, Aurangzeb Bhim Singh, short and squat, mightily muscled, dark as chocolate, walked out in front of a moving car and with his two hands stopped it, pushed it back! And more: he lay down before the stopped car, and all were invited to step forward to confirm that the vehicle was truly sturdy, Empire steel and chrome and rubber. Some of the onlookers took up the challenge and knocked on the panels and bumpers, kicked at the tires, tried lifting the vehicle from either end. The engine was started, and slowly the car began to move, and the front wheels rolled right over the chest and legs of the reposing strong-man! . . . and slowly so did the back wheels! Aurangzeb Bhim Singh stood up to tremendous applause, then graciously allowed spectators to feel his body. It's real, Papa confirmed to an amused Mother, having pressed the man's biceps, prodded his ribs and stomach, pressed his calves.

It was a dizzying day with foods and games and prizes and shows of all kinds. With us, besides my uncle and aunt and their four children, was another adult, introduced as Aruna Auntie. She was slim and pretty, with a long braid down to her waist, and she wore a dark blue shalwar-kameez. She instantly took a liking to Deepa and me, holding our hands as she took us around and bought us candy floss and ice cream. She was a wonder at the shooting range and won a large round doll at a lottery, which she presented to my sister. And she also seemed to get along marvellously with both my parents. After the fete, when she had been dropped off at her home (not without all of us being invited in for more food), the adults couldn't stop speaking about her, and I overheard that she would be visiting us in Nakuru. They all thought that Mahesh Uncle would get along remarkably well with her. I just couldn't wait to see the two of them together, as my uncle and auntie.

The classifieds of the *East African Standard*, appearing alphabetically every Thursday, week in, week out, began with the same first notice: Abraham-son London Gents' Tailor, for your up-to-date Saville Row suits. A new suit from this prestigious outfitter was what Papa, with Mother's permission, had promised himself since Nakuru. And so six of us—my aunt and uncle, my parents, my sister, and I—went into the shop on Government Road. It was dark in a posh sort of way, walls lined with shelves of suiting, illuminated with tube lighting, smelling of fresh new cloth. There were chairs and recliners to sit on, framed pictures of male models in suits. My father was served by an Indian assistant. After a lot of agonizing discussion a material was agreed upon, and finally came the time to take the measurements. There was also in the shop a European couple, picking a suit. When the assistant produced a tape and began measuring my father's inseam (much to the amusement of Deepa and me), the European cried out, Ay, you going to use the same tape on me as the coolie? My father's face crumpled, my mother turned red. No sir, said the assistant, apprehensively eyeing each of his customers in turn, We use a different tape for Europeans. A white man hurried in from the back unravelling a tape, and my family walked out of the shop in silence.

A photograph from that vacation shows my mother and father seated on a sofa, me standing beside Mother, Deepa beside Papa. Deepa has on a striped dress with two bows in front, and her hair has been styled into two braided loops at the back. White socks, black shoes with buckle straps. And I am attired in shorts, a dark blazer over a white shirt, and a wide tie. It is a black-and-white photo, but the tie, I recall, was red and embossed with yellow and blue cranes. My mother was in a sari that day, and she sits up straight, ever so slightly turned toward Papa . . . a beautiful, mysterious young woman. Papa is in a suit and tie. The photo was taken at A. C. Gomes, up the street from Abrahamson's. The suit was made by Ahmad Brothers, the third or fourth name from the top in the Thursday *Standard* classifieds, who also promised London fashions, but at half the price and using the same tape measure for Asians and Europeans. And for Africans?—I don't know.

Long stretches of brown grassland dotted sparsely with thorn trees. A herd of giraffe grazing quietly, staidly; the one closest to us bounded a few steps away. The wonderful thing about these creatures is that they seem quite oblivious to human existence, and unlike impala or gazelle they take only the slightest, the most necessary, safety measures. Zebra in the distance, and the little dik-dik. The train came suddenly to a stop and didn't move for a long time. Elephants had been crossing the tracks, but two youthful ones had refused to budge from the rails, despite protestations from the rest of their herd and the occasional train whistle. Finally some passengers— among them my intrepid father—came out to watch, and as they approached the scene, a couple of adult elephants made a trumpeting charge. The passengers fled inside their train, and the two elephant youths got up sulkily and lumbered away into the bushes. This happened just outside Makindu, on our way to Mombasa. Outside the station was a Sikh temple, to which my mother went to pay her respects. If there was no Hindu temple, she said, a Sikh one could do just as well. She brought for us some halva prasad from there. The train started only when the Indian station master had seen her to our compartment.

The track we were traversing now, whistle blowing, engine roaring, was the setting of my grandfather Anand Lal's favourite stories, and he was with us in spirit. It was on this route that the man-eating lions had so terrorized the work gangs, bringing track construction to a complete stop. We did not see any lions but were assured that they were around. The long journey to the coast, the descent of five thousand feet progressively into a hot and humid climate, the vegetation clotting and greening around us until we were in the midst of dense growth and population, palm and mango trees and villages of mud huts and men in white kanzus and kofias and women in colourful khangas or covered by the black veil, everywhere dusty and dirtier than we were used to but also more relaxed and freer, was a voyage into enchantment. By the light of kerosene lamps men sold roasted meat, cassava, and corn, little dukas stayed open selling the odd item, men sat around on stones or tree trunks or on the ground, as we passed by and slowly approached our destination. We had left early in the morning, at dawn; when we reached Mombasa it was nine at night.

It was such a different world, all abustle and rich in variety and extremes. All the Indians ran small stores, it appeared, including our hosts, who were friends of the family. Boys and girls played on the unpaved sides of the street, beside their homes, barefoot and in rather ragtag clothes. Most residences were behind shops and crowded. The bathroom facilities were primitive compared with what we were used to, and repugnant. Mosquitoes and flies were abundant, as were beggars and crazies, as also were fruits and vegetables of all kinds, sold on the street, brought along by hawkers, or available in the large souk. The language was hard to understand, though it was spoken in abundance among Indians, Arabs, and Africans. Music blared from radios in various languages, people sang as they worked or walked on the streets. There were processions to celebrate weddings, football matches, circumcisions. The Europeans did not come to bother anyone, from their resorts and homes by the beaches. And there was no fear of the Mau Mau. In the evening boys and girls played tag or hide-and-seek outside their open shops, where Indian men also sat playing cards and availing themselves of the enticements of a passing coffee-seller. From nearby roadstands would come the aromas of corn and cassava and meat being roasted on open fires.

But it was unendurably hot and muggy, physically uncomfortable, and even in its own way frightening and mysterious. It was not easy to be a Nairobi boy—as I was derisively called—with my pressed shorts and my shoes and socks, my uncallused feet, my combed and gelled hair, my manner of speaking, my language. Mother, on the other hand, fitted perfectly: this is India, she would say gleefully, walking about barefoot.

We stayed a week in this wonderland—mother had to be pulled away—and then proceeded to our own disciplined and at the time beleaguered world.

After we returned I began corresponding with some of my cousins, and with a friend I had made in Mombasa. There was talk now in my family that I would ultimately go to school in Nairobi. And we all awaited anxiously the arrival of Aruna Auntie. Bill and Annie must have undergone their own profound transformational experiences; we saw them again after four months. We all looked a little bigger to each other now. Bill's games were the same as before, but his movements slower and more deliberate, and I think a little abstracted. Annie was a little thinner; she still stayed close to me and there was still that mischievous, drawn smile on her face, the twinkle in her eyes, as we followed the warring Bill Bruce on the trail of one enemy or another, on sea or land, or in the skies. Bill gave me some comic books. Annie had brought a Stanley Gibbons stamp album for me. I had nothing for her and felt terribly guilty, and Mother, to comfort me, said, What do you give to someone who's just returned from England, and you've come only from Nairobi and Mombasa? There was truth to Mother's words, but I've always regretted my fickleness; surely there was enough to choose for her (and Bill) from among all the exotic wares on sale in the streets of Mombasa. The plain fact is that Annie and Bill had practically vanished from my thoughts during the four weeks of my holidays.

The Stanley Gibbons album remains one of my treasured possessions. As does my memory of Annie.

And Njoroge?

Nairobi had much to offer in the way of presents for someone who had not gone to London, and we brought for Njoroge an eighteen-inch-long pencil shaped like a cane, with frills at the top, and a Mickey Mouse pencil sharpener. This was a present from all of us. But wilful Deepa also managed to give him a paintbox, from only herself. She had got my parents to buy her one at Patel Press, then on our way back from Mombasa, tears flowing down her grimy cheeks, she sobbed, It is gone. A new paintbox had to be purchased. The original item miraculously made its reappearance in Nakuru, and so with Mother's permission Deepa gave it to Njoroge, with a knowing sideways look at me.

The week of our return from holiday, Farmer Hackett and his wife were hacked to death in their home down Njoro way, as they sat down at night to listen to the news. The pun was not lost on anyone; the Mau Mau, it was said, had many educated men among them. One of the Hackett cows was discovered wandering about, its eyes gouged out. More than twenty of them were discovered hamstrung.

A package arrives from Deepa, couriered. It contains a box of Punjabi sweets and a rakhi. The latter is an elegant bunch of coloured threads, a couple of them silver. A sister presents a rakhi to her brother to affirm their closeness and his role as her protector. Deepa always took the greatest pleasure in tying a rakhi around my wrist, as Mother did in giving one to her brother Mahesh, in a solemn ceremony that took place for some reason at the threshold between our living and dining rooms. There would be a wonderful smile on Mother's face as she began the ceremony by covering her head with her dupatta. Mahesh Uncle would extend an arm, saying, Accha, tie me up, sister; gently, Mother would tie the threads, orange, vermilion, and white in those days, round his wrist, patting it when she finished. Then, dipping a finger into an orange paste in a saucer, she would put a tilak on his forehead. Finally, taking the plate of sweets from whoever was attending her, Deepa or I or Papa, she would break off a piece of burfi or petha or shakar para with one hand and put it into his mouth. He would present her with a gift in return: some money, a bottle of perfume, a photograph of our family that he himself had taken and had framed.

That year she suggested that Deepa present a rakhi to both Njoroge and me, and little Deepa went about it with great enthusiasm. Thus, though unwittingly, she made Njoroge her brother, a fact that Mother would use as an argument in later years with much force.

TEN

How is my little boyfriend Vic?

A beautiful face beaming at me as I open my eyes—Aruna Auntie sitting on my bed. She had finally arrived, late the previous night while I was asleep.

You have come, I said. Why didn't you wake me up as soon as you arrived?

Kids need their sleep. And besides, do you think your mummy or daddy would have allowed me to disturb you?

How long will you stay? Stay for long, stay forever!

We will see, she replied pertly, standing up. I took her hand and at the door we bumped into Deepa rushing in. Together, holding her hands possessively, we escorted Aruna to the breakfast table, where Mother admonished us to go and brush our teeth first.

How could there have been a more perfect match for my uncle? She was a beam of sunshine, a great dollop of extra happiness in our household. How different from our dull, picky parents! How lucky Mahesh Uncle was! She got along with simply everybody. She engaged easily and passionately in discussions, so that my father found her companionable at mealtimes and afterwards, when we sat in the living room. She liked to banter with him, and he rather enjoyed the attention. With my mother she sat huddled for hours—so it seemed—until we had to pull her away to play with us.

She was very thin but lithe, always ready for a game outdoors or inside. She had a husky laugh and big, liquescent brown eyes in a fair, oval face framed by dark hair plaited at the back—eyes that all of a sudden turned pensive, and she would be speaking to you. There were tiny, delicate lines at the outside corners of her eyes, and her high cheekbones gave her an oriental look: both features, she said, due to the blood of the Himalayan mountain people in her veins. She was in her late twenties, which I now know meant that she was getting on in years for an unmarried woman.

She had recently come from India to visit relatives in Nairobi, had been introduced to my parents during our recent visit there. And here she was now, a bringer of joy to our home, a prospective wife for our uncle.

On the Saturday following her arrival, we set off in our Prefect for that long-postponed trip to see Mahesh Uncle's place of work, out at the Resham Singh Sawmill in Elburgon. The road leading off King Street was straight, through vast wheat fields, and there was fair traffic mostly the opposite way, with farmers going to Nakuru from Njoro and Molo. Papa enjoyed these road trips, and he was a friendly driver who liked to throw a wave at passing cars, in the belief that it was good highway etiquette, and that some of the people were his customers anyway. He received not a reply in return, and Mother told him to stop his display. This brought them back on track with each other, for it was obvious to the rest of us that they had had a tiff. At the back, however, cheerful Aruna started the game anantakadi, in which the three of us sang in turns, taking our cue from the last syllable of the previous singer. Mother brought out namkeens to eat and joined in the game, and Papa too sang, in his typical way mixing in Bing Crosby and English nursery rhymes with Hemant Kumar and Talat Mahmood. When he had to stop so Aruna could take Deepa behind the bushes, he said to Mother, continuing a conversation it seemed they had begun before, And do you think her family will agree to a match with a communist? Mother replied in exasperation, He is not a communist—and anyway, what communist-shommunist thing can he be up to, out here in the jungle? And what about the family?—they have sent her here, haven't they, so she can find a husband? All he needs is a wife to look after him and settle down, and here you go. Why are you acting as her protector, anyway?

All right, all right, Papa said, as Aruna and Deepa returned, swinging hands together.

The sawmill came as a clearing in the woods, to our left, some ten miles farther from Njoro, where Papa had stopped briefly for a chat with acquaintances. There was an iron gate, where Mahesh Uncle met us, looking somewhat frazzled because we were later than expected. He waved us through and, once we were inside, instructed my father where to park, then asked two servants to carry our bags and bundles to the bungalows. It was breezy as we alighted, and there was a smell of fresh wood, jungle, and smoke. It had apparently rained here a couple of nights before, bringing welcome relief from the drought. Large piles of grey logs and smaller ones of sawed wood were scattered straight ahead of us, in front of two long sheds where a couple of lorries were parked. The two bungalows stood on a rise to our right, away from the main track and the screeching mill, and we walked toward them, my uncle in the lead, explaining the layout. One of the bungalows was for his own use, the other for guests. There was a small log cabin office closer to the gate.

It's lively enough at this hour, Mother remarked, but the nights—

Quiet as a cemetery, her brother said, and dark as dark.

She shuddered.

Do they leave you alone—the Mau Mau fighters? Aruna asked. Are there any in this area?—the Aberdares are in the opposite direction . . . isn't that where they hide?

Mahesh Uncle, as was his way, became thoughtful for a moment, then said, Before I arrived, they had come once and poisoned the dogs and stolen some equipment. But they haven't bothered us much. The dogs bark now and then, and we suspect the fighters are passing through—

I've told him—Mother began, but thought better of it. The conversation had obviously gone off in the wrong direction.

But Mahesh Uncle and Aruna hit it off immediately. Within no time, over tea, he was passionately explaining to her how it was in Kenya. The settlers saw it as another South Africa, he told her, except this would be better, more like Devonshire or Surrey, with the Africans their happy servants or junior partners. And the Indians—

He paused, with a dramatic look at the others.

And the Indians? Aruna asked excitedly, obviously anticipating the nature of his observation.

The Indians are exclusive—almost as racist as the whites—and lazy. Afraid of the outdoors, frightened of wild animals; they will not lift even a spoon but will ask a servant to do so, or to fetch a glass of water—

Aruna was delighted.

But Mahesh, I saw your own tea brought to you by a servant just now, Papa said rather smugly, and Aruna laughed out loud, clapped her hands.

Mahesh Uncle coloured considerably and said, Bhaiya, this is his house as much as mine, there's nothing wrong with giving someone employment; and—

Papa, pleased as punch, was ready with another riposte, but Mother cut in, But Bhaiya, you never told me I was lazy!

Mahesh Uncle was even more embarrassed: I didn't mean everybody—

We know what you meant, Aruna said with a kindly smile, adding, Are you going to give us a tour?

Mother eyed Papa, who said he would look around later, and so she turned to Mahesh, Why don't you show Aruna round the place?

Come along kids, my uncle said, and the four of us strolled out, Deepa holding Aruna's hand.

From a distance came the whine and shriek of machinery slicing through fresh wood. The lorries we had seen earlier were being loaded. The gate was open and a mountain of logs was being dragged in on a hand-cart pushed and pulled by four people straining with all their might. A group of villagers were walking out with bits of bark and baskets of wood chips which they would use for fuel.

How did you get interested in this line of work? Aruna asked.

After I found the job, came the reply. I enjoy the peace and quiet. Though I don't relish supplying the settlers with the material to make even bigger dwellings on land taken from the Africans.

They strode together, Aruna intermittently looking up at him with what seemed to be an admiring, affectionate smile. As we approached the main sawing shed, Mahesh Uncle supplied us with wads of cotton wool to stick into our ears. A circular saw was in operation, lengths of shaved tree trunks approaching it fitfully on a belt and submitting to the angry, slicing blade. A grinning, ghostlike attendant, face masked and arms gloved with sawdust, was guiding the logs on their way, another was constantly pouring water on the blade to cool it, as the dust flew from its sides to form flourlike yellow heaps on the ground.

We walked back, the couple now in front of us and deep in conversation. I thought what a nice pair they made, what a nice auntie Aruna would make, and I confided to Deepa, with a wise nod, They are going to get married.

Why do you show so much concern for the Africans? Aruna asked. Surely they have people of their own to speak out for their rights?

Perhaps I simply need a cause. But—he looked at her earnestly— surely it is the duty of *everyone* to speak out when they see a wrong being done.

And the Indians of Africa? Who speaks out for them? You're not fair to them. Nobody wants them. Not even Pandit Nehru, I bet.

He nodded. I know. I get inflamed when I see their pride going hand in hand with their stupidity. They are naïve and not educated—except in the art of business. They have no idea how the world has changed. They get flattered when a District Commissioner visits their mosque or temple to pray for Our Beautiful Queen and the Empire! In this *atomic* age! After India's *independence*, after its partition!

Yes, she affirmed to him a little later, she too had marched in college for Panditji and Gandhiji and India's independence, and had faced a laathi charge once.

He said: My father was a police inspector in Peshawar. I went around on behalf of Congress explaining to the Muslims that it was not a Hindu party . . . and later I travelled as a Congress observer and placator during communal riots and during the violence of Partition.

Did you see the violence? Women jumping into wells, did that really happen?

He nodded. There was a crazed Sikh in one location who, when we went to pour lime disinfectant into one such well which contained his drowned womenfolk, asked me to remove the gold ring from his wife's finger—he would need it later, he said. And then there were all the lost children and those left behind . . .

I had never seen my uncle speak to anyone like that; he had met a kindred soul. So far he had had only my mother to speak to in such a vein, but she was only a sister; the bond between them was love, and there was always my father around her, from a quite different, colonial world.

That night we were invited to eat at the Singhs' house. It had become incredibly dark outside. A sliver of moon shone brightly, which we all stepped out to watch for a while, admiring its false cheer; then Mother shivered and said, I'm afraid to go anywhere at this hour, why don't Aruna and I cook something for us?

What, corned beef from the tins? asked Papa. Baked beans?

Oh, I do have groceries, and Jonas cooks for me, Mahesh Uncle said, referring to one of the servants.

Then what do you need all the tinstuffs for? Mother asked. Who eats them?

We had brought a box full of tinned food for him, at his request, and whenever he visited us, among the stuff he took back with him to Elburgon there were always some tins of food. But Mahesh Uncle said nothing, and Papa, after watching him pointedly for a moment, said, Let's go to Resham Singh's—we don't want to offend him. Come on, nothing will happen to us.

The six of us squeezed into our car, and we drove off in the dark to Resham Singh's house down the road. It was a nerve-wracking drive, with everyone frantically peering outside in all directions. Attempts at conversation were brief and abortive. The forest was a deep, dark, murky space on our right, home to tall and strange sinister shapes made out fleetingly by the headlights, creatures that could at any moment—it seemed—leap out onto the road and attack us in a fury. Finally, with audible sighs of relief from Mother and Aruna, we reached the house and the gate was opened to us.

The house was a grey stone-brick bungalow with a large veranda; the floors were smooth, polished wood, and there were all sorts of trophies on the walls inside, including a frighteningly immense lion's head and a Masai shield and weapons. The rug in the sitting room was a zebra skin. Resham Singh with his wife and daughter was visiting his son Ajit Singh, who ran the sawmill with Mahesh Uncle. The old man had a greying beard and a paunch, and wore a long-sleeved shirt, untucked. His son was dressed in a safari suit with a vest. All the five women there, including Mother and Aruna Auntie, were dressed alike in Punjabi costume. There was a small kitchen area at the side of the front anteroom that preceded the sitting room, where an African cook was quietly busy. There was deer meat, which my father ate with the Singhs, and a lot of vegetarian fare with chappatis. It surprised my mother that the African had learned to cook so well.

Ajit Singh spoke rather like an Englishman, with a lot of "old boys" and "dear ladys," and talked a lot of politics, which suited Mahesh Uncle and Aruna fine, but the others looked bored. He went into Mau Mau horror stories with a mischievous smile, declaring nonchalantly, My butler James here has taken the oath, I know that, and I dare say also the cook, who has given us this fine fare tonight!

Deepa was fast asleep when we left, and I could barely stand on my feet. Ajit Singh offered to escort us back in his Land Rover and gave Mahesh Uncle and Aruna Auntie a ride, bringing his Alsatian Toby along with him. It was a sombre trip back, Ajit Singh's vehicle with its wide headlights setting a fast pace. He's a brave fellow, Papa said of him, but then you know these Sardarjis, they like to show off that they are afraid of nothing.

I don't think Mahesh belongs here, Mother told him.

·   ·   ·

Pitch darkness around me; the jingle of curtains skidding on their rings; a thin wedge of light seeping in from the side of the door, where it was open a crack. Someone—Mahesh Uncle—moving about on the other side, in the front room. I murmured something, tried to go back to sleep; heard another door, the outside one, close shut, and my heart leapt. All alone, Deepa and I? The two of us were sharing the spare bedroom in Mahesh Uncle's cabin. A little later the outside door opened again, clicked gently shut. I got up and went to peer through the crack. Mahesh Uncle was dressed for outdoors, in a green windbreaker. He was standing at the table, only partly turned away from me, so that I could see what he was up to— intently occupied with an old Indian jute bag he sometimes had on him. On the table were bottles of medicine, packets of Epsom salts—which I knew to be highly recommended by my father as a purgative—tins of various foods . . . a few newspapers . . . and something brown and bulky that seemed to me shatteringly familiar. He carefully placed the medicines and tins inside the bag, then folded up the papers and shoved them in, and finally picked up the last object . . . a gun in a deep-tan holster, simply too much like the one my father had lost!

What was Uncle up to? Was that gun now in his bag really the one for which Papa had flown into a rage, for which poor Amini had been dismissed and was probably languishing in jail, for which the servant quarters had been subjected to yet another raid by the police? Was Mahesh Uncle the one who had *stolen* the gun? Why?

My uncle went out; I heard the door click shut, a little too loudly, and I stepped out into the front room, peered through the window. He was not in sight.

My foolhardy course of action is matched only by the outrageous and distressing nature of that entire episode. How did I pick up the courage to follow him, with such a calm persistence, such thoughtfulness that I turned back from the window, went to Deepa's and my room, picked up my shoes, and closed the door after a glance at her? I put on the shoes in haste, came out the front door, closed it with a softer sound than Mahesh Uncle had made. As I began to walk, I was attacked by a savage cold—I was still clad in pyjamas—and my teeth began to chatter uncontrollably. I turned back and gently opened the door, pulled a shawl from a sofa and, wrapping it around my shoulders and waist, came out of the house as I'd done before. I wished for Njoroge at my side. And I worried lest my sister wake up in the dark with nobody in that alien house. My feet crunched on the hard earth. I breathed harshly the chilled outdoors air, my heart pounding, and I wondered if it could really be true what I had heard, that the heart could choke you from inside if you got too excited.

It must have been not more than five minutes since Mahesh Uncle had stepped out, but there was no sight of him as I trotted along the path leading down toward the gate.

Deep inside me now, for some unconscious reason, from having lived in the same house and having watched him and loved him, and for all the intangible ways by which we sense a person through our pores, so to speak, I knew my uncle to be up to something worthwhile, something secret and dangerous and utterly brave that no other adult in my family would understand. That was why I was here outside, beside the gate in the freezing cold, awaiting a clue to his whereabouts. I wanted to see what he did and whom he met. But I would have to keep my distance.

He was not far. He had gone to mount a horse and soon I heard the clop-clop approaching, coming toward the gate, and I hid behind a bush. Normally it should not have been easy to see me, but the shawl I had picked up was beige and reflective even in that dark. Slowly and then with quickening steps I began to follow. He was not going fast, but even at a trot quite a deal faster than I could walk, and I found myself lagging farther and farther behind and so began a frantic jog. I was anxious to stay close to him now, purely out of a fear of being attacked by a wild animal—what better refuge than an uncle within shouting distance, close by on a horse, and carrying a gun! We were on a vehicle trail that extended a short distance from the sawmill and was used by lorries and tractors and carts to bring in the logs.

All of a sudden a grey dawn had broken. I could see my uncle straight ahead, a couple of hundred yards away, the yellow of the jute bag behind him as distinct as a lamp. He was just then beginning to turn left, into the forest.

I see a boy stooped to seek cover, running in the shadow of the over-growth beside the road: to what end? To satisfy a savage, bursting curiosity about the adults' world, to catch them with their guard down, see them as they are. Just as, some months before, one Sunday morning I had followed a sound from my mother, knowing inside me I was entering off bounds, and caught her and Papa in a grotesque togetherness and asked, grinning, What are you doing, Mother?

In my uncle's case now I wasn't as innocent: he was trotting off into the forest with supplies at his back. And I knew what the jungle portended.

When I reached the spot where my uncle had disappeared, I could see no sign of him, hear no sound. A path, roofed by a tall canopy of tree branches, led off from where I stood. I dared not venture inside that dark wood, follow that trail that could only lead to oblivion. I would never come out alive. Dejected and defeated, for the first time since I had set off after my uncle I was afraid of the consequences of my actions. What would he say if he found out I was spying on him? What would the others, especially my father, have to say about *his* nocturnal activities?

Just then I heard sounds—booming human voices in the distance, the shuffle of rapidly moving feet. Three men had suddenly become visible, where the road took a slight bend; they were jogging together and rapidly approaching. If they saw me, I was dead. In terror I crouched closer to the bushes by the roadside, but they could barely conceal me, unless I fell right into their creepy embrace. Instead, I ran onto the track.

But not very far; quickly, I hid behind a fat tree trunk. And prayed: O Rama, save me and keep your Hanumans away—there might be monkeys around—and all the other wild animals who are your friends, even the mamba, but still . . . keep them away . . . Small flying insects tormented me, getting into my eyes and eyelashes, and I closed my eyes and waited, and supplicated, and the sounds drew closer and were upon me.

The three men were on the track and walking in a single file. They all carried pangas; one had a rifle, another, a dirty gunny sack, the third, a torn rucksack . . . and they were Mau Mau.

I recall a pair of black army boots, laces untied or absent, pounding the earth, sloshing through a carpet of dead leaves; a deep-tan leather jacket, like a fighter pilot's, I thought; a mat of knotted hair on one head and a beard on the face; long carefully wrought plaits tumbling down and partly covering a thin and long face, belonging to the one who carried the rifle on his shoulder.

Any moment during the yuga they took to pass me, they could have seen me, heard me breathe or shuffle my feet or moan in terror where I crouched. There was no single thought in my head, all was one big frightful moment.

Then they were gone, and I waited, gulping, regaining my faculties. Finally I stood up, slowly came out onto the trail, then let go with my feet. The same moment some creature not far away but invisible also took off with a tremendous commotion. I ran without pause.

Deepa was at the door, tearful, saying, Where have you been? I thought the lions had eaten you!

Lions? I said bravely, Don't be silly. When I didn't see Uncle in the house, I simply walked outside to take a peek.

Mahesh Uncle returned much later. Oh?—he said, in response to our questions—I was out in the forest marking trees for the cutters. They'll go and chop them down now and bring them to the mill for sawing. That's what I was doing so early while you two lay snoring!

Was he telling the truth? Perhaps, in part. I knew that he had also delivered supplies in the forest. His yellow jute bag lay carelessly, gaping open on the table, where the three of us were sitting with our morning tea.

I did not bring up the subject of his excursion and of that gun. I had been wrong in following him. He was my uncle whom I loved and trusted, who knew what he was doing. My raising the subject would only cause a quarrel between him and my father and make my mother unhappy as a result.

There was a late and large family breakfast, after which Deepa and I went for a walk with our parents, so that Mahesh Uncle and Aruna Auntie could be by themselves to talk. Early in the afternoon we left for Nakuru.

. . .

It's how you feel, of course, Aruna, that matters. It is your life you have to think of, Mother said.

Aruna nodded. Please don't get offended, Didiji.

Mother shook her head, put a hand on Aruna's.

It was night, Papa had gone to bed after the nine o'clock news. Mother and Aruna Auntie were on the long sofa in the sitting room, gathered by themselves to discuss Aruna's decision regarding Mahesh Uncle. So they are not going to get married, I thought sadly. Aruna Auntie was a heartless Nairobi woman after all, who knew no better. The two of them glanced in my direction, where I sat at the dining room table, watching them. But they did not object to my presence. Mother was used to my listening in this way, in silence, sometimes at hours that were late for me, dismissing any concern with, He's the recording angel, but he doesn't say a word about what he hears.

There were tears in Auntie's eyes.

Tell me why, Mother asked. You two seemed to get along as if you were made for each other.

Something inside me says no. It says, Don't do it, and I always listen to that voice, it's always right.

And you explained to Mahesh, and what did he say?

He agreed, Didiji. He said we were two of a kind and too similar. For a marriage we need something of opposites.

Mother nodded again. You go on to sleep now, she told Aruna, who stood up and went to Deepa's room, which had been assigned to her. Mother sat by herself in that semidarkness, her hands clasped in her lap. I got up and went to give her a hug.

The next day in the afternoon when we returned from school, Aruna was gone. She had already hugged and kissed us goodbye in the morning before we left. Later in the morning my parents had dropped her off at the railway station and she went back to Nairobi.

Those few days she stayed with us were among the most fun-filled in my life.

I saw Aruna again in Nairobi, and more recently and very briefly in Toronto, where she lives, still single. That inner voice of hers may have been overly cautious. But that time perhaps she was right in following it; for in marrying my uncle she would have had to live with the grief and remorse that awaited like karma to haunt and burden his life.

What's wonderful about the summer here, in this northern latitude, are the long days that wane so gradually, reluctantly, hanging on to the last precious ray of the glorious setting sun. This afternoon after walking about for a while, I gardened and then climbed down the cliff to the lake's edge for a swim—a somewhat risky enterprise, because I don't know the water here too well. Seema has taken Joseph to the town's midsummer festival. I declined to accompany them; my recent recollections seem to have dragged me down somewhat and I needed to be alone.

ELEVEN

It comes to me always at night, this tableau, this creation of the mind; there is a sound in the darkness, a child's whimper: No, no . . . Next, light has fallen on the scene and she is sitting on the floor, pathetic, knees drawn up, and looking up and begging for mercy . . . the assailant tall and invisible. Then darkness again—the light, the life snuffed out—and enough, I say, curtain. The mind's demonic theatre abandoned mid-scene, I will take a walk in the dark, room to room, to distract myself. I will look out the window. I may even scribble a fragment of a poem, meagre as my skills are in that area. The trouble is that even though I choose to turn away from the conclusion of that scene, the general picture of the aftermath I carry vividly in the mind: the blood, the gore.

For more than forty years I have been haunted by this image of her.

There's nothing as gut-wrenching, as irrationally tugging, as that plaintive, tragically heartbroken, throaty cry of a child.

Some days ago, late in the afternoon, I heard a child's guttural whine coming from the back porch outside; a girl's plea, to my mind, a sobbing piteous supplication, and out I stormed in a rage. *What* are you doing to her—

Joseph and his two young friends from the neighbourhood stared at me, the latter having taken fright at my outburst. They had begun to play soccer, and I had obviously overreacted to the sounds of what turned out to have been the spoiled machinations of the youngest of them, the boy; I turned sheepishly to go back inside before being invited kindly to stay and be goalkeeper.

Joseph informed me today that he is ready to leave now, to go to Toronto, where he will spend the remaining four weeks of the summer with friends before joining the university. These are new acquaintances, politically kindred souls he has made contact with through the Internet. Perhaps finally he sees me now as an afflicted, weak man, not the cold, powerful, and corrupt monster I have been made out to be by the press back home and in various parts of Africa. Perhaps both he and Ms. Chatterjee—Seema—see me in that piteous manner: I've been stared at sufficiently and suggestively by the two of them the last few days. They have not been easy, these days, for I have recalled the end of that ultimately tragic year of my life.

I have prevaricated enough.

One morning, it was Wednesday, while our family was having breakfast, the telephone rang and Papa went to pick it up in the sitting room. After a few moments we heard a loud cry, Noooo! *Noooo!*

He came back and he was crying. Like a child. Two tears were running down his cheeks. His mouth twitched uncontrollably.

The most horrible thing, Sheila, the most horrible thing has happened—

What? asked Mother, Arré what, but? Is it Bauji? Is it Biji?

No. Send them away, children go to your rooms—please.

Deepa and I didn't budge from our seats. What is it, Papa? What has happened?

He gave a loud moan: Oh my God. Then, to Mother: The Bruces, Sheila, the Bruces, all murdered. Butchered last night. Mister, Missis, children, all—*butchered!*

. . .

I cannot recall exactly how I felt in the days that immediately followed. I imagine a numbness of sorts, a dependence on parents for direction, for emotional shelter. I know that I did not shed a tear. We did not attend the funeral because my father had been informed that it would not be appropriate to do so, it was a family and a European affair. Mrs. Bruce's father and brother were present, having flown from England, as was the Governor of the colony, Sir Evelyn Baring, and the Commander-in-Chief of the armed forces, General Sir George Erskine.

The particulars of the murders, which created an outrage throughout the country, were the following:

The two dogs had been poisoned early in the evening, around dinnertime, and were found the next day at the back of the house. At a few minutes past nine o'clock, two shots were fired outside at the front gate, one of which hit the watchman, who survived. Before Mr. Bruce could get to his gun, some members of the gang were inside, having been let in through the back. The couple were beaten and hacked to death downstairs. Then the gang went upstairs to the children's bedrooms. Bill had been brave, the newspapers said, and put up resistance. Annie had tried to hide . . .

The details of the children's deaths were too gruesome to describe, according to the papers. They printed a picture of Annie's teddy bear, however. It had been cut to shreds.

All the servants except Kihika were accounted for. The police were told by the servants who had been found that they had been locked up in a shed and guarded by two gang members. Kihika however had disappeared, and police were looking for him as a prime suspect. There was a picture of Kihika with Bill sitting on his shoulders at the age of three.

Mother had Mwangi cut the roses from the plant Mrs. Bruce had given her, and she put four of the orange blooms, which had been christened Beautiful Elizabeth by Papa, in a vase in memory of the Bruces.

I know, Joseph, these were only four of a handful of whites killed during the freedom struggle; what about the thousands of Africans who died, you will ask, what about the massacres at Lari, the killings by government forces at Hola? There were children there too, they were black, who remembers them?

All I can say is, these two were my friends. Even bossy Bill. And Annie was my comrade, my secret, innocent little romance. One day they were my playmates, the next they had been cut up in pieces in the name of freedom, of retaliation.

You say, Consider them as casualties of a war, then. To which I answer, reluctantly: Perhaps. The last time I saw them we were blowing soap bubbles and running around in the car park of that shopping centre. Alidina the greengrocer had treated us to New Zealand apples.

Two days after the murders the police came and spoke with my father. The interview, in our sitting room, was grave in tone and lasted a half hour. Lieutenant Soames informed my father that the gun used by the gang at the Bruces' was the one which had been stolen from him. This had been determined by matching a bullet recovered from the Bruces' gate with one my father had fired at the Nakuru shooting range for practice soon after he bought his gun. The police had on file used bullets from all registered guns in the Nakuru area.

Are you sure? Papa said desperately to the departing lieutenant.

Lieutenant Soames nodded, without a word. He adjusted his peaked cap and left. It seemed as if my poor father was somehow implicated in the tragedy. He had not looked after his weapon, now it was in the hands of the very terrorists who had carried out that hellish attack on the Bruces. It was the carelessness of people like him that gave indirect support to those murderers.

What a people, Papa muttered glumly at the lieutenant's back. Every policeman a Sherlock Holmes.

From what I had overheard, I was certain that the murderers of Annie and Bill and their parents were men known to my uncle. He was their friend. I had already seen him taking supplies, including a gun that I was sure had been my father's, out into the jungle. But I said nothing about what I knew.

Meanwhile, during my father's interview, the police had descended upon the servant quarters. Now as the lieutenant left with his men, the trucks grinding away out of our street, a great hubbub began among the servants in the back. We were informed by our help Pedro that the police had taken away two men, one of them Mwangi. It had turned out—and this accounted for all the noisy excitement outside—that this time around Corporal Boniface had emerged triumphantly from a search of Mwangi's room waving telltale evidence: two muddy and torn pairs of khaki trousers and an army-style green jacket copiously stained with blood on the sleeve, all of which had been hidden under the bed.

Mwangi?—a friend and well-wisher of that fiendish gang, those murderers of Annie and Bill? I still ask myself this, after all these years. Over and over I've answered to myself, No, it could not be. They are evil, those who kill children, he had said bitterly, looking into my eyes. By then, most likely he had already taken the oath, like thousands of others. Perhaps this time he had been called upon to abide by it, aid the forest fighters by hiding evidence, and he had no choice? Or perhaps there was an entirely different and innocent explanation for those clothes in his room. The old and wizened man, the wise man who spoke in proverbs, Njoroge's grandfather. The gardener who had tended that orange rose of Mrs. Bruce's creation, who put champeli flowers in Deepa's hair, and once in Annie's. How could he have been party to her death? Though Kihika, who was now wanted for the murders, had also shown devotion to the children . . . and they told you over and over, the police, that every Kikuyu was a potential murderer of children; they gave you examples of treachery, showed you albums of photos of innocent-looking servants who had turned out to be Mau Mau, until you could no longer be sure of your trust.

Our family was stunned by the news. Mother emitted a short, hysterical-sounding, almost involuntary peal of laughter. It was *his* clothes only—she told Papa, in disbelief—and . . . and you know how he is asked sometimes to slaughter chickens for some of the families here! That's where the blood came from! You know how some of these policemen are, especially that European, Soames—he's been after our Mwangi for months. Now they will say it was Mwangi who stole the gun from our house—

Then *who* else? Papa almost screamed at her in frustration.

She shrunk back, as if in terror, and he looked away, scowling and ashamed.

When I think of that scene in our sitting room, the two of them quietly apart on the long sofa, the dolorous, hot, resting hour after lunch having been ruptured by the police visit and now this shocking news, I imagine them both close to tears.

I could have answered Papa's question. If anyone else we knew was involved with the killers for sure, it was my uncle.

It was Friday, and later that afternoon Mahesh Uncle came down from the sawmill. He gave Mother, Deepa, and me a hug of condolence, saying how terrible the news was, and Mother cried, If only we hadn't known them, it would be easier . . .

I quickly squirmed out of his embrace, much to his surprise. It pains me even now to record this, to recall his deeply hurt expression, but something inside me, a core of feeling and love, had withered and died. From that day onward, I refused closeness with my uncle. I squirmed in his embraces, I looked away when he made friendly or tender overtures. I think he knew that I knew something of his involvement with the Mau Mau, something I had discovered that early morning during our visit to him. Once, that weekend, he contrived to be at the table with me alone, and began, If only one could have done something . . . He broke off, looking embarrassed. I was not sure what he meant, but I knew it was said in an attempt to assuage my feelings and win me over.

Njoroge disappeared for a day, following Mwangi's arrest, but then was back hovering about in our yard. For one thing, he needed food. My mother's defence of Mwangi and our own feelings for him were enough to make him innocent in my sister's and my eyes. The plaguing doubts, and the insistent, instinctive denial of them, would come much later.

Now with your grandfather gone, what will you do, William? Mother asked him, having given him puris and kheer to take away.

Jomo will free my grandfather, he said.

I hope so, she replied, with a doubtful look.

He told me years later that he had obtained most of his Jomo stuff from that servant who had sported a Jomo beard and had been detained, never to return. There had existed a cabal of Jomo Kenyatta sympathizers in our housing estate, to which Mwangi however had been indifferent.

People of the estate were wary about Njoroge's fate and their role in it; they knew that this time Mwangi would not return soon, if ever. A new gardener would be sought. What would happen to the boy? Where were his parents? Would he be reliable if employed as a servant?

Ten days after the Bruce murders, two Englishwomen came to speak with Njoroge in the company of Mrs. Van Roost, who was the principal of his school in Nakuru. They told him they had come to take him to a boarding school, where he could wait for his grandfather, and they would assist him in finding his other relations. It was Sunday morning, the scene took place in our backyard. The women were dressed in frocks and hats, as if they had been to church. Njoroge nodded quickly at their instructions and went off to his room and returned with his wooden schoolbag and some clothes wrapped in a newspaper. In the interim, my mother was informed by the waiting ladies that Njoroge's father had been arrested in a riot in Nairobi a few years earlier; his current whereabouts, as that of the boy's mother, were not known. Njoroge came to shake hands with us, and Mother—extremely pleased that he had found a home—told him, Now don't forget to write to us.

Yes, said one of the two visitors, do write to your friends in Nakuru who have been so kind to you.

Deepa ran to her room and brought a paper and pencil, which I quickly snatched from her. I wrote down our address on the paper and gave it to Njoroge, saying, This is our P.O. box number.

Write to us, Njoroge, Deepa said. You can keep the pencil, if you want.

He kept it.

We accompanied him and the three women to the front and watched them get into a car and drive away.

Where did they take him? Deepa asked, suddenly tearful.

Arré we forgot even to ask them, Mother said, pensive. But I'm sure Njoroge will write to us. If not, we will ask that Mrs. Van Roost woman.

But she looked deeply distracted as we slowly made our way back into the house. Poor child, she said. Poor children.

Kihika would never be captured. According to the police he had gone into the forest to join a Mau Mau gang.

One Sunday at our family gathering Mohan Uncle said to Papa, Did you hear, eh Ashok? Your gardener, that old Mwangi, killed himself in prison.

Eh—what? Papa said.

Bechara, Mother whispered, poor soul, then gave a look at Mahesh Uncle, who exploded.

What, killed himself—tortured to death, more likely. Do you see the dignified, proud Mwangi killing himself? For what?

Mahesh Uncle flashed a look at me, as if seeking my approval. Mohan Uncle gave him a sneering reply, with a dismissive hand: There he goes defending the terrorists as usual. Proud and dignified, arré my left foot, your kalu Gandhi was nothing but Dracula-Frankenstein, one to drink the blood of children—

Mahesh Uncle stood up with a roar and another fight almost erupted. My father's brothers departed in haste with their families, and Dadaji and Juma Molabux agreed to go on a short walk, up and down the street.

Our world had changed. We were in the aftermath of a tragedy which had struck suddenly in a furious moment, destroyed the composure of our lives, and departed. Saturdays, Deepa and I stayed at home with Mother and sometimes we would go to the neighbouring estate to play with the other Indian children. There were many presents for us, including a much-anticipated train set for me, which I most enjoyed playing with Papa and Dadaji, who came up with adventurous scenarios for railway journeys. We had constructed all the main stations from Kisumu to Mombasa using matchboxes and pins, and fashioned our landscape and wildlife, including the inevitable man-eating lions, with potter's clay. I recall a family visit to the Nakuru station, where a crowd of townspeople had gathered in excitement to take a look at the new rail car which had recently been brought over (it was said) from the Alps in Switzerland; it had seating capacity only and large windows all around for the passengers to view the scenery. It was full of tourists that day, who looked out curiously and waved at us, and we waved back. I began my stamp collecting in earnest.

Deepa would sometimes wake up at night in terror, imagining intruders outside trying to break into our house. Once, in a delirious fever, she even called me Mau Mau, much to my astonishment. I believe she wet her bed a few times, which my mother tried to keep from me lest I tease her.

Papa gave up his Tuesday night Home Guard duties partly due to Deepa's fears, which were heightened when he went away and Mother had only her gods to whisper to in their corner and her tremulous voice in which to tell us to go to sleep.

For my part, however, I recall a tranquil period. Mother would chide me that I was becoming too quiet. I am not sure if she quite meant it, because I had developed a slight stutter, which quite visibly disconcerted Papa when he was not watchful, and Mother would then have a pained look in her eyes. I was taken to several doctors, including a European specialist in Nairobi; I saw a pandit and a Muslim wahid recommended by Juma Molabux. The only remedy that worked was to remain calm and not get excited or emotional when speaking. That remedy still works.

A year after the Bruce incident our parents told us that for the sake of our schooling, and to forget the terrible events we had experienced, they had decided that we would move to Nairobi.

Joseph has gone. Seema came and picked him up this morning and drove him to Toronto. I can take comfort in the fact that if I could not get close to Njoroge's son, as Deepa desired and I came to wish, at least I found for him someone else whom he trusts, who hopefully will keep him on track, away from the hazards of fruitless and deadly politics.

PART 2

_____

The Year of Her Passion

TWELVE

———————

One day a rather tall and lean-looking young African man stepped some-what hesitantly into the reception room of Mayfair Estate Agents in Nairobi's Indian Bazaar and asked to see Mr. Lall. The secretary, unim-pressed by his deportment, told him curtly to wait, Mr. Lall was busy. The young man sat down, picked up a magazine, and waited what must have seemed an unreasonable time without being announced, and so when the door to the inner sanctum opened one more time in his presence, and the office boy emerged languorously from it bearing another meagre bit of correspondence, the visitor stood up, walked past him, and barged inside. Papa looked up impatiently from his desk.

The year was 1965 and Kenya had finally achieved independence. Great changes had taken place since the stroke of midnight announced freedom eighteen months earlier. Jomo Kenyatta, former political prisoner, was President and father of our nation and his portrait beamed kindly from the walls of every shop and office. The sun shone more brightly than be-fore, and even the sounds of the streets rang different. My father's line of business put him in the midst of the shakeups of Nairobi's many segre-gated neighbourhoods and allowed him to profit from them. The country's freedom had come as a personal boon to him as it had done to many others. European settlers and civil servants were departing, leaving for easy pickings their homes in the posher areas of the city. Indian civil servants were abandoning to the unfriendly market their properties in modest East-leigh, which African cooperatives were quickly buying up. International visitors arrived in droves, sporting sun wear and cheerful optimism, and if they were not tourists, they needed rental housing. Papa worked hard at his job. He managed for the new landlords as he had done for the old; he worked hard for sellers even if they were already resettled in Sialkot, Pun-jab, or Southall, England. This is the time, Sheila, he would say to Mother, if I play it smart, I can make my fortune.

But today was Friday, his short workday, and he was planning to leave for a late lunch at home, then a short siesta, followed by a night of cards at the club. And so the presence of the brash intruder in his office was annoy-ing in the only way it could be in newly independent Africa—you couldn't say a cross word. Sensitivities ran high in the country, the humiliations of colonial rule still smarted; you could be denounced and deported as a racist almost overnight. So my father waited patiently, watching the young man, who was grinning at him insanely with wide eyes.

Good morning, Mr. Lall, the visitor said finally.

Hardly morning, Papa thought, it's lunchtime and not the time to walk into people's offices. He sized up the fellow—modestly dressed, wearing a grey jacket that could have been bought second-hand from Abdulla Fazal, a street away. Not only property but also clothes were changing hands—or bodies.

Young man, he said, having gotten up and come around his desk, there is no vacancy here, the position that was advertised three months ago in the *Standard* was filled long ago, a notice was sent and was printed to that ef-fect. But you seem to be educated, you should have no problem finding something—

Papa had his arm extended to lead the visitor to the door when, prompted by a long exchange of looks with the man, the revelation finally hit him. Like a brick, he would later say.

Njoroge? he exclaimed, in his utter astonishment. Njoroge of Nakuru, grandson of Mwangi? After all these years . . . I can't believe it.

Yes, it's me, Mr. Lall, Njoroge said with a touch of tenderness. He thought my father would faint from the shock. They shook hands and Njoroge held on to Papa's hands.

How are you, my dear young man, it's been a long time . . . your letters stopped coming . . .

You had moved, sir. And how is your wife, and how are Vic and little Deepa?

That last inquiry, as I imagine it, earnest, pointed. How *were* we, what had we become?

Fine, fine—we moved to Nairobi, as you see, in early 1955 after that—that terrible tragedy. What a time that was, I am glad it is over and now it's uhuru.

He stared at a silent Njoroge, who towered over him.

And thus Njoroge came back into our lives—not obtrusively, that was typical of him. He did not want to presume upon us, he told my father, a lot of time had passed since he knew us. Papa stared at the tall young Kikuyu and couldn't have agreed more. An age had passed since Nakuru. But he said, Arré what are you saying? Come home with me right now, I'm going home myself, and Deepa and Vic and my wife will be delighted to see you!

Njoroge declined, saying, Not today, Mr. Lall, I have to be away this afternoon—but do you think Vic and Deepa could meet me in the city tomorrow? I would love to see them.

That afternoon, and again in the evening when Papa had returned home from his club, Deepa and I (but she more so) plied him with questions: What did he sound like? How tall is he? Does he have a high forehead? What does he *look* like, Papa?

Don't forget, Mother said to Deepa, you knew him as a child; he's a grown man now. Don't go and make a fool of yourself tomorrow.

He's a very serious young man now, Papa affirmed.

Nobody can change all that much, Deepa replied, irrepressible and, I thought then, childish as always.

I was somewhat apprehensive about the meeting, as it appeared Njoroge too was. In the past too we both had tended to be more circumspect than my sister. How would the three of us respond to what we had become, as young adults in a vastly changed world? Our meeting was arranged at the Café Rendezvous on the recently renamed Kimathi Street; and as we hastened toward it the next morning, having driven downtown with our father, I had to do all I could to keep up with Deepa weaving in and out between the Saturday throngs. The café had once been a hangout for European teenagers; now tourists and locals of all races overflowed out of its wide doors. Inside was packed and steamy, the latest pop music from England came blaring out. The Beatles had recently become popular. We had stood hardly a few moments at the entrance when Deepa shrieked at the handsome tall youth coming smiling toward us.

Oh my God . . . Njo! It's really you! It's been such a long time, and you stopped writing!

It was as if all these many years she had been waiting for him, to chide him about just that matter.

She rushed forward to embrace him, and held on to his hands and gaped at him, smiling, laughing, and tugged at his arms, back and forth and sideways, as if to make sure he was real. Everyone at the chic Rendezvous had looked up at this wild, unorthodox Asian girl, at the joyous embrace and its aftermath. Independence was here, yes, and Kenyatta our leader had forgiven the sins of the past and we were all citizens of a new multiracial, democratic nation, but still, this was taking integration too fast, too far even for Nairobi!

Did she really recognize him instantly that morning as we stood at the café entrance and he walked over to us, beaming? Did she see in the tall, lanky African with hair parted on the left, wearing an oversized grey jacket and red tie, the boy we had known so many years before? Had she missed him so badly, in private, quietly, all this time?

She was a lovely dark beauty, petite, with sparkling eyes, a long face, and straight hair down to her shoulders; she wore that day not her usual Punjabi shalwar-kameez but a full-length green kikoi dress with a matching dupatta round her neck.

At the table he took both her hands into his, searched her eyes with his, and in that deep voice that was so new and charming to us said, But I wrote to you, Deepa!

Sio! No you didn't. How could you have? I never received anything.

Even her voice seemed changed in this new presence, before this returned avatar of our former friend. The odd bit of Swahili from her—sio—was charming and Njoroge and I both laughed. He took out an old address book from his pocket, pages yellow and curling at the corners, and read aloud: P.O. Box 3312, Nakuru, wasn't that the box number?

Yes it was, I answered.

And I even wrote once—to you both—in Nairobi, someone from Nakuru gave me the address. So?—you didn't reply, Deepa!

They were in love.

They had picked up that spontaneity, the familiarity, in an instant despite all those intervening years of adolescence, in which we had grown up into Nairobi's typical suburban Asian youth. Their closeness simply left me by the wayside, open-eyed with wonder, heavy-hearted with envy. I wonder now that I did not already fear for her.

He had completed primary school in Eldoret, after which he was sent as a promising student to the elite Alliance High School for Africans outside Nairobi, where he had made many friends, some of whom were leaders in government now. He was in his second year at Makerere University in Kampala. Deepa was finishing high school and I was attending university in Dar es Salaam. We were all on school holidays. We carefully avoided delving at length into our days in Nakuru, or mentioning the two friends we had lost. He agreed to come home with us later to see Mother and have lunch with our family.

Life had not been easy for my family when we arrived in Nairobi. Initially Papa opened an Indian grocery store in the busy Ngara shopping area, in partnership with his cousins. But he was alien to the business, and he found it demeaning. He who had sold Gorgonzola, Wiltshire, and Camembert to European customers, and once even brought caviar for them, could never get used to the idea of sitting next to mounds of whole turmeric and garlic, his body marinating in a sweaty blend of a dozen spices by the end of the day (when they cremate me, he would complain to Mother, I'll smell like chicken tandoori), telling people that yes, Monkey Brand charcoal tooth powder was better than Colgate and sat-isab-gol was a traditional remedy for indigestion recommended by ancient Indian yogis and infinitely superior to Eno's Fruit Salts. The only consolation to his misery behind that shop till was the sweetmeat vendor next door, from whom he could order tea and jelebis. Within a year, as he would put it, the money he had brought from Nakuru was all eaten away.

Our life in Nairobi too was a vast departure from the intimate family life we had lived before in a small town. The city was a place of hustle and bustle, of high costs and many temptations. Papa had taken up with regulars at the Indian Gymkhana, and sometimes he came home late in the evenings, having played cards, smelling of whisky. There started to appear some strain between our parents. One or two times Aruna Auntie happened to be visiting him at his shop, and Mother worked up a scene at home, bringing up finally an old grievance she had harboured, that he had flirted ceaselessly with Aruna during her visit to Nakuru, when she had come to be introduced to Mahesh Uncle.

How easy it was to lose the certainty, the simplicity we had once possessed, despite that shadow of terror, in Nakuru: the school, the quiet afternoons, the Sunday family meals and stories, the walks to the railway station. Even the many quarrels of those times between my various uncles seemed like happy, comical interludes. Our saviour in the city came in the form of one Hari Sharma, recently from Punjab and Delhi and now an estate agent in Nairobi. Property's where it's at Ashok-ji, he told Papa; at independence time it's property that changes hands, and the middle man takes away the profit—didn't we see this in India-Pakistan! Don't talk to me of faraway India-Pakistan, Papa replied, in typical fashion, but tell me more about the business here. Mr. Sharma did so, with the result that Papa joined Mayfair Estate Agents, and as Kenya's independence approached and many Europeans put up their properties for sale, fortune smiled once more upon us. But that family contentment, that certainty of my early years, we had lost forever. Suddenly my parents seemed older and tired and disengaged from each other. The love and care I would see in her eyes for him had waned, one was more likely to see her irritated with him; his boyish joyfulness and vigour too were gone. But Nairobi had other pleasures. There were English movies at the Twentieth Century, Hindi ones at the Odeon and Shan, picnics at the National Park, the fetes at the Railway Club. And there was that feeling that you were moving with the times, in this atomic age, and if you were young, the sun was shining on you.

I had started attending the Duke of Gloucester School, a high school for Asians, where I distinguished myself in a few subjects, including geometry. I became a spin bowler for the school cricket team and was president of the stamp club; I was made prefect. We moved from the busy and older Ngara area of Nairobi to a more sedate and green Sixth Parklands, into a spacious bungalow in the shade of a jacaranda tree that became ours only because of Papa's new business connections. The front veranda had a bench-swing of the sort common to many Indian homes, where I recall amidst the scents and soft sounds of the garden sitting by myself in the afternoons reading for my exams, or with Mother and Deepa before dinner waiting for Papa to come home.

If in our new home we spoke about our life in Nakuru, it was always with due caution, certain topics glossed over or gingerly trod upon as if one were on an unstable, narrow rope bridge that could twist and tangle and throw the unwary into the deep chasm below. Those topics had to do, naturally, with the Bruces, our memories of them and of our final, unhappy months there. Sometimes an inadvertent mention would escape from one of us; there would be an uncomfortable moment, a few words of response, and the subject would then quietly expire, like some lost traveller in an empty desert. We never went back to visit, though Dada and Dadi came on several occasions, as did our uncles, Papa's brothers, and their families, for whom we had become the sophisticated city cousins. Mahesh Uncle was already in Nairobi, married. He had arrived a few years earlier, his luck having changed due to a sudden twist of fate. We did not see him very often.

· · ·

Mother, Njoroge says he sent us letters to Nakuru and once even to Nairobi—didn't you, Njo? We didn't receive them, did we, Mother?

We had finally gathered in our sitting room, following luncheon, Deepa and I having brought Njoroge home straight after a lengthy session at the café. Deepa's question was rhetorical, but Mother took it literally.

Don't be silly! Arré paagal, if the letters came wouldn't we have given them to you? They must have been lost, only.

My handwriting did leave something to be desired, I admit, said Njoroge pleasantly. Anyway, here I am in the flesh!

My brothers and my father too used the same post box, said Papa, to explain the mystery further, and who knows sometimes what happens to the mail when so many people use the same box number.

No matter, here I am, repeated Njoroge.

Yes, here you are! Deepa chimed.

A long-lost brother to Vikram and Deepa, Mother told him, beaming happily, and effervescent Deepa blinked rapidly and threw her a wry, almost condescending smile. Which Mother caught, colouring a little, and exchanged a fleeting look with Papa. My parents had their work cut out for them.

Mother now had a streak of premature grey in her hair; she was still young, only a year or two above forty. She had lost nothing of her smooth, fair complexion and ruddy cheeks of north India, but she was thinner and the eyes had perhaps withdrawn a bit, having borne the expressions of her frequent anxieties. Father looked considerably older and darker; his mouth was red from the paan-chewing habit he had picked up; he was balding.

Njoroge entertained us with tales about his schooldays—how the strict Catholic nuns of his primary school would rap his knuckles for getting a sum wrong or for writing badly; how he had to learn to eat with fork and knife and to do his own bed; and those showers he had to take at six in the morning every day with ice-cold water. But he had received much kindness and had even been sent to Europe during a holiday.

That caught Papa's attention: London, eh?

His own dreams of going there had never materialized. He never spoke about them any more. Evidently the dreams now all belonged to the younger people, the opportunities were theirs.

London and Rome, Njoroge replied.

Now he was at Makerere, studying economics. He thought he would work in government following graduation; in the future perhaps he would go into politics. During the present holidays he was an assistant to the permanent secretary in the Ministry of Land Settlement, and in the previous month he had been travelling around Nyeri, investigating land claims. There was much confusion and bitterness, he explained to us, regarding land in the Kikuyu areas. Returning Mau Mau fighters and political detainees had found that their confiscated lands had been turned over in their absence to government collaborators, some of whom were now influential in the new government; the African cooperatives set up to buy land from the white settlers needed loans and the prices demanded were under dispute. Kenya had a great future, it was one of the most advanced countries in Africa. But a lot of work needed to be done first, to lay the foundation for the future.

We all must have gaped at him as he spoke those words. You couldn't help but wonder at his enthusiasm and ambition, the passion in those large eyes, and wonder too at how those words portrayed the passage of time: this used to be the boy who spoke bashfully and haltingly but proudly, the grandson of a gardener, who didn't know much about his mother and father but knew that Jomo was his saviour. Here was now a young Kenyan of today, a leader of tomorrow. On the other hand, he couldn't have seen us as very different from what we had been. We were his old friends, and sort of family; our concerns were mundane and ordinary; and we remained that enigma, the Asians of Africa.

Did they tell you about your grandfather, Njoroge? Mother asked.

Yes, Njoroge replied. They told me he had died in custody.

He gave her a grateful smile. Her maternal instincts, that essential kindness, had always reached out to him.

When the three of us arrived home earlier, she had been waiting for us near the door. She broke into a wide-eyed smile when he entered, unsure how to greet him, and he without hesitation had gathered her into his arms. Now he told her,

Mother, I often thought of you, all your kindness to me—all that food you always had for me, your gulab jamun and sakar pada and chappati—

He didn't pronounce the words quite correctly, but Mother's face turned red, she broke down and wept briefly.

We thought of you too, she said, looking up. We called you William at first, do you remember that? You were like a son to us, and a brother to my two.

Mother, said Deepa, can the three of us go to the Twentieth Century to see a movie—tomorrow afternoon?

The plan had been made earlier, during our drive home from the Rendezvous. This question too was rhetorical.

Later Papa and I drove Njoroge to the Donovan Maule Theatre, where he invited us for beers inside, at the bar, and introduced us to some of his friends. He was putting up not far away, sharing a university room with one of them. Then I drove Papa to the gymkhana. On the way, he said to me casually, Njoroge's a nice boy . . . it's truly wonderful to have him back; but some things are not meant to be. I think you understand that, Vic. Your sister's still immature, it's your job to protect her as a brother.

I was taken aback; how swiftly had come this word of caution. It was a typically parental preemptive thing to do. He threw a glance at me, awaiting my response, and I nodded dutifully, without a word. Like many others of my generation, I was confident that our parents would have to change their ways in our new world. They would take their time, but they would surely change. For now, however, they were too inconsistent and confused about where they stood and who they were, even as they called themselves Kenyans.

———————

I was surrounded by a sea of pure, soft whiteness, as if I had died and been reborn into a new, fairytale world of milky hue. Out back, the snow stretched on endlessly, across the lake, into the mist, and forever, in a scene reminiscent of the pictures of Siberia I have seen, I suppose, or of Antarctica; tree branches hung heavy with the fluffy whiteness, the house lay sunk in two feet of it. The doors were blocked, the phone line cut, the satellite dish out of service. Fortunately there was enough food in the house.

Thus marooned I subsisted for three days, not feeling inclined to dig myself out—into what, I asked myself in a blue moment—and unsure where to start when I was ready to do so. Finally the young father of the kids next door, Joseph's two friends, came over on skis and called out cheerfully through the window: Are you there, are you all right? He helped me shovel a path to the gate, brought out his mechanical snowplough and cleared the driveway; I cleared the back porch. The phone people came, and in the evening a relieved Deepa came through, calling the umpteenth time, as she put it.

Seema Chatterjee has gone to India on vacation.

One morning, some two weeks after Joseph's departure, I walked into Korrenburg town and made straight for the library. There sat Seema, who had not called since she took Joseph to Toronto.

I might never have existed, I said in good-natured chiding, now that Joseph is gone.

Oh? she asked, raising a stern, bespectacled face.

You never called, I explained.

You could have. I was busy, I had things to take care of. As you had, I'm sure, with whatever it is you are up to.

I could have been stabbed in the chest, so unforeseen was the steely barb in her response. I supposed that she had learned more about me from Joseph and did not approve of what she heard. I made the best of the situation, with a few inane-sounding words, and fled. Is it such a big deal to come out and simply state what is bothering one? I asked myself. I thought North America was an open society, where people freely spoke their minds. I decided I was happy to be rid of such an inconstant acquaintance.

The following Sunday, however, she drove up and we had coffee. I could not warm to her, try as she would to be friendly. Finally, as she was leaving, she looked into my eyes and said, Are you always this unforgiving?

She has large, deep black eyes in that round expressive face of hers.

I'm not sure what you mean, I said, and she left.

Some days later she called in the afternoon and said, I actually came over the other day to make up. Ask forgiveness. Look, what I did, how I behaved when you came to the library, was unforgivable, I know—and I'm contradicting myself, aren't I—it was rude, inconsiderate, unfair, cruel. All of those things. I don't know what came over me, I assure you I am not like that as a rule. Look—

It's all right, I said. Apology accepted.

We agreed to meet again, without actually fixing a date. We hung up.

I needed time to thaw. She had formed a definite opinion of me, she had judged me strongly and negatively, without giving me a chance to give my own account of myself. How could she tell me now that all that meant nothing? I did not care to be judged and un-judged at will. But I knew it must have taken a deep sense of honesty and decency to pick up the phone and make a lengthy apology.

Two weeks later I went into the library, and together we walked over to the café across from it and had coffee and cake as a sort of truce. She told me she is an Internet hound and had dug up the dirt on me from the archives of the East African and South African papers and London's *Economist*. I told her, I am not really an evil man. I have not knowingly hurt anyone.

She waited for an explanation, I did not see the need to give her one.

THIRTEEN

———————

Njoroge called early one morning and said, Vic, if you are free this morning I'd like you to witness something important.

What?

Meet me in the city at nine, will you?

We agreed to meet downstairs outside Papa's office building, next to the motorcycle repair shop, and when I reached there with my father at a little past nine, Njoroge was waiting for me impatiently. He shook hands with Papa and then the two of us set off at a pace. He was wearing his grey jacket, with a red shirt, but no tie today. It was a chilly morning.

Where to? I asked.

Uhuru Park, he replied. There's a meeting there of former freedom fighters—Mau Mau, as they used to be called. You will see them up close! In fact, this is your chance to walk up to them and shake their hands! You know they've been coming out of the forest and surrendering. The problem the government faces is how to resettle them.

My noncommittal silence, as I struggled to keep pace with him, was not the response he'd expected, and he added forcefully, It's a historic occasion, Vic. These people fought for our independence.

These were still the early days of our reunion. We were still rediscovering each other. His phone call earlier had reminded me of how he'd beckon at me from outside our back door in Nakuru and take me to share a secret for my ears only, how he'd taken me once to the Mau Mau oathing site behind our house to swear loyalty to Jomo and the cause of freedom. That was the day we had ritually mixed our blood.

We cut past the city market to Kenyatta Avenue and proceeded along it toward Uhuru Park, which lay on the other side of the city's highway. At a lull in the traffic, we trotted across the six lanes of the highway and into the park.

There, said Njoroge, pointing with a finger in the direction we were headed.

In the centre of the park stood gathered a densely packed crowd of men. Behind them, some hundred yards away, had gathered a row of curious bystanders checked by a cordon of a few policemen, who allowed us through merely by our looks. Njoroge and I joined the inner crowd at its edge, but we were a distraction for our neighbours, and spaces gradually opened up before us and we found ourselves nudged forward to the front, where we were deemed to belong.

A few of them still in the thick spidery dreadlocks from their previous lives, one or two draped in a beloved animal skin or a greatcoat, some sporting beards, and all poor and dishevelled and dusty as hobos, the onetime Mau Mau amongst whom we stood looked listless, disgruntled, and weary. They had come here, away from the footlights of Parliament, to meet the Minister for Land Settlement, who had come provided with a padded chair for his ample bottom. He had not asked them to sit, and so they stood before him in a congregation; in any case the ground was damp from early morning rain. The minister—boss of my boss, Njoroge called him—was a round-faced man in a three-piece suit, flanked by assistants. At a spot a few feet to his left, spokesmen of the former fighters came forward, one by one, to deliver a short speech venting their grievances. They had only recently walked out of the forest, members of two gangs, having deposited their weapons at the Nyeri police station, and now they wanted to know where was the reward they had been promised when they left everything behind to go fight for freedom.

We are poor and despised, our land was taken away, confiscated by the Bilitis, the British, given to the Humungati, the dreaded Home Guard, as payment to hunt and kill us; now where is the compensation promised to us, where are the European farms we were told would be ours after uhuru, where are the big houses, where is the wealth? . . .

They couldn't have seemed more irrelevant or sounded more naïve.

At the artificial lake to our right, reflecting a deep copper sulphate blue, a few children ran about under the watchful eyes of their minders, their sharp bright voices just audible where we stood. Skirting the park along one side, lines of automobiles ran smoothly on the Uhuru Highway like columns of ants, breaking up at the nodular crowded roundabouts and then reconverging and moving along. Roads left these nodes for the hub of the city—from where, in the distance, the clock tower of the yellow and brown Parliament building indicated the time as a little past ten. In the opposite direction, tall orange Nandi flame and broad yellow cassia trees and multicoloured bougainvillea bushes lined the avenues that rose gently toward the green suburbs of Ngong and Hurlingham, with their cosy colonial bungalows nestled neatly behind hedgerows. This was beautiful Nairobi, it was an African city now.

The bystanders in the distance, beyond the police cordon, watched the proceedings in silent amazement; even the minister looked a bit cowed in the presence of these mostly middle-aged retired guerrillas who had once given up all to live in the forests, to rule the nights, to draw blood and terrorize in the name of freedom, and to suffer and risk death for themselves; who with homemade guns and machetes had sorely tested the military might of the British, thus hastening independence. It did feel awesome standing among them; it was impossible not to let the mind roam away from the issue at hand, not to stare at this one and that one and wonder what kind of men they were. But they did not look like heroes now; they were here to plead.

A strange, dry musty odour took to the air from this shiftless crowd. Most of the men, their clothes, had not been washed in days and weeks.

They scratched themselves, drew patterns on the ground with their feet in irritation, emitted throaty Kikuyu interjections that sounded like Hear, hear. They did not look very hopeful.

I looked at Njoroge beside me, wondering how hopeful he felt for them. I saw sympathy in his face, and admiration. But even then, as a young student not wise to politics, I couldn't help feeling that my friend was as naïve as the fighters he admired.

Some of the intransigent among the former Mau Mau had resorted to banditry in the townships and when captured had been sentenced to heavy jail terms, ironically by the same judges who would pronounce similar harsh punishments on suspected Mau Mau before independence. Not long ago Mau Mau General Mwariama had been sentenced to a stiff jail term for brandishing a sword stick and causing disturbance; General Baimunge was captured and paraded naked in Meru township. Such news reached our bustling, euphoric capital as a curiosity from the townships. There was grudging respect but not much sympathy for Mau Mau who sought compensation and recognition as heroes of the nation; this was a time of reconciliation and progress, we had been told, a time of forgetting the past, not picking at it.

And yet now a spectre from my own past had stood up, was speaking at me—

The man was small, thin, and wiry, with a deeply lined black face, a thin mat of grey hair; he wore black trousers and a grey tweed jacket. His voice, old and crackling, rose thinly—

We gave up our property, we gave up good jobs with our English bosses who were generous for the times . . . Why do our politicians call us outlaws and bandits, aren't we the army of the people? Even now we are ready to defend them . . .

I didn't know the voice, but I knew instantly that short figure in the worn tweed jacket; the face, scenes from the past, emerged in memory like photographs from a developing film. The venerable-looking elder making his plea for justice was no other than Kihika, the Bruces' former servant long wanted for their murders.

. . . we gave up all that for freedom, for uhuru, he was saying.

He gestured with his left hand and with his right clutched, close to his chest, a thick black book that I guessed was a Bible.

Steady, man, Njoroge said, gripping me tightly behind the shoulder, as if to squeeze out my vision of the man with a teddy bear in his hands, a tender look on his face, walking protectively behind the little white girl whom he would eventually slaughter. Was it so simple? I have never been able to see the murders as anything else. I felt dizzy from the blood pounding in my head; I don't know if Njoroge sensed the extent of my discomfort, but he kept his hand pressed on my shoulder for a long time.

The meeting of the Mau Mau ended with a long hectoring lecture by the minister. The government is a just government, he said, thanks to the wise leadership of our President. All cases for compensation will be heard, no one will be turned away. But!—he raised a stern finger—unruly behaviour and banditry will not be tolerated, even from freedom fighters. Hear this!—the war is over, old grievances must be laid aside! Freedom has come and we must build the nation together! He concluded with the national rallying cry: Uhuru! Harambee!

The crowd echoed its response, slowly began to disperse. The Mau Mau shuffled away.

Some of them, however, turned and came toward Njoroge, to shake hands with my friend, the young educated man who was their saviour who would speak on their behalf with the government of Jomo. They took his proffered hand in both of theirs, or embraced him, and he introduced me to them as their friend Bwana Vikram. Kihika came by too, and I remember shaking a small scabby hand, hearing a dry raspy voice saying to me in English, I am pleased to meet you, sir . . .

I could not meet his eye.

Later, the two of us having strolled over to the Ismailia Tea Room downtown, I asked Njoroge, What would satisfy these Mau Mau?

Land to farm on; some money as compensation. To be treated like heroes wouldn't be bad either, after all the hardships they've suffered . . . some acknowledgement of their sacrifice.

He paused, then said: I know what's gnawing at your mind, Vic. Kihika.

What is he now? Where is he?

Njoroge took a deep breath, before replying,

He's a counsellor to the fighters and their spokesman. He is an elder of the church and has been negotiating between them and the government. Those people we saw today, they came out of the forest and all surrendered to him a few days ago. He is indispensable.

They are evil, those who kill children!

I spoke this with a vehemence and a breaking voice that surprised even me, and Njoroge gave a start.

Your grandfather Mwangi said that, I said to him more calmly. *They are evil, those who kill children.*

And those who go about killing grandfathers?—his voice gruff, flat. It was war, Vic, innocent people die in war, everywhere. We should leave the excesses of the past behind us, that's what Jomo has said. He has forgiven even those who put him in prison. We can't keep on grieving the past, for God's sake!

I know that well, Njo. It's only that I can't always keep those other images out of my mind.

Look around you, Vic, it's all different now.

As if to comply, we both let our eyes wander around the restaurant in silence. The tables were filling up, as noon approached; waiters hurried in between them with plates of hot snacks and lunches. The smell of steaming rice and spicy curry filled the air. Mr. Mithoo, the owner, stood behind the till, unshaved, owl-like in thick round glasses. The Ismailia was a modest place with good basic fare and because it was so centrally placed, just outside the university area at the intersection of busy Government and River Roads, it was a favourite snacking place for students. Soon a group of them arrived and joined us, including an American couple known to be doing research on the freedom struggle, and the daily session of potato pakoda and politics began. Should Kenyatta be President for life? Whither the East African federation? The United States of Africa? Was socialism a good thing for a poor country? For a developing nation, was China a better model or India?

The clamorous crowd at our table had grown to two deep, when Njoroge, noticing my discomfiture, said, Do you want to go? I nodded and we left.

I am not much for politics, I confessed to him once we were outside.

As I'm noticing, he said. I should have remembered. I hadn't realized that those events in Nakuru . . . I'm sorry, Vic, I didn't know they still meant so much to you. I guess we never had a chance to talk about them. To me the Mau Mau murders were reprehensible—they were not many to begin with—but I always knew that they were for a cause and necessary, and that my people had suffered. But we must leave the past behind us.

We all carry the past inside us in some way, Njo, I said. We can't help it.

He didn't reply. What I meant, and he must have known, was that he too carried that past inside him, as did Deepa; how else could they have sparked off their relationship so easily, after all these years?

But Njo, Deepa told him pointedly once. You must have come to Nairobi a dozen times—Alliance High is so nearby!—and you didn't look us up? Or perhaps you already knew where we were, you had seen us!

He returned a grin, told her: Sometimes near Eastleigh I would look at the Indian girls walking home from school, with their long pigtails, in their school skirts and blouses, and tell myself, Now perhaps that one is Deepa; or perhaps she is that other one! Lord forbid, she could be the fat one with glasses—how she loved to eat gulab jamuns!—or she could be the buck-toothed one like a rabbit! And each time I came to the city, I would be looking at girls a little older than the time before. Because I was getting older and I knew you were too! And so was Vic!

We had a merry laugh, but the truth was not so very different. When he came to the city, it had been usually with other boys, on a school trip. And whenever he saw Indian boys and girls on the streets, they would look alien to him, forbidding, and he was afraid that that's what Deepa and I had become—alien Indians with whom he would never be on intimate terms again. He thought of making inquiries, and one Saturday morning he actually did a round of the shops in Indian Bazaar. But he felt too timid to ask about his Asian friends, and instead came away with a flimsy Japanese shirt and a pair of cheap Hong Kong socks—one of which, it turned out, had the heel missing. I'm not joking, he insisted, at Deepa's delighted face. Then finally, after a few more years had passed, he fell into a chat with Mr. Mithoo of the Ismailia and asked, Do you know the Lalls from Nakuru? And the man said, Over there, across the street and opposite the Jivanjee Gardens, above the motorcycle shop, that's where Mr. Lall the estate agent has his office.

And?

As I was walking over to the motorcycle shop—guess what I saw? A lovely Indian girl had come down the stairs followed by her father—whom I had no problem recognizing, though he was older.

She blushed.

I was too nervous, I decided to come back another day. I couldn't believe that it was you, little Deepa, after twelve years. Will she want to know me, I asked myself, will she talk to me?

Gradually the three of us began to talk about our days together in Nakuru, even about Annie and Bill; it took Njoroge, like a magician, to break the glass barrier behind which we had sealed that past.

Deepa once said, making a face: And Vic even has a picture on his dresser of himself as Rama and that girl as Sita—

That girl, is she now, I uttered bitterly.

She whitened. Her excitement had turned her callous and I, jealous but all-important chaperone, had brought her to task.

It was so long ago, Vic, she said in a whisper, almost in tears.

But why *that girl*?

Annie, then—Annie, Vic.

And Njo put his hand on mine and said: Annie, of course. And Bill, Field Marshal Montgomery . . . vroooom! . . . and Kit Carson . . . and pow! pow!

We couldn't help but break out laughing at our memories of warrior Bill in his various guises, the funniest of which had been Hanuman bounding monkeylike behind me as Rama, and fighting Njoroge the ten-headed demon Ravana. Even from such a remove, pompous Bill could entertain.

One day soon after we had arrived from Nakuru, Mother proceeded to remove one by one all the pictures from our family photo album that would remind us of that terrible period, that bloody episode. She was in the living room, the album on her lap, and I stood like a shadow behind the sofa watching over her shoulder. When she was finished, the dismembered album on the armrest, and was quietly looking through the culled photos, lingering ever so long a moment over each, I took from her hand one of these pictures, went to my room, and put it on my dresser. It was the one of Annie and me. When I was in school one day, Mother placed the photo inside a frame which Papa had brought from River Road for the purpose. There it stood, on my dresser, in front of a little brass statue of Ganesh, until later Mother put it away in my top drawer, where it stayed with my handkerchiefs, socks, and ties. I brought it out on the dresser only on Christmas, on Diwali, and on her birthday, March 4. Yet no one at home had ever spoken a word about this little fetish of mine.

During those holidays I worked doing odd jobs for my father. It was my task to take prospective tenants around the rental properties he managed, and on certain days to take the plumber, the carpenter, the electrician, and the mason to wherever they happened to be required. Outside of these duties, my time was my own, and I had set some of it aside to catch up with my academic work.

Njoroge's job took him to the countryside around Nyeri, and whenever he returned to the city the three of us would spend time together. We would soon part, we knew, and were already making plans of how to stay in touch, when to visit each other. We met for coffee during the day, and sometimes in the evenings went to the movies or the theatre or to listen to a public lecture. Prominent Afro-American figures were often visiting our city and speaking at one venue or another. In the afternoons we might sit at the lively bar of the Donovan Maule Theatre, where university students discussed politics and art late into the night. One day Njoroge took us to a house in the African working-class area of Pumwani, where he said his parents had had a room. His father was arrested here during the massive Operation Anvil in 1954; his mother disappeared a few weeks later. Neither of them had been heard from since then. I recalled him telling us in Nakuru that his father was studying in Uganda. Did he believe that then?

When Njoroge and I were together by ourselves, we were like old friends; among the three of us I was the third one, the odd one out, the chaperone. I would wonder if Njo and I would have met so often had Deepa not been in the picture. Deepa, of course, already had several admirers in Parklands, two of whom were rather faithful, accompanying her home from school and buying her snacks whenever they got the chance, and phoning her on flimsy pretexts. Deepa had always enjoyed the attention; but recently, when I brought up these two suitors in a conversation, my attempt at humour had misfired. A deeply blushing Deepa kicked me under the table.

She couldn't wait for Njo to be back in town from his journeys. Her problem was that she was too transparent—as was Mother, who was frantic with worry. Mother, so happy to see him, little insecure Njoroge-William now a big man who would go on to become important some day, and yet so worried that he would compromise, or worse, marry her daughter.

Vikram, bété, do something, say something to her, Mother pleaded with me one day.

What, Mother? She's still young and just an excitable girl. She's simply happy he is back, that nothing bad happened to him. We are old friends. Even *you're* excited that he's back in our lives!

Rabba! I hope you are right.

My sister's situation was the first instance I noticed a certain detachment in myself. Whether she would finally marry Njoroge or not did not bother me. I personally did not favour circumstances—the possible outcome of the relationship—to turn out one way or another. I found myself waiting passively for the situation to resolve itself. I would watch my sister and Njoroge flirting and feel only a bit saddened that I was alone; I would witness my parents' anxiety and comfort them. If I felt saddened by my own loneliness, I did not wish to get involved in a relationship either. Mother called me her brahmachari, a Hindu man who has taken a vow of celibacy for religious reasons, or teased that I had entered early sanyas, the fourth stage of life, renunciation, undertaken after one's householder responsibilities are over. I was very close to her, especially now that she and my father had somehow detached themselves from each other. Deepa, on the other hand, was a firecracker, as both my parents sometimes called her.

And so they had agreed privately that it was time she settled down into a staid, happy family life, with a burden of her own responsibilities.

It was time to call the Sharmas and cash in an old promise.

FOURTEEN

The Sharmas, Harry (actually Hari) and Meena, were among our close family friends in Nairobi. Harry Uncle, like my mother, was a native of northern Punjab, an area that became a part of Pakistan, and this fact created a special affinity between the two. He had met and married Meena Auntie in New Delhi, where he had arrived after the partition of India. He had hinted to Mother once that he had lost his only brother to that bloody event and was only too happy to be out of the subcontinent. Meena Auntie was a science teacher, and the couple easily obtained a visa to come to Kenya. Harry Uncle set himself up in the real estate business, into which he later brought my father, rescuing him from his unhappy foray into Indian groceries. The Sharmas had a daughter, Reshma, who was sixteen and a son, Dilip, who was now in his third year at university in England, studying pharmacy. Soon after Papa joined Mayfair Estate Agents, Harry Uncle left the business to start a development and banking company. We did not see the Sharmas very frequently nowadays, therefore a sudden invitation to dinner at their house came as a surprise to Deepa and me, until Mother's designs revealed themselves.

Deepa, naïve Deepa, had joined Mother in preparing a dessert for the occasion, a bowl of enticing, perfectly round and golden gulab jamuns. She wore a dazzling yellow sari that pleased my parents no end. Mother was so moved by the gesture that she presented Deepa with one of her own set of gold bangles. They embraced, Mother shed a tear. A typical Nairobi Indian family, the women adorned in silk saris, gold jewellery, and Chanel No. 5, the men casual in sports jackets, we set off for the Sharmas' residence in Hurlingham. It was a property well guarded by a cowled watchman hovering at the gate and two fiercely barking Alsatians who had to be curbed before we were let through. The house, constructed on the slope of a valley, was an old grey stone bungalow, which had been modernized recently with a living room extension at one side and a bedroom at the back. As you approached up the hill, it came into view suddenly and surreally past a bend, the brightly lit glass-walled extension glowing like a magical emanation in the thick and misty night. Harry Uncle himself opened the door for us, limping, for he had one false leg, a condition with which he had arrived from India. He was a tall and burly man with a mane of thick white hair on a large, squarish head. The TV was on, but in the background somewhere an evening raga was being plucked out plangently on a tape.

We had come, in a sense, to arrange her marriage, and poor Deepa walked into the setup unaware.

She had a charming, filial manner for such occasions, full of humour and respect, not to say outright flattery, joining the older women in the kitchen and helping to serve the food, yet young and modern enough to banter and joke with the men. Soon she found herself between Uncle and Auntie on a sofa, beaming happily, and Harry Uncle put his hand on her head, part blessing, part token of fondness. Mother asked, How is Dilip doing, how many more years to finish his course? Harry Uncle told her two years, maybe three, then Meena Auntie said, with that characteristic affirmative roll of the head side to side and a singsong intonation, We always spoke of Deepa and Dilip, as if the two went together like a pair.

Yes, said Papa, that we did, little knowing how fast they would grow. Dilip is what?—twenty-two, and already in England. And this one, our laadlee, eighteen—

Already marriageable age, Meena Auntie put in, but Deepa's face had clouded, and she got up, saying curtly, Not yet.

But soon enough, we hope, Uncle said, and as Deepa moved forward to come to sit on the chair beside me, Auntie fondly held on to her hand, only very gradually and by inches letting it slip out.

We had had our dinner and dessert, the gulab jamuns receiving full marks, and Papa and Harry Uncle, skipping brandies, were back to whisky, while the rest of us were left to admire pictures of handsome Dilip in England. The one in which he appeared outdoors after a snowfall, in navy blue overcoat and boots, his cheeks glowing pink from the cold, was admired the most and Mother took a copy for herself.

Isn't it getting late, Deepa said. I had promised some friends to stop over at the Parklands Club fashion show around ten . . .

But you didn't tell us, bété, that you had made this plan, Papa said.

I hadn't known of this plan either, but Deepa's look told me to keep quiet.

It was decided that I would go with Deepa, and Uncle would drop Mother and Papa at our house an hour later. Reshma decided she too wanted to go to the fashion show, and seeing Deepa's face turn a momentary black at this news, I knew what scheme she must have set afoot.

We are to meet Njoroge, she said as we practically rushed to the car ahead of the girl, but I don't want little Reshma to see me with him. So please, dear brother, you keep her company.

The look she gave me then, and that pleading, anxious tone of voice, were the first admission I had from her that she was growing seriously involved with Njo. I said yes, and as soon as I parked the car at the club grounds, she disappeared and I had a sixteen-year-old teenybopper in short skirt and boots to entertain.

Do you like Beatles or Elvis? Reshma asked with great curiosity, apparently inspired by the music of the Fab Four that was playing inside the club hall.

I told her I liked both, and she replied, For me, it's Beatles, Beatles, Beatles! I am mad about them! I would die for them!

The fashion show, with displays of A-lines and miniskirts and sack dresses from London, together with the latest sunwear, was ending as we arrived; six African and European models toting toy pistols in bikinis finished the show to the James Bond theme music and much applause. Dancing started soon after and the two of us went on the floor and twisted away. There was a new dance in town called the Zulu stomp, and we did that too. The hall was packed, uproarious and humid, with people from all the races of Nairobi present. In that mixed crowd was the mood of happiness and all the hope and excitement, at least for the well-positioned classes, brought on by the rush of independence.

Later, when we went outside for a breather and something to drink, I saw Deepa huddled with Njoroge at one of the tables on the lawn, and I had to do all I could to steer Reshma clear of them. Toward the end of the program, around midnight, we went out once again, and this time I saw my sister sitting by herself at a table, fist stuck firmly to her chin in a picture of gloom.

What happened, Sis? I asked.

Some political disaster, she growled. Of all the nights it has to happen tonight.

What disaster? Reshma asked excitedly. She had had a good time and hung close to me.

Deepa gave her a look of disdain and didn't answer. Her ire was the more bitter for the fact that Njoroge was to leave for university in a few days' time, and I was to do the same not long after. Our reunion time was running out.

The next day's screaming headlines reported a disturbance by former Mau Mau in the Industrial Area. Three men had been arrested after a brawl with a hotel manager; they had displayed weapons and assaulted a number of people, including police. It seemed obvious, as I read the front page over the breakfast table, that this was what had called away Njoroge so urgently the previous night. Even as I sat contemplating the drunken-eyed man with distended earlobes glaring out of the page, the phone rang. It was Njoroge.

Your men seem to have made a nuisance of themselves, I said, chuckling.

So you've read the papers. It's not quite like that, though they do tend to be rough sometimes. Listen, Vic, can you come to the city magistrates' court at eleven today?

After a small pause, I said, Of course.

And could you bring with you five hundred shillings, Vic? It's urgent. I'll pay you back in a few days.

I'll talk to my father, I said.

Thanks, Vic.

The anxiety in his voice gave way to perceptible, almost joyful relief. We agreed to meet outside the courthouse.

Five hundred was a sizeable sum to ask of my father; I told him I needed an advance on my college expenses and he did not demur. He did not ask me what the urgency was either.

At the magistrates' court, an Indian judge was presiding, a veteran of the bench whose name appeared often, though briefly, in newspaper notices regarding one case or another. The charges against the three men were disorderly conduct and assault. A young African lawyer spoke briefly on their behalf, arguing that the weapon the men had supposedly brandished was only a kitchen knife, and the magistrate agreed to release them on bail. Njoroge, not wishing to compromise his ministry, had asked me to come forward as guarantor. I did so and paid up, to the surprise of everyone present, and the fighters walked out. The drunken-eyed one who had appeared on the front page was a big man with a catchy charismatic smile and a slyly cynical manner; he called himself Major Simba and wore an army-style jacket, a fashion that had actually been declared illegal. The other two men were small and in suit jackets, each clutching a Bible and looking no more like Mau Mau than my father did. They all shook hands with me.

One more thing, Vic, Njoroge said. Please.

We had come out of the courtroom into the main corridor and were walking out.

Of course, Njo. And then, having guessed the nature of his request, I asked, You want a place for them to stay?

Just for two or three days while I try and get the charges dropped or find them another place . . .

I hurried out ahead of him and called my father and told him Njoroge needed a flat for three days for his friends. Papa said fine, give them something in Eastleigh. Njoroge and his three charges having extracted themselves from the reporters, I drove them to a modest, out-of-the-way flat in Eastleigh that was empty. The three men gratefully shook hands with me. They had not been in contact with many Indians before, and to Njoroge they referred to me as a muthungu, a white man, which rather astonished me. Njoroge warned them to behave themselves and gave them what remained of my five hundred shillings, after which the two of us departed.

We found a place to sit downtown and he thanked me profusely. These men are here, he said, to visit this grand city, this Nairobi they have heard so much about. And they were refused a room simply for what they are—former freedom fighters.

I didn't know what to say. He saw my unease and dropped the subject. We both became silent.

I was not judging the three men or their kind. I knew that they were heroes of our freedom who at the very least deserved respect and consideration in our country. I also knew them as the daityas of my mother, the devils who ruled the dark hours, against whom we secured our doors in the most dreadful fear. The big one of the three, Major Simba, had reminded me of the men I had watched in terror as a boy, in the jungle outside the sawmill where my family and I had gone to visit my uncle. And Kihika, whom I had seen at the meeting in Uhuru Park, was the Kihika of my childhood horror. How could I help the associations? I didn't have a way to cope with them.

He said finally, bringing me back from my thoughts, Let's talk about us, Vic—you and me and Deepa. This has been the most amazing time in my life, six weeks out of a fairy tale. Life is not supposed to be like that!

Yes, it has been the most wonderful six weeks for me too, Njo—and for Deepa, as you well know. She practically changed overnight when you appeared! We somehow never thought we'd see you again. You went away, and it seemed that was that—

Vic—about me and your sister—what are your feelings about that? Please be honest with me, I would like to know.

He had caught me by surprise, though at some point he had to ask me how I felt, and this seemed the perfect moment.

It's up to you and her, Njo, I said. You are my friend and she is my sister. You don't have to worry about me. But you have my parents to contend with, I'm sure you know that.

He remained silent for a while. His hands were in front of him on the table, the fingers loosely intertwined at the tips. I noticed he had big, tidy nails, perfectly cut. His fingers were large and blunt. How rarely we notice these details about our close ones, and how they surprise us!

He said softly, I'm not sure what exactly Deepa thinks about me . . . I just thought I'd ask you first how you felt as her brother . . . and as a friend. I have not given the matter very deep thought—I realize it is a serious matter, not to be taken lightly.

I must warn you, I said, my parents are already looking around for an Indian husband for her.

He raised an eyebrow and smiled. Maybe I don't have to worry then, he said.

I did not see him for a few days. He went to Nyeri, and when he returned he brought back the money to repay me. And then he was ready to return to his university in Kampala.

————————

How amazing it is, this absolute absence of green, of life itself in winter. The pallid sickly green of the conifer is only a ghost of what has been. It is a new world I'm in, a silent world with quiet mornings and even quieter nights, whose heart beats somewhere deep inside the earth. It's a time of renewal, says Seema Chatterjee, who has returned from her holiday; the old has died and the new awaits to take its place. There seems to be a meaning for me, in this adage; I fail to respond, and she adds, more mundanely, But it's also a time to withdraw into a book or a project, to ruminate, or to sit down cosily with a friend over sherry or tea. She has brought me books—a lot of history, some crime fiction.

Back to myself and my labours again, I try to recall a tempestuous passion—not mine, Deepa's—and relive an energetic period from our past. In contrast to the frozen black eternity outside my window, my mind is a landscape filled with sunshine, and the innocent, prancing hope of youth.

FIFTEEN

———————

Deepa once told me, I don't know who has been closer to me, Njo or you, Vic . . . sometimes I can't even distinguish between the two of you in my mind. I replied, somewhat disconcerted, I'm not sure what you mean. I don't know either, she said, then immediately contradicted herself: Oh, you know what I mean, I can share my innermost secrets with you as I did with him. I took this to mean she felt comfortable confiding to me anything about herself and Njoroge—which is as well, for I was the chaperone who looked away, the ear that heard her, the shoulder she cried upon.

Now it was Sunday and she was grooming her nails in the living room, humming along with a Hindi film song on the radio, happy and contented as a child. *If only for a moment you look away, O Moon / Then I will make love to him* . . . You couldn't have told that Njoroge had left for Makerere in Kampala the previous day, but then you wouldn't have known what I did. Papa was doing the Spot-the-Ball competition in the *Sunday Nation,* having bought three copies of the paper to increase his chances of winning.

The phone rang and Mother hurried from the kitchen to the hallway to pick it up. She soon finished, then came to stand in the living room entrance, poised like a herald with her news.

Shall I tell them the good news or will you? Mother asked Papa. That was Meena-ji and she is so excited!

Papa dropped the papers down on the carpet, and his glasses upon them: Tum hi bata do, na, you tell them. You can hardly hold in *your* excitement!

Dilip is coming from *London,* Mother announced throatily, looking from Deepa to me, her eyes sparkling with joy.

How wonderful, Deepa exclaimed. I should ask him to bring me something from there—will he? But what's this—aren't the summer holidays over?

Maybe his aren't, I replied. It was apparent that Mother and Papa had received prior notice of the impending arrival and had only been awaiting confirmation—and perhaps an opportune moment to make the announcement.

We knew Dilip well, he was three years older than I and a wonderful table tennis player. When I first came to Nairobi he was a big brother to me of sorts; I looked up to him and tried to copy his ways. He was already at Duke of Gloucester when I was admitted there and knew the teachers and prefects well as a senior boy, making my life much easier. He was athletic and good-looking and before he set off for England had climbed the summit of Mount Kenya, which was no small feat.

Of course, Deepa, he'll bring for you whatever you ask, Mother said. You have to ask, only! But he's coming for a short time, ten–twelve days. And he'll go only when he's got what *he* wants—it seems London doesn't have everything!

She couldn't contain herself. I looked up with concern at this unsubtle, untimely gambit, hoping perhaps to check her, but she proceeded head on, in the treacly tones of a mother to a child. You know, Deepa darling, we always had Dilip in mind for you . . . in fact, we had made a little pact with the Sharmas when you were young! Deepa and Dilip, we said, Dilip and Deepa, if kismet allows it.

A real catch, that boy, Papa said. Handsome and smart, wah!—wealthy to boot. You'd better not waste time, my girl—there'll be a line of mothers with daughters waiting at the airport, if I know this city at all.

Deepa had turned white. She didn't explode, as she was liable to do, but she knew now exactly what scheme was afoot behind her back. The pact with the Sharmas had been renewed, obviously, because of the threat now posed by Njoroge.

She spoke harshly: I am not going to marry Dilip-Filip or anyone else now, Mother.

Mother's first response was a pathetic attempt at laughter—the short, high-pitched sound she emitted when she was shocked to the core and speechless.

You'll think about it. What's the harm in marrying when a good boy is available? You can go on with your studies after marriage. You can go to London with him, wouldn't you like that?

I don't want to go to London. And I'm not going to marry Dilip.

Can you tell us why? Do you have anyone in mind?

A pause. Then: No. But I'll marry whom I want, Mother, and I'm not going to marry Dilip.

Just like that? Is there anything wrong with the boy? Is he lame or blind, is he a drunkard or a gambler? A U.K. graduate, a handsome boy, of good caste and family—and you have the arrogance to refuse him like that? And your parents—

What do you mean you will marry anyone whom you want? Papa exploded. We are not Europeans, remember that, we are desis, Indians. Proud Indians, we have our customs, and we marry with the permission and blessings of our parents! You will do as you are told, girl!

That was a fine one coming from him, he who had wooed Mother on the streets of Peshawar and taken his proposal to her father himself. Deepa didn't catch on, but my father caught the look in my eye, and somewhat sheepishly he picked up his papers from the floor and sat back in his chair, leaving the battle in Mother's hands once more. Mother never gave up so easily. She gave a deep sigh and glared at Deepa.

Look, Mama, I don't dislike Dilip, I like him, but he's a friend, I can't think of him as a husband! And I don't want to get married now!

It's a good opportunity, Mother said. Think about it. Girls who wait too long ruin their lives. Look at Aruna Auntie, still unmarried, and already old . . .

That last add-on an exaggeration, of course.

Deepa nodded obediently, went to give each of my parents a conciliatory kiss. She was too happy now, had suddenly bloomed the past month. Is there something in parents that sets the guard up against too-happy children?

I'll talk to Dilip, she told me later, I'll explain to him and so on. And you know what, mark my words, he probably already has a girlfriend in London! Some gori blonde called Susan or something. So there.

A triumphant smile on her face.

She and Njoroge had declared their love and committed themselves to each other the previous morning. When she revealed that declaration to me— for as I have said she confessed a lot of her secrets to me—I recall a shiver at the back of my neck, a quiver of excitement, of fear for them both. The die had been cast. She did not seem to understand the seriousness of her offence, not to me but to the values of our times and people. We did not marry blacks or whites, or low-castes or Muslims; there were other restrictions, too subtle for us of the younger generation to follow; Hindu Punjabis were the strong preference always. Times were changing, certainly, but Deepa in her typical impulsive way had leaped ahead of them.

In the morning, Mother, Deepa, and I drove downtown, where we first sat down for coffee, as was becoming the fashionable custom in the city for the nonwhite middle classes. My sister and I enjoyed taking our mother out this way, to draw her out of her frequent low moods, and she enjoyed the outing. She drove us, which also gave her a sense of independence. After sitting with them awhile, having consumed a jam tart, I said I would join Njoroge at the Ismailia one last time before he left. Mother and Deepa had already wished him goodbye the previous day in Papa's office; they told me to take their warm wishes for him. Mother should have been suspicious; the picture of dutiful Deepa, sitting beside her Mama eating iced cake, declining to see Njoroge one last time on the day of his departure, was as real as any of Scheherazade's bewitching tales. But Mother had a remarkable knack for deluding herself. She had still not tuned in to the fact that Papa's call for that first whisky of the evening was now beyond his control; he was turning alcoholic. It had taken her months to realize that there had been a mutual attraction between Aruna Auntie and Papa, when Aruna visited us in Nakuru. Now she had reassured herself that her anxiety about Deepa and Njoroge had been fanciful. And so with a wave at them I left; and gluttonously—because I did not need another snack—I had a tea and potato pakodas with Njoroge, after which I escorted him to Sanamu, a gallery-café not much frequented by Asians, and then went to join Deepa and Mother at the city market, half a block away. With a nod from me, Deepa took off on a pretext (the British Council library) to meet Njoroge in private at the Sanamu, promising to meet us at the parked car in an hour.

At the café Deepa poured out her heart to Njoroge.

Njo, she entreated him, having joined him at a discreet table in a niche away from human traffic, I want you to be honest with me.

Yes, he said, a strained smile wavering upon his face. About what?

Behind him were a few lithographs of masks created by a local artist. The place, serving locally grown fresh coffee for the benefit of tourists, was well known for good but pricey arts and crafts, and was ridiculed for the price labels still on its serving tables and chairs.

I want you to tell me if you have someone special—a girlfriend or fiancée—I will understand that—

Deepa, he said, reaching out to hold her hand across the wobbly cane table and moving forward on the lightweight chair of the same material: Deepa, I have loved you since we were little—you know that. I have thought of you constantly over the last twelve years—only you—even when I was positive you had forgotten me—

He stopped abruptly, looked questioningly at her.

Well, I love you too, Njo, I will come out and say it, though girls are not supposed to be so forward. Now where do we go from here.

She pulled her hand away and placed it with the other on her lap, watched him with a shy smile.

His heart was pounding. He was nervous, even though he was the African, of the new ruling class. Could this be true, this exotic, gentle girl, this tender heart who hid him under the bed once, away from the eyes of the police, without even a blink; this girl precious to her family and her jealous people . . . I only hope this is not a dream, he said to himself.

Your father and mother, he began. They will surely object.

This is a new Africa, Njo, they'd better not. We are the next generation. They will, of course—but I don't think for long. I'm stubborn as a mule, Njo, I hope you are strong too. And what about your people?

There are not that many to speak of. Distant cousins. Friends, yes, they might be disappointed at first—they won't know how to behave toward an Indian girl . . .

They didn't see insurmountable problems. They walked around the nooks in the café, examining the displays, exclaiming and mocking at the exorbitant tourist prices, and in one such corner, observed by no one save the large Makonde old man hewed roughly from Tanzanian wood and exuding the pungent odours of recent polish, they embraced tightly. He brushed her lips with his, squeezed her hand. They promised to write daily. She told him, I'll write first and tell you how to write to me. They parted.

Two days later, Dilip arrived. He was by any standards a catch for any Asian girl. Soft-spoken, well-mannered and -dressed, polished as though arrived from a finishing school. It was my turn now to be the chaperone for him and Deepa, but she turned out to be an ever-elusive eel, slipping out from any circumstance that would put the two of them alone together. And in company she would tease him no end about the girlfriend she had imagined for him. What would your Susan say to this, eating bhajias in such a slum? Would your Susan approve of us eating with our hands like this? She did seem to overdo it, though Dilip didn't mind. The second day his parents had taken us out for lunch thali at the Supreme, and later that day Mother got wind of Deepa's silliness.

The following day the Sharmas were invited for dinner at our home. This was planned by the parents to be the big day, when a large hint would be placed before the boy and girl which they could not avoid.

Meena-ji says Dilip is a rather mature boy, Mother told Deepa that morning. He's grown up quickly, especially after living alone in England—

Yes, he is a bit stuffy though, isn't he, poor Dilip, bechara, Deepa replied, buttering her toast.

Well, stuffy is good! Stuffy is character! You'd better not do anything silly now, Deepa. You've been far too free and childish in your behaviour, ever since Njoroge arrived. One would think you were trying to impress him. Don't mention him in front of the Sharmas now—

What do you have against Njo anyway? All you Asians think is that these African men are after your innocent, virtuous daughters—

Well, I'm glad at least you're not planning to marry him—

I didn't say that—

A mighty ruckus broke out. The shockwave of realization finally swept over Mother, the truth about Njoroge and Deepa, which explained Deepa's strange, giddy behaviour of the last two months, and the previous day's offending silliness at the Supreme.

Don't joke about such things! Mother screamed, almost in tears. It is not a joke, you bad girl—

Mother! I didn't say I was marrying him—but if I was, it would be my wish, wouldn't it? And what's wrong with it, we don't live in colonial times anymore, or in your India-desh, this is a new Africa—

Don't say that! Mother wailed. She looked devastated, a tragedienne of the Hindi cinema.

Father came running out from the living room. He had evidently overheard the proceedings but had bided his time.

Get this in your head, Deepa, he is an African, Papa said. He is not us. Not even in your wildest dream can you marry an African.

What do you mean? What's wrong with an African? *I* am an African. What hypocrisy! And all the nice faces you showed around your Njoroge-William while he was here—

Mother took a deep breath and replied, There's nothing wrong with being an African or Asian or European. But they can't mix. It doesn't work. Njoroge is like a son to me, you made him a brother, back in Nakuru—

That's when you tricked me! Yes you did!

As if I knew you'd be infatuated with him one day.

The voice, unable to hide that slightest trace of triumph, gave her away. I knew then what Deepa also at that instant divined; we looked at each other, and then Deepa screamed at Mother: It was *you* who hid his letters! Admit it, he wrote the letters from school, and *you* with your suspicious, scheming, cunning mind *destroyed* them!

Well, I was right, wasn't I, said Mother.

She began to cry.

(Mother, you went too far. Why this streak of intolerance, this fear of the unknown, when we were living in such exciting times with only a bright future to think of, if we played our cards right? Is it simply envy of the older for the younger who are so free and ready to break the shackles? Did you ever see Deepa happier than she was those two months?)

The dinner was quieter than anticipated, my parents having told the Sharmas to hold off on the matchmaking, the time was not ripe yet; the girl was headstrong about going to university first, but she would come around soon enough. Of course, if Dilip found someone else he liked, he had all the blessings from our family.

But Dilip liked Deepa; he was shown a couple of other girls but declined them. I say, I am not the one for puja and bhajan, all that religious stuff, he explained to us, trying to please Deepa and arouse her jealousy at the same time. He liked her spunk, her freedom. A few times he tried casually to hold her by the arm or hand, but she gently rebuffed him. When he asked her to go out with him one evening, she accepted. But any hopes our families had of making anything out of the date amounted to nothing. She had told Dilip that she had no intention of marrying now.

One morning when the three of us were sitting at the Ismailia, old Mr. Mithoo at the counter handed me an envelope addressed to me. By some happy foresight, I did not open it at the restaurant but waited until after Dilip had seen us off outside Papa's office. When I tore open that envelope, there was another one, smaller and unmarked, inside. Opening that, I fished out a letter for Deepa. Njo had taken the precaution not to address her by name, beginning only with *Darling*—and finishing after three delirious pages composed late on a Kampala night.

SIXTEEN

I returned to the calm haven of my dormitory room in Dar es Salaam. Good old Dar, it was a city that grew upon you, as I am sure it does even now, in a manner Nairobi never could or can. Nairobi has been always an alien city, uneasy home to its inhabitants. It was founded as a way station, after all, a place of convenience, for commerce, and it has retained much of that heartless character. A city I love and yet sometimes feel sorry for.

I had decided a year earlier to go to university in Dar es Salaam on a whim, to get away from home and be alone, but also to escape from the tensions and bustle of Nairobi, its constant striving and ambition, and experience a place very different and organic in nature. Dar es Salaam was African and Asian, disordered and chaotic, hot and dusty, yet in its essence wonderfully relaxed and self-assured. It had a pace all its own, and in Nairobi we had sometimes called it "the Land of Not-yet." It was still common to see people barefoot or in flip-flop chappals in the main streets, men in green or red checkered loincloths and white singlets, women in black buibui or colourful khanga, and nobody hurrying to get anywhere soon. Teashops were where people gathered, with radios blaring African or Indian music over the din of raucous conversation. I remember one afternoon, while out on a walk, coming upon a large crowd of Africans and a few Asians gathered tightly under a tree and wondering what could be the matter. Finally there came a murmur, then applause, and a long, distant shout of *Goal!* became audible, and I realized that the men had gathered to listen to a football match on the only radio around. I would never have come upon such a scene in Nairobi.

In Dar, the Asians seemed to me so much more of the place compared with their cousins in Nairobi. They seemed less well off, but perhaps they were not poorer, simply had a less sophisticated lifestyle. They did not have the Europeans to look up to constantly. There were very few Punjabis, though, most Asians speaking Cutchi and Gujarati, which I couldn't help but learn, to my future benefit.

Momentous political changes had recently taken place in Tanganyika. These had followed the independence of Zanzibar and the bloody and communist-inspired coup less than a month later that sent shivers throughout East Africa. That revolution on the small and torpid isle was the flash that signalled a new and tense reality in our region; the shape of politics, and of much else, in East Africa was never the same again. Our lives would be forever affected, because we had caught the interest of the world's great powers and become pawns in their ongoing Cold War. Tanganyika and Zanzibar became Tanzania, and while the old dream of an East African Federation still merited passing mention, its truth had disappeared like vapour in the harsh sunlight of Dar es Salaam, and we were left with three countries more at odds than ever before. The rhetoric in Tanzania was increasingly anti-imperialist; in Kenya, anticommunist. As a Kenyan in Dar I could hardly escape the occasional taunt or jibe, from friend or fanatic socialist, especially since my style of dressing tended to the formal and easily identified me as a Nairobi boy. Nevertheless, in its essence Dar es Salaam was not much altered; I grew fond of it and tried to hide my origins as best as I could.

I was not—in my father's words and much to his delight—a head-cracking intellectual at university. I was pursuing a somewhat dull degree in commerce—a field of study that stigmatized an Asian because it described his traditional occupation in the region and his caricatured role of exploiter, but that did not deter me. University for me was simply a transition, into what I was not quite sure, though Papa, I knew, had a chair and table vacant and ready for me in his office. Mother would have wished me to become something grand, a surgeon or a "barrister," but I had no inclinations to such greatness and had never shone as a student. I also disliked politics—a hot topic in those times. Politics confused me; large abstract ideas bewildered me; and—what was definitely incorrect in newly independent Africa—I had no clear sense of the antagonists, of the right side and the wrong side.

From what deep source came my parents' reaction to Deepa's involvement with Njoroge was bluntly revealed to me when I myself became the subject of communal prejudice in Dar es Salaam. I was one of about thirty Asian students on "the hill," that is, at the university, most of whom I got to know reasonably well in a short time. Among them I had come across a kindred soul, a girl called Yasmin with whom I became close. She was in the English department and like me somewhat reserved in her ways. She was short, to match me, and quite fair, with long hair falling in a single braid down her back. I still picture her with a sheaf of notes and a book or two in the crook of her left arm, the soft smile of greeting on her face dimpling her cheeks and slightly furrowing her brow as we meet. How are you? she would greet me, with a high inflection on the last word. We spoke in English and a bit of Hindi, though I was learning some Gujarati and Cutchi. She was rather pious and attended the college Shamsi mosque regularly in the evenings; I would wait for her outside this mosque, whose members met in one of the seminar rooms, and when she came out we walked to the dining hall together for supper, past a gauntlet of very pregnant stares. I had been to her house on the way to someplace else, once, and on another occasion for Sunday luncheon. I knew that her parents, although courteous and hospitable on the surface, were intensely against their daughter hitching up with me, a Hindu Punjabi; her two brothers were brief to the point of rudeness—because I was "par-comm," an outsider, and apparently exploiting their sister's naïveté. One afternoon we went to see a film together, it was *Fun in Acapulco* starring Elvis Presley, and when during intermission I went out to the lobby to get us Cokes, whom should I see but one of the brothers jostling ahead of me in the mad crush for drinks; he had a seat by himself, strategically located two rows behind us. But despite the opposition, Yasmin and I continued spending time together, to what end we couldn't yet say—perhaps simply to tempt fate.

I think she liked the foreigner in me—the pardesi of Hindi films, of which we saw several together. There was a part of her that evidently sought to escape beyond the restrictive bounds of her community. It did not deter her that I did not belong to her faith. Once, very discreetly and nervously—lest we be observed by a jealous brother—we entered the confines of a Hindu temple, which rather delighted her, and she did puja in front of the image of Krishna. On another occasion she took me inside a mosque in town belonging to her sect; to my surprise I found it very similar in arrangement to the Arya Samaj temple which my parents sometimes attended.

Dar es Salaam in those days was the site of frequent and endless public demonstrations and parades which all students were required by the government to attend, and Yasmin and I often went to them together. We marched against the timid and placative British attitude toward the minority white government in Rhodesia and watched as the more radical students tore down the Union Jack from the embassy mast; we marched against the Americans, after the government announced it had obtained proof of an American plot to overthrow it, in collaboration with the hated Portuguese who ruled Mozambique to the south (the Americans claimed the papers were Chinese forgeries). We stood in the hot sun among the thousands on Uhuru Street to welcome the motorcade of Chinese Premier Chou en Lai, and we dutifully waved our red Chinese flags at the visitor, chanting his name. The Premier had said elsewhere that Africa was "ripe for revolution," and so he had been made aware that he was not welcome in Kenya. As the slight-figured and, at the time, quite alien-looking premier passed before us, in his grey collarless suit, waving limply at the crowd, I thought for one amazing instant that I had glimpsed, across the street, a too-familiar face: Mahesh Uncle. I even mentioned this remarkable vision to Yasmin, then dismissed it. But late that night there came a gentle but persistent knocking on my door. Standing outside, looking a little furtive and with a wan smile on his face, was Uncle himself. He wanted to spend the night in my room.

It will come eventually either to a hangman's noose or a garland for your Mahesh, Papa had said a few times in frustration to my mother; he couldn't have known how remarkably close his prediction would turn out to be. During our first two years in Nairobi my uncle came to see us three times, over weekends, one of which was during the Holi festival. But his presence had become awkward in our home. The flat in which we lived was less spacious than the house in Nakuru, and our financial capacity much straitened. He was not my object of adulation in the way he had been before. But Uncle's fortunes changed in the most dramatic fashion. First, one day my Rakesh Uncle, Papa's cousin who worked in the Post Office, came home as bearer of grim news. Apparently all letters sent to the Indian High Commissioner Appa Pant received routine screening; one of his recent correspondents had turned out to be Mahesh Verma from Elburgon.

What did my brother-in-law write to that desi busybody? Papa asked crisply.

The High Commissioner was by reputation a former Indian prince who had been specially picked by Pandit Nehru to represent India in Kenya; but his activities, which included consorting with radical Asians and Africans, among them Kikuyu, embarrassed many Asians who had vowed undying support to Queen and Empire.

The ullu-ka-patha Mahesh wrote a long letter saying why independence is a good thing for Africans, said Rakesh Uncle. He said India should give recognition to Mau Mau and assist them. Now your brother-in-law is on the suspect list. Warn him, Ashok. We could all catch trouble.

The next few days Mother tried frantically to contact her brother over the phone, but to no avail, the phone lines to Elburgon were down. In Nakuru, neither my grandparents nor our friends the Molabuxes had seen him for weeks. The fear in our home now was that Mahesh Uncle had already been detained. In the midst of this worry, however, Mother received a phone call, from no less a person than High Commissioner Appa Pant.

Are you Mahesh Verma's sister? Mr. Pant asked. My mother answered, yes she was. Her brother worked in the Resham Singh Sawmill near Elburgon, north west of Nakuru; no he did not like the job very much, he was a university graduate after all, but the Asians would not hire him in their schools or businesses; he could not even get married to a decent girl in the whole of Kenya.

The High Commissioner laughed and said, I have received a letter from a common friend in New Delhi. I will try to help him.

Inquiries by the Molabuxes meanwhile brought the news that Mahesh Uncle was safe. Less than a month later he received a registered letter offering him a job as English master at the prestigious Devonshire School in Nairobi. And it was at Appa Pant's house on Second Parklands Avenue that he met the politician Okello Okello, whose entourage he would join. Both had strong Marxist leanings. It was there too that he met the woman he married, Kamala, one of the four daughters of Vasant Dev, a lawyer who had defended Okello in his trial for sedition at Kisumu.

My uncle was now flying in high circles. At independence, Okello became Minister for Home Affairs, and my uncle left his teacher's job to become his advisor. In the current political climate, following Zanzibar's revolution, it seemed that the only friends the communists had in Kenya were Okello and his entourage. My choice of Dar es Salaam, friendly to communists, as the place to go for university had thrilled Mahesh Uncle. But between us there remained that brief embarrassed look, that dropping of eyes, the silence. I could never completely explain this chill inside me. I did not judge him, he who once had been so dear to me, so tender toward me; even in later years he would never miss the opportunity to embrace me, ask how I was doing. In my mind, however, he had become too tightly bound with the horrors of Nakuru: the wrongful accusation and disappearance of Amini, the ghastly butchery of the Bruces, the detention and death of Mwangi, who I've always believed was innocent—all that which remained still raw inside me, not negotiated yet for a piece of realistic wisdom about the world, a personal philosophy of life.

One morning I took Njoroge to see my uncle at Okello Okello's constituency office on Victoria Street. The talk naturally came to politics, and very soon Mahesh Uncle—a little plumper than he had been in Nakuru, his beard and hair trimmer but greying, his black-framed glasses thicker—had energetically brushed aside Njoroge's open-eyed optimism about the future of the nation.

Njoroge, Njoroge, look around you, said my uncle. Don't you see who's got the prime property now, the lion's share of the Kenya Highlands previously owned by the whites? Why, it's the Old Man and his cronies, some of whom even collaborated with the British! Who's getting fat on the land? Mau Mau are now languishing in prison—because they dare to ask, Where is the land we fought for?

It was the first time I heard the articulation of this argument, that the country was stolen away by an elite, and a traitorous elite at that. This charge has become a constant subtheme in our country's recent history. In time Njoroge too would come under its sway, but that lunch hour as we emerged into busy Victoria Street by the crowded bus stop, the buses grinding their gears before lurching away down toward the river and back up on to Ngara, Parklands, and High Ridge, leaving behind disappointed groaning African and Asian women in the wake of exhaust fumes, as we walked off to the Supreme nearby to meet Deepa for vegetarian thalis, we dismissed my uncle's rantings. I reminded Njo of how Uncle would be the first to take offence during our Sunday family meals, kicking his chair back as he sprang to his feet, fists raised to take on my father's brothers for the sake of his radical politics. Njoroge and I laughed at that memory, doorway to many others that united us as friends.

I've come to spend the night with my nephew, do you have space in your fine abode for your uncle?

We embraced. Why, Uncle, come in, I said. Then: Are you in Dar to meet Premier Chou en Lai?

He smiled, as if I had made a joke, and shook his head. Just to observe the feast, he said, which we in Kenya have been so unjustly denied. I wish Premier Chou could have come and drummed some revolutionary sense into Kenyans.

All he had on him was a small overnight case and his favourite jute shoulder bag that I remembered so well. He sat down on my bed, glanced around the room briefly. Obviously he himself did not want to be observed in Dar, or he would have been in a hotel. I said nothing.

I saw you in town, on the street, waving a flag. A girl was with you—you must have seen me too.

Yes, but I couldn't believe it was truly you. I thought it was the Dar es Salaam heat getting to me.

He laughed.

It was a hot night, and he was famished. He drank a glass of water, then the two of us changed into shorts and took off into the night for the banda down the street, which served tea and snacks practically round the clock, a godsend for students. On the way we passed a man roasting meat, and the smell was strong.

Do you eat meat nowadays? he asked softly.

Sometimes, I hesitated. Chicken preferably. But not much . . . Do *you*?

He nodded. I had to fight my qualms and acquire the taste. You can't be in Kenya politics and not eat meat.

Although he did not mean it that way, the statement sounded rather ominous. He described his first time with meat, at a dinner party in Eldoret, when he discovered on his plate a shank of goat in a generous helping of plantain. His neighbour at the table watched him enviously with his prize, and he had no choice but to pretend to attack it with relish. He had expected to retch up the contents of his stomach before the night was out, like a sick hyena, he said, but he survived and learned.

I did not tell him about my first time, the open land behind our house in Nakuru, the holy mugumo tree, the ritually sacrificed meat, and Njoroge. My first taste of meat was probably rotten, a pinch from the spilled-out intestine of a goat or a sheep. He watched me, went back to his omelette and bread. Later we had maandazi and chai. He lit a cigarette. He mused about his youth in Peshawar, his quarrels with his father. Grandfather Verma, he informed me, was ailing. This was something my mother had not yet told me.

If he dies, I'll have to return to India—for a couple of weeks, he said.

Why don't you go before—see him before he dies, I mean?

He stared at me, in the way he had of lowering his head and looking at you from below, and grinned. His hair was dusty and his salt-and-pepper beard unruly, and he looked a bit wild in the dim light of the tea kiosk outside which we sat, at a small, rickety wooden table.

I will, he said. Thanks Vic, for telling me my duty. I will go and see him. You know what? I will even make up with him. My father and I had deep differences, as you no doubt know.

He watched me for my response and I nodded.

One day I'll tell you about it, he said. It's a painful story.

We became very close that night.

He had reached out to take my hand, and now said, Vic, Vic . . . bété . . . why did you stop loving me?

I did not answer and he turned thoughtful. We were the only customers at the banda. A smell of woodsmoke filled the air as the owner rearranged his fire, perhaps ready to shut it out for a few hours and catch a nap before the morning rush. In the distance, two students called out to each other. Perhaps they were drunk.

Uncle said, I supported Mau Mau, and they took your friends' lives . . . that family of four . . . but I did not condone all actions they took. And all of the fighters were not like that—so brutal. You know that, Vic. Only a handful of Europeans died, while Africans died in the thousands. They suffered. They lost their lands. Should I have stayed neutral, or supported the British?

It's all right, Uncle, I said, squeezing his hand.

I wish I had told him what I had seen that morning at the sawmill: my father's missing gun in his hand, his ride into the woods with provisions and gun for Mau Mau fighters. I wish we had discussed Mwangi, shared our grief, for I am sure he regretted that impulsive theft that turned out so costly; I had never seen him look happy following the incident. I wish I had spoken, and therefore also exorcised myself from that past. This was my only chance; I did not take it. Instead we stood up, waving ahsanté to the tea seller, and walked back, our arms round each other's shoulders, Indian style, drunk on nothing else but tea and emotion.

Before we went to sleep, we spoke briefly of Deepa.

What exactly is going on, according to you? he asked.

They want to marry, but Mother won't have it. And I think she'll have her way.

He nodded.

What do *you* think—about the affair? I asked.

I think it's a wonderful thing, he said. If my daughters Sarojini or Natasha were to do it, I would approve. But your mother won't let it happen. I've spoken to her. Our people are not ready for it, what can we do?

Early the next morning I accompanied him to the bus station. And that's how he left for Nairobi.

———————

My leg is in a cast and I find myself propped up in a chair and staring out the glass back door of this house rather like the hero of an old Hitchcock film—except that what I look at is the empty expanse of frozen lake before me as I delve into the memories inside my head. I had a rather nasty slip on the back steps. Unable to move, I thought I would freeze to death in the cold, no one in sight to rescue me. I found the situation distinctly funny: vilified by the press from Nairobi to Cape Town, hit men and the Attorney General in my home town perhaps still on the lookout for me, the World Bank demanding details of the government's dealings with me, here I was out all alone in the Canadian winter, dying in the snow. I started to laugh hysterically, silently, even as tears from the pain and the cold streamed down my face. Perhaps in this ironical situation I had found my fitting end, worth embracing happily. A freezing death is not painful, I've been told, except during the first minutes.

A half hour after my fall, as if hallucinating in my dazed, semiconscious state, I caught the barking and yelping of dogs, and high, rollicking children's voices, and glimpses of bright yellow and blue and red leaping like pennants in front of my eyes. The two neighbour kids like angels had appeared to my rescue.

Next of kin? asked the receptionist at the hospital. I gave the name Seema Chatterjee, and immediately happy faces bloomed all around me, and I was in the tender care of several friendly women, until Seema herself arrived and brought me home. She'll spend a few nights here, she says, until I am mobile.

Of all my characters she likes Mahesh Uncle best, he is her hero. But she once said of him: How typically Punjabi! Fight first, ask questions later! She is intrigued by his relationship with his father, my Grandfather Verma the police inspector, whom I had once overheard my uncle describe to my mother as a "traitor." She says there is information she could access through the Internet about the role of the Indian police in India's long independence struggle. I am intrigued, as much by her curiosity as by what she will uncover regarding my maternal grandfather.

SEVENTEEN

———————

Dilip wrote to Deepa, as he had promised he would, and she replied. His letters came regularly, reaching her every two weeks on a Tuesday, having arrived by the London post and been sorted over the weekend. Over Diwali he slipped in a thin gold chain with his letter, and another time a pressed flower. There was nothing embarrassing or overbearing in his approach, nothing unsuitable or not meant also for the eyes and ears of my parents. He was proper, always the gentleman. He wrote about how he had spent his time since he last wrote, having visited a cricket or football match or a play at the West End, and sometimes he mentioned a girl or two of his acquaintance at the university, in an attempt to tease her and perhaps my mother too. To both my parents he was the ideal suitor for their daughter, whose impulsiveness and quickness of temper, whose undue extroversion they watched anxiously lest these excesses spill over and poison the golden matrimonial prospect unfolding like a boon from the gods.

Njoroge too wrote to her, of course, letters in a humorous vein signed "Bugsy" and also not unintended for my parents' attention. They found his posturing awkward and disconcerting. His secret love letters to her, however, were frantic and frequent, delivered by a messenger in school.

He missed her desperately, and he found the secrecy unbearable. He had no one to talk to about this love in his life and sometimes, reflecting on it all by himself, away from his many friends, away from the heated political debates and the literary gatherings Makerere University was famous for, he even doubted his ability to nurture it. Perhaps he was deluding himself with it. He wasn't even sure at times what level of intimacy to adopt with this alien girl. Wasn't she still a child? And yet how easy she found it to handle the situation!

Doubts and fears assailed him like hostile spirits as he lay awake in his bed at night: how would he convince her family to relent, permit him to marry their daughter; if they didn't, would he have the strength to defy them, whom he loved and respected? It was not going to be easy at all. And later still, how would his African friends treat her, when they could still recall bitterly the past racism of her people? How would her own people treat her . . .

Perhaps, he wrote in dejection once, we should call it off. I know your Indians too well, they will never allow their daughter to marry an African. It's no good, my Deepa, don't you see? I've become an African terrorist for your parents, who once loved me so much. I sometimes wonder how it is even possible that we've come this far, from our respective ends, that we are able even to talk so intimately, share so many thoughts. The most wonderful thing about us is that we've learned, we've discovered a new terrain in human relationship, a new trait of the heart that proclaims that we can get as close to another human as to become one in body and spirit—no matter how different the details of our birth! Do you see this?

How can you say that! came her reply to him. How can you have doubts! If you stop loving me I will die! Let's run away to London, she pleaded, that's what Indian girls do to marry outside their community or religion. You're right, they will never relent!

He answered categorically, No, Deepa. This is a historical moment for Kenya, for East Africa, don't you see? It's a time for Africa finally to become great in the world! We have arrived. I have to be here, you have to be here, to witness that greatness; to make it *possible,* my dear. I have a role to play in that future, I feel it in my very bones—how can we run away to seek refuge in the arms of our former colonial masters?

In panic, she drove to the General Post Office one night, soon after receiving this letter, and from one of the bank of phone booths on the sidewalk outside she called him and apologized: I am sorry, Njo, how could I have been so thoughtless, to ask you to run away from Kenya for my sake?

She was in tears. They had trapped themselves into a corner of hopeless despair and pessimism, and she was suffering. He had misjudged her strength: their secret, forbidden love was exacting a pitiless daily toll from her life. Her pent-up passions cried out for release, yet at home she had to put on a complete performance to deny her true self. The good humour with which she bore my parents' awful hints and jokes about her "romance" with Dilip; her self-control at the increasingly presumptuous attentions of the Sharmas; the charming, mature girl she tried to become, only so that Mother and Papa would bend her way, but which made them believe she was finally acquiescing to theirs; all this, and she wanted to scream out to the world, But it is Njoroge I will marry! Don't you see? Let me live my life! She stayed up late nights to read and reread his letters and to write to him with matching passion. Mother was ever watchful, not completely taken in by the show of compliance, and she would sometimes tap on Deepa's door with an anxious Soyi ho na? Are you sleeping, beti? Just finished reading, Mama, I'm going to sleep now, Deepa would reply. His correspondence she carefully rolled up and concealed in a cardboard tube, which she inserted into one of the hollow metal legs of her bed; and she was careful not to leave any guilty impressions of her love on the writing pad.

Outside on Kenyatta Avenue, the only pedestrians were the sidewalk prostitutes, bargaining with tourists in taxis, and the occasional straggler drifting homeward. In her phone booth, she did her best to keep her eyes away from curious stares.

It's all right, Njoroge told her on the phone, I would escape anywhere in the world with you—if it worked; but it wouldn't . . . do you see that, darling? You also don't want to run away from everything you love?

She agreed. You're right, Njo . . . let's wait then as we planned.

I love you, Deep, he said as they hung up.

But a worry tugged at her: Why was he so reasonable, not burning up like her?

It was nine o'clock and my parents had grown frantic with worry. Finally, in an act of desperation, Papa and a neighbour took off in the latter's car to comb the plausible streets of Nairobi to look for Deepa. The sparsely lit suburbs of Nairobi take on an eerie look at night, but much to their relief the two men saw her near Forest Road, racing back home in the family car, and they turned around and followed. Papa and Deepa walked in together, he severely scolding her; she would not explain where she had been, instead went to her room and locked herself in. What made her come out finally was my telephone call that night; she broke down over the phone, saying, Vic, they are tormenting me, Mama and Papa, they are destroying my life!

A doctor was called, who sedated her.

Njo, did you have a fight with her? I asked.

It took me a few hours and a lot of expense to get hold of him that night. It was not easy to make a late phone call from the Dar University campus; my call home earlier had been from the post office downtown. I sought help from a Danish lecturer, from whose apartment, under the watchful gaze of his suspicious wife, I tried to locate Njoroge over the telephone. A search was set in motion after my first call to Kampala; thereafter I called the number, a public phone used by students, every twenty minutes to check for progress. Njoroge had been observed at the library, then traced to a friend's room, and later to a pub in the company of this friend and others, and was finally located arguing politics outside Lumumba Hall and brought to the phone.

No, we didn't have a fight, he replied to my question. Why do you ask? What did she say? My God, did I give that impression to her? Tell her, Vic—

I told him that she had hardly spoken to me, that she simply had been in a state.

Tell her, Vic—tell her that I shall see her on Tuesday at the gate of her school. And that I care very much for her . . . nothing has changed.

Don't do anything risky, Njo. I can explain to her what you tell me; I'll tell her everything's all right.

Just tell her, Vic, that I'll see her Tuesday in Nairobi outside her school. Please.

On Tuesday at lunch hour he was waiting for her at the gate of her school. She saw him, tall and lean and black, wearing a white shirt, and gave a shrill cry and flew toward him like a gazelle, barely catching herself from giving him a public embrace. Still, a fair-sized crowd of curious boys and girls were there to observe them as they strolled off. The news would get around.

Where could they be together that was respectable enough for her and also private? She had planned to attend school in the mornings and spend afternoons with him.

I don't want to meet you like a harlot, she said, when he suggested a hotel or a friend's house. I'm surprised you even mention something like that?

I was only testing you, Deep, he teased.

They were immensely happy, need I say more?

They had to control themselves in public, keep their trembling arms from brushing, their hands from seeking out and clasping, their heads from coming together in unguarded moments brimming with love; but they couldn't, and their violations were furtive, quick, full of guilt and fear. He couldn't keep his hands off her hair when it blew on her face; impulsively he would reach out then drop his hand. These were their first hours together since they had declared their love in a café that Saturday morning and parted, brave and confident. They sat out two afternoons on a bench in City Park. On Thursday at noon they took the bus from Ngara to Temple Road and she took him to the Sanatan Dharma temple, which she and Mother liked to frequent.

It was a wonderful temple, where all the gods' statues were displayed behind glass and worshipped equally, and to which even I have had recourse sometimes. They could have been a young couple come to worship together. But they were black and brown, a Kikuyu man and a Punjabi Hindu woman of the Banya-Kshatriya caste. He strolled inside with wonder-filled eyes, everything was so dizzyingly colourful, almost gaudy, even the ceiling. She walked beside him, her head covered with a dupatta which she had brought, keeping a small formal distance between them, occasionally coming close on the pretext of explaining something. A young man from the temple came to guide them after a while, taking them from right to left, from Vishnu reposing under the cobra, to Krishna killing the snake, to Shiva and Parvati, and Ganesh their son and Ganga from Shiva's hair, to Radha-Krishna and Rama-Sita-Lakshman, to Amba Devi the goddess and Kali her other form, and before each of them they joined their hands in pranam, and Deepa closed her eyes in a momentary prayer. Then the guide took them to pay respects to all the ten avatars of Vishnu that were displayed at the back, including Gautama, and finally to the great souls Shankaracharya and Vyasa and Mira Bai and Guru Nanak.

The young man's name was Yogesh, and he told them he was a graduate in astrology and palmistry and could tell their futures.

Njoroge quickly agreed, and just as quickly Deepa said, No—not today. Yogesh left them at the doorway, and just as they prepared to leave, the temple priest called them from where he was seated on the floor, against a side wall. When they went over to him, curious, he offered them prasad. They went down on their knees before him, bowed together, and accepted the sweet; then he put sandalwood paste on their foreheads. Finally, joining their hands to the gods, they left. Deepa uncovered her head.

What did this mean to them?

I considered myself married to him, Vic, she stammered out once, years later, her face flushed.

And he? What did he make of it?

He too, I'm sure . . . We both made vows as we stood before the gods. We vowed that we belonged to each other, nothing would come between us.

She asked him if he would prefer her to go to a Catholic church with him some time, or—a twinkle of mischief in her eyes—climb Mount Kenya, the abode of the Kikuyu God, Ngai.

We'll do both, he promised, pleased at the idea.

Joyful and confident, foolishly on Saturday they went to eat an Indian thali at the Supreme and were seen by none other than Mrs. Sharma, our Meena Auntie. Deepa's future mother-in-law, if our parents had their way, waved from her table, then barrelled over with a friend and sat down with the couple, crowding them and thus spoiling a tender, emotional farewell, with further endearments yet to be uttered, strategies yet to be completed. I knew, Mrs. Sharma told Deepa when a fuming Njoroge left the restaurant by himself, I knew that that African must have forced himself on you. Don't you know, they've had eyes on us all along, on us and our businesses.

The goodbye with Njoroge, who was waiting outside the restaurant, was short and strained, under the watchful and grim eyes of the two Indian matrons, who drove away with an almost tearful Deepa.

Mother, when she found out about the rendezvous, was beyond control. When did he come to Nairobi, this man? How many times did you shamelessly see him? Without telling us! How dare he come and meet in secret with you! Sala badmaash! What kind of a faithless man he has turned out to be, after all we've done for him—

Watch what you are saying, Sheila, Papa spoke sternly. It is Njoroge you are talking about!

Papa, when he wanted to, could be a very sensitive man. He didn't want her to say anything she would regret later. But he was also the cause of much of Mother's unhappiness, by his late stays at his club; she would look at him with distaste the next morning at breakfast, when he would be the worse for wear, obviously still hungover. Recently he had hired an assistant, an English widow who appraised properties and antiques for him. Her name was Mrs. Burton and he rather flaunted her; word had reached Mother that he had been seen having coffee with her at the New Stanley patio restaurant on more than one occasion.

I don't know what's come over Mama, Deepa wrote to me. She who was so gentle and loving, such a harbour for our little sorrows, the voice of reason in our home, how could she have metamorphosed into such a fury and fiend? Please, please invite me to come and visit you, dear Bhaiya, let me get away from Nairobi for even a week.

And so, expecting a respite in my schedule, I invited her to visit me; in fact, hoping that away from home she and Mother could arrive at some intimate understanding, I invited them both to come and see balmy, relaxed Dar es Salaam, the fantastic Land of Not-yet.

EIGHTEEN

You fool, Vikram, she told me when I picked her up at the airport, it was from *her* that I wanted to escape, and you had to go and invite both of us together!

I looked at her, surprised, amused, a little sad.

So how did you manage to leave her behind? You told her not to come?

I censored your letter—didn't read out the part where you invited her to come too. I hope you don't mind.

But I also invited her on the phone.

She became quiet. Mother had actually told me by way of excuse that it was better that my sister and I had a chance to be alone to talk things over. She listed a litany of Deepa's sins, the most grievous of which was her treachery and sheer recklessness in meeting with Njoroge, when Meena Auntie of all people had seen her.

In a restaurant, in public! Her whole future!—she wants to throw it away like that! With a click of the fingers. And then she looks pleased with herself and pert as a new bride—tauba! I'm not going to live through this, mark my words, Vikram!

But I guessed that Mother had declined to come also because she didn't want to leave Papa by himself, with the Englishwoman Mrs. Burton lurking close by.

Later, as I got Deepa's things out of the taxi and paid the driver, she informed me matter-of-factly: You know, Njo is also coming to Dar this week.

You didn't tell me. And he didn't either.

He assumed I would, and I didn't get a chance, Vic. It doesn't matter, does it? . . . And Mahesh Uncle left today, I guess you know that.

I nodded. That I knew.

Our uncle had been named to a delegation, led by the minister Okello Okello, which was leaving that day on an official visit to the Soviet Union. It was a momentous occasion for him, a prize for someone who had always kept communist sympathies, for which he had been taunted and called names. Uncle had come to see Mother in great excitement a few days before his departure and announced his decision to stop over in Delhi on the return leg of his journey. He was hoping he could convince his boss Okello—who had studied engineering in India—to do the same, though the latter, being a government minister, desired an official invitation.

I wish I could come too, meet you in Delhi and see Bauji, Mother said. Wouldn't it just be wonderful, Bhaiya, the three of us together again!

But of course she couldn't go, with the home front being what it was, and especially not when both Papa and Deepa had insisted too keenly that it was a good idea. She had not been back in ten years, though, and Uncle not since he arrived in Africa. He had spoken to her about his visit to me, the evening we had spent together in Dar, and that pleased her immensely. Family is all you have, she would remind me and Deepa whenever we quarrelled as children.

I will only go to India after you are married, she had said to Deepa this morning. Both your Papa and I will go, then. And perhaps you and Vikram can come along too and meet your nanaji.

That will take a long time, Mama, and Nana can't wait that long. You should go and see him before he—

Your nana will wait for me, Mother declared confidently. He would always wait for me—if I was late from school, he wouldn't eat his lunch until I was home—do you know that? The love of a parent . . . we don't realize what it means when we are young. My Vikram knows it, but; but you, Deepa—do you know what a mother's love is?

Deepa left the torment of the breakfast table in tears. A few hours later my parents dropped her off at the airport, and there was an emotional farewell. And now here she was, in another act of betrayal and love.

So where's this girlfriend, this Yasmin of yours?

Not girlfriend—just friend, remember.

What kind of friend? Do you hold hands, do you bite her ears—haven't you promised to marry each other?

No. Just friends, like I told you. Special friends, but no commitment.

Dar es Salaam was a small city and gave a couple no privacy to speak of, save for the university on its isolated hill, where Yasmin and I could go off on walks in the evening. Sometimes we held hands, yes; and sometimes after much cajoling she would relent and sing a filmi song or two—she had a beautiful voice.

Ours was a relationship straining for definition. We spoke about many things together, even about how the other Indian students looked askance at us. Yet we assiduously avoided the subject of exactly what we meant to each other. I was aware, though, that she had left the onus on me. As a boy, I was supposed to take the initiative, declare my intent.

Beside me, Deepa trudged thoughtfully on, leaving me to my musings. We were on our way to the refectory for lunch, having dropped her luggage in my room, where she would stay with me, and it was dazzling hot. Once she muttered, breathlessly fighting the sandy trek beneath our feet, How can you stand this heat? The sand itself is boiling!

I believe they roast peanuts in the sand here, I said wisely, without too much exaggeration.

More silence later, Deepa turned to me and asked with concern, Are you afraid of commitment, Bhaiya?

I'm not sure, Sis.

The truth, which I did not tell her then, was simply my failure of heart. I could not find that passion within me, even a small and reasonable portion of the tempestuous, uncontrollable, unbearable spring of love such as she had found in herself, to take me over my hill with Yasmin. There was a frozen core buried deep inside me that I could not dislodge or melt, that held me back. Thus even the question of what Mother would think of my relationship seemed somewhat beside the point.

But I will meet her? my sister asked.

Of course you will.

Do her people know about you?

Yes.

And? They like you?

I don't think so. Nobody in Dar likes to see me walking around with a Shamsi girl. So you see, Sis, it's not just our mother and father, it's what we Asians are, even with each other. And if you think about it, others in this whole wide world are not much better.

I know, even in America, with those riots and marches.

Yasmin's neighbourhood had actually turned more hostile toward me in recent days. I couldn't help the feeling when I was there that I was constantly being watched. Once while we were walking together on Upanga Road, beside the low brick wall outside her mosque, I had the distinct impression that a car had passed us a few times. She saw me staring after it but didn't say a word. And then only the previous Friday evening, having dropped her off at her home, as I came strolling down the same road headed for the bus stop, a partly eaten mango came flying at me from the shadows, grazing and soiling the front of my shirt, accompanied by the pejorative epithet, Banyani-dengu!

I have often recalled that scene on suburban Upanga Road: a gentle evening breeze blowing, wafting in the salty smell of the ocean, which was a mere five minutes' walk away down a side road; a faint whiff of incense; a few cars on the road; and a distant chorus of singing voices floating out the upper windows of that imposing prayer house a hundred yards away. A few stragglers, well dressed, hurrying toward it, through the gates and into the garden. And then from behind the hedge close to me, that filthy missile, that vile invective.

That afternoon President Julius Nyerere was addressing the students; it had taken a lot of inveigling with university authorities to be excused from attending the public meeting so I could meet my sister. Yasmin of course had to go. And Njoroge, who had arrived earlier in the day unbeknownst to me, was also there, and by coincidence briefly met my "special" friend Yasmin.

Njoroge and Deepa were together three days; they spent time on the campus mostly, but they took the bus to town one day and strolled on the main avenue, walked into restaurants, and later visited a nightclub. They held hands, they danced together. They were stared at, of course. But nobody knew her in Dar; she was doubly a foreigner. As a Punjabi she did not have a community here; and in her clothes, her speech, the accented Swahili she spoke, she was so very obviously a Nairobi girl—westernized, fashionable, and presumably free in her ways. And so, except for a few poisoned arrows from the loafers who hung around the Odeon, an area best avoided in dubious situations, she was not harassed.

What bliss to be loved, and to love in kind. I never experienced that, but then I have saved myself from that aching shadow that always dogs such ecstatic reaches. There was no doubt in my mind that Deepa and Njoroge's declaration of their hand in the open, in Dar, would eventually make news in Nairobi—the two cities did talk, after all. And so a council of war was called for.

Deepa liked that term:

Yes, Bhaiya, a council of war, that's what we need—how to *proceed* now, how to convince the mai-baap to *relent*. We don't live in the Stone Age anymore.

I looked from Deepa to Njoroge. He was sitting sideways at my desk; my sister and I sat facing him in our chairs, across my sloping coffee table—fashioned by the carpenter who worked next to the tea kiosk down the road when he was undoubtedly drunk. Beside me, as I also recall, was the three-legged low stool with a zebra-skin saddle-top—such items were not banned then—with a newspaper upon it, looking much as it does stooped in my presence now, thousands of miles away and decades later, bringing them both close to me in my memory, closer than she actually is across the lake in Rochester fretting about his son . . .

Suppose our mother doesn't come around, I said. Then what?

She will. She has to. If she doesn't, then . . . we just . . . elope.

I turned to Njoroge.

She will come around, he said confidently. She must. I will go and speak to her myself. I will go and present myself to her. What do you see wrong in me? I will ask her. What harm can come to your daughter if she marries me? I have a bright future. I can become a permanent secretary or a minister some day, our country has a great future. And intermarriage is inevitable.

And suppose—

Suppose she doesn't like the idea of half-breeds, I thought, suppose she wants to be able to speak to her grandchildren in her own tongue, in Punjabi or Hindi, and she doesn't want to be the talk of the Indian community in the whole of East Africa and be subjected to the contempt of other women, who will say she has a pukka kalu for a damad; suppose she wants to be able to hold her head up high in temple in front of these women, and to take her daughter and her family to Delhi to see her father and feel no shame . . .

You talk to her, Bhaiya, my sister said to me. Take a stand in my favour, for God's sake, Vic, she pleaded.

I turned red under that look, those large black beseeching eyes with just a hint of reprimand in them.

I will talk to her, I said.

We agreed on a plan of action. As soon as the college term ended, in May, we would all meet in Nairobi and coordinate our moves. I would first speak firmly to both my parents. Mahesh Uncle would be prevailed upon to speak to Mother. Then Njoroge would come and meet them. He would bring a granny along, some elderly and utterly respectable Kikuyu relative, and also the Minister for Land Settlement. My parents could not but be convinced. The minister would promise to have the wedding of their daughter blessed by the Old Man, Mzee Kenyatta himself.

How could that not work? We celebrated by giving a multiracial party in my dormitory that night.

Deepa and Yasmin hit it off straight away like long-lost cousins. Yasmin was charmed by Deepa's mercurial nature and Nairobi mannerisms, and touched by the present my sister had brought for her, a skirt and top. Nairobi fashions were always prized in Dar. Nairobi was still little London. I saw them once walking hand in hand discussing something and laughing; for some reason I imagined that they were talking about Njoroge and me. One afternoon the two went off to the city together and returned, having had tea at Yasmin's house.

I love your sister, so, Yasmin said to me later in that typical manner of speech that sweetly echoed her Cutchi inflections.

We were out on a walk in the evening, on the campus grounds, and we had allowed Njoroge and Deepa to take the lead. We must have been a sight to behold for the curious onlooker, examples of flouted conventions, but it was a late hour and sparsely lighted where we were; not many people were about.

Oh yes? I replied. She likes you a lot too, I can attest to that.

She is so lively, so full of *spunk*! But it takes a lot of courage, what she's up to, nuh?

We had slowed to a stop, a momentary unconscious one, and I flicked her pigtail affectionately, met her flashing black eyes and her tight-lipped smile. What she herself was up to, with me, I could have told her, required no less courage than my sister's. This was the moment, we both knew, when we could have sealed our relationship and our future together. She was waiting for me only to take that first step. I pulled away, and we strolled on.

On the Friday evening, Njoroge having left the previous day, Deepa and I had just walked Yasmin home after a movie and were strolling back along Upanga Road for our ride back to campus, promised by a young Canadian

professor. It was a quiet night, the lights in the windows and open doors of
the row houses just visible over the hedges, faint strains of western pop or
Indian music drifting to the ears, a voice or two calling out in the distance.
We had spoken about Yasmin, how much Deepa liked her; my sister was
certain Mother too would like her, regardless of her faith and background.
We agreed that Mother needed understanding and care, emotionally warm
but fragile as she had always been; and we agreed that Mrs. Burton was a
passing phase and harmless, over whom Papa was fawning in his typical
manner as he had sometimes done over Mrs. Bruce in Nakuru. The remi-
niscence made us laugh, turn thoughtful. It was one of those moments of
absolute closeness, rare, ephemeral, whose fullness of emotion sends a chill
down your spine, and you wonder if you will ever be able to reproduce it,
if it will ever seem as real and intense as you want to remember it.

Bhaiya, do you think of Annie often?

I replied slowly, after a pause, I guess somehow she's always there at
the back of the mind. It's hard to explain.

She was such a sweet girl. She meant a lot to you, I know.

I don't know, Sis. We were so young then. But somehow I never got
over her. It was the killing, the horror and suddenness of it, how unreal it
was, like a nightmare.

Deepa put her arm through mine, asked softly: Do you think
Njoroge's grandfather—Mwangi—had anything to do with it, Vic? I am
sometimes frightened by the thought.

I don't think so, Deepa. Do you remember how he would put flowers in your hair . . . and once he put a champeli in hers too, that day she
and Bill and their mother came to visit us and brought that rose plant?
And she sang that Latin song from her choir? *Laudate dominum, laudate
dominum* . . . I have never forgotten it. Sometimes it just keeps playing in
my mind, over and over. Like a record that's broken . . .

I felt a tremor in my sister's arm.

Before us, at the intersection, the mosque stood towering in all its
grandeur, outlined in a brilliant series of decorative light bulbs in honour
of some celebration; its clock tolled the half hour at ten-thirty. A dog
barked somewhere, and in perverse reply came the sound of a bicycle bell.

The image of old Mwangi was floating in my mind, of him tending the garden patiently, when suddenly a terrifying, unearthly squeal came from the shadows, followed by a hoot. My sister and I froze in our tracks. Oh God, Oh Rabba, she whispered, digging her fingers into my arm. Out leapt before us six youths, howling like wild dogs, gesturing like demons, mouthing all manner of obscenities; they surrounded us. I took hold of Deepa's hand and made a dash for it in the direction we had come, only to meet a leering Elvis face, shirt open, pants crotch-tight, wielding a tree branch. I lurched sideways, ran forward, to no avail. We should have screamed, but terror froze our throats. Backwards, sideways, forwards again, and our paths were blocked in a horrifying checkmate and what awaited was only the kill. But then at the intersection appeared a white Mercedes; it turned left onto the main road, swerved left again toward the gate where we stood trapped, and the six scampered away into the dark like cockroaches. The man at the wheel was a local millionaire, Mr. Bapu; he rolled down a window and asked us who we were and what was the matter. We explained our predicament, and he told us to spend the night in his house, he would have us driven to the campus the next morning.

There was no doubt in my mind, from the obscenities I had heard—in a mixture of Cutchi and Swahili, that Tanzanian specialty—and the faces I had seen—that buck-toothed horse, the curly-haired half-caste chotara— that our attackers had known me, and most likely seen my sister before. I, a Nairobi Punjabi Hindu, was dating one of their girls; to make matters worse, I had a sister who was going out in the open with an African. When men develop contempt for a woman, the vilest, filthiest language escapes their lips. All night I smarted from those insults. Deepa was close to hysteria and I spent the night in the same room with her.

The next morning Mr. Bapu drove us in his white Mercedes to the campus, but not before a lavish breakfast and a tour of his quite wonderful garden, which he obviously had a hand in tending, though there was an elderly gardener with whom he chatted amiably. Mr. Bapu cut for Deepa a red rose. On the way he hummed a tune, some sort of bhajan, which we could not quite figure out, but it seemed completely out of key and Deepa and I had a job keeping up straight faces.

I realize that my contempt for those nocturnal attackers has not waned a bit; I have called them names, but this is how I have always recalled them and that terror-filled eternity that must actually have been two or three minutes. Mahesh Uncle comes to mind: when we were little he once said to us, in his typical manner, Henh, henh—see how memory makes monkeys out of our enemies, as one of my teachers used to say. And what does it make out of our friends, Uncle? we asked. He said, It gives them a tint of rose, or it saves them in amber—do you know what amber is, children?

Mr. Bapu, whom we never saw again, is preserved in amber.

Seema doesn't spend the night here anymore, now that I can move about quite nimbly with support. She does visit sometimes after work and we have dinner together. She brought some information recently about Inspector Verma, my mother's father. In 1942 a trial had taken place in Peshawar of some captured officers of the Indian National Army; the INA, under Subhas Chandra Bose, had taken up sides with the Japanese against the British. Many of its members were deserters from the Indian Army. In that trial, of among other people the well-known Colonel Jamal Khan, my grandfather had been a prosecutor. All INA men were found guilty and handed out death sentences, which, however, were never carried out.

There are books on this famous trial, Seema tells me, but I am not interested. She has stories about the heroic deeds of Colonel Jamal Khan and his men, stories about blowing up bridges and gymkhanas in far-flung places and about thrilling ambushes of British troops. Jamal Khan, like Bose, she tells me proudly, was a Bengali. There is a street in Calcutta named after him; the airport is named after the redoubtable Bose.

This trial is what I assume my uncle referred to when he would remind my mother about their father's traitorous deed. Mahesh Uncle had promised me a full revelation about himself and his father; but as fate would have it, we never had a chance to regain the intimacy of that night in Dar when he made that promise.

I wish I had known Grandfather Verma better. Every year he would send us Diwali and birthday cards from Delhi, where he ended up, and we would write to him occasionally. There was always the anticipation in me and my sister of meeting him one day. I wonder now why he didn't come to see us himself; perhaps, as for many old people, the thought of dying somewhere away from his homeland daunted him; perhaps he was waiting for an invitation from Mahesh Uncle. Traditional propriety certainly demanded that if he came he stay with his son. Lately he had moved to an ashram, a retiree commune run by a swami, and sometimes he sent Mother little snippets of Vedantic philosophy whose abstractions more often than not only puzzled her. She was a practical, emotional person. When she tried them on my father he would become irritated; Deepa and I found them distant and amusing. In Nakuru my nanaji's photo had been prominent in our home; high on a wall, he looked imposing to my young eyes, in his police uniform and with his smart military moustache and combed-back hair. In Nairobi he hung in the dimly lit corridor outside the bedrooms, faded and barely noticed.

Joseph visited last week. He had changed his hair, now it was gathered in small knots spread out over the head, a startling style that rather ominously reminded me of a famous picture of Mau Mau leader General China at his trial, a police constable standing on either side of him. I did not make a comment and understood that he is still very much involved with the MuKenya Patriots, the self-styled Sons of Mau Mau. Seema took him skating once; he wore a hat and was spared the stares he would inevitably have attracted.

One late sleepless night, as I sat watching the darkness outside at the back of the house, my infirm legs propped in front of me on a stool, he kindly brought me some herbal tea. As he stood up over me, having put down the tray, and I looked up to thank him, I discerned more clearly than ever before the shadow of his father upon that long face, its high forehead. And (credit this to too much whisky late at night) the spectre of Deepa wafted across the waters of the lake and came to stand beside him.

NINETEEN

———————

The short rains had come and that year's East African Safari motor rally was more gruelling than ever; of the seventy-nine cars that started out, eleven finished, arriving in Nairobi mud-splattered and beaten up in every way. Taking the same plane as Deepa back to Nairobi that Monday morning was the ace rally driver Mohindra Singh, known to Papa through their common club. His Peugeot had skidded and hit a tree, avoiding an obstruction on the road planted by thrill-seeking villagers; it was later savaged by an angry rhino while parked, but fortunately while Singh and his codriver were not inside it. Yet here he was in the waiting lounge, cheerful and chirpy as a parrot, anxious to get back to civilization, as he put it. The *Daily Nation* had a front-page picture of this year's winning Safari team, the chubby, blond Erikson brothers of Sweden, reclined on the bonnet of their Saab, sharing champagne from their silver trophy cup. They hate each other, Mohindra Singh confided to us about the Swedes, but they make good partners.

Deepa was in excellent company it seemed and I prepared to leave.

The omens looked good for her heart's wish to come true that bright Dar es Salaam morning, the warm air redolent of salt and sea, the sun already broiling hot. The charismatic Kenya minister Tom Mboya, at a public meeting in Nairobi on Sunday, had called intermarriage a good thing for racial harmony. Njoroge knew Mboya distantly, Mahesh Uncle knew him even better, through Okello Okello. And this morning's paper reported that Carl Erikson, the younger of the Safari-winning brothers, had announced his engagement to a Swahili beauty queen from the coast. All these, signs of our galloping times that our parents could hardly ignore.

I waved goodbye to Deepa as she boarded the shuttle bus; she wore her blue school blazer over white slacks, and brown leather sandals; an East African Airways bag was slung over a shoulder. Beside her towered the beaming, pot-bellied Mohindra Singh in crimson turban, obviously flattered by her company. I was happy for her, and felt almost certain now that she would get her way. I was filled with admiration for her. I thought that she and Njoroge would be an example and inspiration for what was possible in our new society . . . We were young still.

Less than three weeks later Njoroge suddenly arrived in Nairobi, to be interviewed by the Ministry of Land Settlement for a permanent job to follow his graduation in a few months. This was the same ministry where he had worked during the holidays. Full of excitement, the morning of his arrival he drove to our home in a borrowed car, looking forward to the delightful surprise he would surely see on Deepa's lovely face. It was Sunday. Deepa, seeing him through the window, rushed out joyfully to the driveway to greet him; Mother watched them. The lovers came inside, sat side by side on the living room sofa, and quite innocently let slip out the secret that they had met earlier that month in Dar.

Njoroge of course had lunch before he left.

You children have broken my heart, Mother wailed at me that night when I called.

Mother, I lied, Njoroge's visit to Dar was simply a coincidence! After all, I did invite you to come with Deepa!

Then why did you keep his visit a secret from me? You encouraged them, Vikram—you, her brother, who should have known better. How am I going to explain to Meena-ji? She already suspects—

Suspects what, Mother? And surely you have to respect Deepa's wish to—

What wish? There's no wish without parents' approval! We shall see about this, you will see what I am made of, you two.

What are you saying, Mother?

She hung up the phone.

What would she do now? Fortunately Dilip was not around for her to arrange a rush engagement. There was still a month to go to the end of term, which was when the three of us had decided to begin our moves to win her over. We could only bide our time meanwhile and treat her with utmost consideration.

Fate, however, had in mind another course of events, which it had already set in motion.

The next morning Papa returned less than an hour after he had left for work, with a telegram from New Delhi. Grandfather Verma had died. Mother collapsed on the floor immediately when she heard the news. Thereupon, having been helped to the high-backed chair in the living room, for several hours she sat motionless, staring vacantly ahead of her, tears forming intermittent streams down her face. Papa dared not leave the house until Deepa came home from school. Finally, at around four in the afternoon, Mother went and took a bath, and she put on her new purple sari and her wedding jewellery. She lit a candle in front of her father's framed photograph, which she had brought from its place on the wall to the coffee table, and sat staring at it for half the night. She had not spoken a word since the news came of her father's death. Meanwhile Papa had had a phone message sent from Okello's Nairobi office to Mahesh Uncle in Moscow.

The following morning Njoroge came to pay his condolences just as Mother was preparing to leave for temple. With Deepa not around he thought this would be a good opportunity to meet Mother face-to-face, even if nothing else was said. If he had been a minute late, she would have missed him. But they met, and that meeting changed everything. That's why Deepa for many years afterwards would blame fate and so cynically condemn God—they conspired to the very last minute to betray her.

Mother listened to Njoroge's sympathies with a blank face at the door, where she met him, and she formally thanked him for his concern. She was on her way to the temple, she told him, But come in, she said and took him inside the house and bade him sit. Tea was brought for him. It became clear that her father was not on her mind right then, as she stood over him, and Njoroge knew he was trapped. Looking him sternly in the eye, Mother issued a command: William, Njoroge, I forbid you to see my daughter in the way you have been seeing her. You have been like a son to us, she is your sister.

But Mother, he began.

No. No, I say. I have no one in the world except my brother and my children. I want you to understand that. I have lost my home in Pakistan. I have no cousins or uncles or aunts, no parents. At least let me have a normal family, where I can see my grandchildren grow up as Indians, as Hindus. I had dreams too, of children and grandchildren—whom I can understand, can speak to . . . and bring up in our ways. I have nothing against Africans. But we are different. You are a brother to my son and daughter, you are their best friend. But a husband for Deepa—no, Njoroge.

The world is different, Mother, he said, but she didn't reply, simply stared at him with her large grief-stricken eyes.

I have a lot of opportunities in this country, Mrs. Lall . . . Mother . . . a lot of exciting times ahead that will help to heal my hurt. But Deepa— she's a girl—you'll break her heart, Mother. You'll never be able to give her happiness your way.

I said I forbid you, but no, I go down on my knees and beg you. Please. Let her go!

Her voice ending in a whisper, there was nothing he could reply to that. He drew a deep breath. They embraced, and he left.

Outside the temple, the same one where Njoroge and Deepa had made their secret vows before the gods, Mother gave five shillings to every beggar who sat there. She thanked the deities, especially Rama and Ganesh, her favourites. The priest who had previously blessed the couple now received a bonus for his gods' intercession against them.

How to orchestrate the break? That was Njoroge's problem. Their commitment had been complete. All their doubts and fears they had left behind, now they were only looking forward to the future. Deepa knew him too well, there was no lie he could tell her about his change of heart that would convince her. He picked one, however, against which she was quite helpless.

He met her at the Rendezvous, then they walked to Uhuru Park by the artificial lake, and there in relative quietude he told her that he had happened to consult a Kikuyu elder, a famous mundumugo, about his affairs. It was customary to do this before embarking on a special venture—an important job or a marriage, for example. This mundumugo—Bwana Daktari—had divined the presence of a stranger in Njoroge's life and had commanded him to forgo marriage to this stranger, or he would bring disaster to his entire clan. Njoroge could not spurn that advice—it was an order, really, for the elder was a consultant of his own minister and also of Mzee Kenyatta himself. Let's cool it for now, Deepa, he said.

For how long? she asked, wild-eyed and utterly shocked.

For a while, he said, but she knew from his face, his manner, that it was over. No hug, just a gentle, almost neutral squeeze of the hand. No look in the eye. Could this be real, what was happening?

I betrayed her, he would tell me later, I betrayed Deepa in the worst way . . . having extracted sacrifices from her . . . but I couldn't deny your mother's plea, I couldn't watch her suffer. Her suffering loomed so large and inhuman, it frightened me.

You can't do this, Njo, Deepa whispered. We were ordained for each other, you know it, ever since Nakuru . . . and the vows we took—you did take one, didn't you, in the temple, and . . . and . . .

She said she would go to see Bwana Daktari, the mundumugo, herself, and let him convince her. Njoroge said no, Bwana Daktari would not sit down with a woman, which was a lie.

Is it my parents, she asked softly, eyeing him intently, did they make you do this?

Don't you have faith in me? They don't know. But it's for the best, my dear, take their blessings. We will always be friends—more—we were *first* with each other, no one can take that away. In a way you will always be mine, and I'll be yours.

I don't know about you, but I'll always be yours, Njo. I have given myself to you and I will always be yours.

What exactly she meant by that last statement I never dared to ask. She never told me.

He drove her home. On the way she asked him if he was certain of what he had told her, couldn't they consult another mundumugo, who might contradict this one; if she was willing to defy her parents, why couldn't he defy this witch doctor; and so on, pointlessly, for she knew too well that she had lost. Her dream, her plans, had collapsed suddenly and completely like a child's fantasy world when confronted with reality.

At home she sat down at the table where Mother and Papa were having afternoon tea. Mahesh Uncle had sent a telegram, Papa told her, he was now on his way to a place called Haridwar to deposit Grandfather Verma's ashes into the Ganges. It was a place Uncle had always wanted to visit, Papa said. My mother and father appeared calm, and Deepa staring at them with her big black eyes divined their adult victory. Her hands shook when she picked up her cup of tea; she attempted a few sips, put down the cup. Then she silently went to her room, closed and bolted the door; and from behind it, thus sequestered, she gave out a long, piteous howl.

Yes, Joseph, she did know happiness in later years, but that happiness would always be laced with bitterness, regret, sorrow; there would be memories, filled with sadness and the occasional tear; and there would be above all the abiding knowledge of having loved once, but passionately. What a chance was lost there: a romance as pure and natural and spontaneous as a starburst, smothered by a fear of the unknown, of what-is-not-done. My mother was a kind woman, a sensitive, gentle soul; but in this matter she was immovable and cold as stone. And Papa, who had hurt Mother in other ways, dared not cross her; all he could say was, My poor daughter, little Deepa-Deepika, what has happened to her?

But there would be a chance to reignite that passion, if only for a momentary, illicit flare. All was not lost, isn't that why we talk, you and I?

TWENTY

On the third day after her painfully conclusive meeting with Njoroge, Deepa disappeared from our home.

She had shut herself up in her room previously, coming out rarely to go to the bathroom across the hallway; she picked up a few crumbs from the full tray our servant Pedro lovingly placed three times a day for her outside her door. The first night and day had been the most terrible for our parents; Deepa would wail and sob, she beat herself, tore at her hair. Mother or Papa would go to her door to plead with her to eat, to come out and talk: Béti, please, my darling hear me out, I am your mother not your enemy; but mostly they needed to reassure themselves that she was still whole, behind that door. Deepa had scissors and a penknife in her room, a bottle of Aspro, a school compass box with hideously sharp objects inside. On the second day she was quiet, seemed finally to have fallen asleep; but Mother couldn't be sure, so she had a ladder put up against the wall outside, among the roses, and she climbed up and peeped inside the room. Deepa seemed safe in her bed, but at that moment she looked up at the disturbance outside to see Mother's gaping face at the window and she let out a scream. Mother lost her balance and fell on the flower bed, spraining her wrist and skinning her arms with thorns. Perhaps that was her way of sharing my sister's pain. Papa came and took Mother to the Aga Khan Hospital nearby. And late that evening, as if a spell had lifted from our home, Deepa came out of her room and took something from the fridge to eat. Both my parents came rushing out of their room. Mother wept. Papa rushed over and took Deepa clumsily in his arms, getting butter and jam over his pyjama shirt.

The next morning Mother took off for the city market in the safe assumption that all was well at home. When she returned, Deepa had disappeared. She had left a note: Don't look for me. My feelings didn't matter to you. You have changed the course of my life without my consent and I want to go away from you forever.

I flew home that same evening.

Mother was in a state. What could I have done, Vikram, tell me, what was a mother to do?

It's all right, Mother. We'll find her. She's not said she's going to do something to herself. So she's only gone away somewhere.

Papa had already made scores of discreet phone calls to people's homes inquiring if his daughter happened to be dropping by at that moment. Publicizing the disappearance was of course out of the question, at least for the time being. So it fell upon me and my father to look for Deepa.

Njoroge was back in Kampala.

Of course she's not here, Vic!

If only she were, Njo, then I'd know she was safe and bring her home.

I'm taking my finals, Vic, but if you need me, Vic—

It's all right, Njo.

I'm here, Vic. Just tell me, I'll do my best. And Vic—

Yes?

If you need help with police, or just manpower, I know a few people there in Nairobi.

Thanks, Njo.

Vic . . . I couldn't take the pressure, it was just too much for me . . . all the secrecy and going against the wishes of your family, and . . . and the thought of later, people staring at you . . . and raising half-breeds . . . I just chickened out.

I couldn't help thinking how easily he had given up. Deepa's reaction, her flagrant and absolute passion, shamed him. It was impossible to believe how he'd suddenly re-entered our lives and now just as abruptly had left it, though we promised to continue to see each other.

My parents and I could not imagine where she would have gone off to. How long could she remain safe by herself? She had taken no money or clothes. Had we read the note wrong, had she simply gone and drowned herself in the river? I found myself paying heed to every word on the news. Papa seemed to be doing the same. We had no one to turn to but ourselves, and the three of us would be each lost in our private broodings.

See how much she loved him, Papa muttered once. Is sé ishq kehete hai. Heer ki tarah nikli, hamari béti.

Heer, the Punjabi Juliet who also died for her love. And Anarkali, who would be buried alive but not deny her love for the emperor's son. There were enough legends to draw depression from.

Papa would have relented, I thought, for his darling Deepa. He would have accepted Njoroge as son-in-law; he had hardly been strong on tradition anyway. But it was Mother who still said, We have to think of the samaj, the community, don't we; the world watches us . . .

But she sobbed; she loved her daughter no less.

Five days passed, of utmost horror. Mother spent day and night on the sofa, in a stupor: every phone ring a jangle of frayed nerves and renewed stabs of anxiety. Papa would call from the office: Any news? Not yet, Papa. Twice everyday, morning and afternoon I roamed the downtown streets desperately hoping that she might decide to show herself there, amidst all the bustle. I would drive round the Indian areas of Parklands, Ngara, and Eastleigh, where boys and girls wandered about in happy, clamorous droves after school. There was no Deepa anywhere. One day discreetly— or so I thought—I interviewed some of her school friends, and the next day Meena Auntie the prospective in-law appeared at the doorstep: Is everything all right? Arré, what has happened to you, Sheila, you look like a very corpse! Mother said she was sick, and that Deepa was at her grand-parents' in Nakuru, her dadi also being sick. That saved the day, but it was becoming impossible to keep the disappearance a secret, even servants talked, and it was perhaps illegal not to report a missing person. Pedro had been instructed to keep his ears peeled in case he heard something over the grapevine in his neighbourhood.

On the fourth day, while Mother and I were at the table with our morn-ing tea, Pedro reported rather tactlessly that a girl had been found under Ngara Bridge the previous evening; she looked like a Muhindi. At this last word, Mother closed her eyes and collapsed, falling sideways with her chair. The family doctor arrived and gave her an injection and prescribed glucose. Broken and dazed, she was explained that the dead girl, according to the radio, was an Arab from Mombasa, not an Indian. But Mother, who had not eaten a meal in three days, remained close to a coma, prepared for the worst.

As a last resort, I called up Njoroge.

You've not found her yet, Vic? You should have rung me earlier—

I wasn't sure what you could do from there. I thought she'd turn up, we'd find her. But it's four days now, Njo . . . You said there were people you knew who could help—

Actually Vic, there's someone in the police you could contact there—someone you know well, from Nakuru.

He didn't look older, but then I couldn't have observed him so closely as a child.

Ours is a small country, it was much smaller in population then. Hardly a momentous coincidence to be seeing Lieutenant—now Chief Inspector of Special Branch—Soames again, this time in Nairobi. Yet it was un-canny. To get the appointment I had identified myself as a scion of Lall's European Grocery of Nakuru and said the matter was urgent. The CI had sent word in reply, telling me to come back early the next morning, and here I was standing nervously at his door. He was in khaki uniform and looked up from his desk as I entered his office, a cheerful smile on his familiar, handsome face, and he bade me sit.

The office was large and drab, in size more like a lecture room; two tables at the walls on either side of it were strewn with folders; dust motes danced in the morning light streaming in through the window over one of the tables. The floor was cement, the ceiling high and suspended with tube lights.

Ah, you must have been quite young then, when you were in Nakuru, he said as I sat down. How is your father?

He is well, I said.

What are you doing here in Kenya—have hopes of going to U.K. or perhaps returning to Bombay?

I said I was a Kenyan citizen and currently studying in Dar es Salaam.

Well, well; it's an African country now, you know.

I wished it had been anyone else but him in front of me, this man with that superior smile whose every presence, every visitation upon our housing estate in Nakuru had filled me with so much dread. This was the man from whom Njoroge hid under Deepa's bed once; who took away Amini, having scolded Papa for losing his gun; in whose custody Mwangi had been tortured on one occasion and had died on another. I was here because I didn't know where else to go to locate my sister. Behind him on the wall a picture of the President, Jomo Kenyatta, in black frame; next to it a gold-framed letter of commendation from the Queen. There was also a faded map of Kenya, and another one of Nairobi and Central Province with little white squares of paper tacked on, to mark points of interest. The Special Branch, of course, was in hot pursuit of recalcitrant Mau Mau who refused to put down their weapons; oathing ceremonies had been reported in the papers, mostly occurring around Nyeri but some even on the coast, and the government had issued strict warnings against such rebellious practices.

He saw me staring at the wall and said, So tell me how I can help you.

I told him about my sister's disappearance, without mentioning that the boyfriend in question was a Kikuyu named Njoroge whom he might also know from Nakuru, so as not to complicate the situation. He said he would ask his askaris to keep a lookout for her and would phone me as soon as he heard anything. He sounded confident; he smiled and waved as he dismissed me, saying not to worry, he understood the need for discretion. Whatever else he reminded me of, I thought it was kind of him to have listened to me and promised to help.

This was Saturday morning. There was now only the wait. Mother was surviving on glucose, Papa on Scotch. We hardly spoke. On Sunday Dada and Dadi came from Nakuru to help alleviate our suffering; Papa had told them what had happened, and it seemed now the news would spread, through his brothers and their wives. But Dada and Dadi were essential to us that weekend, without them we might not have survived it intact.

Early Monday morning CI Soames called, asked for me.

Mr. Lall, an Asian girl has been seen in a house in the Kariakor area, she could well be your sister. He gave me the address and told me a constable from the Pumwani police station would be waiting for me on River Road later that morning to accompany me. It's not a nice area, Mr. Lall, he warned. I thanked him.

I took Pedro along with me.

River Road is one of the oldest streets of Nairobi and the earliest Indian shopping area. We walked past the thronging discount shoppers and idling layabouts, ratty pickpockets, and desperate Tanzanian youths looking to buy Kenya shillings or pounds sterling on the black market, all this a hallmark of this street. There were the rows of chappal stores, hawkers selling fruit and vegetables, sidewalk vendors of newspapers or roasted corn or cheap toiletries. Some of the stores now had African owners, who had replaced Asians who were denied licenses, for one reason or another, by the new regime. Indian women chatted boisterously across balconies strung with washed clothes flapping like banners. At a mithaiwallah, where a halwai outside the doorway was removing whorls of dripping orange jelebi from hot ghee, we met our copper, as promised by Soames. I bought him jelebi in a gesture of friendship, which he quite expected, and Pedro and I too had some of the sticky delicacy. I couldn't help wondering what Mother would say if she saw me eating celebratory sweets at such a time. I also bought grateful Pedro some Gujarati chevda and gathia from the fragrant pyramids on display at the counter, after which we set off in the direction of the river.

In spite of the sweets the mood was grim, we hardly spoke. We descended the valley first onto Grogan Road with its rows of motor spare parts shops and parked trucks, some of them with their guts spilled out on the ground. According to local legend, you could come and buy a tire rim or headlight on this street, to replace your stolen article, only to find yourself inspecting your own property in the first place. If you were fool enough you would also lose your second headlight while you waited. This was Grogan Road, air reeking of oil and dust, unknown to tree or plant, the sun now beating down on broken pavement and street. At the end of the street was a Hindu temple; a low-caste was sweeping the sidewalk, the priest in singlet and dhoti sitting at the door threshold, expectant. His stare, and Pedro's, trapped me in a moment of guilt and I had no choice but to go inside and pay my respects to Rama and Krishna and Ganesh.

Farther down from Grogan Road we came to the Dhobi Ghat at the river, full and burbling now, where not many years ago Indian washermen in the scores came to wash clients' delicate cotton clothes. Now two women were washing sheets and saris, beating them upon rocks, hanging them out on a line, as a long, frothy trail of suds drifted slowly downstream. We had to cross the river. Why didn't you tell me we were coming so far, I grumbled, isn't there a bus? It's not far, Bwana, reassured the constable; even if you take the bus you have to walk afterwards. We are taking a short cut, he said, this is where the workers from Pumwani, Kariakor and Bondeni walk everyday, across the field, to go to the city. They do? I said, but I knew I had no right to complain, I would have gone anywhere on earth this guide took me. This is what I had entreated the gods: Take me to my sister, please . . . and I will put up a temple for you. I don't know in what spirit I meant that promise then, but I have been able to keep it.

We crossed the river at a shallows, stepping on a path of large smooth and slippery rocks, and began a long climb up the other side. The constable, my guide, was tall and bony, with an oscillating, camel-like gait; intermittently he would look back at me and smile. He had the proud but kindly look that came from knowing he was assisting someone in dire need. We were on a sparse, desperate terrain, an unfriendly no man's land connecting two parts of our city, a poor Indian and a poor African quarter. It was strewn with sticks and whorls and pellets and splatters of human turd, and dark bottles of beer and home brew, and carpets of yellow and white cigarette stubs; pages of newspapers flew about, yesterday's news idly skimming the ground; we passed by stenches of urine and alcohol-spiked vomit, a mountain of rotting rubbish attacked by dogs, and at the end of our path, a heap of condoms like dead white worms in a patch of dead grass. And finally the grey street bordering the valley we had crossed.

We walked awhile then turned into one of a bunch of smaller streets. It contained dilapidated settlements along its length, interspersed with makeshift beauty salons and hotels. On one such street, beside a carpentry shop exhibiting garish red-varnished furniture up to the edge of the road, we came to Our Kimathi Hotel, Bar and Dancing Club, the name painted on a board above the door and also, more prominently, on the wall beside it. All three of us went in. The lobby was so dark that, walking in from outside, suddenly and for a few moments I was totally blinded. Gradually a young man with parted hair and wearing a jacket became visible behind the counter. A few women sat around, one walked out stylishly in high heels, wearing a cloud of perfume. I could well imagine what the dancing at this club was in aid of.

Do you have an Indian girl staying here? I asked with a beating heart, uncertain whether to hope for a yes or a no.

Bhaiya . . . , she called out softly behind me.

She was at a table in the far end of the room with a bottle of Fanta, looking small and sad and lost.

She came forward and I took her in my arms. Sis, what hell you've put us through.

She had made friends with a female street vendor outside her school and asked her to recommend a place to stay. The hotel keeper had given her a room in the knowledge that she would eventually bring in a profit. I paid him a handsome three hundred shillings, well deserved because he had not harassed my sister, and we left in a taxi.

I stayed a few days at home after I brought Deepa back from her little exile, so I could be with her during her transition back to normal life. I let Njoroge know she was safe, and I wrote a letter thanking CI Soames for his assistance; I even spoke to him on the phone. But the sister I brought home was not the happy, exuberant girl of before; some vampire had sucked all the joy, the life out of her. All her movements were now carefully subdued, as expected of a woman; no longer would she dash off to the phone or the door or the car, share a joke with a waiter, tell jokes at family gatherings, argue with the men.

When I returned to university in Dar es Salaam, I had missed more than two weeks of classes, and my exams were at hand. But nothing seemed important after what I had recently experienced. Yasmin was deeply shocked by the news I brought with me. It was difficult for her to accept that the spunk (as she had described it to me before, with admiration) and defiance she had seen in Deepa could have been so completely crushed.

I always knew that if either could be convinced to break their romance up, it would be he, she said.

Why do you say that?

I got to know her, didn't I, she replied, with a wise, knowing nod. Njoroge was much too nice and reasonable—he could be convinced.

Before I left for the holidays, we promised to write regularly to each other. I promised her also that I would invite her to come to Nairobi; she could come with a friend or a cousin, and I would show them around Kenya.

It was summer in England, and Dilip came home, and he and Deepa went out regularly on dates; their engagement was announced on July 4, a day I remember because after the ceremonies the three of us all went to a fete or-

ganized by the United States Information Services in Uhuru Park. Dilip
knew that she had come to him on the rebound, and from her looks and
manner also that she had suffered terrible unhappiness. Always the gentleman, he showed patience and understanding. It was Deepa he wanted,
above all the other girls Meena Auntie paraded before him. I never got to
know him intimately, I wish I had. I think of him now as a tragic figure, in
the way a second best in love always is, gnawed at constantly by that fact.
But then, at that time, I didn't see that in him. We all watched a lot of
cricket that holiday, because he had been recruited into the Asian
Gymkhana team, and in his ducks he cut a dashing figure, striding to the
crease, or fielding in slip, his thick dark hair ruffled by the wind. I once
heard Meena Auntie say, at the cricket field: He could have the Nawab of
Pataudi's sister if he wanted!

Njoroge phoned one Sunday at our home and spoke to Deepa. They
had a lengthy chat, during which Mother remained on the edge of her seat,
her eyes wide with anxiety. We had just finished lunch, and Dilip too was
present. Deepa gave a gurgle of laughter once and Mother's fork fell on her
plate; otherwise our table had become quiet. Then Deepa returned from
the phone and announced: He's getting married. She looked happy, that
was the wonder of it.

Njoroge's wedding ceremony took place at All Saints' Cathedral on a
Saturday morning in September. The bride, Mary, was a lovely Kikuyu
girl, a student at the university and daughter of Njoroge's boss, Cabinet
Minister Joseph Kamau. Deepa, Dilip and I went to pick the present which
Papa had suggested and bought, a Queen Anne chair from Mutter and Os-
wald, and the three of us attended the reception on the terrace of the New
Stanley, where among the guests, though briefly, was the President of the
country, Mzee Kenyatta. As the stocky Old Man, in a black suit and beaded
cap and surrounded by a small retinue, made his entrance at the far distance
from where we were sitting, Deepa's eyes briefly met mine, then turned
away.

Deepa and Dilip married December of that year and she went to live
with him in England.

I was now quite alone in my life. For by this time I too had accepted the inevitable, the unhappy resolution to a relationship that I was unable to consummate.

Earlier in the year, after the holidays, on the first day of term at Dar es Salaam, I set out to look for Yasmin, taking a route we had often walked together. It led out of the women's dining hall and I expected she and I would have lunch together. I was looking forward to seeing her again. When I saw her, from a distance, she was standing chatting with someone. Her single long braid was flipped forward, in front of her, and in the crook of one arm, characteristically, were a couple of books. She was smiling. Her companion I recognized as a Dar boy from her own community. Her fleeting, guilty glance in my direction as I approached them made me lose a step; slowly I arrived, and with a slight blush she introduced the boy to me. It was more than evident to me that the two had hitched up in the holidays, during which I had written her but one letter.

I was saddened considerably by my loss. I realized then that I had lost a chance as good as I would get for real happiness. But I could hardly regret that outcome or be too surprised by it. Although we had belonged so much together, that spark of love for which I had so long waited had refused to ignite in me. I was unable to make my commitment to her, while she had been under constant pressure from her people to find someone of her own kind. She did well for herself, ultimately, for I was to understand over the years that she was a happily married woman, who ended up, like Aruna Auntie and many others, in Toronto.

———————

I had a nightmare recently. Joseph appeared, a tall and bony caricature of himself, wearing dreadlocks and a bright yellow shirt. Pointing a long accusing finger, he said: You stole the country from us! All of you! Instead of waiting to be enlightened—whom was he speaking to?—I opened my mouth to defend myself. But no words would come out, however hard I tried. It was as if I was caught at the start of an endless stutter. Seema appeared on the scene at this point, a detective-woman with white hair, and apparently sitting in a rocking chair, in her lap an open book or a piece of knitting. She looked at me with a demented smile and mouthed voicelessly something I couldn't quite catch.

I woke up in a sweat and angry at myself.

Easter is here, but the long-promised spring is yet to arrive. All looks dead outside, the lake grey, the sky cloudy, the trees barren. I have reached a stage in my recollections when I often wonder, considering my existence here, if there was a certain moment in my life, a single turn I took, which determined that I would end up precisely here, now. I was never much for predestination, you see.

PART 3

The Years of Betrayal

TWENTY-ONE

In a thick cloud of clinging hot steam in the early morning chill of the Kenya Highlands, the 5607 "injun," as the Sardarji engineer calls his locomotive, pulls off under the watchful eyes of Kijabe station crew and soon arrives at the lip of the Great Rift Valley—the expanse of grassland stretching vastly before us in the mist down below, virgin as God created it, endless and endless until the Red Sea, as Papa would describe it to my childhood wonderment. Beside me stands Dadaji, shaky on his feet, clutching my arm as he too looks down at the valley, which we descend at a slow ten miles per hour, his eyes glazed with grim nostalgia. This is the route he toiled on sixty-five years ago with fellow Punjabi labourers, here he lost the tip of his pinky finger as the rails were laid down one after the other on the muddy slopes during March rains. Down we come, and pick up pace, whistling steaming racing ecstatically on the flatland toward Naivasha— the deep green Aberdares looming to our right, beyond which lie the Kikuyu highlands from where Mwangi had arrived once, and on our left at the foot of solitary, nipple-shaped Mount Longonot stretch the dusty Masai plains where once Dada witnessed his friend Juma Molabux's wedding with the Masai girl who would become our Sakina-dadi. A weak old man now, Dadaji walks with the aid of a stick, one eye near sightless; he gazes at the plains knowing perhaps that this could be his last look down at them.

As he stands lost in thought on the gleaming footplate of the locomotive, the downy white hair on his small head blowing softly in the wind, I am snatched by a true and rare sense of pride and accomplishment; this trip is a treat from me, Vikram Lall, newly hired at the Ministry of Transport, Nairobi; it is my gift for a grandfather who would take me to watch the trains on Sundays, and whose name is supposedly etched in wriggly Punjabi script on one of these rails he helped to lay down.

This is definitely the last voyage out of the 5607 "Sir George," yet another steam locomotive fated for the ignominious scrap heap, to be replaced by a newfangled diesel engine. And so it is also the last voyage home on the engine footplate of Sardarji Hardev Singh, native of Nakuru. The occasion is momentous, both engine and driver have a long history in the railways. Sardarji Singh is silent and contemplative, like my dadaji; his father like him had been an engine driver. The 5607 was brought to Kenya in 1949 from Burma, where a fierce guerrilla war had rendered the "bechari"— Sardarji said—useless and forlorn. It was, famously, an articulated locomotive of the Garratt type, made in Manchester, wheel arrangment 4-8-4+4-8-4 in the jargon, the heaviest most powerful locomotive in East Africa when purchased; the design, with the boiler and cabin suspended on pivots between the fuel bunker and water tank, was one specially adapted for use in the British Empire, to go up and down the winding routes of its colonies, on steep gradients and narrow gauges.

Stuck crudely with glue in front of Hardev Singh, among the brass handles and knobs and the many twitching monitor needles is a wrinkled picture of Guru Nanak, right hand raised in a blessing, and a smaller one of grinning elephant-faced Ganesh. We pull into Nakuru to a clamour of welcome shouts and clapping and the careless clanging of a bell. Dadaji is helped, almost carried, down to the ground; I leap out, then the engineer. His wife, a big woman in white salwar and shirt, steps forward, pulls the dupatta tighter round her hair and puts a garland round his neck, saying with a shy smile, Wahe Guru di mehar! You reached safely. For good measure she garlands Dadaji. And then she and the other Punjabi women present shower the 5607 "Sir George" with rice, anoint its sweating crimson-painted iron body with orange paste, accompanying the process with a cheerful though discordant song that I surmise is about a gaja, an elephant. Tearfully, Sardarji goes down on his knees, joins his hands, and bows farewell to the 5607.

Thus the marking of time passed, one generation yielding to the next—with grace and thanks, some nostalgia, some sentimentality, why not. But it belied the reality elsewhere, this last voyage of the 5607 and the farewell ceremony in Nakuru station, it was time out from the practical, real world around us. In this new decade of the 1970s which had just set in, when I found employment that would alter my life in previously unthinkable ways, our times were actually turbulent and reckless, in a manner I can only describe from a personal point of view and in hindsight. But I make no moral judgement on the time or its people, I am quick to add, I am hardly in a position to do so.

Independence had brought an abundance of opportunities, the British and the Europeans vacating lucrative farms and businesses and well-paying jobs, foreign aid and loans promising contracts and kickbacks; this was a time to make it, once and for all, as a family, as a clan, as a tribe—the stakes were mountain-high. And this in the tinderbox Cold War climate of the period, foreign governments peddling influence, bribes, arms. Many of the newly powerful had never been in close proximity to such authority before, such organization, such influence, such access to wealth as had become possible. From pit-latrine to palace, was how one foreign journalist crassly described these changes in fortune; he was quickly deported. But his fault was more his limited imagination; if I say that by the end of that decade it would be possible for a politician to own real estate on the French Riviera or interests in Manhattan, I would be closer to the truth. Money and power were all around me, the one dizzying and glamorous, the other intimidating and coercive, and the two often went together.

In the first-class cabins of Hardev Singh's train that day were a team of West German engineers, whom we dropped off at Naivasha; they were out to survey the tracks and the lie of the land for which they wished to supply a new generation of diesel locomotives. The Americans, the Canadians, the Japanese, and the British also desired to do the same, all promising long-term loans for our young nation to make its purchases.

How Nairobi had changed by then. Among its Asian communities a devastation had taken place. Half the stores on River Road had new, African owners; from the remaining Asian shops you would catch the vacant looks of owners expecting any time someone to walk in with an official writ ordering them to vacate the premises and hit the footpaths.

In 1968, the British government, apparently in a bid to preserve the authentic nature of British society, hastened a bill to curb the flow of British Asians from Kenya. A date was set beyond which they would lose the right to enter Britain as its citizens. Their applications for Kenyan citizenship had been held up or were no longer accepted, and as noncitizens they could not work or do business. A mass migration began, as thousands took to the planes almost overnight, to beat the British deadline.

The Nairobi sky reverberated with airplanes leaving at all hours, where previously only one or two would leave for Europe on overnight flights. At the airport, overflowing with passengers and well-wishers, the GSU, the dreaded General Security Unit normally used against rioting students and rowdy strikers, was sent for crowd control. There had descended a sort of numbness upon the city we knew, the Little London of old. So many friends and acquaintances left; families were torn apart; stores which had been landmarks for decades vanished, personalities who had been fixtures in our social lives departed. Property values in Asian Eastleigh, the Punjabi haven, had plummeted. Previously arrogant men, regulars at the fashionable clubs, were reduced to quivering, stammering victims, begging my father, Please accept the keys to my property, Mr. Lall, whatever price you can fetch for it, Mr. Lall, will be acceptable, and send the money to such and such a bank account, in Southall, Brixton, Greenwich. Meanwhile if you can advance some cash for tickets and such . . .

One morning Papa came to his office to learn a piece of news that crushed his spirit, at least for a time. His friendly assistant, Mrs. Burton, had left for London the previous night, having transferred to her own account there twenty thousand pounds, which he had entrusted her to deposit into an absent client's account, also in London. He spent much of the day at his bank trying to place a hold on the transfer; but the misappropriation had taken place a few days before and the cheque, which had carelessly been made out to cash, had gone through. Papa came home in the evening tearful and still incredulous. She had been such a friend and so solicitous to the plight of the Asians; she had wholeheartedly condemned the British government and was a fount of helpful information for Papa's departing clients, who would arrive in London to greetings from hostile demonstrators and a blistering winter.

Mother's look of gloating when he told her the news was a sight to behold, a portrait of the cold-hearted contempt she had developed for him. This was the darkest time of their relationship, and it was painful to watch. Having observed Papa and Mrs. Burton in the office, I knew there was nothing sexual between them. She had been merely an ornament for him, a happy, carefree diversion, and perhaps a fantasy. He and Mother had continued to drift apart. After Deepa's departure Mother had become even more religious, attending the exclusive gatherings of the most devout women at the Arya Samaj temple Saturday mornings, where they would sit around a tape recorder on the floor and sing along bhajans with it, declaring their devotion to Lord Krishna. Papa had simply lived his life at work, where there was friendly and smart Mrs. Burton, and at his club, in the company of cronies and whisky. But that evening he had, in a sense, come home to her, hoping for comfort and reconciliation. She replied only with taunts.

Deepa had returned from England with Dilip at about the time of the Asian Exodus—as the migration came to be called—with two-year-old Shyam in tow and pregnant with her daughter Alka. Dilip acquired a pharmacy on Government Road, and the two seemed well settled and happy. It was a joy to go and see her those days, preoccupied with her boy and her pregnancy, mature and less impulsive than before, contented and philosophical about life. She lived with her in-laws and there was a cool but not hostile relationship between her and Meena Auntie. She and Mother had made up and often got together, and she would come and look up Papa on

Sunday mornings as he sat down with his paper, listening to Hindustani music on the radio and working on the Spot-the-Ball competition in the *Nation*. He needs the prize money for sure, Mother would comment sarcastically, to make up for his British woman's theft. Deepa would lecture Mother on the need to look after him, and Mother would hmph and retort with something like, He'll be all right.

I had seen only a little of Njoroge in the last few years, since Deepa's wedding and her departure. He was a rising government bureaucrat specializing on Kenya's infamous land question, and I was aware that he had been overseas on training. He had found his calling and was well set to achieve his ambitions, it seemed to me, while I was nowhere close to even a life of my own. After graduating I had apprenticed in Limuru at a shoe factory and in Kisumu at a tire retreading company, before settling in uncertainly with my father in his business. Therefore it came as a pleasant surprise when Njoroge phoned me at the office late one afternoon to ask whether my family or anyone else close to us needed help in these trying times of the Asian departures. I replied that we were unaffected, we all had become citizens long ago, adding somewhat arrogantly (and, I am ashamed to say, perhaps to gain approval) that it was only those who had hung on to colonial coattails who were now in trouble, on their way to an England that despised them. We agreed to meet, and during our lunch together, hearing of our real estate woes and Papa's recent humiliation and money loss (he couldn't help a loud guffaw at that), he said he would set up a job interview for me in government, if I was interested. I very much was.

It was that short innocent meeting with a childhood friend whom I had not seen much since his involvement and breakup with my sister that set me off on my life's path and the career that I have followed. There are doubtless those who will say that, intrinsically corrupt as I am, I would have no doubt reached the same degenerate end through some other means. You will judge for yourself. Here I was, a young Asian graduate in an African country, with neither the prestige of whiteness or Europeanness behind me, nor the influence and numbers of a local tribe to back me, but carrying instead the stigma from a generalized recent memory of an exclusive race of brown "Shylocks" who had collaborated with the colonizers. What could I hope to achieve in public service? Black chauvinism and reverse racism were the order of the day against Asians.

With a strong recommendation from Njoroge, though, I won a job at the Ministry of Transport. For three months I was the comptroller at the ministry offices, a duty given to me, I believe, under the assumption that as an Indian I was naturally adept at handling large sums of money. Behind a bulletproof glass cage with my heaps of newly minted notes and coins, I also did not have to be dealt with socially. We Asians were considered strange in our ways. (Though, to be fair, in the Nairobi offices of those times, a Boran, a Turkana, or even a Masai would have seemed equally if not more alien.) My break from this boredom came, however, when I volunteered to join a team of auditors setting out to evaluate the complete worth of the Kenya portion of the East African Railways. With Tanzania having taken a stridently socialist direction, rumour was that it would not be long before common services among the three East African countries disintegrated. Every section of rail, every locomotive, defunct in its shed or operating, every bogey, tanker, and flatcar, all the signals and relays in the store yards, and even the eucalyptus trees imported and planted next to the tracks in the old days of wood fuel received a price tag from us. The auditors were the venerable company of Anderson Peacock from Nairobi, working in collaboration with an engineering outfit from Manchester in England.

According to my family, my arrival at the East African Railways was pure destiny—kismet and karma combined, sheer good fortune and just reward. We had come full circle, from my grandfather laying down rails at the inception of the railway to myself, assistant auditor and inspector on the line in independent Kenya. No other job could have thrilled me so much. As a boy I had dreamed of speeding on a railway engine from lake to coast, crossing the country back and forth, head and shoulders leaning out proudly to appraise the world flying past before me, like those Sardarji engineers I admired. I would imagine trains travelling west from Nairobi to Lagos and Accra, south to Cape Town, north to Khartoum and Cairo, uniting all Africa. Now I had the rare fortune to fulfil that childhood dream as closely as possible in the circumstances. The country was mine to explore, on this mysterious metal highway stretching from the coast into the interior, its iron rails reaching to diverse, far-flung and strange places; stories clung to it and ghosts still haunted its path. It could well have been called the Thousand and More Miles of Fantastic Lives and Ghost Stories.

For a month, initially, a Scottish auditor, an English engineer, and I scoured the old Mombasa station for inventory and came away with scores of items untouched for half a century or more, most of them now quite worthless: ancient tool chests; a crate full of fragments of rat-eaten rupee notes, a portion of them apparently indigestible by rodents because of the kind of ink used; partly eaten rugby balls and boot soles; tinned food; a barber's handbag, intact, containing among the tools a little Quran. One of the most intriguing finds was the remains of a hand-bound notebook: the pages inside had almost entirely been nibbled away, but the inside front cardboad cover had the remains of the signature "Patterson" inscribed upon it. We imagined it to have been an early draft of the famous memoir, or a diary, of the man by that name who had shot the equally famed man-eating lions of Tsavo on the railway; one of my companions took away the relic, presumably to check the handwriting against a known manuscript by the famous man. I never learned if he had any luck. The railway shed still had one of the hand-operated trolleys that served to take passengers around old Mombasa town in the pioneering days of colonial rule; they could seat one to four and were quite open to the elements and to curious gazes. There also lurked rusting hulks of old locomotives that had been technically scrapped, each of which we inventoried; each had a year of birth, a pedigree, a biography. Those in good condition were designated for the proposed railway museum in Nairobi. And once a week, with a lot of attention and ceremony, like a mighty and fierce god—Jupiter or Ngai—on wheels, the earth atremble under its iron weight, one of the 59 Series Garratts, the most powerful steam locomotives ever, would head off for Nairobi, pulling up to an altitude of fifty-five hundred feet a long train-load of imported goods to service our voracious capital.

Some seventy miles out of Mombasa all trains slow down to a crawling pace as they pass the mosque at the small McKinnon Road station, out of respect for the sufi saint Sayyed Bagh Ali, who lies buried there. Not to observe this token of respect is to hazard an accident, a supernatural road calamity. Even on the parallel highway motorcars, buses, and trucks observe this token of respect. The saint is said to have been a railway coolie, giver of spiritual solace to fellow workers; my dadaji had spoken about this mentor, though I don't know if he had actually met him. According to legend, when the saint carried karais of sand or cement on his head, they would not actually touch but rested balanced in the air a few inches above him. This was because the djinns carried the karais for him.

About fifteen miles beyond his grave my two co-workers and I came upon an unused railway siding curving off mysteriously into the savannah. We had our little inspection train pulled into this track, where it stopped a few yards inside; our interest piqued—the place was not marked on any map—we decided to follow the track on foot. Our engine driver advised us against this, with a shake of the head. Bad luck, he said. But we were undeterred. We walked through waist-high yellow grass (the rains had not come yet) following the old track and singing—*Sixteen men on a dead man's chest, yo-ho-ho and a bottle of rum*—this having become our theme song ever since we discovered the money chest with rat-eaten rupees in Mombasa. About half a mile in, we entered a grove of trees. Here the track abruptly ended in front of the remains of a small European-style cottage constructed out of stone, complete with chimney, embraced between two large tree trunks, their branches reaching out like grasping arms. Parked in front of this house was a small train: a tank-type locomotive and two carriages. There was nothing save dust and debris inside the house—no furniture, no curtains; no remains, animal or human; no snakes. Everything had been removed, nothing had entered to seek shelter. The locomotive was an old American Baldwin made in Philadelphia in 1902, according to its nameplate. Its cabin was caked in leaves and dust, but the brass still shone when wiped. One of the carriages was empty, perhaps it had been used to carry luggage and servants; the other one, in front, had been furnished for private use, with bunk beds and a table. We were simply flabbergasted by the sight. The locomotive, numbered 63, was designated "scrapped" in the railway books for 1920; yet here it was in front of us, completely intact, as if ready to go if its water tanks were filled and the furnace set going with firewood. When news broke of its discovery, an Italian film company purchased it to revamp and use in the making of its popular westerns.

Sometimes I was sent by myself to take stock of stations or even inspect lonely stretches of track on rarely used, almost forgotten routes. On the northward branch line that goes from Nakuru to Solai, I was asked to stop at a tiny defunct station once called Jamieson. The station house was now dilapidated. An old railway clock lay broken on the floor, fallen from the crossbeam above. Old ledger and receipt books were scattered among the debris around it. Behind the station, between steep grassy banks, flowed a thin stream, and on its opposite side stood a ramshackle tin-roofed house, its whitewash faded, its warped, discoloured door swinging open from an equally warped frame. As I stepped off the log crossing, a large white woman in khaki shorts and shirt came hurrying over from the side of the house; wisps of white and gold hair blew across her face, she was breathing hard and her neck was red from exertion. Hullo, she said in a throaty voice. Behind her came to stand an African man, shorter, somewhat older, and balding. Her name was Janice, and his, Mungai. Her husband Jamieson had been the town station master, before he was killed in 1952 in a robbery; along with their two children, she added drily, with a nod and a look in my eye. The station had been renamed after the dead man soon after, and then closed a few years later when the white settlers of the area all started leaving. Janice did not go. She and Mungai eked out a living farming on the land. They were having lunch and I was offered okra and plantain, with warm homemade beer, on a table in the backyard. In a far corner of the yard lay three well-tended graves, side by side and marked by stones. I had been sent here because the Nakuru office had reported receiving tickets issued at nonexistent Jamieson and did not know how to proceed. Janice said the locals often waved down trains and liked to have a ticket in hand when they did so. She and her husband (she meant Mungai this time) had been issuing old unused tickets to whoever needed them, without cost, and the conductors on the train seemed to honour them. The only thing I found of value at Jamieson was a reel of copper wire. It was railway property and accompanied me on my way back.

I recall, on another occasion, on another track, coming across a railway siding that led to a former poachers' haven—a grim and eerie killing field, dotted with bleached elephant and rhino remains, overseen by empty log cabins and fiercely guarded by wild dogs; my companions and I beat a hasty retreat, fearing less the dogs than poachers who might be around. Another time I was shown a rail car, on the Kisumu-Butere line, that had fallen off a viaduct into a deep ravine many years ago and never been re-claimed, dead passengers and all. The car was brought up following my re-port, and the bodies were buried in a mass grave at the nearest railway station.

I had taken to my wanderings well. I know that I was lonely at times, especially when I found myself travelling alone; but I carried with me a constant sense of wonder and discovery; there was the cold thrill, when I stepped off the train, that I was about to uncover yet another hidden life on the railway. In that intermediate state, between place and place, one life and another life, perhaps there was also a kinship with my own inner nature. For some reason I became particularly attached to Jamieson and its two in-habitants, and in the future I would find occasions to visit there again. Pos-sibly it was to be reminded of the dark nights of Jamieson that I came here, another seclusion, where I now write these notes.

Finally, however, I was brought back to a desk job in Nairobi, an out-come with which my anxious family were more than happy. My new duties were to assess the tenders and proposals received by the Ministry of Trans-port, Railway Division, and I was directly responsible to the permanent secretary, Ben Oletunde.

Often during my travels for the railways I stopped over in Nakuru to visit my grandparents and uncles. Both my uncles' children had grown up and gone on overseas or to Nairobi. The neighbourhood in which I had lived with my parents and sister now looked somewhat worse for the wear, though in other respects not very different. The old servant quarters, where Mwangi and Njoroge and the others had lived, and which had been subjected to frequent and nasty police raids, had been built over and let out to tenants. At the back of the development, a slum had sprung up, proceeding to a bustling Bondeni and thence in raucous lines of dwellings and unpaved potholed streets to the beautiful pink lake of a myriad flamingos. Nakuru was much more populous than before, and many formerly empty lots had been built over or simply occupied. It was behind our house, where the slums now were, that Njoroge had once brought me, and in a crude ceremony involving stripping and cutting ourselves made me swear an oath and pledge myself to Kenyatta. But our former house still had a thriving garden in front. I walked there one day, right through the gate, and spied under the window, in the flower bed, a rose which I had no doubt whatsoever was Beautiful Elizabeth—named by my father on Coronation Day, still growing where Mwangi had planted it. Its orange and red shades were unmistakable. Mwangi had planted it under the watchful eyes of Mother and Mrs. Bruce and Annie, who had sung for us that Sunday. *Laudate dominum.* Praise the Lord. Scenes from that childhood came rushing to my head, more real for me because more intensely felt than the life I now lived. How fragile, life; and how doubly so for that girl, like the wings of a butterfly, so easily crushed. She lived for me again, as I walked the old neighbourhood and relived the past. I thought of Mwangi and that whole episode sitting like a wound on my soul; a scar that did not hurt yet cast a gloomy shadow and would not ever disappear, by that very persistence making claim on a part of my life.

Mother had taken a cutting from that rose plant with her when we moved to Nairobi, but she could never make it grow. That day I knocked on the door, a servant opened it, and I asked for a flower and put it in my lapel.

Juma Molabux, my grandfather's old friend, had died; his wife Sakinadadi lived with her elder son, who had returned from his Masai existence to manage his father's businesses. He was a prominent member of the town council now and would be seen in tie and jacket at the Nakuru Club. The younger son Saeed had left for England, one of the many Asians who retained British status and took up residency there.

Dadiji, my grandmother, died not long after my secondment to Anderson Peacock the auditors had ended and I began my new duties in Nairobi. I recall a scene at the gathering we had organized in her honour at the club grounds after the cremation: Dada sitting on a chair, Sakina-dadi standing beside him, each looking far away and quite alone. Behind us, serving drinks, was the bar shed, its walls covered with group photographs of all the teams that had represented the club. How the past was slipping away; soon the untold stories among the older Molabuxes and the Lalls would simply have disappeared into the winds. Hardly a month before that, as a senior and now valued official of the railways, I had treated Dadaji to that ride on engine 5607, the Garratt "Sir George." He died not long afterwards, within a year.

———————

Taking a long walk from the house, on a cross-country trail I have been directed to, I come upon the tracks of the Canadian railway system. It's not long before a low rumble is heard, like distant thunder, and then after some delay there appears from the east the electric "Sir John A. Macdonald," in the blue and gold colours of the sky, bound for Toronto. Smoothly gliding on its shiny rails, it goes past and disappears among winter's grey gnarly woods, stark and beautiful, quiet as these bleak surrounds on this cold and clear day.

I walk back to the house only partly satiated, nostalgic for the feel and sound of roaring steam.

TWENTY-TWO

Straight after smashing successes in London, Cape Town, and Madrid, so the promotions assured us, Pamela Jones was entertaining at the Sombrero nightclub on Duke Street. Alluringly attired in a shimmering black swimsuit costume, with matching lace veil, boots, and top hat as accessories, she had a husky voice and an arrogant manner, and, as was the general consensus around our table, was as big and meaty as Africa likes its women. There were ten at our table, six from the Ministry of Transport and the rest from an Italian firm seeking business. Wine and beer flowed freely, and a lavish course of starter foods preceded the steaks and pizza. We don't mind friendly, generous gestures from our richer friends, PS Oletunde had more than once reminded us at the office, but we make our business decisions with a calm and studied neutrality; we shall not be bought. The Italians were the most friendly of the foreign business visitors who entertained us, and the most fun, any veneer of formality peeling off at the sight of the first drink or woman. The others preferred genteel lunches or lavish, formal dinners. Eyes popped up as Miss Jones favoured our table, stopping by for tips, and the gaunt PS attempted to reach out and put a handsome baksheesh into her revealing and tempting white bosom, but she archly straightened up, caught his hand with a smack, and pushed his bills in her hat instead.

At that moment four women, having just entered, were spotted by one of our Italians; he called out in happy recognition, waved, shouted, and invited them over. We moved chairs to accommodate them among us. That was how I came to meet Sophia; she was the petite one who sat next to me and introduced herself.

Sophia, like Loren, I smiled with a brave effort, intimidated by her closeness, the smell of her perfume, the low cut of her tight-fitting white dress.

Like Loren, she agreed, returning the smile. She had short black hair and ivory-white skin; an upturned nose, a cherry-red small mouth.

The four girls were all Italians working for the airline Alitalia. In such circumstances the women are always prey, and in those times race was always a factor. White women were even then, some years after independence, the exotic and forbidden fruit, and reputedly freer in their manners than our own local girls. But we handled ourselves quite honourably at our table, subtle and not-so-subtle hints notwithstanding, and the women left together appreciative and unoffended.

The next afternoon Sophia D'Albertini phoned me at the office and asked me if I would accompany her to a dance at the Italian Club on Saturday. I said I was not really much of a dancer but would be delighted to accept her invitation. We had hit it off well at the dinner and needless to say I found her very very attractive. Before that Saturday of our date arrived we had already met a few times. She was an airline stewardess, on vacation. She was charming and demonstrative, prone to draw attention wherever she was. (Spicciati, Vittorio, vieni o non vieni? Haraka! And she halts on the Kenyatta Avenue sidewalk, arms at the waist, all eyes taking her in before coming to rest enviously on me.) She had appeared like a genie and transported me spontaneously and magically into a youthful ecstasy I had not known before. She came home for lunch once and met my parents, who were delighted by her informal ways. It turned out that Sophia and I did not go to the Italian Club on the Saturday but went to the drive-in instead, where a rather comically dubbed Italian western was being played. It was here where we first made love. I did not go home that night but spent it with her at her hotel. I had been a virgin so far, and that first experience of sex was—well, what such an experience always should be. It was wonderful to be alive and I was in a state of thrill; it was wonderful to be so physically intimate with, so bound into, another for a moment that is eternity, and then feel emotionally close afterwards, the heart brimming with happiness.

The following day, Sunday, when I returned home already showered and shaved and sat in the living room, my face still glowing, as I imagine it, Papa said, So you spent the night with the Italian girl, hunh?

I nodded, in embarrassment.

Shabash! he said, Well done!, with such a boisterous warmth in his enunciation as to totally flabbergast me. His son had become a man, but so untraditional was that response that I started uncontrollably and silently to snicker, tears streaming down my cheeks, and he did likewise. Mother of course knew what I had been up to, how could she not? Surprisingly, she had not objected to Sophia—not to her different race and culture, not to her occupation—though her inquiries on my behalf and her pressures upon me to settle down, meaning to get married, were well under way.

I took some days off from work, and Sophia and I spent an extended weekend at a beach resort in Mombasa. This was her treat, she having access to special rates and favours through her airline. Where were we headed, Sophia and Vittorio? Precisely nowhere, of course, though I would have been loath to admit that. Deepa had already warned me that if knowledge of my loose moral conduct, that is, being constantly seen with a beautiful white woman, were broadcast among Nairobi's Asians, I would find it hard to settle down. But did I want to settle down the traditional way anymore? I was smitten, and so it seemed was Sophia. We couldn't stay away from each other.

It turned out that Carlo Cortina of Lettieri, the company which had hosted the outing at the Sombrero and whose tender to my ministry was currently under appraisal, was also in Mombasa that weekend. Carlo was a darkly handsome, athletic man in his forties, always flamboyantly dressed: a red or black shirt open at the neck, white duck pants, a light jacket and a panama, is how I remember him then. We met him under a Cinzano canopy for lunch on the porch of our hotel by the sand, the sun hot and glaring, a Goan band playing jazz, the waves chasing each other in quick ripples in the distance, crashing gently on the shore. Grilled meat and fish of more than a dozen varieties were offered us, with the better wines from France and Italy. After we had eaten and chatted awhile, Sophia stood up to go for a nap, ruffling my hair and caressing the side of my head as she left. I held on to her hand a moment, then watched her fine behind as she alluringly walked away to our room. She wore a colourful khanga wrapped round her waist, with just a bikini top above. There followed an interlude of silence, during which Carlo and I sipped our coffee, our eyes briefly on the sea and the sand, before he turned and casually inquired if everything was in order regarding the Lettieri application. I said it was, just as he raised a hand in apology, saying, No business talk, sorry. And then he asked me if, regardless of the outcome, Sophia and I would be willing to join him and his wife at a holiday resort in Sardinia.

I said I would love that, if Sophia was game. We left it at that.

It was Monday night when I left Mombasa with Sophia, provoked and bothered. The following day was the meeting with the PS regarding the Lettieri application, and I looked forward to that conclusion, to bring to an end those lingering doubts I had begun to feel regarding the legitimacy of Sophia's and my relationship.

Lettieri, better known for their sports cars and their jet engines, had proposed through their coach division to supply sleek ultramodern first- and second-class carriages, chair cars, and observation cars to service the Kenya portion of the railways. They also proposed new kitchen and dining cars. But there were obvious drawbacks to the proposal. First, the level of traffic on the railway, even if a tourist boom were to take place, did not warrant spending on new luxury-type passenger coaches, however stylish and sleek their appearance. Moreover, the proposal did not come with attractive loans attached, the company proposing to acquire development rights to some beach property in Mombasa in lieu of partial payment. And finally, Lettieri's prototype models had been developed for Europe and not Africa, where steep gradients and narrow gauges were the norm, raising concerns about the stability of their product. I had diligently consulted with mechanical engineers at Nairobi University regarding this matter and even written to retired EAR engineers in England. A team of us put these arguments forward with all the earnestness of young people having been assigned an important project involving our country's development and scarce financial resources. The financial expert, a man also recently from university, and I had met a couple of times and carefully thrashed out our reservations. His name was Juma Omari and he revealed to me that Carlo Cortina had taken him to the Nairobi Casino a few times, offering to pay for his excesses, but being a Muslim Omari declined to gamble.

Lettieri was sent the letter of rejection stating our reservations. The next day Carlo left for Rome and I never saw him again. I spoke with Sophia briefly over the phone, immediately following that afternoon meeting, before I headed for home. She seemed a little taken aback at the news, but we promised to meet tomorrow, as we had previously planned. The next day however I could not reach her in her hotel room. I called every hour from my office, left messages, and later called her from home. It was midnight when I stopped dialing. I recall my humiliation, sitting by the phone pretending nonchalance, idleness, Mother pottering about the vicinity with obvious though unstated concern. The following morning Sophia finally picked up the phone and to my anxious inquiries, said simply, Vittorio, caro, I have been having second thoughts about us. I don't think it is a good idea for us to see each other any more. We are too different, no? So please don't call me again. Ciao.

Just that. I smarted from hurt and humiliation. It seemed that everyone at the office was aware of my situation, looked up and down at this smart young bureaucrat who had been taken for a ride by the Italians. Had I been so utterly toyed with? Was Sophia no more than an expensive prostitute, who had been used in an attempt to buy me? There were no answers, because she had none to give me, and she too disappeared from Nairobi.

I saw the PS's wife in a tiny brand-new Lettieri 650, the Bambina Sports as it was called, not long afterwards, cruising around downtown's Kaunda Street desperately searching for parking, as one tends to do there. I don't think Oletunde had accepted a bribe, he was always an honest man; he had acquired the vehicle, I presume, the same way I had come upon

Sophia, as a bit of unbelievable good luck; but his green Bambina Lettieri did not drive away. His wife would use it well into the next decade.

One day Oletunde called me to his office and said, Minister Paul Nderi has been rather impressed by your integrity in the matter of the Italians and he wants you as his personal assistant. To my look of confusion, the PS said pointedly, That's a promotion. You have done well.

But there was a wariness in his long look at me. I knew I did not have a choice.

Well, well, said Njoroge when I gave him the news. You certainly are going places, Vic. Personal assistant to Paul Nderi himself—high up there, in the Inner Circle, close to Mzee and possible successor to the throne! But then Njoroge turned serious and said: *Refuse the offer.*

Why? And turn down my chances? I could become a PS myself, one day, for heaven's sake!

You don't know what Nderi's like for one thing. And it's wiser to keep out of the way of the top brass. It's dangerous and murky up there. What's not wanted is thrown away and falls a long distance.

I've been posted—I don't have a choice. But this is Vikram Lall, remember—I am the least political person you know. *I survive.*

He grinned. You're right. Remain that way. Just stick to railways. And finance. Stay away from politics.

Neither of us could have known what irony lay embedded in that advice.

TWENTY-THREE

_____

Africa's Anglican ministers had gathered in Nairobi at the city's new pride and joy, the Kenya Conference Centre; church observers from other countries of the Commonwealth were present, and the meeting which had hitherto been dull and routine suddenly erupted in an uproar. A motion had been put forward recommending that Africa should resolve never to develop nuclear weapons, hands were up for the formality of a unanimous vote, when Paul Nderi, the country's Minister of Transport and self-styled Minister of Science, leaned forward into the nearest microphone, tapped it a few times for attention, and dissented: Mr. Chairman, Archbishop, if I may put in a word here . . . Let's not be in a hurry, my dear reverends. The motion is pointless, surely . . . And then, his voice rising, the round-faced minister exploded into proclamations: Africa must and will have nuclear weapons! We should leave behind the ridges and the forests of our fathers, eh my dear sirs! Come out into the world! I will go so far as to predict that we will explode a nuclear device, namely a bomb, by the year 2000!

When calm prevailed, the motion nevertheless passed. And the government minister had once again left his controversial stamp on a public proceeding.

I choose to introduce Paul Nderi this way—perhaps presumptuously—to highlight how expectations and self-image have changed with time. What confidence and pride our new country had then (what cheek the minister showed), whereas now like a waif in a poorhouse it awaits handouts from the rich "Donors" who regularly raise stern fingers of admonition at it, as at a naughty boy.

My new boss was a charismatic, intimidating man. He was a bulky five-eight, with round jowls, smooth face, and an impressive, deep forehead in the manner of many Kikuyu. I was asked to meet him, following my appointment to his office, at the railway yards in Nairobi. When I arrived he was standing in a group with a few EAR officials, viewing a locomotive; it was approaching under a trail of steam, an ugly hulk of ancient steel emitting shrill, short whistles. He had just been explained the difference between burning oil to fuel a steam locomotive and the combustion process of a diesel locomotive. But the minister was a proud man of science and already knew the difference; the explanation was only stoking an already raging temper. There had been a cock-up, for he had come to view a diesel, one of the older series that had given much trouble ever since their hasty purchase by the colonial administration. The day was hot and the approaching engine belched a great fog of steam, as it gave an ear-piercing screech and came to a halt.

The engineer, one Eddie Carvalho, stepped out of his cabin to report to his superior, who was standing next to the minister. On his way he turned around and shouted to his assistant, Ay! Wipe the engine, you!

A rather rude and foolish mannerism, reminiscent of arrogant colonial attitides.

When Carvalho reached us, the minister asked him why he was treating an African subordinate that way.

Even I have been asked by my superiors to wipe and clean, said Carvalho in a knowing manner, giving a cheeky grin, at which the minister said, White superiors, ndio! and almost leapt upon the skinny dark Indian in a fury, landing a couple of slaps on the unfortunate.

It was a shocking incident by its sudden intensity, and it left in me a deep impression of the power and passion of the man, and a fear of that maniacal temper. My heart was still thumping as I followed him into the black ministerial Mercedes and we were driven to the Norfolk for lunch.

He smelt of sweet cologne but his recent exertion had left him breathing heavily, and he wiped beads of perspiration from his forehead with a large white handkerchief. He spoke little on the way except to say that we were meeting to get to know each other and discuss my duties. When we arrived at the hotel, his secretary Rose Waiyaki was waiting for us at the terrace restaurant, and the minister was soon a transformed man. Waiters hovered deferentially behind him, tourists gawked at him. For lunch he had oxtail soup, which he grimaced at, and shepherd's pie; Rose and I had maize-meal ugali, a local staple cooked specially for the benefit of tourists. You can get better ugali at the kiosks down the road, he told us in good humour. He tasted a couple of white wines and picked one. Over lunch he told me my duties, which amounted essentially to being an assistant to him as required.

Paul Nderi was obviously not the beastly man I feared he might be from that display at the station. He was educated, suave, and had a sense of humour. He could be generous. And as I came to realize, he feared no one except the Old Man of Gatundu, Mzee Kenyatta himself, to whom he was devoted, and—according to rumour—his own wife, to whom he was routinely unfaithful. He had a master's degree in physics from Rochester University.

Almost from that first day on the job it seemed to me that I had been shunted aside to run petty errands for the minister. I was supposedly the intermediary on railway matters between the PS Ben Oletunde and Paul, but this arrangement was a mere formality, a salve to my ego, for the PS also spoke directly to the minister. In due time this charade was dispensed with. Paul Nderi was active on many fronts. Often I was on the phone setting up meetings. Rose, who was also his distant niece and mistress, was present at the more private and politically sensitive meetings. I was secretary at the innocuous ones. My hands would reek from the perfumed purple ink of the cyclostyle machine that Rose and I used to make copies of notes and minutes. The Olympic Committee met once every two weeks, and the City Transit Commission once a month. One of Paul's other ambitions (besides the African atom bomb) was to bring the Olympic Games to Nairobi in

1980. Urban planners with rolls of drawings appeared at these sessions and businessmen promised all manner of benefits; the upcoming games in Munich were a subject of many discussions. The afternoon Transit Commission meetings on the other hand were so dreary that two of the senior members present actually snored, and Paul was often late or absent. It seemed to me I had become a sort of Asian batman for Paul Nderi to show around; still, he was the minister and I received the respect and attention due his assistant. As I sometimes stood listlessly about while he dictated a letter to Rose at her desk in the outer office, she would watch me with a thoughtful smile. I was convinced that she felt sorry for me. She was a beautiful, long-legged woman with a soft oval face that she lightened with creams. I found her attractive, but she was the minister's girl, and also perhaps too tall for me.

Was this job a punishment of sorts? Had my forthrightness in the Lettieri case been viewed negatively after all?

I had left a wonderfully fraternal and challenging working environment; my work had inspired me. I loved trains, I dreamed locomotives. Before I left I had been drafting a report on the feasibility of converting the Mombasa-Nairobi traffic from steam to diesel; the conversion would be expensive, I concluded, especially with the current global oil crisis and tensions in the Middle East. There were already standing orders for Indian steam engines and for a new class of 61 Garratts. But the drive to diesel was led by Nderi himself—man of science—to whom steam spelt Stone Age, irrespective of performance, and he was damned if Africa would remain there. He was already looking to an electric future. I wondered if he had brought me out of harm's way of his plans. But I was small fry; my report could always be shelved, as no doubt it ultimately was. I could have been transferred to another department, why had he brought me right under his nose? It turned out he had other designs for me.

One day I knocked and entered his office at four in the afternoon, a time we had earlier prearranged for a meeting, and caught him at his large desk with beautiful Rose Waiyaki on his lap, his hand somewhere up her clothing.

She stood up and left the room, ruffled but not without a smile, and he too stood up, part sheepish, part arrogant. Such situations, I told myself, would sooner or later land me in hot water. I was, however, as composed as an English butler, impervious to his master's indiscretions.

I wish I were as cold as you are, Vic, he said to me. You are quite quite the Frigidaire aren't you? And I bet you take pride in that.

Smarting, I recalled my hectic deflowering at the hands of the Italian beauty Sophia and said in an affected Jeevish tone, No, I don't believe so, sir. Only, I prefer to keep things under control.

Yes, you are a cold tilapia, he said emphatically, adding: I on the other hand, much to my own embarrassment sometimes, am white-hot underneath. In any case, I apologize for putting you through that . . . that . . . nani, show. But the damned woman is so finger-licking good, you see.

He beckoned for me to sit on the long cane sofa on the far wall across from his large desk, and stepped out of the room, returning a few minutes later wiping his hands in his handkerchief. He came and sat beside me, the cane of the sofa groaning under his bulk, his expensive cologne as strong as ever, and said gravely: I am going to bring you into my confidence, Vic Lall. I am going to give you an important assignment, of vital necessity. Our country is in great danger from the communists, as you no doubt are aware. As you have read in the papers, arms have been discovered now and then in the hands of the opposition, money flows constantly into their coffers, from Moscow and Peking. All they have to do is win an election once—yes—and bingo, we are a one-party socialist state like our neighbour Tanzania to the south—where they have nationalized the banks and the private properties of your Asian brothers, I don't have to remind you.

This was totally beyond me. Like any ordinary citizen I had read the news reports he mentioned and assumed that, if correct, they would be acted upon by the government. I did not know how they concerned me, specifically. I looked at him expectantly. I realized now that he had placed an attaché case on the coffee table before us, over the strewn copies of current newspapers and magazines. He flicked the two end locks of the attaché case open, flung the top back in a quick motion, and watched for my response.

Stacks of American twenty-dollar bills met my astonished eyes, neatly and exactly fitted in rows into the cavity of the case, and looking strangely unreal—a foreign and very potent object with their dull green colour, their narrow size compared with our own large and flamboyant legal tender.

By now my palms had broken into a cold sweat. Dollars, I said lamely, flatly, inwardly recoiling from them, wondering desperately to myself: Why is he showing me these?

He said softly: these are donations to our party from well-wishers abroad. If the opposition found out, they will yell blue murder, call it bribes—foreign interference, American imperialism. But they are honest-to-God donations from private individuals. I would like you to find your Indian contacts and have them change this money and stash it; like in a bank. You with your brilliant mind will keep track of the account. And when our different constituencies need money for their operations, they will be paid by those Indians. Umefahamu? You understand?

Dumbfounded, I simply gaped back at him. What would have happened if I had refused the assignment? I would have been sacked and warned off. Nothing else, though could one be sure?

I was sworn to secrecy, yet I couldn't do the job without seeking help; what did I know of Indian merchants who traded in dollars? And so I called up my father and we met at a coffee shop below his office. There I took him into my confidence. He was mortified.

Baap ré, you are not meant for this kind of shady business, this looks dangerous, son.

What could I do, Papa?

He took a long moment, drumming a finger on the glass-topped table, before replying calmly, You can quit your job—but later, in the future. Now you have this attaché case, and you have to get rid of it.

That night after dinner we went and saw Harry Uncle. He immediately understood what was required: Go to Narandas Hansraj first thing tomorrow. I will call him meanwhile and tell him you are coming.

And so Narandas Hansraj, of Muindi Mbingu Street, dealer in curios who came into frequent contact with tourists, became the banker for this foreign currency. He was a short thin man with a small moustache and round glasses—a typical banyani of modest habits, shrewd mind, and accumulating wealth, whom I must have seen a dozen times in the past in his little storefront across from the market, staring out in the way of all such shopkeepers at the world passing by. This was business for him only a shade out of the ordinary.

Don't worry, bhaisahib, he assured me genially. Fikar nahi, we'll handle it, discretion guaranteed!

I had made his world a little more exciting.

The beneficiaries of the fund simply had to identify themselves to Narandas, who would have received a prior phone call from me, and money would change hands.

In those days Njoroge and I would meet at the coffeehouse on Mama Ngina Street, and Deepa would on occasion join us, coming over from the pharmacy. The three of us worked within ten minutes of each other, in the bustling hub of Nairobi. I sensed that Deepa decided to meet us the first time in order to test herself with Njoroge, and it seemed to me that she could deal with his presence. She had a mature, controlled manner with him now. She was no longer the headstrong girl of before, after all, but a woman in her own right, and married. She sported a Sassoon hairstyle, with short, straight hair at the sides and back, and liked Indian cotton shirts over blue jeans or jean skirts and wooden beads and bangles. She drove a red MG convertible. And yet as they sat across from each other at the low wooden table in the crowded coffee shop humming with business and political têtes-à-têtes, it was impossible not to sense the electricity between them, charged with the memory of that previous relationship; it escaped in the occasional spark in her banter with him. Her repeated assertions of the fickleness of men, or how happy she was, could not go unnoticed by him. Attired like me in the bureaucrat's grey or blue suit, he would sit straight and upright, watch her with a smile on his long face and a gleam in his eye. I was a little frightened for them. But I knew that my sister was an Indian wife, she would not do anything indiscreet to jeopardize her husband and her children. How carefully she had been held together following that devastation she suffered in love. I would always remain aware of it, in her presence. She had shown exemplary courage and resolve to emerge out of the chaos of a mental breakdown. Njoroge never mentioned that episode, but his pointed avoidance of coming to our home was indication enough that a lot remained unsaid. There was an element of unhappiness in his own marriage. His father-in-law, after a falling out with the ruling party, had been denied a seat in the last elections and was now a plain businessman minus the privileges of office. Mary had had a couple of miscarriages, and they had no children. Therefore, when Deepa brought along her family pictures, picked up apparently from the studio down the road, I thought perhaps the scene was contrived to take a stab at him.

I did not tell Njoroge about my assignment from my boss Nderi, even though we became very close in those months. I was leading a carefully orchestrated double life, only for the good of the nation, I had been assured. There was perhaps some truth in this. Occasionally after work we met at the bar of the Nairobi Theatre, across from the Norfolk, and sat on the terrace. This was where, I suppose, student and faculty dissenters from the university down the road also met. Njoroge had become a cautious admirer of Okello Okello and more recently of the Member of Parliament J. M. Kariuki, a fellow Kikuyu from Nakuru. Influenced by these politicians, Njoroge too was beginning to believe that the freedom movement and the Mau Mau had been betrayed—that ours had become a country of ten millionaires and ten million paupers, as J. M. himself had loudly proclaimed, and those who had collaborated with the colonial police were now in all the high posts and had taken for themselves the best land and opportunities.

We spoke of our childhood days in Nakuru and I apprised him of the recent developments in the town. We had a chance to analyze our strange friendships, among an English boy and girl, an Asian boy and girl, and an African boy, grandson of a gardener suspected of being a Mau Mau by the police. I told him about Mahesh Uncle—how I had seen him with my father's stolen pistol at the sawmill and then later riding off on horseback with supplies for the forest fighters; how I thought him responsible for our servant Amini's fate and Mwangi's arrest and death.

I have never believed Mwangi was a party to that murderous attack on the Bruces, I told him.

He waited a moment, then said: You know he gave Mau Mau oaths.

I was silent, uncomfortable, my heart thudding inside me. Why did he tell me this? I did not want to hear doubts cast upon old Mwangi: my faith in him, his look, his touch, his gentle voice, was absolute.

But giving oaths . . . that didn't make you a murderer, I said desperately.

Njoroge sat watching me, then he went on slowly, in an even voice:

Some Mau Mau used to put the body parts of their enemies into the stew they used for their oathing ceremonies. That's what I heard from a few of the old men I came to meet. I don't know whether to believe that or not—I understand it, as a binding ritual, and yet I don't . . . It's not the kind of thing we like to talk about. The truth scares us . . . instead of simply acknowledging us as a part of the cycle of human good and evil. I've tried hard to understand Mwangi, and through him, myself. What was he like, my grandfather?

He watched me awhile, musing, then added, Don't worry, Mzee Mwangi was no murderer. I lived with him, I knew him. I knew everything he did . . . You know they used to torture their suspects—Lieutenant Soames and his men, especially that Corporal Boniface? They would tie fishing lines around the testicles of their suspects and pull, one man on either side of the victim. My grandfather's battered body was buried in the police compound. I've heard it said that the testicles were missing.

That night I went home and cried. I didn't know why the tears streamed down my face, uncontrollably, in the darkness of my room. Papa was watching *Bonanza* in the living room, Mother listening to Indian music on a tape recorder. I suppose it was because I felt my childhood's years to have been so blighted, in a way I could not fathom. And that evening, with the memories dredged up, the cold carapace of my composure cracked and the tears leaked out in streams.

I don't intend to be sentimental.

The next time I saw Njoroge he gave me a brown government envelope, stiff with the contents inside.

They were in the court records, Vic. You know the British destroyed many police records before they left. But these—they are the only extant photographs of that attack on the Bruce house—they were in the high court archives. Two servants were brought to trial for the murders, but the case was later withdrawn. These pictures are gruesome, I advise you. But they are for you to destroy and lay to rest. Burn them in the Hindu fashion. They were your friends, Annie and Bill, let's face it—more than they were mine.

Gentle taunt; echo of a sentiment long harboured. And I the guilty one in the middle, the perilous in-between.

Paul Nderi did not soil his hands handling dollars after that day he passed me the attaché case full of them. He said the party's well-wishers preferred to send their donations via two Americans who worked in Nairobi, and I was to be the intermediary. They were Jim Perkins and Gerald Cornwall and I met them for the first time one day in a booth of a steakhouse. They were friendly and informal, as Americans tend to be, one lanky and the other somewhat muscular and squat. It amused me that they were always together whenever we met thereafter, perhaps due to a rule in procedure. Each attaché case they gave me contained two hundred thousand dollars. I wondered naturally who these benefactors were who sent so much money to the country, and—as I would not do now—how Narandas Hansraj, dealer in tourist gewgaws, could so easily muster the equivalent sum in shillings.

One day the two Americans told me there were ten thousand dollars extra in the briefcase. Let's face it, said Jim, the job is risky even if it is above board—these are what we call campaign funds, all politicians need them. They are the grease that smoothes the democratic process. Now as our token of gratitude we would like you to keep the extra ten thousand.

I refused, saying I was only the minister's minion.

In the future I would know better, for that ten thousand surely didn't end up in a worthier pocket.

TWENTY-FOUR

If I say I married out of boredom, I would not be far off the mark. This is not to devalue the marriage, nor to say I never loved her, in a manner, and she, me; there was never passion in it, true—since when is that required of arranged matrimony, anyway? An arranged marriage is an alliance, a prudent exchange of duty and understanding and care that leads to the growth of mutual affection and even a restrained species of that thing called love. It is comfortable, not extravagant, and consequently less painful. It was perfect for me, at a time when a sense of listlessness hung over me cumuluslike in its oppressive weight. And so I became husband and lord of the manor, which meant I looked after its material well-being. In return, I was looked after from my morning wake-up tea to the steaming buttery chappati straight from the tawa to my plate at mealtimes, to the nightly glass of milk and the pressed pyjamas on my bed; when I had a stubborn headache I could look forward to the pain deftly stroked out with medicinal oils, and when my feet and legs ached they too received ministrations from her small, dark, soft and cool hands.

And yet she was a highly educated woman.

The offer of marriage had come from her family of jewellers, called the Javeris, through our friends the Sharmas. Deepa was delighted at the prospect of seeing me finally settled. Without forewarning me about the offer, she took me to the jewellery shop on Kenyatta Avenue on a pretext, on a Saturday morning. Past the unfriendly, steel-reinforced glass double-doors unlocked from the inside by a switch, and the uniformed guard on duty, we were attended to by a young woman with a husky melodious voice smooth as silk; she was petite and dark, had large, deep, deliquescent black eyes. She offered us masala tea with burfi, and an assortment of diamond-studded gold jewellery sets was displayed before us on a counter. My sister, in the manner of the bourgeois wife she had become, bargained and haggled but bought nothing. And in the manner of the skilled saleswoman, the young woman at the counter did not attempt to pressure her, but remained friendly and charming throughout.

As we left the shop, a revelation hit me:

How did she know my name? She called me Mr. Lall.

Deepa gave a devilish smile, said, You are not unknown, you know, Bhaiya, and she giggled delightedly, took my arm, and guided me to a coffee shop nearby where Mother and Meena Auntie awaited us, picking anxiously at the cheese pies before them.

They asked me if I liked the girl in the jewellery store, a proposal having come from her family that the two of us were well suited to get married. Neither of us had been aware of the proposal in the store, though I recalled two men and a woman in sari taking peeps at us from an inside doorway.

England-educated, Meena Auntie said. Cambridge University, isn't that so?

Deepa agreed. Very smart girl, Bhaiya, and she likes you too, I think. I saw you staring at her. The only hitch is she is Gujarati—but you're fluent in Gujarati, aren't you—kem che, and all that—after your Dar es Salaam experience?

She was enjoying herself. Nothing else in an Indian woman's life quite approaches the sheer ecstasy of arranging a brother's wedding. She turns into a child again. Many a young man has gone the marriage route through the happy wiles of an enthusiastic, busybody sister. Deepa was of course not a little envious at the freedom I still enjoyed, but she was also concerned about me, especially after my aborted affair with Sophia.

But what's her name? I asked my sister.

Shobha Devi, she answered, unable to hide the tremor in her voice. Call her Shobha and may she be a shobha in your home!

There was a wistful, almost resigned smile on Mother's face, as she watched me for my response. She had already, in my absence, expressed reservations about the match. She would have preferred a Punjabi girl—there's no dearth of good girls in Punjab, is there, she had said. And she thought the Javeris, who were from Mombasa, were somewhat compromised castewise (this was according to a rumour) and the girl in addition was a bit too dark.

Deepa watched her impatiently and blurted out, What's the matter now, Mama? Do you want an Italian or Seychellois daughter-in-law? Because that's precisely what you'll get if you go on being picky—some Sophia or Gina Lollobrigida or—

Meena Auntie put it succinctly: Better an Indian and respectable Hindu in hand—

—than a Punjabi in the bush somewhere in India, Deepa completed.

I agreed to meet the girl. I saw her over coffee the very next day and we spoke about our lives and our aspirations. At some point in the future, she said, she wanted to return abroad and do her graduate studies, but for now she wanted to be in Nairobi. She had come with two other young women, one of whom was her sister, and they sat at a table away from us, conversing and looking up to watch us furtively. I was surprised and charmed at this bit of chaperoning. I liked Shobha and I didn't find her very traditional. In this I turned out to be badly mistaken. We parted and informed our familes that we liked each other. Our families met. Finally, a few days after our first meeting, I took Shobha out to dinner with Deepa and Dilip. At the end of that dinner, which was very pleasant and turned more intimate as the evening progressed, Dilip asked the two of us, So can we assume that you two are agreed . . . er . . . to a union? We all laughed and Shobha and I looked at each other and said, Yes.

When I told Papa the news later that night—he had waited up for me and greeted me as I entered the house—Papa looked me squarely in the eye and asked, Are you sure, Vic? You're not letting the ladies push you into this?

No, Papa, I told him. I think it's time to get married. And the girl is good.

He nodded with relief and a far-off look. Mother came on the scene, dishevelled from sleep, and upon hearing the news pressed her knuckles against my head and cried with happiness, her reservations all gone.

Is that all it took to get married? Yes, barring a few details like the horoscopes, which were found to be compatible, and some negotiations about what the bride would be bringing to the new home. The wedding was well publicized, a photo of my bride and me appearing in one of the Sunday papers in its nuptials page. The bride's sari, it noted, was a brilliant red threaded with gold, and her jewellery shone like the sun, as befitted a jeweller's daughter. The best man was Dilip, who gave a suitably sophisticated speech on my behalf, in the right accent. The reception was at the Nairobi Club, where prominent Indians delighted in rubbing shoulders with the few of the ruling elite who were known to me and were present. I was touted as a new rising star in the Nairobi firmament, and my in-laws were proud of me.

The Javeris were a large extended family who had branched out across five continents, in the true and caricatured Indian banya fashion, in order to minimize risk to the family's assets. Thus my wife was a British citizen. In Nairobi the family consisted of old Bhimji Javeri and his wife, and their three sons and two daughters, all with their own families. Shobha was the daughter of the eldest son; she had two brothers and a sister.

I enjoyed their company and they treated me royally, as a son-in-law. They were simple and unpretentious folk who had amassed their wealth only recently, and their interests were rather limited. The talk at their home was money in all its facets, and every adult and most children among them understood the vicissitudes of the daily gold price, the value of the pound sterling and the dollar, and of the Tanzania and Uganda shillings. For my dowry I received a gold ingot, which remained in their safekeeping until I had a reliable safe of my own. On Sundays after the family meal at Bhimji-dada's house, the men all liked to disrobe into pyjamas or dhotis before napping with their wives, then later would get together in the living room to watch wrestling programs from England, while chewing paan, drinking tea, and smoking cigarettes. The family was so extended, with uncles and aunts and cousins, I sometimes forgot whose wife was who, and the noisy and boisterous children seemed only to have proliferated since the previous time I took note of them.

My wife had a degree in economics and I would learn much about banking practices from her. But her heart was set in making a home. After our marriage we lived with my parents in their Parklands house, but less than a year later she insisted we move to our own place. Mother had aged, with grey in her hair and lines on her face, but she was still mistress of her home. The food cooked there was Punjabi, and Shobha was not only the junior wife but also an alien. She had to ask permission to include her Gujarati curries at mealtimes, which my parents evidently did not enjoy. She found my mother's home economics too liberal and my parents' relationship unnerving.

Before we departed the home, Shobha and I said our farewells to the gods on Mother's puja table; Mother anointed our foreheads and put sweets in our mouths, and we bent and touched our parents' feet and received their blessings. We gave a gift to our servant Pedro, who broke a coconut in the driveway for good luck, upon Mother's instruction, and as we drove off to our house on Riverside Drive, Mother's face was actually beaming. She was happy, if only for my sake, but her dreams of her grandchildren growing up in her lap were now gone.

By this time my wife was pregnant with our son Ami, short for Amitabh. Soon after we moved, my in-laws had a safe installed for me in the new house, behind our bedroom closet; it was a walk-in affair that could do a bank proud, and I would be forever thankful to them. I could now keep my gold ingot on a shelf inside, under the watchful eye of Goddess Lakshmi, whose picture Shobha had provided, and occasionally take a look at it and tell its worth from the daily gold price which I could not escape.

So this is it, my friend, marriage to a virgin Indian girl, a pack of children, and the straight family life. Rice and daal and chappati forever.

Paul Nderi was disappointed, he had meant to draw me out of the Asian quagmire as he called it. He had hopes for me, but hopes of what? Rose too was disappointed; I had sat with her sister Grace at two parties and driven her home, and Rose rather hoped something would come of that. Grace was pretty but a less flashy complement to her sister. I have wondered sometimes if I took the easy way out, but always come out with the answer, No. To the African I would always be the Asian, the Shylock; I would never escape that suspicion, that stigma. We lived in a compartmentalized society; every evening from the melting pot of city life each person went his long way home to his family, his church, his folk. To the Kikuyu, the Luo were the crafty, rebellious eggheads of Lake Victoria, the Masai backward naked nomads. The Meru prided themselves on being special, having descended from some wandering Semitic tribe. There were the Dorobo, the Turkana, the Boran, the Somali, the Swahili, each also different from the other. And then there were the Wahindi—the wily Asians who were not really African. What would Nderi draw me out into, when the week of my son's birth he gave a speech, which I proofread, calling for all government jobs to be Africanized, meaning kept for blacks only? I brought him to task, telling him even Julius Nyerere of Tanzania had made a distinction between citizens and noncitizens, regardless of race—that was the democratic constitution of our countries. He answered that what he had said was what the unions wanted to hear and not to be taken seriously.

Nderi seemed always in the thick of secret meetings and conspiracies, whose major preoccupation, I gradually was coming to learn, was the Presidential succession: who would be the new father of the nation, the President, after Mzee, who was old and ailing? From which of Kenya's many peoples would this man emerge to bear the shield? My boss was said to belong to a secret Inner Circle of the President's men, who had sworn to keep the Presidency among themselves, or at least within the Kikuyu people. This was a subject I dared not show my awareness of before him, especially as the existence of the Circle and its dark machinations had been hotly denied by the government.

One day Okello Okello came to visit the minister. Okello, a charismatic politician whose colour dimmed only in the presence of Mzee Kenyatta, had been the latter's strongest supporter when he was in prison. In the past Okello had been seen as Kenyatta's heir. But with his socialist leanings and communist friends, he had gradually fallen out with the President and the government, and he had organized a strong opposition with the support of his people, the Luo of Lake Victoria. The meeting with Paul Nderi was secret, though outside in reception Rose and I and Okello's two men could hear loud arguing. Okello finally came out in a huff, saying, Don't think you lot can bribe or threaten us and keep the power away from us. Trailing his long robes behind him and adjusting his beaded cap, he left; a flustered Paul stood watching outside his door, muttering for my benefit:

Says the President did not eat at his house in Kisumu. The President is no fool, does he want to eat poisoned fish? These Luo people are smart, beware their hospitality. They extract poisons from the lake, which even the Americans know nothing about. Now he's threatening riots in Kisumu, the devil.

Wouldn't the Luo hosts eat the same fish as the President if he accepted their hospitality? I asked just to be obtuse.

He glared at me. Then he said, He's not the man to help your uncle.

Mahesh Uncle had been living in India for several years now, ever since he went to Delhi for Grandfather Verma's funeral rites. Having deposited the ashes in the Ganges and toured the country for a few weeks, when he returned to Delhi he was refused a permit by the Kenyan Embassy to return home. In vain he explained that his application for Kenyan citizenship was pending; that he was an assistant to the minister Okello Okello, whom he had accompanied in a delegation to Moscow; and that he had a wife and children in Nairobi who were all born there. Our efforts for him in Nairobi were to no avail either. A decision had evidently been made higher up in government to keep him out. Finally his family had to join him in India.

Earlier, as Okello entered our office and I was introduced to him by Paul, I told him I was Mahesh Verma's nephew and received a hearty handshake. But when I told the man how desperately my uncle wanted to return to Kenya from India, Okello had shaken his head: I think it's best for him there.

This attitude only confirmed the bitter conclusion my family had come to, that Mahesh Uncle had been shamelessly let down by the man whom he had served. Okello's office had done nothing for my uncle's case.

Why don't you help, then? I said to Paul.

He eyed me again. Maybe Double-O is right, your uncle is better off there, in the homeland.

Next you'll tell me I'm better off there too, in the land of my ancestors, I muttered.

Touchy, touchy, he said.

I knew I had trodden on thin ground. But I had Paul's confidence and this had made me bolder.

Rose suddenly appeared, having changed into an imitation leopard-skin outfit with matching purse and red beret and shoes, looking quite striking. She was a couple of inches taller than he. Want to come out with us, to the Casino? Paul asked, rubbing his hands as if ready to grab his mistress. I shook my head. Grace is waiting downstairs, Rose put in, and I shook my head again, as Paul watched with a sardonic grin and a nod.

I admire you, he said, unable to resist a taunt, but I wouldn't be you. Life is way too short—but you folks believe in reincarnation, don't you? You should return as an African when you die. By the way, how are the funds doing? Tell that man it's Johnny-O this week, he said, talking in code and referring to Narandas, and then explained blithely to Rose: A little bit of betting on the side, my dear. She put her arm into his, and they walked away to the elevator, her Italian high heels echoing down the corridor.

The code was simple. The recipients of the foreign grants that I managed were designated Johnny-O, Tommy-One, Phil-Three, Sammy-Four, and so on. I simply had to call Narandas and say in Gujarati, Johnny-O na char, and whoever was Johnny-O went and picked up four hundred thousand shillings from the shop on Muindi Mbingu Street. Sometimes Gerald, who was a teacher at the Maxwell International School, would call me when a donation had arrived and was ready for pickup; sometimes Narandas would tell me that the account was running low or was in overdraft, and I would call Gerald. A meeting would be set up.

I did not query who the mysterious code-named personages were who had been designated to receive the grants. My role required secrecy and discretion, and I was aware that the less I knew outside of that role, the better it was for me. I was simply an intermediary between the donors and the beneficiaries.

Unwittingly though, I did find out who one of these beneficiaries was.

On a Saturday I took a family friend of my in-laws, who was visiting from England, on a visit to the downtown stores to hunt for curios. As we left the city market, loaded with kiondo-baskets, and crossed the street to Narandas's, where I could presumably expect a good discount on the likes of carved giraffes and African combs, who should we bump into than Paul Nderi with a bulging briefcase, waving a hasty goodbye to the smiling shopkeeper. I would have made something of this accident even had Paul not looked absolutely startled and Narandas looked away in shame.

It was Rochester-educated Paul who was Johnny-O, the largest recipient of those grants. He had a palatial house in Muthaiga and a vast estate outside Naivasha, and he was one of the owners of the new JQS Tower rising ever taller on Kimathi Street, in that constricted heart of our city that could only burgeon skywards. I was truly shaken by my discovery; though I realized that Paul could be using the sums he collected (how much of them?) as Johnny-O for any number of the political activities he was involved in. There the matter lay as far as I was concerned. In all, I believe two and a half million dollars of those foreign grants must have passed through my hands, a staggering sum in those days, yet not so very great on the scale of my involvements later in life.

I was doing well in my job with Paul Nderi; the salary was modest, in accordance with government schedules, but the Christmas bonuses from Paul, in thick flabby envelopes, were hugely generous, and I could hardly refuse the car and house allowance he gave me. One day in my absence the two Americans Jim and Gerald left a thick manila envelope full of hard currency at my home as a present for Shobha's birthday and I let her convince me to put the sum aside for a rainy day, just in case. Perhaps I was influenced by my boss Paul Nderi's cold calculations. Once he had uttered an aphorism: If you don't take it, someone else will; but if you take it, my friend, at least you could do someone some good.

How right that sounds.

Total corruption, I've been told, occurs in inches and proceeds through veils of ambiguity.

Recently, Seema asked me in all seriousness, How does one swindle a sum like three hundred million dollars? This is the sum associated with my publicized misdeeds that she's gleaned from the Internet. I answered her, It's simply a matter of scale, you can play poker with penny chips or million-dollar chips, the game is the same.

She gave me a brief, hard stare to check if I was serious. I very much was. I puzzle her. I have no explanations for myself either. My life simply happened, without deep designs on my part. Perhaps this narration of my life will explain me to myself. Perhaps it won't.

Spring has arrived; we've had some deliciously sunny and warm days. I've been tending the garden a bit, tidying up the beds, turning or replenishing the soil. The Agatha Christie Society, under Seema Chatterjee's direction, will soon adjourn for the summer. Lately they occupied a local inn for a mystery weekend. The event ended with a masquerade ball, in which there were quite an assortment of Poirots and Marples. I went in a plain brown suit, and she told me it was perfect and straight out of a beloved Christie yarn. The society is planning a Caribbean cruise in early winter.

I don't think I will last that long here, I tell her in reply to her invitation, I have to face my accusers and start functioning again.

This is the first time I have hinted that I might go back to Kenya. We are sitting out on my porch with beers, enjoying the bright clear weather; children have come out to play in the ample and mostly bare backyard that stretches right out to the lake; a nursery rhyme from my own childhood comes to mind; steam from the nuclear reactor in distant Darlington appears to have drawn a long white arc in the blue sky. Seema looks up sharply at my comment and says:

Don't you have a whole squad of hitmen looking for you there?

I'll have to find a way around that, I tell her.

I could be found here too, but I don't say that out aloud. Joseph has only to mention my whereabouts on the Internet, either inadvertently or out of righteous indignation at my misdeeds against the country. I have received some silent phone calls, which are probably wrong-number calls, but still. The neighbours' dog, who barks at every shadow and whisper of wind, is a good alarm signal, and I have an emergency hideaway, just in case—not as excellent as the steel-walled walk-in safe my in-laws installed for me (it has still not been discovered), but it will do. And I subscribe to the *MuKenya Patriot* newsletter on the Internet under a false name, in case I get mentioned there. Its contributors continue to demand an end to corruption in Kenya. Their obsession, though, remains the "genocide" of their Kikuyu compatriots in the Rift Valley; calls for revenge and the overthrow of the government refuse to fade away. Where will they lead?

TWENTY-FIVE

Mzee. The Old Man with the white goatee and deep-set magus eyes.

So much has been said of him, mostly negative nowadays . . . the greed and nepotism, the selling of the country, the purported deal with his British jailers, the betrayal of the freedom fighters . . . even the acquiescence to murder in his name; yet he was, remains, Mzee Jomo Kenyatta, the one and only; we delight to quote him to each other as we would an old father; we agree we would have been a lot poorer without him.

He was fatherly, this man the British claimed masterminded the Mau Mau uprising, whom they convicted in a kangaroo court. We know he didn't mastermind the movement, his name merely lent prestige to it, and its reputation in return gave him the aura of menace and power.

Paul Nderi came rolling and puffing into the offices one day, checked for messages with Rose at her desk, then turned around and said to me as I approached, Come, hurry, I'll take you to meet the Man himself.

I looked up in confusion and he said, The President—Mzee Kenyatta—he wants to meet and thank you in person, Vikram Lall.

I could only gasp incomprehensibly and follow him out, with a helpless look at Rose. My heart palpitated all the way to the State House. I racked my brains for words I would say to Mzee. How would I address him? What would a man such as he think of someone like me? Beside me Paul smiled wryly. He had no explanation except that Mzee had said he wanted to meet me. In silence we both stared out the car windows. He seemed a little on edge himself, as he always did before his meetings with the President.

The Old Man started his days late and so we had gone at eleven. I had never been to the State House, a lovely-looking white colonial building glimpsed in parts from the road outside, over its trim deep green hedges and through thick canopies of cassia trees with their yellow flowers. It was the rainy season and the morning air everywhere in Nairobi smelt of damp earth, and more so at this arboreal address. The sun, though, was beginning to shine through at that hour, the day was warming. Past the gatehouse, at various points on the driveway and outside the building, stood languid-looking soldiers in camouflage outfits carrying automatic weapons; they would look bigger, more threatening, and greater in number as the years passed. A policeman waved Paul in at the entrance and searched me, then I followed my boss as he swung past two mammoth elephant tusks mounted on stands and into the VIP reception room. We drank Coca-Cola and waited, Paul bantering with the secretary, inquiring from her what mood to expect Mzee to be in. Cantankerous, was her answer; his stomach was bothering him and he had been receiving complaints about his ministers. And "that Nakuru man"—meaning the outspoken MP J. M. Kariuki—was causing him ulcers; he should be taught a lesson. They joked about the Old Man's rather frank public utterances; Mzee was not one for niceties and euphemisms in his speeches to the people. Once, he had pronounced to a crowd of thousands, There are those who say I am no longer man—eti I cannot get it up—but you just ask my wife here if that is true! His beautiful young wife stood giggling behind him. The crowd roared. Then there was the time when he asked the young women of the nation why they willingly opened their legs all the time and then complained about the men when they got pregnant.

The room we were in was high-ceilinged and panelled; the leather-upholstered chairs were old and the centre carpet somewhat threadbare. There were framed paintings of Kenyan tribesmen and women all along one wall; on another wall was a large official picture of Mzee in beaded cap and suit, waving his fly whisk. Under it was a somewhat faded, blown-up picture of him taken outside his prison quarters, between two wardens, and beside it was one of him with the Duke of Edinburgh taken during the independence ceremonies at the midnight hour of 12 December 1963.

There was an abrupt hush in the building and looks were exchanged in a quick, silent relay to pass the message, He has arrived. A policeman came and sat in our room.

There was one man waiting ahead of us, Jonas Wabera the education minister, and he went in first. Ten minutes later he hurried out, eyes lowered, evidently after a verbal thrashing (the national School Certificate examination papers in two regions had apparently been leaked), and the look on Paul's face could only have been called a smirk. We went in next. We had to pass a small room where sat a bald giant of a man at a table next to an inner door, which he indicated with a brisk nod, but not without an expertly searching look at both of us.

Jambo, Karimi, Paul greeted the giant, then opened the inner door and let me go in first.

Hitherto I had been consumed by curiosity and wonder; I had been admitted into the abode of power from which the British governors had ruled the colony. Now, as beckoned, I stepped in through the open door—and turned to stone. Jomo, the President, was walking slowly toward me, with the help of a cane. Not ten feet away—the god and demon of my childhood, in flesh and blood. The cane thudded on the antique red carpet.

He was not much taller than me, though a great deal heavier. He wore a grey striped suit with a handkerchief in the breast pocket, his head was bare and the hair grizzled somewhat; there was a twinkle in the eyes and his mouth opened in a large smile.

Many have said that you could not look into those big yellow eyes; they mesmerized you. I did look into them, and I say this not to prove my bravery or arrogance—my knees were buckling, my voice trembling as I said, Good morning, Excellency, and shook hands. There remained that typical tiny smile upon his lips and he seemed to be looking through me into some distance beyond. Had I said something wrong already?

Lall-jee, he said in his rich gravelly voice. I told this Nderi here I wanted to take a look at this young Asian who is doing an important service to the nation. You are doing good work, Lall-jee.

Thank you, Excellency.

He looked at me, growled derisively without raising his voice, What is this *Excellencee* the British have taught you? I am a father to my people.

Yes, my father, I said in the African manner, to which he replied, Yes, abstractly putting a hand on my shoulder and dismissing me with, But you must learn to keep your mouth shut too.

Yes, my father.

That was all. It was enough for that day.

I left the room in a daze, Paul staying behind to finish his meeting with the Old Man. The two had sat down, Mzee behind his large desk, under the Kenyan coat of arms, saying, I heard the students booed you once again, Nderi . . .

Paul, fancying himself the man of the future, liked to take on the university students, make the conciliatory paternal gesture in the face of their constant criticism and protests against the government, and more often than not they heckled him.

I felt transformed by my experience; I was now a higher initiate, one of the chosen few among the nation's multitudes. I had stood close to the abyss, been touched by its mystery and power. I recall, as I was driven home in an automobile from the President's office, the trite thought, Njo must have shaken hands with Jomo, but I bet not in such intimate circumstances . . . the Old Man asked me to call him *father;* he put his hand on my shoulder, I can still feel its weight and the grip was hard, like a claw . . .

But Njoroge of course had begun to turn away from the Old Man.

Recently he had gone to see Deepa, in the pharmacy on Government Road that she ran with her mother-in-law, Meena Auntie. Dilip and his father were into manufacturing pharmaceuticals, and Dilip often visited Germany and England, from where he purchased his manufacturing licences. Njoroge came into the shop on a whim one morning. He asked for Valium for his insomnia, and Deepa advised him against depending on medication to put him to sleep. The shop had, typically, showcases running all around, and glass cupboards higher up on the walls. A watchful Meena Auntie sat at a small table behind the side counter at the front end, and Deepa stood halfway down the opposite side. The pharmacy employed two shop assistants. Njoroge seemed reserved in the presence of Meena Auntie, whom he remembered, but Deepa was her effusive self, and the two talked animatedly for half an hour. At the end, Njoroge held both of her hands in his as he said goodbye.

The result was a furore in the Sharma household.

A married woman! Meena Auntie raged. We don't even shake hands with men, we do namasté, does she know what that means, and she allows him to hold both her hands! And people staring at us from the sidewalk! It is the husband's job to control his wife. Is that all you are going to tell her, Dilip? She has come into this household, when we turned away queues of decent, traditional girls, she should maintain its sanctity. A husband is a god—

But he is a friend! I've known Njoroge since we were children. He is like a brother!

An African! What kind of brother? Do you take me for an ullu? A pagal?

Then *you* tell me what kind of brother, you tell your son that!

Poor Dilip, like a betel nut, as they say, between the contrary edges of a nutcracker. He had to trust his wife, or else he had no marriage; his mother wanted him to punish Deepa, in the old-fashioned way, to beat her. At least one slap, like a man, she screamed at him, bring her to heel!

Mother was understandably distraught. She went to speak with Deepa in the shop when Meena Auntie by prior arrangement had slipped away to the bank.

Why throw away everything, Deepa? There are ways of behaviour for a woman. This is not it, talking to a man intimately—where is our lajj, our dignity in that?

Mother, I only spoke with him. He is my friend, you know Njoroge! Didn't he do what you told him to? (Mother reddened.) Should I turn him away if he comes to the shop? The rest of the world doesn't behave in this manner.

Explain to Dilip, Mother pleaded, and behave in a proper and reserved manner if Njoroge comes to the shop.

The tables slowly got tipped against Meena Auntie for not trusting Deepa and behaving like an old-fashioned suspicious mother-in-law. It was Meena Auntie who eventually had to ask for Deepa's pardon. She had not liked Njoroge the first time she saw him, in a restaurant with Deepa while Dilip was wooing her, and his presence again had raised her ire. His eyes tell me everything, she said in her defence.

How right she was.

Those eyes looked unhappily at me as he said, Five years married and we cannot pop out a child.

What do the doctors say?

Believe me, we've tried everything, including some things you don't want to know about. We've been to mundumugos and maalims, and those Asian quacks in Pangani. It's not destined . . . You know, I went to Deepa's shop the other day.

I heard.

She looks happy, eh? Two kids, boy and girl. And you—also a boy and girl. You Indians certainly do it right. You could go on reproducing this way forever—boy, girl, boy, girl—

Yes, and in twenty years we could be a majority in Kenya and there could be an Indian President, as one MP has already warned Parliament . . .

He laughed out loud.

We were sitting at the Ismailia on River Road; from a distance not too far away came the occasional thudding of tear-gas explosions. The customary clamour of River Road was eerily absent or subdued; the single truck grinding its gears up nearby Government Road could only be a military one; perhaps there was a zing or two of rifle bullets. The university students were once again protesting, but this time more vehemently, and the GSU were out in full force to contain them. Apparently, the previous night the police had raided and closed down the performance of a play, purportedly seditious, and detained the playwright, who was also a professor. The students lost no time coming out of their dorms; the GSU were waiting for them. Where we were now, people had moved from the street and sidewalk to stand closer to the doors of the establishments, in case the riot came our way.

I told Njoroge I had met the President, before I realized that he did not know the nature of my recent activities.

So what did you see Mzee Kenyatta for?

My boss Nderi took me to meet him. He told me I was serving the nation well, I couldn't help boasting.

Keep in mind, as they say, you need a long spoon if you sup with the devil.

The devil? You used to worship him once.

Jomo is Moses, Njoroge would say, and he will bring all the cattle home and . . .

We exchanged a long look, the same scene perhaps going through his head as mine: the two of us leaning against the back wall of our house in Nakuru, or sitting on the pavement, Deepa flying on the swing, singing. Happy, innocent Deepa.

He said: I don't know what to believe any longer, Vic. The world's too much beyond our control; we thought we could make a difference to it, we could make Kenya great, make Africa great—and it's all slipped away, the ideals and the hope . . . Look what's happening outside—GSU clubbing down students, one of our best writers detained like a criminal.

He was on his way to Scandinavia for a few months for a training program in land management, and he told me to inquire after his wife, Mary. She has people, but just in case, you know, give her a ring. She will appreciate that.

I said I would call her, touched by the request. I knew that Mary had her own group of friends associated with the Catholic church, which she attended. The two of them lived in a modest government flat in Hurlingham, though they also had a farmhouse near Nyeri. Outside, the city's business seemed to be proceeding but at a slower pace, ears cocked and eyes watchful for possible trouble from the riots. The danger always was that they could spread to include the jobless and poor. We walked up to Government Road, where we stood and observed the scene, our eyes smarting from the tear gas in the air. Diagonally across the street, next to Jivanjee Gardens and alarmingly close to where my father's office was, police trucks and cars were parked and a barrier had been put up, cutting off the university area farther ahead. Two senior GSU officials were hurrying up the road beside the police cars. Njoroge and I exchanged a glance; we both knew the big one. His face was in the papers occasionally, whenever there was a disturbance in the city and the GSU were called; he was former Corporal, now Major Boniface, the Grimm Giant as I've come to think of him—once the terror of Nakuru Africans, now the bane of university students. We had both noticed how people from our past had a strange way of popping up in the present; CI Soames had retired from the police a couple of years before and had departed for England with a well-publicized and rousing ceremonial farewell at the airport. Kihika, once wanted for the Bruce murders, was a District Commissioner in Naivasha.

Give my regards to Deepa, Njoroge said with a sigh as we parted company.

At home my prestige had increased, my wife showing no inhibition in broadcasting that her husband was intimate with the President. Jyare president ne maila, to enu khambu pakaidu. The President put a hand on his shoulder. Like a traditional wife, she never called me by name. My in-laws took to seeking my advice on coming political trends, and on such matters as the loyalty of the army and the health of the President. They had acquired interests in mining semiprecious minerals in both Kenya and Tanzania; there were rumours of gold finds in Tanzania.

The power latent in my new status was brought home to me in the most amazing fashion.

One day a young man, straight from university, it seemed, walked into my father's office bearing a letter from a city official. The letter stated, You are required to hand over your business to the bearer, Mr. Peter Ogwell.

Papa phoned me.

Just like that—he wants to take over the business, Papa said, utterly distraught. Can you believe it? He thinks it's easy to do this business? I will have to train him or what?

It was not unheard of for petty politicians—and some not so petty ones—to force out Asians from their businesses through sheer intimidation. Now my father had become such a target.

Papa had stuck doggedly to his trade; property values, especially in Eastleigh, were finally picking up. It was time to recoup his losses due to the Asian Exodus. Many of his clients were the new African landlords in the area, whose properties he managed. He was well respected.

That same afternoon, from Papa's office, I telephoned Ogwell's patron. We are citizens of this country, I told him, the business is legal, it cannot be simply taken over. By what authority, may I ask?

I could not keep the nervous edge from my voice; you do not normally take on a politician in our country.

The man actually screamed at me: You cannot talk to me like this, you Indian! I will have you deported tomorrow!

Simple blackmail. But I played through my gambit. I replied calmly, I have recourse to the courts of law and the constitution, to defend my father's business and his rights.

Brashly, the man replied, You try it, my friend, you will not even reach a hundred feet near the court—

I said, In that case I will speak to Mzee himself.

There was no answer; I could hear the earpiece humming its high note, but no human sound emerged. Just as suddenly there was utter silence all around me in the office, among the two secretaries, my dad, and Peter Ogwell, the man who had come with the letter. I could hear the hum of traffic on Government Road half a block away. A bus groaned, and in that interim it seemed so close I wondered why a bus was running in the street below. After less than a minute, I think, the party at the other end put the phone down with a click. Peter Ogwell walked away, never to be seen again.

Arré Vic, Papa said, Budhe sé tum aise-hi baat karsakte ho, just like that you can talk to the President?

I don't know, Papa, I replied.

I was left profoundly affected. Can such power reside in one man? Was this the only way to get justice for a minority? Then only the well-positioned among them could gain access to it. And the others? The Africans? If you were connected, through family or communal allegiances, even penniless you were protected and favoured. Otherwise, suspicion and intimidation could make a victim of anyone. Try as a coastal man to open a pub in Nakuru or as a Luo to look for a job in Nyeri. But we Asians were special: we were brown, we were few and frightened and caricatured, and we could be threatened with deportation as aliens even if we had been in the country since the time of Vasco da Gama and before some of the African people had even arrived in the land.

This abhorring of a people, holding them in utter contempt, blaming them for your misfortunes—trying to get rid of them en masse—could and did have other manifestations on our continent. Idi Amin cleansed Uganda of its entire Asian population by deporting them, and many African leaders applauded him. Little did they know what a slippery slope it was from that move toward genocide in Rwanda, and then elsewhere. Now in Nakuru, the place of my childhood, it is the Kikuyu who have become the unwanted exploiter-demons, and on the Internet the MuKenya Patriots vow, if not revenge, then self-defence.

The JQS Tower on Kimathi Street was completed and opened with much fanfare by the President, who called it a credit to our country, an example of the harambee work spirit of its citizens. This skyscraper, said Paul Nderi in his grandiloquent fashion, in his speech following the President's, was proof that Africa was on the march. Few were wise to the fact that the Minister of Transport was part owner of the tower. It was an impressive monument, one more addition to the handsome phalanx of concrete giants that now dwarfed what remained of the squat grey stone structures of the colony that had housed its banks and showpiece library, its one Woolworths and its modest shops, and given the city its elegant tropical character. Among the first occupants of JQS Tower was Mermaid Chemicals of

Dilip and his father, and in a photo opportunity they stood with the President and his ministers.

As I walked back in a thin drizzle from the opening ceremony, on Kenyatta Avenue, outside the Bata shoe store, to my utter surprise I ran into Sophia.

Vittorio, how nice to see you, she said softly.

Cheating is cheating, says Seema, my confessor. Her visits have become more frequent as the days lengthen, and I have even begun to look forward to them.

Is it? I ask her.

Yes—she catches herself, as if a doubt just intruded upon her mind, then says again, Yes. And she adds, Your sister and Njoroge, and you and Sophia—do you think by any chance you used her as a substitute for little Annie?

I quickly reply, I did not stop to think. Annie was not much in my mind in those days. And I don't know if Deepa ever really cheated—

I get a stare that says, Meeting Njoroge in secret was cheating, and I suppose it was. But Deepa couldn't help herself. My whole being lighted up in his presence, Vic, she said to me once, pleading for herself.

TWENTY-SIX

Njoroge stayed six months in Sweden and Norway, the last three of which Mary went to spend with him. We met less frequently after he arrived, and curiously there was less to say to each other. He had taken a leave of absence from his ministry and was assistant to the radical politician J. M. Kariuki, champion of the poor and a critic of the government. I sensed that Njoroge did not think much of my work for Nderi, the nature of which he probably had found out from his own boss and their dissident circle. Occasionally, during mid-morning breaks, I ran into him at the Kenya Coffee House; he would be with people, and he would wave or come over and join me. Usually I went alone there, for some private time out of the office, and perhaps also because I hoped to see him. There remained that bond between us; we would linger with each other over the low coffee tables of that establishment, at times in silence, and when we parted it was always with a feeling, in me at least, of loss, a sense that we seemed to be irrevocably drifting apart. I noticed that he had stopped wearing a tie to work. He was on a mission. Once he boasted, I am researching—I am taking account of the personal worths of all the higher-ups in government, all that they own: land in the villages, houses in the city, ranches in the Rift Valley, shares in industries, hotels, pubs, brothels. But keep that between your ears, it's a secret for now—until we come up with a full exposé. How naïve and earnest he sounded, adding, as he leaned forward hoping to shock me: Do you know, your own boss owns an entire block of Eastleigh, behind Saint Teresa?

And a part of JQS Tower and much else, I said to myself, I wonder when you will find that out . . . Such knowledge as he divulged left me cold. To me the world was what it was, a far from perfect and a tangled manifold. It was not for me to change this world. Moral judgements, therefore, I shied away from, and this became the secret of my success. As an eight-year-old I had seen my beloved Mahesh Uncle take up a moral cause. He desired a different world and ended up abetting the slaughter of my friend Annie and her family and being responsible for much more. I never recovered from the shock of those events, and I don't believe he did either. I therefore prefer my place in the middle, watch events run their course. This is easy, being an Asian, it is my natural place.

Mermaid Chemicals had grown into a major industry, with factories in Mombasa and Nakuru, and the Sharmas no longer needed the little Mermaid Chemists on Government Road; but Deepa said *she* needed a shop of her own and so she attended to it, her own private domain, while Meena Auntie applied her talents to managing the staff at the posh main offices in JQS Tower. The shop on Government Road was where I could stop to have a brotherly chat with Deepa sometimes, taking time off from my work; it was also where, on Saturdays, Njoroge made a habit of quietly dropping by. He and Mary now had a daughter—the result apparently of their stress-free stay in Scandinavia—and he would sometimes, in a bold moment, take them along with him to Deepa's. I don't think Mary knew then of that intense past relationship between her husband and this Indian woman that was beginning to awaken, the bitter, yearning ghost that would soon tie a noose around the two of them.

One day, at Mother's insistence, I spoke to Paul Nderi about Mahesh Uncle, who after four years had still not been granted permission to enter the country as a permanent resident. Paul told me to take my complaint to the Old Man himself. Naturally I was hesitant. How could I take a personal gripe to the President? It was one thing to threaten a bullying small-time politician that I would complain about him to Mzee, but actually to request a personal favour from the Old Man was surely another matter.

Paul scoffed at my reservations: He is our father. If you think your uncle has been treated unfairly, you should tell him. He expects that. Give him a chance to do something for you. He will like that.

I wrote a long and careful letter to Mzee. Your Excellency may not be aware, I wrote, that my family's service to the nation did not begin with me. I informed him that my grandfather had worked on the construction of the railways. I described my uncle's activities, first in India with the Congress during the independence struggle there, and later in Nakuru, supporting the freedom fighters. He had married the daughter of a nationalist lawyer who had defended many Kenyan nationalists in their fight for independence, including some members of the present cabinet. Surely such a man deserved better treatment from the country of his adoption where the rest of his family had deep roots?

Within days I was summoned to the State House, and spent an hour sweating in the VIP reception room. This was my second visit to see the President here, though I had met him at a few public functions by now.

Finally I was escorted to the small annex outside his office, where the bald giant Sam Karimi sat at the little table, with a pad, a pencil, a newspaper, and a phone, his upper body rising up like a tower behind it; Karimi stood up and opened the President's door for me. The door shut behind me and Mzee himself stood up, from a couch at the far end where he had apparently been relaxing with a sheaf of papers. He was in a short-sleeved bush shirt that day, and he shuffled a few small steps in his sandals—his gout often bothered him—breathing heavily with the effort.

How are you, Awaa, I said and went toward him in alarm. There were rumours that he had a heart condition too.

Ndimwega, he replied softly, I am well for an old goat. And you?— you look well too.

He eyed me, put his hand on my arm, pumped it; he had a firm grip this way, though when he shook hands, I had noticed the previous time, it was rather soft. He held my letter in his other hand.

You have a shida, and you have written to me, he said.

Yes, my father—

Is this how you speak to your father, he growled, like this—eti with a letter? Na cheti kama hicho—*Excellencee!* he scorned, brandishing the letter with contempt.

I'm sorry, my father, I was embarrassed. Niliona haya, I said in the Swahili I had learned in Tanzania.

Nyinyi wahindi wenye adabu, kwa kweli, lakini. . . . You Indians are brought up well, but a letter is not the way. But now—sasa—it is done. Go. Tell your uncle to get on the plane and not do foolish things here in Kenya. Look what his friend Double-O has done to our Kenya.

How could one not think of this as sheer munificence—at least for the times and the mores involved? He was like a father, and his faults, his reputed acquisitiveness, his quirks we—those of us who loved him—saw as those belonging to a father and an elder. Yet he had been seen by the colonial government as having directed killers, having inspired and encouraged the butchery of hundreds if not thousands, and there were those who had loved him in the past but now called him a partly senile but ruthless dictator who would stop at nothing—including giving the nod to the assassination of Pio Pinto, a Marxist activist, and of the popular politician Tom Mboya. It was whispered that he was so afraid of losing power that he had resorted to calling for secret oaths of allegiance from his Kikuyu compatriots; busloads of people apparently had been taken to his home in Gatundu to swear allegiance.

But that day it was I who initiated the oath: I promise he will not do anything foolish, I said, and I added, I swear I will always keep your trust, Mzee.

I bowed my head, and he gave me his hand to accept my oath of allegiance.

What drove me to make that strong gesture? It was the power and charisma of the man and my willingness to serve him. I wanted to come closer to him. That moment I was totally under his spell. I fear I could have done anything for him.

Somewhat embarrassed and with apologies, I brought out three photographs of him and a copy of his famous book on the Kikuyu people, which Shobha had asked me to have autographed. He obliged with a laugh, just as Sam Karimi opened the door to escort me out.

So, what gift did you take for our father? asked Nderi a few days later in the office. It's our custom, isn't it yours?

Yes, but—

It had never occurred to me to take a gift for the President. Evidently I had blundered in the matter of a simple protocol. Red-faced, I promised my boss I would send something. But what does one give the Father of the Nation? I hit upon the idea of a diamond-and-gold jewellery set from my in-laws' shop.

My in-laws, businessmen to their nail-tips, wouldn't hear of payment for the exorbitantly expensive set, thus compensating me for the advice they constantly sought from me and my influence in government, which they might use yet. I took the present to the State House, where I asked to see Karimi, who came out and took it from me with a perfunctory nod. A few days later I received a card of thanks, saying, In appreciation for your services, and signed Jomo Kenyatta, which was mounted, framed in gilt, and hung prominently in our living room by my wife.

I have taken you from that . . . that railway office, said Paul contemptuously, to the corridors of power and the sanctum sanctorum of this nation. You should be thankful to me.

I am, I said. What do you want me to do?

Was he expecting a gift?

No, no, no, don't give me diamonds, he scoffed, reading my mind.

You are welcome to go to my in-laws, I said, you know they'll give you a handsome discount for any purchase.

Because they will be shitting in their pants worrying I will have their licences revoked. But I believe I will buy a present for Mrs. Nderi from them, one is overdue, I think. Yes, a present is definitely overdue to the wife . . .

Presents were moving around in Nairobi like offerings, redeeming sins and buying indulgences.

Shobha: You were seen in the company of a white woman downtown.

What do you mean, *I was seen*. I am seen with all kinds of people, that's my job.

You were seen entering the Hotel 680—

Where Paul Nderi the minister was waiting for me—

And you came out *four hours later*! My brother saw you!

As I saw him. Paul was there with me—

Your Paul Nderi gave a lecture this afternoon at the Lumumba Institute, where he was booed again by the students . . . So you feel the need to seek sexual comforts from white prostitutes—

That woman is not a prostitute, I retorted. And very uncharacteristically I muttered a crudity about my wife's sexual reticence, to which she replied very archly another crudity that I would never have believed of her. We never resorted to such language again. And we never touched in bed after that.

No doubt Sophia was a hooker, though of an expensive and exclusive (I flatter myself) variety. She had come to me in the first instance, two years before, as an offer of a bribe, but I didn't know that then. In the months in which we saw each other again, I did pay for many of her expenses. But we had something magical between us, as we had already recognized two years before: we could talk, and we could laugh together. She liked to sing when she took a bath in the hotel room I rented for her, from Italian opera or something utterly frivolous like "Che sera sera" or "Never on Sunday." She told me about herself—her family's small farm in a village outside of Naples, her brothers and sisters, her schooling, her job as hostess with Alitalia, which she had obtained when a bunch of girls from her class had sent their photos to the company offices. She had been taken off the Rome-Nairobi route soon after we broke up, and was now very happy to be back—in Africa, with me. She had liked Boston, where she had flown to in the last year, and Montreal. Her father had fought in Ethiopia with

Mussolini's army, been captured by the British, and become a POW in Kenya, building roads and working on a pyrethrum farm. He had told her many stories of the beautiful wild country where he had spent two years as a prisoner of the British.

More than the sex—which came near the end of our meetings, and was brief but satisfying—there was our friendship. There were entire weeks when I did not see her because her route had suddenly changed; I would receive the odd postcard from her ("But what am I doing in Benghazi?"; "Cape Town—how beautiful but sad.") in my office, to let me know that she had not forgotten me. Then she would reappear. Shobha and I did not talk about this affair following our argument. I was discreet, and my family life remained unchanged.

One weekend afternoon as I was searching through my socks drawer I discovered that the old chocolate box which contained some of my memorabilia had been gone through. There was no photo of Annie inside—that small iron frame with the picture of me and her, play-acting Rama and Sita one Diwali week in the car park of the shopping centre in Nakuru, was missing. In despair I looked everywhere I could think of where I might have placed it, but to no avail. I was certain Shobha had taken it. This was her way of wounding me. She walked in while I was frantically searching, met my eye, pointedly said nothing. How had she known what that photo in the box meant to me, had I inadvertently revealed that? Or had my mother or my sister talked about my childhood hurt and obsession? The thought that I would never look on that face again profoundly saddened me. I was a grown man with a wife and family, whose safety and well-being were my constant concerns; I had a mistress; and yet it seemed to me that the cruelest thing had been done to me in the wilfull removal of that childhood picture from my private box.

I rather liked my wife, and there were moments when I loved her, for her silky, singsong Gujarati voice, and her kind ministrations, and her brilliance. Love takes many forms, and I have confessed to no passion. I don't think she disliked or hated me either; there was an element of condescension perhaps, for the fact that I was a mere middleman, a dalal as she called it, an agent of others. But she believed in the sanctity of the family and the home, which remained a contented one. There were outings with our children Ami and Sita, there were the large extended family gatherings on Sundays, there were the films.

Mahesh Uncle arrived with his family amid much fanfare and emotion. As soon as he came off the steps from the airplane, wearing a white kurta-pyjama, he threw three kisses into the air, in three directions, and went down on his knees and kissed the ground. Airport workers and fellow passengers watched him in amazement, no doubt taking him for an Indian guru. Obviously he had lost none of his dramatic flair. Papa muttered, That is our Mahesh Bhaiya all right. Mahesh Uncle had always kept him on edge, and now here he was again. But Papa had also admitted a few times to missing my uncle. The two families, ours and his in-laws', had been allowed the privilege to stand on the tarmac to watch the arrival. Uncle with his family got on the shuttle bus, which zipped over the short distance and brought them among us. There were shouts and cries of joy. Deepa's two children ran out and put garlands round Uncle and his wife; tears were shed, a shower of rice was thrown, and ladoos were handed out. It was around noon, and the sun was pleasantly hot. It was five years since Mahesh Uncle had left from this same airport, and the years had altered him. He was fat, and his beard had turned partly grey. We shook hands and he gave me a long and large hug. You're a big man now, Vic—I understand you arranged all this within a day? Not quite, I told him. He spoke more slowly than before, his entire manner seemed more composed and deliberate. He was preoccupied with his family.

This visit, however, was not a permanent return. When Mother joyously cabled him that he was now free to return to Kenya, he had sent his reply: Wonderful! But then he wrote a long letter saying that much had changed, and he realized there was little he could do in Kenya now; he was not sure if his children would be able to adjust to another move. They had become Indians. It would be best if he brought his family for a visit first. And here they were, overjoyed but uncertain. The country had changed and not only had Uncle been warned not to get involved with Okello,

Okello himself did not seem to have use for him. There was nobody from Okello's office to greet him at the airport, though there was a face lurking in the background that definitely bore the look of Special Branch.

Mahesh Uncle decided he could not return to live in Kenya. His departure with his family, after a festive and hectic three weeks, during which none of us slept much, was as emotional as the arrival had been. In all those days the two of us never found an intimate moment together. It seemed to me that in the swirl of his domesticity, his sansaar as he called it jocularly, he had found a certain happiness, in which the past had no place.

But once, there was a fleeting, embarrassed exchange of looks between us, when something got uttered at one of those noisy gatherings . . . and it was that past, I figure, unable to resist sending its unhappy signal from its subterranean home.

You see, Paul Nderi derided me when he learned of my uncle's return to India, you people have your feet planted in both countries, and when one place gets too hot for you, you flee to the other.

I felt provoked enough to retort:

Wasn't my uncle denied entry to Kenya even when his wife's family had been in the country eighty years, and didn't he plead for years for a permit? It's rather that "we people," as you call us, don't have a place anywhere, not even where we call home.

This was one of the few times I let my anger get the better of me. But Paul had only mouthed a sentiment common to many of our politicians, that Asians did not really belong, they were inherently disloyal. Such statements we had learned to grin and bear, the occasional but inevitable ill wind.

Hmm, Paul said, taken aback at my outburst. You do make a point, Vikram Lall . . . though I'm not sure it's the same point your Asian brothers would make.

Mahesh Uncle went back to his job as principal of a private school in a hill station outside of Delhi. I never saw him again.

———————————

TWENTY-SEVEN

Mother had visited her homeland India twice since her father's death, and there was little doubt, especially now with Mahesh Uncle's decision not to return permanently to Kenya, that India was calling her, that she was ready to end her African sojourn and return finally home. What kept her in Kenya for the time being were her children, Deepa and I, and our own children. She had already been on a few religious pilgrimages in India, and the mother who had returned to us was one who had come to terms with her growing years. She still looked radiant and fair, still a little fleshy, and she had retained her thick long hair; age had blemished her only by the shadows round her eyes and by the tired look she sometimes carried. The years had not been as kind to Papa, however, who looked more visibly aged, having turned jowly and partly bald. He had kept his business going. He had his nights out at the club, and Mother had her time at the temples and the women's satsang meetings, where she would meet my wife Shobha, who was much in demand as a devotional singer. Our parents slept in separate rooms now. Deepa and I tried to bring them closer, by meeting at their home once a month in a family reunion, and inviting them to our homes. It was more than Mrs. Burton, however, who had pulled them apart; it seemed that Mother had become aware of all of Papa's failings during their years of marriage. This seemed not quite fair, because my sister and I could recall the happy times we had had as a family together, especially in Nakuru, when we were young; and Papa's stories of how she had bewitched him riding her bicycle in the streets of Peshawar, and how he followed her home and ultimately won her from her stern father, Inspector Verma, could charm a smile and a blush from her. He seemed bewildered and a little hurt by her recent manner toward him. See how he drinks, she would say, as Papa would appear with a glass of Scotch from his drinks cupboard, and Deepa would reply, And who has driven him to it? Mother would turn to me in protest.

It was Saturday afternoon after luncheon. Papa came into the living room with his drink and sat down. Mother turned to him and, continuing their discussion of before, said, You go with Vikram, I don't mind. I have no desire to see London, anyway.

I had been asked by Paul Nderi to go to London on business and had offered to take my parents with me. Deepa and I had come over in a bid to convince Mother to change her mind and not act the spoilsport.

Mother, you must! Deepa protested.

Hanh-ji, Papa said, and you can see the best doctors there.

The doctors here are fine, Mother replied.

London had been Papa's Mecca once, and she would have accompanied him there, or anywhere else, in another time. She was due for some medical tests, about which she was acting too nonchalant and secretive, and we were all a little worried. Mother persisted, she did not want to go to London. She wanted to rest and go through with the tests in Nairobi.

Over the last year the political donations, as they were called, brought by Gerald and Jim from whichever organization had sent them, had become irregular and finally they stopped. The account with Narandas Hansraj of Muindi Mbingu Street was closed. In retrospect, the reason seems obvious: the sums I had handled were a mere pinch compared with those now moving more efficiently through other channels. The two Americans had become my friends, however, and I would meet them in the city sometimes. I had even done a small favour once for Gerald and the international school where he worked, helping them to obtain papers for an expatriate teacher. All I had to do was make a phone call. But it seemed evident to me that I was no longer required by Paul Nderi. He seemed distant and worried, and there continued the strong political undercurrents in the country, which, happily, did not involve me. It was no surprise when he asked me to go away on a trip that was more related to the work I had done earlier, in the railways department.

An official from the British High Commission had approached Paul covertly, with a request from the railway authority of Rhodesia, with which country we had no diplomatic relations because its white government was not legal. The Rhodesians, because they had coal in the country, had decided not to dieselize their railways and now were proposing to buy some of our steam locomotives. They wanted a meeting.

Who else but you, Vic, the soul of discretion itself, Paul told me, ending my briefing with him, and when I looked flabbergasted in response, he added, Go to London and meet the Rhodesians, or their agents, and give yourself a holiday with your mistress.

That casual aside was unnerving; it was the first time he had mentioned Sophia. Was I being watched? I never found out.

But go to London I did, accompanied by my father. It was my first visit abroad. Papa had left the country only once before, for India, where he had met and married my mother. But this was his first time on a plane. He was excited as a schoolboy on vacation, and he had come with a list of all the places he wanted to visit, and suggestions and advice from both Deepa and Shobha, who had lived in London. He had bought a black beret to cover his baldness and an army-type jacket for the autumn weather we would meet.

Remember, remember?—he told me on the plane—when those goras in Nakuru, the . . . the . . . our customers . . . they visited England—

The Bruces, Papa, I said gently.

Yes, they visited London and the children sent a postcard—

I remember, Papa.

He had kept the postcard, which had been addressed to me and Deepa, and stuck it next to his table in the grocery shop. I always wondered what happened to it when we closed the shop. Bill had written the card, and Annie had scrawled her message below his. It was curious that Papa had forgotten their name, that they seemed so distant to him.

There was a quiet hint of sadness, though, in Papa's triumph, in this fulfilment of his dream to go to London, for his partner of a long time, his wife, was not with him. But he would not have missed London for the world. As soon as we landed he was taken in hand by the people he knew, friends, relatives, and the clients whose properties he had managed faithfully and sold in their absence, after the sudden Asian Exodus. He had already arranged to stay with a cousin in Greenwich and left me immediately upon our arrival. I did not see him until the last few days of our visit.

I met two white Rhodesians in London, both engineers in their thirties, friendly athletic-looking fellows who seemed to have taken the opportunity for a brief respite from troubles back home. We spoke a lot about our respective countries. They both loved Rhodesia and did not support Ian Smith's unilateral declaration of independence, which had made their country a pariah in the world. As a student in Dar es Salaam, I had had to go along in the loud student demonstrations against both Rhodesia and Britain. But there was an affinity between these two Rhodesians and myself in a way there wasn't between them and the people of their race in England. Our business discussions were at an elementary level. I had been told to sound them out and provide them with a list of locomotives we expected to sell and at what price. The sale would have to be accomplished through a British intermediary. Little did I realize that this dialogue with the two engineers would count as espionage when I returned home.

I spent two of my evenings in the company of a large extended family of in-laws belonging to two of Shobha's uncles, where in traditional manner I was accorded royal treatment and presented with a gold watch and a gold chain. It took some struggle to maintain my independence from their well-meaning but grasping intentions. I also met with old classmates from the Duke of Gloucester School, during a very nostalgic evening that turned emotional and tearful, as the drinks began to have effect. Kenya was in their hearts, they would never become British. And yet, even as this was evident in their nostalgia and their tears, they found it odd, and even an insult to their integrity, that I was still in Kenya, with no plans to leave.

Sophia did not visit me in London. Instead, she instructed me to make the best of my time with my father; I would always remain thankful to her for that consideration. We would meet in Nairobi anyway, though not as freely as London would have afforded. And so my father and I spent our final two days together walking the streets of London, seeing places which once had carried powerful meaning in our lives. This is where the Queen was crowned, he said emotionally, as we stood upon the cold stony floors of Westminster Abbey, and I recalled the holiday when he had stayed glued to the radio, giving us a running commentary on the proceedings of the coronation. He stared wistfully at Big Ben, the statue of Sir Winston Churchill outside Parliament, the guards at Buckingham Palace, Number 10 Downing Street, Scotland Yard. He had arrived on the scene a decade and a half too late; everything we saw seemed almost immaterial now, devoid of the charge it had once carried in a British colony far away and long ago. I felt that if she had known about him, the Queen would surely have granted this man, this admirer for so long, an audience, to discuss with him the passage of time and the end of empire, and how they both had aged. I took a lot of pictures. We did a lot of shopping.

During those two days we spoke intimately in a manner we had never done before, would never do again. Our happiness was complete in this one manner, and yet in another it was a one-winged bird in awkward flight; we both missed Mother, she belonged here with us. We called her in Nairobi and told her we missed her. She was touched and, much to my surprise, told me to take care of my father.

It was Sunday, after dinner, and we had just finished that call. Mother had been alone in Nairobi and Papa and I both felt a little depressed. We were exhausted too from touring the city all day, having changed trains, ridden taxis and double-decker buses, and hiked; it was now time for a quiet drink, a final filial-paternal moment of closeness, before we departed the next day to resume our normal lives. We had been ten days in London. I noticed that Papa had discovered the subtle pleasure of drinking wine during this trip; back home, like most men, he would head straight for the quick knockout punch of hard liquor.

So your business is finished here, he said.

Yes.

Satisfactorily?

Sort of.

There was a long silence between us, during which he attempted a couple of fruitless discussions about nothing important; finally, looking me straight in the face, he spoke his heart.

Listen, Vic . . . About your mother—I want to tell you something. I've not been perfect but I have always loved her and my children. I want you to know that. I have been a fool in some ways, but still—don't forget that.

I know, Papa, you have always loved us.

I recalled him preparing to go out on Home Guard duty in Nakuru in the dead of night, instructing Mother yet one more time what to do in case the Mau Mau attacked and where everything was kept, especially the police whistle and that fateful gun.

I don't know why, but at that moment I told him what I had resolved before never to reveal to my family, had revealed only to one other soul, Njoroge. I told him what I had seen that morning at the sawmill: Mahesh Uncle with that missing gun.

His mouth fell open. Really—he uttered, and he grasped my hand across the table. Slowly he said, Then at that killing, at the—

At the Bruces, Papa.

Yes. The same gun, he whispered, shook his head briefly. And what a scolding that inspector and the judge gave me . . . You must have suffered, keeping that secret, Vic, all bottled up.

And we sat there momentarily, our hands clasped together.

When we reached Nairobi, late in the night, we were met by the family. Deepa embraced Papa and then me, and I hugged my mother. Shobha came and stood beside me; we were not in the habit of hugging. Dilip shook hands all around. Papa went toward Mother, and quite suddenly he took her in his arms and they embraced emotionally.

On the way home with my wife it occurred to me that the whole scene minutes before at the airport had been rather strange, as if it had been staged. After all, Papa and I had been away only ten days. We did not need to be welcomed home by a family retinue. Now on the dark airport road, the streetlamps few and far between, the occasional factory dimly lit and moribund as a graveyard, my wife sat quiet and grim beside me in her car. No news of the home, the children. No questions about London or the flight back. I turned and gave her a long stare. Only then did she break her silence.

About Ma—I have to tell you something.

What about Ma? I asked, my throat suddenly constricting, my voice giving.

She told me that Mother's medical secret was in fact a lump she had discovered on her body a few weeks before. It had been diagnosed malignant in my absence and she would need a mastectomy.

That night Shobha and I became the closest we had been in a long time, as we sat together and talked about assorted subjects, including the options for my mother. She also told me that Paul Nderi had sent word that I should see him first thing in the morning.

It is espionage, all right, said Paul Nderi to me. You know that black Africa is in a de facto war with Rhodesia and South Africa. Our friends the Tanzanians are training guerrillas and there is always a threat of South Africa sending its bombers up north.

But *you* sent me, I said, I was merely following your orders!

That was before the South African papers got wind of the meeting— you must not have been prudent, my friend.

And I thought you were only kicking me down the stairs back to railways.

You cannot be seen in government, Vic. I must disavow you.

Just like that? Sacked, for obeying an order? My ticket was authorized by you! Oletunde himself came and briefed me!

The Old Man wants this; it's for your own good. His orders, specific. And you are not to discuss the matter in public.

And then as I sat lost in hopeless contemplation behind the closed doors of his office, Paul Nderi said to me, So what will you do now?

I don't know—

Join your father—I have a property in Eastleigh you could manage. And I could send you other business too.

I shook my head and wondered if he had despised me all along. His occasional jeer I had thought was simply a mannerism, but I had earned his trust and therefore surely deserved his respect. Rose gave me a smile as I passed her desk on my way out, then abruptly she got up, came around, and gave me a kiss on the cheek. Take it easy, she said, squeezing my hand. Paul Nderi, standing at his doorway, watched me leave.

I received a nod from the giant Sam Karimi and proceeded to enter the office of the President. He was sitting behind his desk, in a brown striped suit, looking rather formal.

My father, he said softly in a rasp, meaning in his own way, My son. How are you keeping? Sit down. Keti kidogo.

I sat and answered appropriately, My father, I have been keeping well . . . having just returned from government business in London.

You liked it—this London?

It is a great city, my father.

A great city, yes—from where they ruled us. I spent many years there, in university. I liked it too, this London.

I had asked for a meeting with him, following my dismissal by Nderi, and had very quickly been granted this audience. There was a query in the blunt, momentary gaze he turned toward me now, with that tiny enigma of a smile located only on the lips. He was not in a good mood.

That was bad business, Lall-jee, he said, talking with our enemies in London. And now they have made it public—

My father, I was ordered—

You were ordered. So you want me to fire one of my ministers for making a blunder. How will that look? Ministers are like wives, they do not get sacked. But you . . .

I did not answer, and he said, waving a hand, Go, Lall-jee. I cannot help you.

Yes, my father, I said, deeply shocked by the abrupt dismissal, its casual cruelty, and prepared to stand up and depart.

Our eyes met, and he seemed to take pity on me; his look softened and he said in that low grainy voice, Remember, sometimes it is better to have sipped the beer than to have eaten your bellyful from the pot. Your place is not in government. Go. And if you have any shida, Lall-jee, come and see me. Any time. Unasikia?

Yes, my father. I have brought this offering from my in-laws, if you will be kind enough to accept it—they are your admirers and have benefited from your wise rule.

It was a jewellery set and he accepted it.

My in-laws the Javeris begged me to join them in their business, but I declined. I would spend my mornings around the house, then visit a few places around town, and return home to play with the children. I took an interest in gardening. Shobha found me an annoyance at home, nagging at me that a man's place was out in the city working. As if I didn't know. Sometimes I went out to meet my parents. I did not know what to do with my life. I debated going overseas, even emigrating. I was depressed. There was nobody I could talk to. My wife assumed I had done something wrong to fall so easily out of favour. Neither Deepa nor Njoroge was in a position to sympathize; they did not know of my secret assignment under Nderi. I had been, simply put, dropped—because I was the convenient scapegoat, the disposable outsider, and my usefulness had run out. It was as well that Sophia had not arrived in town since my return from London, for I would have made poor company. My stutter, which I had developed in childhood and learned to master, was back in force, and the irritant it was I could see on the faces around me. One day after a bitter quarrel with my wife, in which I did not lose the opportunity to accuse her of stealing my private possessions, I called up Jim and asked him if I could hitch a ride with him to Nakuru, where he had told me he was going, when we met a few days before in town.

I left home for the period of a month, an abandonment that my children and wife never forgave. Where I headed was not arbitrary, I knew exactly where I was going. I did not even pause to ask myself, why there. I was heeding a call, from somewhere so deep inside me, I did not understand it.

After treating Jim and Gerald and their girlfriends to drinks and dinner at the Nakuru Club, whose old colonial ambience delighted them, I quietly took a goods train on the Solai branch line the next morning and asked the driver to drop me at Jamieson. Yes, he told me, the old couple, the white woman and the African man, still lived there. He let me ride in his cabin, and as I watched the red earth pass beneath us, and the dense forest up ahead, and the green hills to my right where monkeys frolicked in the tree branches, and the odd gang of half-dressed children who had stopped on the paths to watch us, as the driver hummed "Onward Christian Soldiers" while adjusting his controls, and the engine went clackety-clack on the rails, I told myself how desperately I loved this country that somehow could not quite accept me. Was there really something prohibitively negative in me, and in those like me, with our alien forbidding skins off which the soul of Africa simply slipped away?

The driver blew his whistle, slowed down as we approached the deserted broken-down village, and with a big grin watched me jump down onto a mound of grass and rubble; then the train went along its way.

The old couple had seen the train, waited for it as they sometimes did, and as I stood up, dusted myself and came around the old dilapidated station and down the ridge toward them, they stared at me in stupefaction. They were attired similarly in ragged shorts and shirt; Janice had on a straw hat and looked rather red. I told them who I was, and Mungai nodded his head slowly a couple of times with a look of what I assumed was recognition. He opened his mouth, but said nothing. I told the couple this was not an official visit. I had tired of city life and come to spend a few days in the quiet of their surroundings, if they did not mind.

They stared a moment longer at me, then at the duffel bag in my hand.

Come along then, said Janice and led the way.

We would sit outside at night by the fire, often in silence; the couple would later retire to the inner room and I would stay outside, throwing dried branches into the fire, watching the moon go down behind the trees. The stars and planets shone brilliantly, tracing, I imagined, their wide elliptic orbits in the firmament, itself rotating against the earth. This equilibrium, this rhythm, was called the music of the spheres, I remembered being taught, and was the inspiration behind all the music in the world, and a reflection of the cycles of our lives. Did I perceive cycles in my own life? Yes, in the end of childhood and the onset of the middle years, the birth of children and the aging of parents. Many years later I would look at this same firmament from another part of the world, on cool, clear nights . . . and feel connected to this place. The only disturbance in the night now was the sound of wild dogs fighting over scraps at the dump, a safe distance of a few hundred yards away. I slept on a child's broken-down cot in the veranda, which was in front of the house and enclosed but three-quarters of the way up. I was afraid my first few nights there; as I closed my eyes I comforted myself with the thought that all the animals in the forest were doing the same, except for the wild dogs and the owls. I was woken up every morning by the shrill cry of a kite. And as I peered out at the cool blue slice of morning sky visible outside from where I lay on the cot, I could just discern the pale, white, and now fading sparkles of the stars. There would be the smell of wood burning; the light thump of footsteps on the earth somewhere; the call of the rooster.

I went out hunting with Mungai, a spear in my hand, but the weapon was for form and only rudimentary protection, I did not know how to use it. We came away with a small deer once and a rabbit another time. The former was roasted and the latter went into a stew. But our main diet was ugali or rice, with beans or spinach.

One balmy afternoon after a rainfall, while the three of us were playing cards on the veranda, there came loud trumpeting from behind the
house, not far away, and the sound as if of a hundred warriors stamping
their feet. Janice looked up impatiently and said, Oh those ruddy tembos
again. We all raced to the back of the house.

It seemed that people in a nearby village had cleared some of the
woods in their vicinity to make space for a football field and rally ground.
In the process, they had encroached upon the route of an elephant herd.
The elephants in their confusion had changed their route several times,
sometimes stomping through cultivation. The grey beasts were waiting in
a group at the far end of the couple's plot, as if conferring before beginning their mischief, and the three of us wailed like banshees, beat on ancient four-gallon tin cans and aluminum sufuriyas in order to distract or
dissuade them, but to no avail. Slowly they traipsed into the cornfield, covering its entire area, and trumpeting joyfully—so it seemed—they system-
atically and thoroughly uprooted it, before ambling their slow deliberate
way to find their lost route.

You big devils, muttered Janice tearfully after them, you should try
and work for your dinner sometimes.

The next few days we spent repairing the damage done by the tembos.

Every afternoon I went to the graves in the backyard and watered the
wildflowers growing there.

This is Janice's story, which she told me one day:

One October night after attending a meeting in the local school to plan
the town's Christmas festivities, she had gone for drinks to the home of
some friends, a couple of miles away. Her husband John and their two sons
were at home and asleep. The year was 1950 and she was forty years old.
The two boys were eight and ten. When she returned she was met by three
of the servants who were standing outside the house; they looked frightened, one of them began weeping. Fretfully they took her to the chillingly
quiet aftermath of a bloodbath in her home. It looked like a setting in a
tragic drama before the heroine arrives on the scene and tears out her hair.
Robbers had attacked and killed, and everything of value had been taken
from the house. She did not know if any of the servants had been involved

in the crime, she did not care. There was nothing to go back for to England, and she simply stayed where her husband and her children were buried. This was where she too desired to be buried.

She confessed to the indescribable grief which caused her to be admitted to the Nakuru European Hospital. There were pressures on her to return to England thereafter, more so after the abandonment of the area by the other Europeans during the Mau Mau period, and the closing of the station. She stayed on, a ghost in the house, which slowly began to come apart around her. One day Mungai, a former clerk at the station who had kindly helped her cope with daily routines, brought his things and moved in with her. He too was alone and far from home.

I watched them together, he sitting on the ground like me, she on a three-legged low stool. There was a quiet, gentle intimacy between them, and also a deep difference they did not pretend to bridge. For example, she would apply fork and knife to pick at a sizeable bone, even though her prematurely wrinkled skin, the frazzled, curly hair, and the gnarled hands hardly bespoke daintiness.

What brings you here? they asked. I was betrayed by my father, I said cynically at first. More seriously, I told them I had been deeply impressed by this place when I first saw it. It drew me perhaps because of the tragedy of the murdered children, which touched me in a way I could not consistently explain. It spoke to something deep inside me.

Once a week, on Saturday, the train would pass, going north to Solai and the next afternoon it would return on its way back to Nakuru.

One day, a month after my arrival in Jamieson, Dilip walked up to the backyard where we were sitting after our midday meal. He had come by car, with a companion, through a back route. It was not hard to find me. An inquiry in Nakuru had revealed that I had bagged a ride on the Solai train. Furthermore I had already spoken to him more than once about this mysteriously affecting place.

I said my goodbyes to Janice and Mungai, full of foreboding that one day I was sure to be back.

When I reached home the next day, my wife greeted me with a smile and a cup of tea; my box of memorabilia was on my bed, with the missing picture of Annie and me back inside it.

Thus Shobha declared her truce with me, having been scared witless by the prospect that she had become an abandoned wife or even a widow. Still, she had to tell me, as the chappatis kept coming on my vegetarian plate from the kitchen, where the cook baked them, I smell meat on you— I hope you will not mind if I keep my distance from you for a few days. My children, Ami and Sita, hovered around me all the time. They were now four and three years old and I was moved by their attention to me, their dependence on my own attention and my love. I had never thought of them as insecure or needy; so orderly had been their lives and so complete a control had Shobha on their existence, with the aid of two efficient nannies and an expensive nursery school, that I had sometimes felt myself superfluous to their lives. But it seemed that the uncertainty and acrimony at home after my dismissal by Nderi, followed by my sudden mysterious exit about which their mother had no answer but an anxious look, had considerably unsettled them. They had been unhappy.

In the spirit of Shobha's truce, and to bring the former stability back to my home, and because there were no other options, I agreed to join my in-laws in business. The terms were generous and a new episode in my life began.

———————

The photos are old and brittle, six by four inches; they are yellow and easily curl up; the edges are serrated in the fashion of their time. Their contents are everything I expected. There are four of them, one for each victim. In the first one, Mr. Bruce lies on the ground, where he was shot; one knee is raised. There is a black stain next to him that is most likely blood; it disappears under a sofa. The next picture is of a boy's headless body; he is wearing shorts and shirt, is partly on his side on the floor. There are machete marks on the calves, and perhaps a leg is broken at the shin. The third picture. A girl in her bed, lying sideways, the head separated by an inch from the neck. Both arms raised. The fourth one shows Mrs. Bruce on the kitchen floor, lying face down in a pool of blood; like her husband she had been shot. The children's gutted teddy bear lies on its back in her blood.

They burn reluctantly like old bones, these photos, and they hurt in their burning. They hurt not only at the thought of what happened to those children but also for what remains in me, the stain I cannot erase. I don't have a suitable prayer to utter, at this point, except to murmur, May you be resting in peace, wherever you are, dear friends, I wish you had lived and we could have known each other more—I will always remember you.

With tongs I pick up the ashes from the grill on the porch and put them in a plastic bag; then I walk in the dark to the lake and drop the ashes into the water. I look out across the lake and imagine Deepa there.

I have burnt those pictures, Deepa, I tell her over the phone. Just as Njoroge told me to, when he gave them to me. I gave them a cremation and put the ashes into the lake.

She waits a moment, then says, Good. I'm glad you did that, Bhaiya.

I know she has tears in her eyes; tears for me.

Seema walks in a little later and I tell her I've given the photos a cremation. Her eyes light up and she comes and gives me a tight hug, as if in condolence. Good for you, she says. It's the closest we've come.

She was about to speak as she came in, I realize, before I interrupted her. Now she tells me, There's news on CNN, about Kenya. Joseph called and he's very disturbed.

According to the news, there's been a massacre in Nakuru. A Kikuyu MP has called it genocide and ethnic cleansing, adding, We shall fight with weapons, if necessary.

And on the Internet, the MuKenya group, the Sons of Mau Mau, have declared war on their enemies who are unnamed but could be the government and its supporters in the Rift Valley. No more machetes! says a rallying cry. We have guns! Come to Kenya and fight!

TWENTY-EIGHT

––––––––––––––––

We had spoken about it, occasionally, Sophia and I. She might be posted on another route for a long time and not be able to come to Nairobi; she might meet her ideal man to settle down with somewhere; my wife might give me an ultimatum. Sooner or later our relationship would come to an end, and che sera sera.

One morning Rose Waiyaki called me at home and said that a letter had arrived for me at Paul Nderi's office; there was no sender's name or address on the envelope, but the stamp said South West Africa. I think it is from that woman who sends you postcards from abroad, Rose ventured confidingly.

She was right. Caro Vittorio, Sophia wrote, I am sure you will understand. I have married a businessman from South West Africa whom I met on a flight to Johannesburg . . . Ciao baby and remember me sometimes.

As I finished reading the letter, in a coffeehouse downtown, I began to realize just how attached I had grown to my petite Italian mistress, my own private spark of life and joy in an otherwise apathetic existence.

Ciao, Sophia, I wish we had burned our flame a little brighter and longer; only I lacked that passion to feed it, as you well knew and understood.

The mouse blows kisses as it nibbles away, was the Javeris' modus operandi. You ate and let others eat, was the more widely quoted adage of the day, to which all our city's business people subscribed. Bribes were extorted, offered, paid until they became casual as handshakes. My brother-in-law Chand explained the situation this way, with his businessman's cynical humour and folksy wisdom: Bribes were a form of taxation; before the Europeans arrived, the Africans collected a tax called hongo which you paid if you passed through their area. Missionaries and explorers had all paid hongo in the past, having learned from the Swahili, Ukiwa na udhia, penyeza rupia: when in trouble, offer a dollar. A bribe today was simply hongo tax, payment for services rendered, or for permission to pass on unobstructed to the next stage of your enterprise. Since the government paid so little to its employees, they simply collected their own hongo, calling it "tea money." In most of the countries of the world, he claimed, people were used to paying this surcharge.

I had been appointed the Javeris' facilitator; I could open doors for them that would otherwise remain shut. My influence reached far, for I had been chosen: I had recourse to the fount of all power in the country, I had the ears of the Old Man. For with his abrupt and hurtful dismissal of me had come also a partial benediction, and an offer of lasting friendship.

Consider.

A panic-stricken and terrified Dilip came to my office one Monday morning and said, My head is on the block, Vic. Save me. The past Friday he had received a terse phone call, telling him he was required for a private conference with Mother Dottie in Nyeri, to hear a business proposition. Mother Dottie was like the legendary predator python who, by simply drawing in her evil breath, could suck you in from afar and ingest you within her coils. Mother Dottie's awesome power derived from the fact that she was a favourite of the Old Man; she had perhaps been his mistress in the past. She struck ruthlessly and her victims were all of the vulnerable sort. Now the evil summons had arrived for Dilip. He flew straight to Nyeri the next day, dread in his heart, and was met and driven to Mother Dottie's residence. It had been a country club in British times and included a golf course and tennis courts. Mother Dottie, tall and beautiful, dressed that day in a slit Malay-style dress, had a heavy accent in English. She was a graceful hostess, meeting Dilip in person at the driveway, offering him coffee, and then leaving him in the library with her two male advisors to discuss business. In the midst of the discussions, she sent over a club-style lunch, with beer, more coffee and cheese. What impressed Dilip about the library were two ceiling-high elephant tusks on either side of the antique desk, and bookends and numerous other knick-knacks of carved ivory. Mother Dottie was known as the principal dealer in the country's illegal ivory trade.

There was not much for Dilip to say to the two henchmen, one of whom was a lawyer. They laid before Dilip Mermaid Chemicals' annual reports and particulars of business on file with the National Bank and the Tax Office. They laid before him information regarding his family, who had bribed officials on several occasions, and one of whom (Mahesh Uncle) had collaborated with communist enemies of the state. They laid before him an agreement he should sign, handing over Mermaid Chemicals to Mother Dottie for a nominal sum.

This extortionist procedure was well known in Nairobi and dubbed "sign on the Dottie line."

Dilip immediately refused; then, extremely frightened by the chill that met his answer, he said he would think about the matter. On his way out he saw Mother Dottie from a distance, in the company of a stocky Anglican priest. She waved like a queen, and Dilip bowed in reply and departed almost at a trot.

What can she do? he asked.

Plenty, I answered. Your factories could be closed for any number of reasons.

He stared at me.

Or it could be worse, I added, you can never tell.

Dilip was sitting on a gold mine that was the envy of many. He had licences for beauty products, pain killers, and sleeping tablets; he manufactured antibiotics, which people in Nairobi had acquired a habit of prescribing for themselves. He was expanding into garden and agricultural products. He wanted to hang on to his chemical empire, not sell it at a tenth its value.

Sam Karimi admitted me into the Old Man's office. The President and I greeted each other in our manner and I sat across from his desk and told him my shida, what troubled me. I narrated at length the story of Dilip and Mermaid Chemicals, up to the events of the previous weekend, which had brought me here. While I spoke, he would rub the backs of his hands as if they itched; the jewelled ring he usually wore on his left hand was removed and placed on the desk before him. Arthritis often bothered him. Now and then he would dart a glance in my direction or grunt to acknowledge what I had said.

Ahh! he said finally, when I was finished, and shook his head sympathetically. Then softly, indulgently, he went on, Sio nzuri. This is not good at all. They actually told him to sell them his business, and at a tenth of its value? How greedy people get in our land . . .

I suppressed a smile. It was not as if he was unaware of Mother Dottie's doings. It was just her bad luck that Dilip was my brother-in-law.

He picked up his phone and asked for a line. When he was connected, he spoke to Julius, the lawyer-henchman of Mother Dottie.

Julius, wewe, said Mzee. This, this Mermaid Chemicals . . . she is interested, but why? . . . And you have advised her so? . . . Huna adabu. You have no shame. They are an asset to our country; they export to Uganda, to Tanzania, to Ethiopia. Now what do you have to go and do your ushenzi for and harass them? Call this Muhindi—this Dilip—you tell him you are sorry, it was a mistake. Yes, a mistake. Sasa hivi, mpigie simu, mwambie ni kosa lako tu.

Thus the Old Man. Only he could do that. And I could have bet that Julius was shaking in his dripping wet pinstripe trousers at that very moment.

And what else can I do for you, said Mzee, watching me with benevolent amusement.

Thank you my father, I said, you have been kind and fair. You have given me of your precious time, for which I am immensely grateful. I stood up and presented him with a jewellery box. Please accept this token of friendship from my in-laws.

The goldsmiths, hmm, your in-laws. He smiled, opened the box with mild curiosity and observed for a moment the brilliant necklace and matching earings inside. Yes . . . they give what they value, the shiny things. But it is good. And what token have *you* brought for your father?

If it doesn't sound like an affront, my father, Dilip has requested that you accept a ten percent partnership in Mermaid. Just like the British manufacturers say, By appointment to Her Majesty the Queen, et cetera.

He stared at me craftily, then said, That is good—by appointment. I accept.

In gratitude Dilip offered me also a ten percent partnership in Mermaid.

In contrast to his ilk, the Javeris pre-empted extortionist demands through gifts and politic partnerships. Their duty-free airport shops were owned partly by the redoubtable Mother Dottie and did a brisk dollar business on the side.

My prestige round about town was large though somewhat shadowy. I was the famous facilitator, with access to the powerful and the immeasurably wealthy. I was not in any business for myself, yet I gained a stake in many enterprises that I had helped to make a success. A year and three months after Paul Nderi dismissed me, I was put on the President's New Year's Honours List and was awarded the Order of the Burning Spear (second class). I was touched by the Old Man's gesture. When I went to receive the honour at a State House outdoor function, he gave my shoulder a warm, affectionate squeeze. Mother Dottie, incidentally, received the Order of the Golden Heart, the country's highest honour, at the same time. Paul Nderi, as far as I know, was never publicly honoured.

Shobha exulted in our status as members of the country's elite. She who wrinkled her nose and smelled meat on me if I had consumed even a sliver of turkey on a canapé (and scrupulously avoided me for a day or two while I became cleansed through abstention) could not herself resist a garden party at the American, French, or Saudi embassy, or a dinner-dance courtesy of the Koinanges or Njonjos, all serviced with mounds of beef and other meats and alcohol. She would come elegantly attired in lavish silk saris, winsomely coiffed and laden with gold and diamonds. Her dark, smooth skin was an asset and her silken, melodious manner of speech was seductive. She was considered smart. When someone asked her at a party why she wore foreign clothes, she answered that the men who were present in suits were not in Kenyan dress, nor were the women clad in London and Paris designs.

My wife and I had moved a tolerable distance apart so that the household still functioned. After every carnal—which was her word—party, she would go to temple and beg forgiveness; her donations to the temple funds were generous. Your Bhagwaan seems to forgive readily, I would say. She of course had her own opinions of me. One day our daughter Sita asked her, as a test, what a figure with zero sides was called, and Shobha answered, with a sweet smile, Darling, ask your father, he is one; paradoxically, he is also a man of many sides. She also called me the Thin Man. Whatever I was, she continued to thrive on it.

One day the president of the National Bank called me up and told me overseas aid money had arrived for the drought-stricken northern district of the country, but it was in dollars and the Bank did not have enough shillings in hand to convert them in an emergency. Could I help. Immediately, my brothers-in-law, whom I set to the task, began scouring the shops of Nairobi, Mombasa, Nakuru, and Kisumu, offering dollars for shillings, new currency for old, and the shopkeepers emptied for us their safes and trunks and turned over their mattresses. The required currency was made available in two days. Later the Bank needed to buy back some of the dollars from us. In this way Aladdin Finance Company—now vilified across Africa—was born. I have not denied, when challenged, that our charges to the Bank in such instances have been high; I have argued, in reply, for the morality of the marketplace, adding moreover that our slippery local currency needs large commissions as a buffer to absorb dealers' risks. What I have not revealed, though obvious to anyone with a head, is that with every transaction a certain percentage worth of service charge—in other words, a bribe—was demanded in private by officials and was happily paid.

Money was pouring into the country, liberally sloshing around, benefiting those it touched, and pouring out to private banks and investments overseas. A well-placed, discreet finance company like Aladdin could work miracles for its clients and for itself. The sums I had been handling for Jim and Gerald (the former was now in Dar es Salaam, the latter in Lusaka) were mere loose change in comparison.

Meanwhile, the popular Member of Parliament J. M. Kariuki continued to condemn corruption in the country. As did the students and faculty at the University, but more noisily and in the streets; frequently the GSU would rush up to State House Drive to meet the demonstrations and whack heads and throw bodies into the paddy wagons. The writer Ngugi went into exile, never to return. And rumours began to circulate of that Dissenters' Hotel, the basement torture chambers of Freedom House, right behind JQS Tower, where I had my office.

Says Seema to me: In my estimation, half of that aid money you and your in-laws handled for the Bank went into your pockets—money that could have gone to feed starving children, those poor kids with their bellies distended with kwashiorkor, those little hearts caged inside naked skeletons . . . Her imagination, I tell her, sounding annoyed, has obviously been fed by too many sensational images of poor babies on television. Not that there is no starvation in the world. But does any aid ever wholly reach the poor, without the aid of middlemen? I spare her my brother-in-law Chand's thesis about hongo tax and service charges. But I do ask her, How right is it for the fat people of the world to consume ten times what the poor of the world consume—and then preach to others on morality? And are you sure you know exactly where your retirement funds are invested? Perhaps you own a bit of Aladdin Finance after all, with all its sins. I have offended her; perhaps my manner was brash and contemptuous. I did not intend to draw attention to her stoutness, which in any case is only slight and rather becomes her. She leaves, red in the face, and I am sorry to see her drive off into the night, engine purring, headlights catching the shrubbery across the road before fading away. I return to my own lonely vigil.

I think of Sophia, who succeeded in completely engaging my soul. After she had left me, as I lay awake beside my wife in that loneliness that only couples know—while she lay deep in a sleep that dare not be disturbed—I would dream of Sophia . . . her embraces, her sweet smell, the kisses from her small cherry mouth, the tender Italian endearments. I believe she meant them. I would wish then that I had made more of that relationship; but it was too late, and in any case I was caught in a web of family relationships with their many expectations. It would take years for that web to finally break.

I think Seema and I could make something out of our relationship, take it further—we see each other often enough and she does take care of me, as an Indian woman is wont to do with a single male—but her moral qualms about me stand in the way; and I have kept my distance because I know not how long I will remain here. I call her the next day to apologize for my rudeness; she says it's all right, maybe I had a point. And so we make up.

Deepa calls in the evening. Bhaiya, I'm worried about Joseph, she says. All he speaks of when I call him is the massacre in Nakuru . . . and revenge, and war. He seems totally consumed by these thoughts, Vic. What shall we do?

Leave him alone, Deepa. He's not a child. He's not likely to run off to Nairobi seeking revenge, is he?

But this is exactly what she fears. And she wants desperately, more than anything else, to keep Joseph safe—for Njoroge's sake, who died, and for Mary's sake, who was betrayed.

You know he is headstrong, she says softly, like his father was . . .

The last time Njoroge went with his wife Mary to Deepa's pharmacy, Mary was pregnant again, this time carrying Joseph. Thereafter he went alone, on Saturday around closing time. He would pick out what he needed, the two shop assistants would quietly leave, and then Deepa and Njoroge would be alone.

We held hands, Vic, she said once, but there was nothing more . . . nothing much more.

Much more? Meaning exactly what? This was not a question I could ask my sister, and it did not really matter any more.

I did not know of his visits to Deepa at the time; we rarely saw each other, but we arranged to meet one Sunday afternoon at my parents', when he came to visit my mother.

Mother had had both her breasts removed and the cancer seemed to have been arrested. The disease had brought my parents together once more in a rather touching manner. Once Mother was home, Papa doted on her. He made breakfast for her, returned from work early whenever he could. I know I shouldn't treat her like she's sick, Vic, but I can't help it— I feel I want to be nice to her, share moments with her. Didn't we share some precious moments when you were little, in Nakuru—weren't we in love, Vic, your mother and I?

Of course you were, Papa, it was nice and comforting to watch the two of you, it meant a lot to Deepa and me.

She still desired to return to India, and he had told her he was ready to go with her whenever she was ready; but meanwhile here they were in Nairobi. Mother seemed to have realized that in spite of her past quarrels with Papa, he was what she truly had in her life, and moreover he loved and cared for her.

Njoroge had seen Mother at the hospital after her second operation, but this was his first visit to our home in many years. It was Sunday, tea time. The sight of frail Mother sitting on the straight-backed chair in the living room, strands of greying hair loose on her forehead, overwhelmed him as he arrived, and as he gave her a hug in her chair, he couldn't hold back a sob. She told him: It's *my* job to cry, William.

She used his other name and that made the moment even more intimate. She had made gulab jamun that day, which had been his favourite since our childhood. For some while he sat beside her holding her hand, telling her about his wife and daughter. You should take some gulab jamun for them, she told him, and he said he would. She said she had some Indian medicines that would ease Mary's pregnancy; he smiled.

She seemed gay and detached that day, and not quite among us, as if she now belonged to a different, more fragile existence, a limbo to which Papa had more access than we children. She was still under medication. I longed for her to return to her more normal self, as we had been assured she would by the doctors, who had also told us she had many more years to live. She was still the precious centre of our small family, and Njoroge's presence now beside her seemed appropriate, he had been so much a part of us.

Vic—Njoroge said, as we departed my parents' home and stepped out into the front driveway—Vic, my brother, mind where you tread these days . . . who your friends are. The present regime may not last long, and you may find yourself out on a limb.

I looked at him, surprised. Njoroge's mentor J. M. Kariuki, it was said, was rooting for the succession to the Presidency when the Old Man died, but so were the several others of the Inner Circle. And I had heard nasty exchanges on the subject of Kariuki—who had said famously that ours was a country of ten millionaires and ten million destitutes. It seemed to me that if anyone it was J. M. who should exercise care. He had powerful enemies opposed to his populist ideas regarding the redistribution of wealth. He had mass support, but at the top, he was an isolated man, and marked. I told Njoroge this, and he looked away, his face clouding, as if I were confirming what he already feared.

A cool spring breeze blows in a dark and clear night; a low susurrus of waves fills the background as they roll and ripple onto the shore a hundred yards away under the cliff. And out here on the porch, looking out on the water as I like to do, wrapped in a Kulu shawl that is a present from Seema, I think of the country I have left behind.

A small war ravages the north, Somali shiftas ambushing vehicles and attacking drought-stricken villages; in fact, the entire belt of land from northern Kenya through Sudan and Uganda into Congo cries out in an agony of rape and abduction, war and pillage. An ethnic war, a politically inspired cleansing, threatens the Rift Valley. In Nairobi's South Sea, Muslims and Christians, including perhaps youth from the MuKenya movement, or perhaps simply the idle and unemployed, of whom there are plenty, have gone at each other, burning mosques and churches. AIDS has decimated villages in the Lake Victoria region. Throughout the country rains have failed to come in their usual abundance, for which blight rampant deforestation may be the cause. In the midst of all this I made my millions; tens, hundreds of them. It would appear then that something is wrong with me. But that is too easy a judgement, surely.

I ask, would it have made a difference if I had declined the fortuitous role that happened my way? Surely there would have been another to fill my place. The game of money requires the presence of someone such as me, the neutral facilitator.

Does a bank need be moral? Or a croupier? Or indeed a genie of the fabled lamp, as I sometimes saw myself?

I have said that I could not engage morally in my world. Without actually looking for it, or even desiring it very much, for I am not one of extravagant habits or needs, I found myself on an easy path under the patronage of he who mattered most in our land. My friend Njoroge, on the other hand, had a conscience that engaged; but if anything, his life only proves the quixotic nature of that engagement. Our world functioned according to its own rules that no one—perhaps not even he who mattered most—could control.

Applause. Too long and strenuous a defence, you say. And perhaps you are right. You see, the woman who comes to talk to me in the evenings under the stars, over tea and whisky or wine, has found a way of gently but persistently needling me, probing that cold hard carapace over my heart that I have come to see as my strength.

Perhaps Seema is right in her liberal attitudes; they may be simplistic but contain a germ of Gandhian truth. If enough people cared, she explained to me . . . Cared, and did what, I challenged. She blushed, then said cautiously: Cared and did little things that perhaps could add up?

Do I feel at last the stirrings of a conscience?

TWENTY-NINE

The outspoken J. M. Kariuki, as predicted, was murdered. An unclaimed mutilated body which had lain on the slabs of the city morgue for at least a day was finally confirmed by one of his wives to be that of J. M. It was March 1975.

The previous two days the man who was seen as a saviour of the country's poor, the politician who had become Njoroge's mentor and his friend, had been declared missing, and our newspapers had dutifully reported a planted story that he had been sighted in faraway Lusaka. But we all knew, all Nairobi whispered, that the Old Man's emerging nemesis, the antagonist in the sidelights, had been got to by his enemies. A cloud of foreboding lurked over the country as it awaited news about J. M. The university students were restless, and it became fearsome for motorists from the suburbs to come down State House Drive, where the seething, angry dormitories lurked; army and GSU jeeps prowled the City Centre and the slum areas. The body of the beaten and shot politician meanwhile had been discovered by a Masai herdsman in the Ngong Hills, where it was dumped in the hope perhaps that the hyenas would get to it. It arrived at the morgue badly mutilated; had someone from Kariuki's supporters not checked at the morgue in time, the MP would have been buried anonymously and his disappearance would have remained a mystery. When the news of J. M.'s killing broke, as expected there were riots in the streets and calls for the President to resign.

There was a story going around, which is still repeated in the country to this day, of a secret meeting at the President's home in Gatundu. At the meeting, according to this version, J. M. Kariuki, who had been the Old Man's secretary once, was strongly told off by his former boss and idol for his scandalous speeches against the government; in a fury, the Old Man lashed out at J. M. with the top of his ebony walking cane. The top of the much-celebrated Presidential cane was a carved elephant head with gold trim; it knocked out three of J. M.'s front teeth. As he went reeling to the ground, the President said to those around him, Take care of him. Which is what they did. J. M.'s body, when found, had the front three teeth missing. And, the story concluded, the Old Man's cane now had a telltale dent on the gold trim, where J. M.'s teeth took the hit.

What are you looking for, Lall-jee? the Old Man said to me in his gravelly voice, a twinkle in his eye.

It was only a week since J. M.'s body was found, and I had come to see the President on a mission. I had not seen him in six months. He looked gaunt, his cheeks withdrawn, eyes sunken; his sparse white hair looked woolly and unkempt. There had been a rumour of a heart attack, and a bad fall, and the newspapers were said to have long readied their obituaries, which apparently lay locked away in editors' safes.

I did not believe the story of the President knocking off J. M.'s front teeth in a fury, yet I couldn't help peering at the cane now leaning against the bookshelf next to his desk. The gold band didn't show a blemish from where I sat, the gleaming white ivory tusks of the elephant head curved to their ferocious tips without hitch.

I'm sorry, Excellency . . . I was distracted . . .

He knew well what I was looking at and why. Whenever he called me Lall-jee, I took that as a sign that there was a formal tone to the relationship that day and accordingly called him Excellency, which did not meet with the contempt he had thrown at it before. The President was extremely pre-occupied these days, and this meeting had not been my idea. But, at this precarious time following the Kariuki murder and with the ongoing rumours about his delicate health, I had been sent by a group of Kenya's worried business elite to affirm their undying support of him. As a token of good faith I had come bearing gifts—some local handcrafts, a cheque for a leprosy hospital, and a briefcase full of cash donations. I detested the crudity of that last offering, stacks of hundred-shilling notes, but today I was simply the messenger. He was in any case appreciative.

Sam Karimi nodded at me as I left the President's office, and handed me another briefcase as a gift on behalf of the leader. It contained a large sum of money in Deutschmarks and a signed photo. The Old Man was nothing if not generous; even the humblest village petitioners would leave with something from this father, when granted their group audience. I glanced at Karimi and met his eye as I closed the door of his little anteroom shut behind me. He was a frightening man of few words, and he seemed capable of anything to defend the President, his Mzee.

Karimi turned out to be one of the last people to see J. M. alive; there were witnesses to that, and one of them was J. M.'s disciple Njoroge, who was frightened for his life.

On the Sunday of his disappearance, Kariuki had set up a meeting with Njoroge in the late afternoon at the coffeehouse in the Hilton. J. M. was late, but even before he arrived, there were policemen outside the Hilton, shooing off the parking boys and clearing the area of taxis. Njoroge didn't give much thought to this police activity; it was not unusual and indicated perhaps that some foreign VIP had been put up at the hotel. At around seven p.m., J. M. hurried in to Njoroge's table, looking extremely nervous. The Special Branch had visited him at home that morning, he said. As he looked around to call a waiter, a man appeared at the table and said, Excuse me, J. M., can we talk outside. Njoroge recognized the man as Mathu, the head of the GSU. J. M. got up, excused himself for a few minutes, and walked out with the visitor. Waiting for them at the doorway loomed the silent figure of Sam Karimi. Njoroge knew immediately something serious was up and he followed the three men, all of them in dark suits, J. M. in the middle, as they strode through the hotel lobby and headed toward the street entrance. He kept his distance, and just as he reached the entrance and passed through the glass doors, he saw a blue Peugeot station wagon quickly drive away; J. M., sitting between his two abductors, had leaned forward momentarily to look out the side window. The look of fright on his face was something his young disciple could never have imagined. Njoroge ran to a taxi and told the driver to follow the Peugeot now speeding along Kimathi Street, but the driver, after a look at the policemen hanging around the hotel entrance, refused. The Peugeot disappeared. Njoroge turned to the cops and asked them if they knew where Mathu and Karimi could have taken Kariuki. At first they grinned good-naturedly at him, as if he were a bumbling rustic who had lost his way in Nairobi; then one of them muttered to him to go home if he valued his life, and to keep his mouth shut about what he had seen.

He went home in tears, as the realization gripped his heart that he had seen the last of J. M. Kariuki; that terrified look on J. M.'s beloved face continued to haunt him. The man had been so confident, so fiery and energetic. He would have made a great President. He was a man of the people. But *this* President's men, a gang of thugs, did not wish that a better man than theirs should arise. He recalled the past murders of Tom Mboya, another populist leader, and the socialist, Gama Pinto; the shootings of stubborn Mau Mau generals; the numerous detainees in jail. Anyone who dared challenge Jomo's authority had been dealt with ruthlessly. Now it was J. M. Kariuki's turn. He was gone; his promises to the poor would vanish like vacuous dream clouds; and life in affluent Nairobi would go on as usual, in the well-guarded estates and planned colonies of Ngong and Kileleshwa and Riverside and Muthaiga and Gigiri. The wealthy and powerful desired no changes.

I've never seen him like this, Vic, Deepa said to me in my office.

You're not supposed to see him, Deepa, not like that in private. People are beginning to talk. Mother knows.

He's terrified, Vic.

Her voice soft and pleading. What could I tell her? To give a thought to Mother, who was sick? To her own family—Dilip and the children? He had come to her seeking comfort, shattered by J. M.'s murder and terrified for his own life.

He has a wife, Deepa, I said, you can't take her place.

I am not trying to, Bhaiya. But he needs me, and I will not turn away from him.

She had agreed to meet him at Sanamu, the gallery café where in another stolen moment they had first declared their love long ago. In one of its quiet, partially hidden nooks, under the vacant gazes of tribal sculptures and masks, he told her what he had witnessed at the Hilton. He had lain low for a week in his home, before venturing out again into the city. He had sent his wife and daughter away to Nyeri, for their safety. He was certain he was being watched. As he sat there before her, his shirt was barely tucked in, his eyes were red, he had not shaved.

I should leave the country, go to Tanzania maybe. Come with me, Deep!

She gasped. I can't go, Njo, can't you see? And you can't either. What would you do in Tanzania?

I could go to Sweden from there—seek exile—I know a few people in Sweden and Norway.

He had been the calm voice of reason when she had wanted to run away from home; now it was she who had to talk sense, while he, all his dreams shred to bits, desperately begged her to leave with him. The circumstances were completely different now, both were married, with families.

He knew it was futile, yet he persisted: They'll come after me, Deep, if not today, then tomorrow; I am not safe.

Can't you do something, Vic, she pleaded with me. Talk to Mzee?

And tell him what—Now that you've had J. M. Kariuki snuffed out, could you please leave my friend Njoroge alone, he has seen nothing, knows nothing, and will say nothing about the affair?

Yes, she said tearfully, *yes*! Something like that, can't you do that for Njo? Tumhara bhi jigri-dost hai, Bhaiya!

She shamed me. Of course he was my dear friend; but he had been naïve like his mentor, and obstinate. My influence did not reach into politics. I feared that if I was seen to dabble in matters of no concern to me, I would lose my favoured status and earn the considerable wrath of the Old Man. Still, after my sister had left, I made a nervous phone call to State House and asked to speak to Sam Karimi. What is it? he asked gruffly. I told him that my friend Njoroge wa Thuku had been a friend of J. M. Kariuki but he was also a loyal Kenyan. I knew that because together as boys we had both taken an oath of allegiance to Mzee. He wanted to repledge his loyalty to the President. My friend was very dear to me.

There was a short pause after I had finished what was basically a plea. In effect I had said, as I was sure Karimi understood, that Njoroge had told me what he had witnessed, and he was pledging not to talk. I will tell Mzee, Karimi said, having heard me out. I don't know if he ever did. And if he did, what that meant to the Old Man.

Why don't we meet for coffee, Njo, I said, when he called to thank me for my efforts on his behalf. Deepa had apparently told him about my phone call to State House. A month or so had passed since J. M.'s murder and the turmoil in the country had abated. A parliamentary commission had been set up to investigate the murder. Njoroge felt safe now, he did not think he was being followed anymore, and he would soon go back to work. He was in high spirits. Yes, we should, Vic, he replied, let me call you in a few days. He never called, but he continued to see Deepa at her shop.

Fortunately for Deepa, her in-laws Meena Auntie and Harry Uncle were away on a world trip. But Mother was concerned. She had heard of the rumour about Deepa and "that Kikuyu."

Is it true, Vikram? she asked me.

Mother, Njoroge has been through a difficult time—his friend and guru has been murdered. It's a difficult period for the entire country, you know that. He just finds it comforting to talk to her.

But she is a married woman, Vic.

She is responsible, Mother, let her deal with it. I put my hands on her shoulders, looked into her tired face. Mother, she'll be all right. Everything will be all right.

Hé Rabba, I hope so.

On a Saturday morning, a few weeks after I last spoke with Njo, the *Nation* carried a report that Njoroge wa Thuku, assistant to the late politician, would give the first "Celebrating J. M. Kariuki" lecture organized by the University Students' Union. The lecture would take place the following Tuesday and was titled "The Promise Unfulfilled: J. M.'s Vision for Kenya." The report went on to say that the young man, educated at Alliance and Makerere, was well poised to enter politics himself.

I read this news item, short but boxed inside one of the inner pages, in my office at JQS Tower. The political tenor in the nation had so changed recently that it seemed there had never been a better time to speak out. But I knew, and Njoroge knew, that he was on reprieve from J. M.'s killers.

A little worried, I picked up my phone, called Njoroge's house. The Bwana had just left, the house maid answered; the Bibi—Mary—was in. I said I would ring back in the afternoon for Bwana, and what was she cooking? Chicken, she replied, why don't you come and have some? It was eleven-fifteen.

Njoroge came to Deepa's shop at a little past noon. At half past, the two assistants left by the front door, pulling it shut behind them. Njoroge was wearing a polo neck white sweater, which she had told him she rather liked, and dark grey pants. He sipped from the Coke that had been brought for him; she chided him that the drink would do his toothaches no good, and showed him a new medicated toothpaste. He took her hand gently and she let him.

She felt an intense ache of guilt inside her; her eyes glazed over, withholding tears, holding his eyes. She couldn't pull away from that warm, that rough hand, that look she knew so well and loved, and she knew she must.

Don't take the risk, Njo, she told him, composing herself, referring to his proposed address to the university students. The police and GSU will be there, there could be gunfire—

They dare not touch me now, he said confidently. The public knows how J. M. died, they will not allow any more nondemocratic nonsense from that despot in Gatundu. Changes are afoot, Deep, J. M.'s death will not have been in vain.

This was their private moment away from the eyes of the world; it was impossible to peep into the shop from the outside; and it is not easy for me to invade that privacy now, from here. She said later that they were intimate and close to each other, when hell's gates burst open upon them and two gunmen were suddenly inside. One of them covered her with his gun, wrenching her roughly away by the arm, and the other shot Njoroge at point blank range, once, twice, three times, and the two escaped through the back door to a waiting car.

Deepa screamed, loud and recklessly, missing an angry bullet from the escaping thugs, and people rushed inside.

She was photographed, her mouth open in a long wail of grief, kneeling on the floor of her shop, Njoroge's head on her lap, his white sweater dark with blood, her raised hand dripping with it.

In that scene he was finally hers. But she who had saved him from the clutches of Lieutenant Soames and his police had to deliver him up first to his assassins before she could have him.

One of her shop assistants, it appeared, had failed to ensure that the lock had firmly caught when she pulled the front door behind her while leaving. The murderers, according to the police, had been loitering outside and probably planned to get Njoroge as he departed from the shop, but noticing the door not quite shut, they went inside to do their deed. It was not clear why they decided to escape from the back, where the getaway car had gone on to pick them up. Fortunately for them the back door was also unlocked.

Njoroge's death did not raise the stir that J. M. Kariuki's had; he had not been a people's man, though he could well have become one. The police held one of the shop assistants for a few weeks then released him. The case remains officially unsolved.

I had always realized that Njoroge and I were essentially different; yet we belonged to each other, we had been nurtured in the same soil. We were drawn together when we first met as boys, and later we would seek each other out, with care and affection. I found it painful to talk about him. But he was embedded deep in my life and experiences. Deepa too, after that wail of grief captured so vividly in our papers, expressing so much so openly, did not much speak about him. I recall how he re-entered our lives, when we met him again at the Rendezvous after so many years, and how joyfully Deepa had rushed to him, Njo! Njo! She would blame herself for allowing him to be killed in her presence, and for escaping unscathed herself.

I was used to set him up, Vic, I was bait, she said once.

But it wasn't your fault, Deepa, they would have got him anyway. You barely survived yourself.

You don't know . . . I wish I could explain, Bhaiya.

That last bit of abstraction went past me. Her grief was understandable; but I could never have imagined what painful knowledge kept gnawing at my sister's mind.

———————

Using binoculars I have traced the trajectory of Saturn in the sky for a few hours. One more thing for which I am grateful to this hideaway is that it has brought me in touch with the sky and the earth, and through them, with myself. The moon's reflection now is a shimmering stab wound in the dark water; there is a craft in the water somewhere, its motor emitting a low drone. The neighbours' dog barks. The glass of Scotch in my hand has warmed, and there is a crunch of gravel which in my state I don't quite register until it is too late. Sharp metal, as of a knife point, is pressed hard against the side of my neck. I twist my head foolishly to take a look behind me, and draw a painful stream of blood from my neck.

If I kill you now I would do a service to my country, Joseph says in his deep voice. He is obviously drunk. The thing in his hand is a three-inch penknife.

If you could have read my thoughts just as you came, I reply to him in my mind, you would probably have pushed that penknife right through and into my veins.

He staggers inside to the fridge and picks out a beer, comes out, and announces, in Churchillian tones, We will not fight with pangas this time but with guns . . . we will battle them in Nakuru and (hiccup) Nyeri and (hiccup) Nairobi, for we . . . we are the sons of Mau Mau, the true patriots of the land—

Seema hurries toward us from the side of the house, casting long shadows by the outdoor lamps, and says, Oh there you are.

The two of us help Joseph up and she guides him to her car. She returns to say goodnight as I put a wet cloth on my neck wound.

Are you all right? she asks. He came unannounced, he's so very disturbed by the events in Kenya. He's planning to go back.

He doesn't know it yet, but we killed his father, I announce to her, quietly.

She doesn't comprehend, shakes her head, and leaves.

I return to the silent summer night outside in which to confront once again my past.

THIRTY

Goodbye my father; kwa heri Mzee. You depart like a comet, leave us fumbling mortals to manage as best as we can in the darkness. Those who follow you can never bear your glory and so its brilliance lies shattered in a thousand pieces. But me—you gave me the privilege to share your presence, to call you my father, my father, to experience your enigma and wonder at it. What exactly did you think of me? Once you said to me reproachfully, when I the outsider presumed to offer an opinion on local politics, You think we are simple, but we are as deep and varied as the forest. I often wondered what you meant by "you" and "we." I never saw you angry, yet there were those who said your wrath was profound. You terrified us, but why? You toyed with me, you knew this Muhindi would never belong to your games; yet I know you liked me too, you would never have hurt me. And my friend Njoroge who is dead?—who first taught me to utter your name like a prayer, to sing in your praise, you the Moses of Kenya who would bring home the honey, lead your people to freedom? What secrets did you hide in that forest behind that wistful smile, those deep eyes? Did you know he would die, my father, this worshipper who turned bitter apostate; or did you delegate measures that sealed his fate; or did they simply take matters into their own hands, Karimi and the others, and you looked away? I did not know you as a man, but as a father, a god. And as such I take leave of you.

He lay in state in the banquet hall of the State House, on purple velvet under the great chandelier, in a purple-striped black suit, and socks and sandals, the famous elephant-head cane under his left arm. No sinister tell-tale marks on the gold trim. At his right hand was his fly whisk, the symbol of a great chief. He looked haggard but seemed at peace, that forest that was his mind now quiet forever. I couldn't help a smile, though. Even in death he was enigma and mischief: this was my second visit to see him; the first time, two days before, I had brought some Asian leaders to pay their respects, and I was certain that between the two visits the handkerchief in his breast pocket had been changed, from white to red!

As I was walking on Kimathi Street, having paid my respects to the late President this second time, as I approached JQS Tower, I collided into a rolling, puffing Paul Nderi at the entrance. Lie low, my friend, he growled breathlessly, and not without a certain conspiratorial sense of humour, beware the line of fire as the new regime settles in. He had been among that select group of politicians, the notorious Inner Circle which had schemed and plotted incessantly to restrict the Presidential succession to their own members, or at least to those of whom they approved. Circumstances had beaten them. The old succession law stood, and according to it the leadership of the country had just slipped from their hands. The new President, called the New Man, was of a different tribe and had the support of the army.

But Nderi was influential and he would survive.

I had always been of two minds about him. I liked his wit and his energy. He was smarter than most other politicians. But he was also shamelessly unscrupulous. Mephistopheles-like, he introduced me to the path of power and corruption, and he dropped me when he needed a scapegoat and I was no longer of use. But I had survived, for which he grudgingly respected me. He was now one of my clients.

See you at the funeral ceremonies tomorrow then, he said as we parted.

I am not invited, I replied.

Oh. He gave me a brief look and a thin smile. We understood each other.

The city was full of dignitaries who had arrived from all over the world for the ceremonies. The funeral procession, with pomp and circumstance not before seen in our capital, would leave the State House bearing the flag-draped casket on a gun carriage and proceed to the Parliament grounds, the final resting place of the President, where he would receive tributes and a gun salute. It was a blow to my prestige, and a sign of uncertain times, that I would not be among the dignitaries to witness this farewell ritual as the country and the world watched.

I spent a nervous night at home, worried by Nderi's ominous words. Without my almighty protector, I realized, I was naked, easy picking for any enemy I had casually made on the side. An arrogant word dropped in the past, a business deal declined, the Old Man's favour to me that was a disfavour to another: any of these could turn up to exact a price. As I had discovered once before, I was an easily disposable commodity. I had to take more care than simply duck the line of fire. The next morning I removed some documents together with a large sum of money from my safe and packed them into a trunk; in the evening I boarded the Nakuru-bound train. Shobha and the children had gone to stay for a few days with her parents. I did not journey all the way to Nakuru but got out in Naivasha, where I stayed the night with friends of the family, and in the morning I borrowed a car and drove to Jamieson. It had been five years since my last visit to this dead town, but I knew that Mungai and Janice were still there. After my previous visit, I had sent them packages every Christmas, and once I had helped them with their bank account in Nakuru. This time I spent four days with them, and before I left I asked them to keep my trunk in their safekeeping, it was valuable. They did not ask me what it contained, but they must have guessed. It was pushed under their bed.

Nairobi was calm when I returned. No riots had broken out, no coup had occurred. Our house, however, had been broken into. There were bullet holes in the walls; jewellery and significant amounts of cash, which I had deliberately left lying around, had been taken. Some of my papers had also been removed, but the walk-in safe had not been discovered. I called retired Chief Inspector Harry Soames to complain: what kind of security was his company offering, why had the guards not seen anything, the alarms not gone off, and the police not been called? The former Mau Mau hunter was back in the country as head of a new British security company, SecuriKen. His experience of the country and influence with the police made him a useful asset. Soames told me the break-in looked like an inside job; one of the servants must have been involved, did I want him to come and interrogate them? I said no, and the ensuing silence told us we both understood the situation: there were certain intruders his security guards could not stop. This was as I expected.

I called my wealthiest clients and informed them that I feared I might be targeted by influential parties who were anonymous, and I dropped hints that if anything were to happen to me . . . well, I had secrets, and there were signed documents in the possession of my lawyers that many people might not like to see publicized. I was reassured that I was only imagining my terrors, fearful Asian that I was. I was an important and valued member of the business community and had nothing to be afraid of. The wheels grind on as before—perhaps even a little faster, sio?—for we have a hungry, impatient lot in the new government who've waited long for their turn at the honey pot to come. The hegemony of the Kikuyu is gone, but business is business is still paramount. Would I like to be a member of a delegation that was being struck this moment to visit and pay homage to the New Man? I said I most certainly would, realizing that I was being given the opportunity to establish my status in the new regime. I was told to await instructions, but meanwhile to prepare a briefcase of donations to present to the President, in aid of the lepers of Kenya, the basket weavers of the Rift Valley, or whatever, even the fallen women of Mombasa. This was spoken with such cynicism as to startle me. At least in Mzee's time some niceties of form were observed.

. . .

So many prominent yet nervous Asian businessmen desired to contribute to my briefcase, my membership in the delegation having been amply broadcast, that to accommodate all it had to be filled with notes of twenty-pounds sterling instead of the local currency. The names of the signatories were embossed in gold on a card and highlighted with small but handsome red diamond bullets by a goldsmith in one of my in-laws' workshops. There was no doubt for whom the donation was intended.

The meeting with the President was to be at Nakuru State House on a Sunday. Some twenty of us flew in a single plane the previous night, road journeys considered unsafe because of all the suspicious car accidents involving prominent people that had occurred in the past. Early the next morning, at six a.m., we drove in several cars through the gates of the State House. Unlike the Old Man, the New Man evidently was an early starter.

The grounds were scattered with army personnel. Three tanks stood guard in the distance among the jacaranda trees, their guns trained toward the main gate through which we had entered. A helicopter stood by on a lawn, where tea was being served in silence. As soon as we alighted from the cars, the message went around that we were supposed to wait, and that while we waited we should take care not to make noise. Some of us stood quietly with our teas, exchanging a word or two here and there with caution, others went to stand in awe before the copter.

Suddenly the cool Nakuru morning air was filled with loud choir music, which someone opined was that of Bach, the President being a very religious man.

The nervous tinkle of teacups on saucers ceased in a moment and the President, the Right Honourable Patrick Iba Madola, was amongst us. He went around briskly, grimly shaking hands, accompanied by two bodyguards and followed by a golf trolley that collected all the briefcases of donations.

Mr. Madola was a small man who hailed from the coast. He had a quick, dry handshake and a look to match. He nodded briefly when I introduced myself. We had of course met before, but he did not acknowledge this. The Old Man had patronized me, with a glint of humour in the eye;

this New Man, I realized, would simply tolerate me. He did not smile easily.

There are those who say that if the Old Man showed greed, then those who followed under Patrick Iba Madola took that attribute to its zenith, squeezed the country dry to its rind and core. I rarely met the New Man, which was just as well, for I was too much identified with the old regime. But I came to know well those under his patronage, the perpetually up-wardly mobile businessmen and politicians. I was their banker of choice, the alchemist who could transmute currencies, the genie who could make monies vanish and produce gold out of thin air.

And thus the 1980s wore on.

On the anniversary of Njoroge's death my sister and I would meet in town for a private remembrance of our own. She would have been to temple be-fore that, the same old temple where she had taken Njoroge, where the priest had blessed them jointly as a couple. Once she asked me to drive her there and insisted that I go inside with her. When we came out, dupatta on her head, she proceeded to give shillings to every beggar sitting outside on the sidewalk. We then walked down to the Ismailia on River Road; this modest tea shop had been a special place for the three of us. Ancient Mr. Mithoo still sat behind the cash; the potato pakodas tasted the same as they had for decades; foreign researchers sat in noisy groups with local friends. It was here, at its counter, that her first letter from Njoroge had arrived and been passed on to me.

Thus it was, every year, we would meet at a place that reminded us of him, and we would chat quietly over tea or coffee. This annual ritual of grief was important to her. No one else could belong to it, or even know about it.

One year she brought along photographs, one of which she had ob-tained from Mother. It was a picture of the five of us, Deepa and Njoroge, myself and Annie and Bill, taken outside our store in Nakuru. We reminisced, but carefully; detailed memories were painful.

Now there are only the two of us, she said softly.

Yes, I replied. We survived.

I wonder . . . had Annie lived . . . if you would still be in love with her?

I don't know, Sis. We were young then.

Poor Vic—

Why poor?

Sometimes I wish that you had known real love, complete and passionate love. It's a gift, Bhaiya, to be possessed like that.

But a curse too, Sis, it doesn't come without a price.

But it doesn't have to be that way, does it? You have to take a chance.

As she did, and paid the price, while I chose safety.

What about your love for me, Sis, I said, I always had that?

Yes, Bhaiya, you've always had that. And I've had yours, for which I am grateful.

Ten years after Njoroge's death, Dilip died in a car crash in Germany while speeding on an autobahn in a sports car. He had just reached his forty-fifth year. He had become well known and liked in Nairobi, a fixture at sports and charitable functions, a handsome and gracious rich man always ready with a cheque to donate, and the news of his death was shocking. Among Asians it inevitably raised ugly rumours, pointing accusing fingers at his widow, my sister, recalling the scandalous front-page photograph of Njoroge with his head on her lap after his shooting. That picture had driven Meena Auntie and Harry Uncle out of the country in shame. They went to live in London. Now when grief-stricken Meena Auntie returned for Dilip's funeral ceremony, a wave of communal sympathy greeted her; at meetings of condolence in people's houses, in tragic tones she would roundly condemn "that whore" for her son's death.

Deepa lived in the large family house in Muthaiga with her daughter Alka, their two dogs and a parrot, who sometimes disturbingly broke out in

Dilip's voice, calling out the cricketer's cry: How's that? She was a director of Mermaid Chemicals. Her son Shyam was in America studying, and Alka was soon to follow suit. In Nairobi Deepa couldn't be seen at Asian functions without being made to feel embarrassed. On one occasion, at a qawali concert, she had been spat at.

A few months after Dilip's death came the tenth anniversary of Njoroge's death; Deepa and I agreed to meet at the Sanamu this time. She had already been to the temple, and her driver dropped her off outside the gallery café, where two tourist vans had also just deposited their charges. She was in a white sari that day, wearing dark shades against a brilliant sun, and as I watched her step inside from the cluttered street I was reminded that she was doubly a widow. She joined me where I sat and opened for me a small packet of prasad she had brought from the temple. The granules of sugar powder shooting savage pains into the gums, I sought quick refuge in a sip of bitter black coffee. That made her smile: it was exactly what Njoroge would have done, as she'd told me on another occasion.

It was an awkward moment. I couldn't help wondering if Dilip should not be uppermost in her mind right then; but what did I know of passion—as she had pityingly observed to me, I had never known real love. Today was Njoroge's day. She could recall every detail of it, up to the time he had lain in her lap dying, and she had wept and pleaded, Stay alive, please, Njo, *please*!

It was now ten years almost to the hour since that moment.

There is something you should know, Vic, she broke into my thoughts rather sharply.

Yes, Sis? I turned toward her. She had been on the verge of tears and they started copiously to fall.

Take it easy, Sis. What is it?

There is something you should know, she repeated, in a quavering half-whisper. Help me forget it, Bhaiya, no one else can . . . it's monstrous and it eats into me . . .

I'm here, Sis, tumhara bhaiya ko batao na.

She took out some tissue paper and wiped her eyes; some of the makeup had run and smudged. She looked petite but older in sari, which she had taken to wearing after Dilip's death, to present an appropriately sombre appearance to a keenly watchful Asian public. Her sadness touched me as no one else's could. Still little Deepa, I thought, taking on the world.

She said, That day Njoroge died, when the two men rushed into the shop waving guns . . .

She assured me she had actually checked the front door of her pharmacy after her two assistants had gone, and ensured that it was locked; and she was positive the back door too was locked. It had not been opened since the previous day, when she had locked it herself. But according to police reports at the time both these exits had been inadvertently left unlocked.

You could have been mistaken, I told her.

No. They had keys, Vic, that's how the two killers must have come in the front door, and I heard them unlock the back door when they left! *They had keys, Vic!*

What are you saying—who gave them the keys? Why didn't you tell the police?

A long pause, then in an even voice: Dilip had the spares, Vic.

What are you saying, Deepa? Your husband?—

My husband had the spares, which he gave to them. There was no other way.

It's not possible. There must be another explanation.

No. Remember, the getaway car had gone to wait at the back—the police had no explanation for that. It was all prearranged. I am certain, Vic, the killers obtained the spare keys from Dilip.

But she never let on at home that she knew of her husband's role in the murder. For the sake of her children, and for him whom she had betrayed and made suffer, she kept the knowledge to herself. He had never once been cruel to her, he was the perfect husband. She must have driven him by her indiscretion to seek her lover's murder. She must even consider herself partly responsible for that murder. What point was there now in making a public fuss over the event and seeking further ruination? So she remained the dutiful, loving wife and mother. But the knowledge of his guilt, and hers, was acid in her heart, the pain muffled only by the little joys and the busyness of family life. She thought that he must have guessed that she knew something, that he must glimpse sometimes the fleeting edge of the shadow that suddenly and momentarily darkened her demeanour. Perhaps for that reason he tended to go away frequently on business trips.

But why, Deepa? I asked her. Why murder . . . something so extreme?

To keep his family intact, she said.

I could not imagine Dilip hiring gunmen to commit murder, let alone knowing how to do so in our city, and in secret. The police attitude to the case had always suggested a political assassination. But Njoroge was a minor figure and quickly forgotten in the tumultuous wake of J. M. Kariuki's murder, and the persistent, titillating rumour of our President's possible hand in it. I had gone to see Mzee immediately following that event, somewhat cravenly bearing good wishes from the business community. I managed to see him again only once in the years that followed, this time with some investors from India who needed political backing. He had looked extremely frail and rumours were rife of his impending death. There were even rumours of a plot to assassinate him, so as to snatch the succession. I could not in any case have broached with him the subject of my friend's murder—why would I do that unless I thought he might know something about it? It was unwise to leave such an impression. I recall the sinister Sam Karimi's eyes following me out that last time I left the Old Man's office.

Now, a decade later, I began my own quiet inquiries regarding Njoroge's end. I could do that because I was in good standing with members of the new regime; furthermore, Sam Karimi had been retired. What I learned finally I had to buy at a steep price from a former captain of the Special Branch who was made known to me by my contacts. It turned out that Dilip had actually been approached with a proposition. He was in the habit of playing tennis Thursday evenings at the Muthaiga Club, following which he sat down at the bar for a lemonade. This time a club member from another table walked over and joined him. He was a large, imposing man, none other than Mathu of the GSU. The two other men at the table he had left were Sam Karimi and the captain, now my informant. Mathu put a snapshot before Dilip on the table and said, in effect: Your wife is having an affair with an African, who also happens to be disloyal to the country. This is what we want you to do. Or else the story with revealing photos will be splashed all over the *Daily Nation*. Dilip obliged. The next day the captain collected the keys from Dilip and handed them over to the assassins.

Poor Dilip, I've always thought. Poor all of us; poor children, as Mother once said when Njoroge left us that day in Nakuru, taken away by the two European ladies.

Mother died six months after Dilip. Deepa's widowhood had devastated her. This was not just because of Deepa's loss but also for the shadow that her widowhood cast upon her, the shadow it turned her into. It was Deepa's luck, Mother said to me a few times, it's what was written, the karma your sister brought with her to this world. Mother could not have forgotten, and she saw the look in my eyes to remind her that she had been the most forceful agent of that destiny, the karma that joined Deepa with Dilip. Njoroge died early too, she would end such exchanges, as if to comfort herself with the thought that Deepa could not have avoided tragedy. I came to believe that my mother was ultimately sorry for causing Deepa the unbearable pain that almost took her away from us, the unhappiness from which we all knew my sister never recovered. For by the time Dilip died the world had changed and interracial marriage did not appear as offensive as before. Mother suffered from the last stages of her illness for about three months, during which Papa was always by her side, and my sister and I spent all our free time with her. We had moved Mother's puja objects to a table in her room, and the Indian gods looked upon her from their home in the Himalayas as she lay in bed. I want you to have my Shri Rama, she told me, he always meant something special to you. Shri Rama and Sita, she smiled.

Mother left behind a broken and disoriented Papa, who carried the desperate demeanour, it seemed to me, of a sailor lost at sea without a compass or a destination; thereafter he was a resigned man who would say his innings had run out. He seemed to possess none of his former authority, his endearing certainty, that cockiness with which he had visited Grandfather Verma to ask for his daughter's hand, or asked his own father whether he had had a Masai girlfriend once.

One day Deepa told me that she had received overtures from parties willing to buy her portion of the shares of Mermaid Chemicals and had decided to sell and go to the United States, where she could be close to her children. She had observed a man in the city who, she was sure, was one of the assailants who had come into her shop and shot Njoroge. She was frightened. I encouraged her to go, telling her I would visit her regularly.

I remember one cold midnight bidding her farewell at the airport and thinking, The world as I knew it has now totally ended.

You had nothing to do with the murder, Seema says, why did you blame yourself the other night?

I suppose there is the burden of surviving a friend who died so young . . . and pure.

Before us is that maligned photo of grief-stricken Deepa, Njoroge's head on her blood-soaked lap. His open eyes look up at her, send a chill through me. He had warned me once to be careful of changing political tides; a few weeks later here he was, riddled with bullets, in a scene screaming out with the agony of broken promise.

We have sat through an evening, Seema and I, looking at pictures, discussing memories. Balmy night breezes waft in through the screen door, carrying strains of distant music, laughter from a late party. The time she spends with me, I realize, cuts into her contributions to the cultural life of little Korrenburg.

He had striking eyes, Seema says.

And forehead, which his son inherits from him, I add.

She looks at me thoughtfully, then replies to my silent query, It's a pity you and Joseph never came close.

Like father and son, as Deepa hoped? I would like to sound hard and cynical, but fail, I think, as I go on to explain, No . . . too much history, too much of the past stood between us.

I recall the morning last August when he left to begin his studies in Toronto. Seema, who was to drive him there, was in her car. As we shook hands at the door, I reminded him to call on me for anything he might need. Remember, I said, you are like a son to me and—

I saw him recoil momentarily, felt his hand go tense. We nodded our goodbyes to each other.

I was deeply humiliated at this instinctive rejection. I had believed I deserved to be acknowledged as a concerned adult, a friend of his father, and therefore a father. You should have known better, I chided myself as I closed the door. You are still an Asian.

Quite suddenly I desperately need this woman who is my friend, not just to talk to, but to be close to, to be one with. I beseech Seema with my eyes—perhaps I am drunk—and I take her hand as she gets up to leave and I hold it. I pull her back down. She stays the night.

THIRTY-ONE

―――――――――――

The days are long and warm; the air fragrant with the smell of grass and leaves and earth, the squirrels seem tireless, the birds are clamorous every morning, and spring bulbs in cheerful bright artificial rows have put their gaudy but no less authentic signatures on the season. It's the heavenly, joyful spring and summer that lull you, Seema told me once—explaining herself, her immigrant life—that keep you here until you are suddenly trapped by the winter months and anxiously await the next spring and summer—which have never failed so far, let me tell you; and so the years pass and before you know it you've lived here decades and unwillingly, unwittingly, belong.

Belong, I echoed her word and asked myself, Can I too learn to belong here?

But now the night is still and we sit this side of the screen door, this side of the dark, over a bottle of wine, listening to the murmur of the waves on the lake, the rustling of the new leaves on the trees, contemplating the future.

She sits with me on the long settee, my confessor, leaning back at the other end, her two small feet on my thighs, as if to ensure I stay put. She has on a shalwar-kameez in soft warm colours, her perfume is nice, and she has a ring on one of her middle toes. I never paid attention to these little details about her before.

Do I belong here—in this wonderful country where the seasons are orderly, days go past smoothly one after another? This cold moderation should after all be conducive to my dispassion? No. I feel strongly the stir of the forest inside me; I hear the call of the red earth, and the silent plains of the Rift Valley through which runs the railway that my people built, and the bustle of River Road; I long for the harsh, familiar caress of the hot sun.

I feel the press of her feet upon me, sense the deep gaze from that soft round Indian face gauging my thoughts. She says, You've gone away, haven't you, Vikram Lall. You are truly a cold man.

I'm sorry. It's time for me to face my accusers, I tell her.

She pauses to gather this in, then says: And get your name off the List of Shame?

I'm not sure if she's being sarcastic.

That List of Shame has long intrigued her. It does sound so dramatically damning. It counts me the most corrupt man in our country, itself ranked one of the most corrupt nations in the world. What does that make of me? During the first months of our knowing each other, this stigma stood like a wall between us. Aided by Joseph and the raucous headlines of the Nairobi papers, she made me into an evil genius, but then quickly and with touching honesty revised that judgement. I am actually quite the simpleton. I long believed that mine were crimes of circumstance, of finding oneself in a situation and simply going along with the way of the world. I've convinced myself now that this excuse is not good enough; as she put it so graphically and forcefully, That's what many of the killers in Rwanda would also say. Thank your stars you did not find yourself there during the genocide, going along, as you say. But I would never kill, I objected, to which: There are different ways of killing, Mr. Lall.

I did not have the heart to risk a quarrel; but then perhaps I had no quarrel to pick. I recalled Kihika, how uncompromising I was in my judgement of him, as a young man. Now Joseph was my judge.

The Gemstone Scandal, now synonymous with me and my activities, was what put me on that shaming list. But that arrangement of business deals was not even my idea. It simply fell into place like a fortuitous hand at poker. All we had to do, my partners and I, was to pick up the cards and play.

One day a man came to visit my brother-in-law Chand, at the Javeris' retail shop on Kenyatta Avenue, bringing with him a number of items, beginning with a sample of earth in a metal box. Jewellers entertain a lot of mysterious business propositions, very few of which pan out. The visitor, made comfortable in the confines of Chand's inner office, threw his soil sample into a strainer and poured upon it a solvent, apparently a new product from America; he let the liquid drain away into a bowl. Chand saw in the glistening wet residue in the strainer a generous sprinkling of blue gems. Tanzanite, the man pronounced drily, an expert stating the evident. Tanzanite was the recently discovered rock much touted as the gem of the future. Chand, no fool in the matter of precious stones, knew that the gem turned blue only after heat treatment. The visitor's dramatic demonstration was obviously a con. The man claimed to offer a small but lucrative Tanzanite mine for private sale on behalf of some unnamed local bigwig. A meeting was held of the Javeri brothers and myself; we were all of one mind: Let's get hold of the mine; dud or not, it will come in handy one day.

So it did. For the government of Patrick Madola had a scheme in which it offered handsome commissions to exporters for selling local commodities abroad and bringing into the country precious foreign exchange. Solomon Mines, our new company, began exporting nonexistent or worthless gems at high prices from its little mine in Tsavo to its subsidiary in London, earning immense sums in commissions in foreign currency. What Solomon paid to itself were worthless equities inflated in value. The pounds sterling won as commissions from our government were deposited in British and Swiss banks on behalf of some of our elites, into their secret accounts, garnering further commissions for us; the local currencies so collected were sold to the National Bank at premium during cash-flow crises. Needless to say, transfers of funds were handled by our affiliate, Aladdin Finance. But in a country such as ours, such large profits, the manufacture of money out of thin air and paper, as it were, plus a bogus mine, do not go unnoticed. Agents of powerful interests haunt the corridors of commerce and banking, feelers out for the smell of success, for rich veins to bleed and possess. Solomon Mines duly attracted its share of well-placed partners. The scam operated for a period of three years. It came to be called the Gemstone Scandal.

But my financial involvements were varied and many; they were a game that offered me comfort, prestige, and the friendship of the powerful. They made my name legend outside the country. Consider. One day a man walks into my office offering gold and diamonds for sale, cheaply, on behalf of a company in Uganda that is obviously a front. The payment is to be deposited into the account of another front company, in Europe; I also have to facilitate the arrival of certain metal goods in Mombasa port and their transportation in covered trucks back to Uganda, from where presumably they will go on farther north or west, where the civil wars are fought. Nothing could be easier to arrange. Another day brings a hand-delivered letter from a deposed general or his son or one of his wives. There have been dozens of coups d'état in Africa. Every coup releases its share of unwanted flotsam—generals, prime ministers, presidents, politicians, widows, orphans, with stashed-away millions and uncollected kickbacks that need the assistance of a finance company such as Aladdin to see them safely to their new homes.

This chummy bazaar of the discreet telephone call and the party circuit came under stress when the Cold War ended, and along with it the threat of international communism; countries of the West which had supplied aid and loans aplenty, turning a blind eye to abuses, now demanded accountability from the government; the press discovered its guts. The Gemstone Scandal became public knowledge and a symbol of corruption; its audacity provoked outrage. Consequently, when my name became reviled as the Fu Manchu of corruption and the King of Shylocks (our newspapers, under the thumb of the government or otherwise, have always been creative), my life seemed, at least in the initial months, cheap to all those I had offended or in whose way I stood.

Two days after the story of my degeneracy broke, while I was at dinner with my wife, a phone call arrived from Harry Soames, warning me that a midnight raid had been planned on my home. I had promised Soames a large sum of money for just such a timely warning. My son Ami and daughter Sita were out partying with friends and I prayed they would take their time returning. We turned off the lights in our home and waited, the children uppermost in our minds. Ami was twenty and attended a local college; Sita was finishing high school. At eleven the phone lines went dead; my wife and I headed for our closet, behind which lay the walk-in safe which had been a present from my in-laws. We did not go immediately into the safe, for it was a cramped space, but sat down on the floor beside the open closet door and waited. At one a.m. Shobha tugged at my hand; I woke up to hear violent commotion outside the house, at the front door and windows. We quickly entered the closet, then the safe, and closed both doors behind us.

The next hour was a punishment from hell. The safe was shallow, with two tiny air passages, and in our enclosure we gasped painfully like two large fish trapped in a small tank. To make matters worse, Shobha and I had not been so physically close for a very long time. We sat down, and our bodies touched. We heard the front door crash open, one of the bedroom windows too, then the sound of booted footsteps and threatening roars and shouts. The attackers seemed frustrated; furniture and objects were thrown around, and in a final angry fit a couple of machine guns were let off randomly, in all directions, two bullets tearing into the wood and metal of the door that enclosed us. Shobha wet herself and worse, and in that intense humiliation I saw tears of frustration coming down the cheeks of my very proud wife.

The next morning I invited reporters to take a look at the unlawful attack and destruction of my property. I told them that if required I would be happy to come clean about my business dealings, and that my papers were in the keeping of my lawyer Mr. Sohrabji, who would know what to do with them if my life was threatened.

The President made a speech that very day, while on a visit upcountry, in which he reminded the public that we lived in a democracy and vigilante attacks on private individuals would not be tolerated. He invited the Attorney General's office to lay charges against Mr. Lall if it had a case, which of course it couldn't without implicating members of the government. I was safe, for the time being. But Shobha had had enough, she departed for the safety of England with our two children.

———————

And why didn't you go with them? Seema asks.

After our experience in the closet, we could not even face each other without turning away in embarrassment. In my presence, Shobha seemed always out of breath, as if reliving the torment of the closet. Obviously, according to the unspoken rules of our household, I had not provided sufficient protection for my family. We thought at this point that a legal separation was a good idea. I didn't want to leave the country, in any case. I had business to attend to. I didn't believe I was any more guilty than a hundred others, and I was certainly less guilty than many I could name. Perhaps there would be a general amnesty, as was widely rumoured, allowing businessmen and politicians to come clean and start afresh under a new and strict code of ethics. What would I do in England or North America?

With your money? Plenty, Seema says. What made you leave, finally?

I give this one a long thought. I would like to say that Njoroge came to me in a dream and said, Vic, I'll give you a new oath of allegiance . . . let's go back and start all over again . . . And reluctantly I pushed myself off the wall on which I was leaning and followed him to the woods behind our house . . . I would like to mention the letter I received one day from a girl called Happy in Kampala. Dear Mr. Vikram Lall, she said, I have heard you are a big charitable man in Kenya . . . Her village had been raided by rebels in northern Uganda, her entire family had been killed except herself and her little brother; she was raped and abducted by the rebels; she was taught to fight her own people and became mistress of a commander. She was now in Kampala and needed money to pay her fees at a convent school. There was a letter from a principal and a transcript showing very good grades. I sent money, of course, I have always given to charity. I would like to say this was my transformation, my redemption, this terrible knowledge that I had been party to supplying guns to that area where Happy's village was attacked.

But no. I left for neither of those reasons. I saw not light but the darkness of plain fear.

I left because I was afraid. Representatives of the donor countries, who underwrite social programs in our part of Africa, and of the World Bank, came to Nairobi, having frozen all aid and loan instalments, and demanded an immediate account of the hundreds of millions of dollars that had disappeared from the national kitty. The government set up the independent Anti-Corruption Commission to satisfy the Donors and the Bank, and the Commission published its List of Shame; Vikram Lall's name was first. I was invited to testify about my questionable business dealings, in particular the Gemstone Scandal. But if Vikram Lall spoke, as everybody knew, a lot of prominent people would get skewered. I possessed information that could help indict a platoon of politicians and a hive of senior bureaucrats. The country, goaded on by the newspapers and the government's opponents, held its breath: would I come forward? Meanwhile hitmen, I was warned, had been paid for my blood. And so Vikram Lall absconded for this town on Lake Ontario where he had earlier invested in a property.

I look at Seema, this new lover who understands my race, my needs, my loneliness, but not my career. There can be no reconciling between her idealism and my sins; her home here in a zone of temperance, and mine far away in the tropics.

There is no choice but to return to Nairobi and meet my destiny. Papa is alone there; and Joseph, I have learned, was arrested in Nairobi as soon as he arrived there on his foolhardy venture.

PART 4

Homecoming

THIRTY-TWO

Mr. Lall, a man says as I come down the stairs into the arrivals lounge, and I get the fright of my life. My passport says Victor De Souza, and it is as such that I expected to be addressed. He nods as I look up and says, Everything is taken care of, and bids me to follow him. A slight-figured man in the careless khaki attire of a low-level bureaucrat, he leads me past the grimly intimidating, high-pedestalled immigration wickets, then down the stairs, past the carousels and the chaotic customs counters. If this man knows who I am, who else does too, and what is my life expectancy this precise moment? But nothing happens. Papa is waiting for me in the reception hall; he has been chatting with a large Somali woman and looks up with a wan smile as I arrive. He has on a red sweater over black pants, a black beret. My son, he says to the woman. We quietly embrace and quickly head for the car park outside.

There is something immeasurably familiar in the feel of the cool Nairobi night that tells you you are home, that for better or worse, this is where you belong.

As we drive away from the airport, Papa keeps nervously looking behind in the car mirror, in case we are being followed. The road into the city is for the most part dark and deserted; the factory names we pass seem oddly cheerful; the police car by the lonely, barely lit gas station promises either comfort or menace. A haze hangs in the air, vestige of a prior rainfall.

It's taken me a while to adjust to where I am, but finally I turn and ask my father, How did that man know me by name?—he called me Mr. Lall.

Papa replies, I gave the game away a little bit, Vic, I introduced myself as Mr. Lall, and he guessed the rest. He was paid well, let's hope he keeps quiet.

I had asked Seema to make a carefully worded phone call to Papa, with my travel plans and assumed name, and he had done the rest, arranged for my rush processing at the airport.

We agree that I should not stay with him in his apartment. It is where I would be expected to go.

Papa, you should act as if I am not here, I tell him. You've not seen me. In fact, you should go on holiday to Mombasa for a few days, until I have my business sorted out. This way you will not be bothered.

He agrees, too quickly.

All right. But bété, Vic, be careful. Why did you return anyway? It's completely foolhardy—

I would like to secure the release of Njoroge's son, Papa. And I have plans to speak to the Anti-Corruption Commission and make my peace with them. Everything will work out. I promise.

He eyes me, doesn't say a word. His look reminds me there are those who would have me silenced first. I have come here hoping to convince them that I pose no threat to them. They are people I know well, we have eaten and drunk together. One of them is Paul Nderi, the former minister, my old boss.

Papa takes me to the New Stanley, where I have no problem finding a room. I cannot stay here for long, though; the man at the airport will no doubt be seeking bids for his information, even now. Papa and I sit down at the lounge and exchange bits of family news.

He looks small and dark, elfin in a manner I had almost forgotten, though it's been only a little over a year since I last saw him. My recent memories of him have been of a much younger and fuller man, when

Mother was alive. He smiles as I watch him rub his bald pate, brush the sparse hair on the edges, dart curious eyes around the room where we are served our coffee. He asks for cognac with his.

There was a time when we couldn't lay a step inside this place, he says to me. We would stand outside and watch the Europeans carousing.

I remember . . . and are you well, Papa, have you had the checkups we agreed on before I left?

I am fine. You just make sure you look after yourself. I don't know what's come over you, Vic, but you should promise me one thing—

What?

That you will leave the country if things get too hot.

I promise.

Deepa is well, I report, I spoke to her on the phone before I left. Shyam will soon finish his residency in Rochester, and Alka is studying journalism at Columbia University in New York. Deepa will go wherever Shyam finds a job, at least for now.

I don't tell him that she cried over the phone when I said my goodbye.

He asks, You did not get a chance to meet Shobha and your kids?

No, I do not think she wants to see me. We are getting a divorce, Papa.

He nods. Sohrabji told me. She's demanding equal share in the wealth—a goldsmith's daughter after all, and pukka Gujarati on top.

Vintage Papa, in his prejudices, he beams back at me.

I have to speak to Sohrabji, Papa. And Papa—all the wealth, the money I have made over the years, I am going to give it up—most of it— part to the Commission and part to a foundation. I will start anew. I will come clean on the Gemstone Scandal. That should satisfy them and the Donors and the World Bank.

He's turned quiet, thoughtful; I sense him taking his time, choosing his words. Then: I hope so, son. What's wealth, so much of it, anyway? You know I've started going to temple—but occasionally, just to come to terms with myself; and to remember your mother . . .

He breaks off into thought again, then adds wistfully, You know, Vic . . . if we had kept British citizenship after independence, and gone to England, we might all be together in one place, she might even be alive.

There's no guarantee of that, Papa. We stayed because this is our country. And Mother would have gone to India, not England—you know that.

He nods. But it's hard, he says. You don't know what troubles we've faced here in the last year. Water shortages, power outages, robberies. We would get up at midnight just to collect water for cooking and drinking and to wash ourselves. Nairobi!—it used to be the jewel of Africa. This is a city now where even to take a walk is hazardous.

We embrace, and he leaves, promising to call me as soon as he's reached home safely.

––––––––––––––

The next morning I sit down for breakfast on the patio under a canopy and immediately realize my folly, for during my dealings in this part of the city hundreds of people have come to know me by face and name. A few startled looks go past me, where I sit close to a potted acacia—there is the manager of Land Rover, and a clerk from Barclays, and even the vendor of newspapers on the sidewalk eyes me familiarly. What made me think I had been gone a very long time? It will be perhaps only minutes before the Special Branch drive up. I hand in my keys at reception and step outside, walk over to Kimathi Street where Papa said he would park the car which he has hired from a friendly mechanic. It is an old Fiat in a somewhat dubious condition, but I nevertheless head in it for the Limuru road and the long drive north out of Nairobi.

The road along the escarpment edging the Rift Valley was constructed by Italian prisoners of the Second World War, one of whom was Sophia's father. There is a lookout point on the way, an unpaved siding upon which stands a small grey stone church that the POWs built. I have passed this solitary church on numerous occasions but never stepped inside it. I decide to do so this time. I enter an empty room; there is no place to sit, the air is hot and dusty and the floor gritty with the red clay soil that's blown in from outside. But there is a Madonna with child, made of limestone, on a pedestal up front and I stand before it a moment. I recall what Papa said last night, about coming to terms with oneself. In place of a Hindu murti, a Catholic one will do, I presume, and stare at it. Sophia comes to mind; she too must have stopped by here some time, this place where her father had worshipped and which perhaps he had even helped to build; few and far between but warm and precious moments of joy, that had been my Sophia from a far-off land. Annie, too, I recall, the little girl who in some inexplicably innocent way stole my heart when I was only eight, and the gentle Yasmin of Dar es Salaam, waiting for me, her books in her arm. Deepa comes to mind, and Njoroge; and even Bill, perhaps we had misunderstood him completely.

It is cool and drizzling outside, a mist overhangs the valley, covering a good portion of Mount Longonot in the distance. This is Kikuyu country historically, neat and ordered little vegetable farms fringe the highway; here and there produce has been laid out for sale. A young vendor waves sheepskins at passing cars, another holds up brown bags of peaches. We used to buy plums and peaches from roadside youth when we came to the escarpment for drives with Mother and Papa, and we always wondered what anyone would do with sheepskins. From the flask which Papa had placed in the car I pour myself some tea. A Masai youth comes by and gives me the traditional handshake, checks the time on his watch against mine, and asks me, for curiosity, what is my line of business. I was a railway inspector once, I tell him. My grandfather built this railway that descends into the Rift Valley . . . He looks at me in disbelief.

For lunch I stop over at Nakuru's Bombay Sweet Mart, where the world's best kulfi was made, or so I believed as a child. The street outside is cluttered with idle youth, giving it the feel of a wild-west town at high noon, waiting to erupt. Actually, many of the young men have emigrated from the outskirts, following the recent ethnic strife, and I understand there to be many guns in town awaiting use. The Nakuru Club is right across the street, behind the brick wall topped with multicoloured broken glass, and my membership there is still valid, but it is vegetarian fare and anonymity at Bombay Sweets that I crave.

I speak to Sohrabji, my lawyer, over the cell and he is relieved to hear from me. How nice to hear your voice, Vic, you should at least have had lunch with me and my wife before you left town, he says, in his honeyed manner, knowing full well that it would have been impossibly risky. A brilliant lawyer, he has represented politicians and businessmen of all stripes; he came to teach law in Dar es Salaam when I was a student there, though I did not get to know him well. Once he and his wife had invited all the Kenyan students at the university to a garden party in their home. Even then his resemblance to Gandhi was remarkable; it has only increased with age. We talk business and I tell him about my plans to propose a deal to the Anti-Corruption Commission.

It may not be easy, Vikram, he says. There are people who see you as a wedge they can use to topple the government. But I'll do my best for you, I have my contacts. This very moment I'm going to start the ball rolling in that direction.

With Sohrabji that could mean in a week, or a month, and I can only hope for the best.

Sohrabji, I ask him before hanging up, can you find a safe place for me to stay in Nairobi, meanwhile?

He chuckles. Vic, currently the only place safe enough for you would be in Eastleigh, in Somali Town!

Three young men have surrounded my car as I approach, giving me the tacit understanding that they have stood guard over it for me. Which could well be true. I give them twenty bob each and depart this town that once cradled me and now seems to be crawling with menace.

The road north to Jamieson, where I am headed, is full of rain-filled potholes and slippery with mud, and the drive in the old Fiat is slow torture. Three matatu-taxis filled to capacity, horns blaring music, almost push me off the road into the bushes as they pass me, though to see so many people on the road is also pleasing. Finally at around four o'clock, after some difficulty I see the turning that I seek and enter a forest road that is barely more than a walking trail. A couple of miles from Jamieson my way is blocked by a large fallen tree, and so I lock up the car and walk to the village. The old dilapidated house behind the defunct railway station still stands, and Mungai and Janice are both alive and look well and are delighted to see me. I have come unannounced. I last saw them years ago here, and once after that Janice had come to Nairobi to meet a visiting nephew from England and I had put her up in a hotel. They are both greyer and shrunken, but knotty and still nimble on their feet. Mungai comes with me to clear the offending tree, which we accomplish with machetes and the help of two boys, and I bring the car into the village.

It is not simply to hide for a few days that I have come but also to collect the little trunk I left here a long time ago when the Old Man died and the New Man took over and I feared for my safety. I ask the couple if they still have it and they say, with much alacrity, Of course we have it, and give meaningful looks at each other. Do you want it now? I'll take it when I leave, I reply. They must have known that they had in their keeping a very large sum of money. On my previous visit I asked them if they wanted their dwelling rebuilt; the only convenience they had in their home was a stained seat toilet over a pit; everything else had been makeshift and broken, and was much more so now. They had declined, but now they tell me they wouldn't mind moving to a small town, like Nakuru, closer to conveniences, though they are fearful of the dangers that might lurk there, especially for old people. I tell them it would not be a bad idea to move to Nakuru, better still Nairobi, and live in a well-guarded, secure apartment complex.

For dinner there is only peasant fare, ugali and spinach; there is plenty of tea and, later, a modest round of whisky. I had wondered on the previous occasion where the money for the whisky came from, before concluding that obviously Janice must have some money in the post office, insurance she collected after the death of her husband. The three graves at the back are still well tended, in the full shade of a tree that has matured over the years. If she wants to move from here, then she must not mind abandoning the graves. We sit outside by the fire, making small talk about our childhoods. As I glance up at the night sky I think fleetingly of Seema and that house on the lake in a far-off country . . . where the seasons progress in order and the world seemed safe. I notice that Janice does not see well at night, in spite of glasses, and Mungai rubs his leg with a rather

rough-looking home-prepared ointment. They go to neighbouring Sarotich sometimes when a travelling clinic comes by, I learn.

I wonder to myself if I kept the money here because I wanted to be
able to return one day to this simple primitiveness. As we sit watching the
glowing embers and inhaling woodsmoke, hearing the bark of a wild dog,
the crick-crick of insects, a radio far away crackling out strains of traditional dance music, there are no complicated questions between us. It is the
forest, in whose shadow we are, that owns us.

During the next two days I follow Mungai as he goes about his
chores. We dam up a branch of the stream to divert it from the back
yard. We set an overdue fire to a refuse heap and let it smoulder. We
plug leaks in the roof and walls of the house. There is a tea break and a
late lunch with homemade beer, following which we lie down for our
naps. In the afternoon, when the sun is low behind the trees and the air is
cool, we tend to the vegetable plot. It takes effort to recall the world I have
left behind. Perhaps it is here, I tell myself, that I should start my life anew,
a life as simple and pure as a mountain stream from the green misty
Aberdares. An empty, desperate dream, I know, for I am very much tied to
my world.

The morning of the third day I make an arduous trip to Sarotich,
where there is a post office with a pay phone, from which I call up Sohrabji.

Sohrabji says, Joseph's release should not be much of a problem, Vic.

Have you seen him?

Yes, and he's all right. Roughed up a bit, but what do you expect in detention. They like to use the water hose there, and starvation. His activities
in Canada are known to the Special Branch, they want to find out what
these MuKenya Patriots are up to in foreign parts—

Can you get him out?

Yes, provided he agrees to stay out of the country for a few years;
though the price of freedom, Vic, is steep. A lot of cash. Green.

I'll pay you the dollars, in cash. But is he agreed to the condition not to
return? Does he know it's I who am springing him?

Yes, and no. For the present he knows that it is his mother who is bail-
ing him out, with the help of friends and family. A few nights of detention

and interrogation under water torture have convinced him he doesn't want to return in a hurry. Did you know his girlfriend was killed in riots last year?

No, I did not know that.

A fleeting image comes to mind, the two of us sharing that house by the lake.

In the middle of the night—we have gone to bed after sitting around the fire telling proverbs—Janice lets out a sharp short scream. A heart-stopping terrifying scream in the still night, as if a small animal has been suddenly caught by a cruel predator and is now in the silence that follows being torn to pieces. The next morning, while Mungai and I sit in the back-yard having tea with bread, he confides that Janice has been having night-mares for about a year now. Sometimes sitting by herself she will start to cry. It's when she remembers her family, he says. Your presence and our talking together brought back memories. Once this happened after she picked up a foreign newspaper that chanced to be flying in the wind right here in this place; how the newspaper came here is a wonder. She had a few troubled nights then.

Have her relations with you altered? I ask.

No, he replies, it's just that her past life continues to haunt her. It will not be easy to leave those graves behind, but what can be done?

We find ourselves staring at the graves. A full-length one and two small ones. They have been covered with small shards of stone, carefully laid; and I notice something very strange: upon the stone blankets of the smaller graves have been placed a few random-looking objects—a couple of carved animals, a plastic ball, a police whistle . . .

Mungai says, We care for each other very much.

She happens to be passing by, on her way to throw out old water from a can, and she says, mutters, Yes, that we do.

She is a diffident woman, very British, but of a previous generation. She reminds me of some teachers I had who also never went back home to England.

Five days after my arrival, in the morning we drive to Sarotich, where they visit the market and post office, and I take my leave and head back to the bustling sansara of Nairobi with a heavy heart.

Craters cover the wounded lawless roads of Eastleigh, once the main Indian quarter of the city, and cars, buses, trucks, and pushcarts negotiate them painstakingly, riskily, one by one. Multitudes swarm these dusty streets, turned out in jeans and shirts, full-length veils with eye slits, head-and-shoulder scarves, long white kanzus and embroidered kofias. Sidewalk stalls add a dizzy brilliance of colour, selling everything from televisions to perfumes and toiletries, clothes and jewellery, furniture and mattresses; tall wooden frames loiter precariously at the street corners, like jugglers on stilts, tossing up in the air every variety and colour of track shoe; qat and bhang and Kalashnikovs too, says the lore, have sellers at this market clamouring with chatter, car horns, and music. In the quieter sidestreets, hair salons vie with bars and tire shops for space and attention. I remember staying with relatives a long time ago as a child of eight, in one of these houses that's now a bar and perhaps a brothel, and in later years coming with my father to collect rents for his Asian clients. This is a different country now, an alien planet, and the first language is not Punjabi but Somali. It is here that I have come to hide next.

I park the car inside the wide-open gate of an old apartment complex, in a gravelled greenless yard in which a few kids are at play among a couple of broken-down cars. They watch me with curiosity as I look around for a while, discover the staircase at the side of the leftmost building, and slowly go up. There is a screened partition halfway up at a landing, with a door, which I enter to see yet another door, to my right, opening into an apartment rich with the aroma of fresh garlicky chicken pilau. The landing floor is being scrubbed by a cleaning girl and two large cockroaches lie on their backs. I knock gently on the door and an African woman carrying a child bids me in. Is Ebrahim here? I ask. He's praying, she says and takes me to an old-style sitting room with gleaming linoleum on the floor, a prominent TV on a table, two armchairs with white knitted lace on the head-rests, and a bed. The woman, who is Ebrahim's wife, turns the TV on for me and leaves the room. A children's quiz show is on. Soon Ebrahim arrives, a broad, clean-shaven, medium-height Mombasa Arab, with a young bearded cousin in tow. He is friendly in a quiet way and has been expecting me as Victor De Souza. We shake hands, and immediately he invites me to have lunch; in such a household hospitality is not spurned, and bashfully I allow myself two helpings of pilau with kachumbar. The talk at the table is about public safety, the economy, and religion. After the meal, Ebrahim walks me to the apartment he has reserved for my use, a block away, above a shopping centre called the Mogadishu Mall.

The mall has been constructed, using lumber, as an extension and modification of a traditional Nairobi Indian dwelling once occupied by several families. We go past a sweet-smelling hallway full of young and old Somali women selling eastern perfume, into a maze of narrow passageways lined with all sorts of shops and sounding with at least three kinds of music, at the end of which is a staircase leading up to several apartments. The flat allocated to me belongs to one of Ebrahim's younger brothers; it is exactly at the head of the stairs and consists of two rooms. A window looks out at the noisy street below.

Ebrahim and his brothers are clients of Sohrabji, who represents them in a dispute with a car dealership that happens to be owned by a government minister. Ebrahim says he hopes that after this favour Sohrabji will be induced to hasten his case somewhat; it's been dragging on for a couple of years at least. I sympathize. He walks to the door and hollers down the stairs. A lanky youth from an electronics stall downstairs comes up. He is Salim, the brother who owns the apartment. Ebrahim instructs Salim to look after all my needs. Salim bows and shakes hands with me, then the brothers depart, leaving me to myself.

Vic, Vikram my friend, says Sohrabji warmly, how nice to see you after such a long time. He takes my hand and squeezes it. Listen, I would like to take you—when all this is over—to a sensational new Ethiopian restaurant in Hurlingham, a veritable treasure that brings an absolutely original addition to this city's cuisine . . .

And I am thinking there is no one as soft-spoken in Nairobi as this Parsee who looks like Mahatma Gandhi but eats and drinks like Falstaff.

He has come to see me at the apartment above the Mogadishu Mall, my first afternoon here. Salim has kindly brought up two teas for us and we sit beside the window facing each other, the clamour from the street down below audible in all its glory.

A far cry from Hilton, eh, Sohrabji says with a naughty smile, putting his cup to his mouth, but you can hide here till doomsday and no one would know. You know my own place is open to you, only it is watched all the time.

He looks anxious for a moment.

Don't worry, Sohrabji, this is fine here. I am grateful.

He nods, gratified, and says, Joseph is out, and he will be on his way to Toronto in a couple of days. His mother thanks you, and she says one day he will know what you did for him.

His father was the only true friend I had, I tell him.

But did you have to come all the way to Nairobi only for this, Vic?

Sohrabji, I told you to sound out the Anti-Corruption people—

He smiles sheepishly, says,

That I am doing, though I don't know why you want to bother. You should have stayed out there in the West. In any case, I have spoken to a couple of people already. As I understand it—and tell me where I'm wrong—you are willing to meet with the Commission and answer questions about some of your business dealings, specifically those related to the so-called Gemstone Scandal. As a goodwill gesture you will dispose of most of your wealth, part to the Commission and part to an approved foundation—and I assume you will keep enough for yourself and also to pay my fees. You have done things unethical but not illegal, and these were done with the approval of public servants. For your troubles you would like the Commission to declare publicly that it has no case against you.

You think they'll buy that?

One can only hope. It's a brilliant plan, but. You were the perfect scapegoat, an Indian without a constituency, whom they could hold up and display to the World Bank and the Donors as the crafty alien corruptor of our country. But they never expected you to talk. They cannot charge you without also charging an army of public servants and friends of government. If they prepare indictments, the evidence will disappear. And where do they start with indictments, corruption in this country goes back thirty years, reaches the very top, and even into the ranks of the opposition. Already there are whispers of a truth and reconciliation commission after the next elections—so we can start anew in this beautiful country that's been run off the tracks.

And you spoke to the businessmen? To Nderi?

To Nderi, yes, and a few others. There's the rub, Vic. They are scared of being made scapegoats like you, for a condition that's rampant. I've told them they have nothing to fear from you, you are going to focus only on Gemstone, as the Commission requested, about which it knows enough already. I believe they'll call off the goons; they feel safer with you here, amongst them. They do respect you—you are one of them after all.

From somewhere close by comes a call to prayer—a long, wavering arc of sound rising above the rooftops, a reminder to the faithful, a call to the Almighty. We find ourselves staring at each other, lost within the spell. How insignificant we seem at this moment, a shady businessman with his clever lawyer, in this hideaway reeking of paint and wood and youthful sweat.

At length, as the call subsides, Sohrabji smiles at me and says: Well.

I follow him downstairs to the street and we walk along the sidewalk market awhile. He pauses at a few places to inspect the goods, reading out designers' names for my benefit, bargaining with the vendors though not prepared to buy.

You know, he tells me, there are things you can buy here that you would not find downtown or in any of the fancy new malls you see going up in the suburbs. Stuff comes here all the way from the Persian Gulf, by ship and camel, road and railway. My daughter Roshnie will shop only at these stalls—they come here, the teenagers, though it's not really safe. Do you know, Ebrahim was carjacked only last month? They took him along with them on a spree of robberies, then left him tied to a tree in the woods near Ngong. He was lucky.

Sohrabji takes my cellphone, which I have hardly used, and gives me another, a brand-new one, as a precaution. Then he leaves.

It is impossible to believe that the bustling street down below could empty, but it did so, in the course of the night; now dawn's dull shadows emerge wraithlike from the walls. There comes the muffled chatter of the day's first newscast over the radio, perhaps from the restaurant down the block; then the sound of a child crying; the smell of fresh bread. The room feels claustrophobic, and there are bedbugs in the mattress, so I have slept only fitfully. I wish Deepa would call, or Seema. But Seema wouldn't, we parted with a finality that was absolute. She was bitter. The thought of her brings memories of that house by the lake: the pure, cool air, the clear night sky. I wonder if Papa has my new number. I had told him not to call except in an emergency.

I wonder, not for the first time, if I made the right decision, returning. By all the measures of practical common sense that I can summon, it was a foolish decision. But I could not have lived out the rest of my days an escapee from my world. I had to come back and face it—though I still await to emerge safely from this weird underground. Meanwhile I have prevailed upon Sohrabji to act for Joseph, and that has been a good outcome, surely. Ultimately I will have my say; and I will make my peace with my world.

The muezzin's call to prayer, then the street begins to fill up, the bustle rises to a crescendo and, to paraphrase the idols of my youth, I feel fine. A refreshing morning scene: children in uniforms traipsing off to school. I recall that Saint Teresa's is here, and the former Indian Primary School. Salim informs me there is a restaurant on a sidestreet a couple of blocks away that is owned by a Somali who returned from Canada. I tell him I will go there later perhaps, but meanwhile I have breakfast at a tea kiosk. For a lark I get a haircut at one of the beauty salons, then, carried away, I buy a kanzu and kofia and wear them like a devout Muslim. I don't know what is happening to me. In the evening Ebrahim takes me to his home for dinner. We eat by ourselves, the two of us, and the fare is mutton curry, Swahili chappati and rice. Ebrahim tells me that his wife is actually a Luo and theirs was a love marriage. He runs a charitable organization that sends teachers to the north of the country; he also collects sponsorships for the slaughter of goats during Eid. I don't fancy sponsoring the slaughter of a goat but I tell him I will donate to his charity. We watch TV until late and then he walks me back to my apartment. On the way he says to me casually, How did you manage to fool the National Bank like that? I stare at him, startled, and he says, I know who you are, Vikram Lall of the Gemstone Scandal. But don't worry, I will not give you away.

I dream of cockroaches. They are crawling all over the floor and climbing up my legs. Some of them fly and there are a few in my hair and one in my ear. All the while Ebrahim is entreating, have more curry, the coconut in the rice is really very fresh . . . I wake up in a sweat, my heart beating violently.

While I'm having a completely unnecessary lunch of spaghettini and tomato sauce at the Canadian Somali restaurant, Sohrabji calls.

Vic, he says, hardly able to control the thrill in his voice. About your offer to the Commission—it's settled. They are agreed.

Wonderful! Exactly what, but?

What you are offering is enough for them. The Donors and the World Bank will be pleased, all they want is some admission, after all, some accountability. You come clean on the Gemstone Scandal, you need not name names, you hand over the money; and you get a clean bill of health—you start anew. This is the first real break they've had since their mandate, Vic. The Commission is excited. Now they can hope other individuals will be persuaded to follow your example—and this could be the beginning of truth and reconciliation. Done, my friend!

We agree to talk again later to discuss details. Perhaps we'll go to that Ethiopian restaurant in Hurlingham that he was raving about.

And so when Deepa calls that night from Rochester, she couldn't have found me in better spirits. We are laughing. A new start, Deepa! Yes,

Bhaiya, a fresh start, a clean bill of health, how wonderful! I am so, so happy!

We plan the rest of our lives over the phone. She says she will call Seema and give her the news.

Friday at noon, Somali Town. Brilliant sunlight bastes the street down below, itself festive with the holiday spirit. It is one hour to jumaa prayer, men and boys in kofia and kanzu bustle about hither and thither. A man in shirt and pants walks by under my window singing, apparently in English. A young woman in a brown veil gives another, in a blue veil, a short chase; suddenly, as if sensing my gaze, they both look up at me, startled.

My cellphone rings. It is Sohrabji, and he sounds frantic and shrill.

Vic, did you hear? The Commission—the Anti-Corruption Commission has been declared illegal and disbanded!

What does that mean?

I don't know—for one thing, there is no one you have to explain to.

I am not sure that is what I want, Sohrabji. That's not a good thing at all.

Eh?—he sounds surprised but knows very well what I mean. We don't seem to have more to say to each other, and he says he'll ring again later.

For a long time I stare out my window at the tumult down below, turbulence of humanity swirling in the street. The two young veiled women have disappeared. A Land Rover is being pushed out of a pothole, the crowd flows smoothly around it. A boy of ten (I guess) waves at me. Finally the call to midday prayer begins, rises up over the rooftops, and languorously weaves a canopy of exotic sounds over our heads.

I can see no way out of my predicament.

I have been left dangling. I have been outsmarted. It's clear that powerful people close to the government prefer me to keep my mouth shut. I have no friends and my former partners—rightfully—don't trust me. I came ready to shed a large load off my shoulders; I was naïve in my expectations, which were inspired perhaps by an alien environment, but I also know that I had no choice. Now there is nowhere to put that load. It only makes me a target.

I spend the rest of the day reading papers and walking about the stores, a denizen of Somali Town in kanzu and cap. At four, time for the afternoon prayer, I walk into a small mosque in a sidestreet. It is dark and cool inside and I go and stand against the back wall. I cannot follow all the motions of the devotees but I sit and stand and turn left and right as they do. Once again I don't know what is happening to me, perhaps I simply long to belong somewhere. Later, at seven, I have dinner with Ebrahim, after which we walk about the streets. He asks me if I want to visit a prostitute, a clean one, guaranteed. I decline. Back in my room I cannot sleep.

In the morning Papa calls, tells me Sohrabji was taken away by police the previous evening. He insists on seeing me and comes in his car and drives me out to an Indian restaurant in Ngara. Like everything else in Ngara it has seen better days. Next door, Papa had his first business in Nairobi and hated it.

They took him away on Friday so they could keep him till Monday, says my father.

All I can do is nod back glumly at him. For all I know, Sohrabji is in front of a water hose right now, his thin body pinned to the wall by the force of the jet.

You know, Vic, you can stay with me, says Papa.

No, I told you, Papa. In fact I told you to take a holiday in Mombasa.

He is silent awhile. Then: Vic—you know, I'm living with someone—

I am aware, Papa. Deepa told me.

How did she know?

She finds out things.

You know, she's African, Vic.

I nod.

She is a comfort to me and looks after me. Do you think it's wrong of me? A man gets lonely . . . Is it wrong, son?

He desperately craves approval, acknowledgement—a lonely old man who wants to be loved. All I can do is tell him, You did the right thing,

Papa. There's nothing wrong with it. You have to go on living, Mother would understand that.

We go to the temple, and we do our round of the murtis separately, each to make our peace with our gods. Then we take a walk, a few times briskly round the temple grounds. Finally he drops me off at the apartment in Eastleigh. He gives me a tight hug before he leaves.

————————

Sunday night. I wake up sweaty and hot. There is violent banging on the door.

Fire! Moto! shouts Salim at my face when I open the door.

Where, Salim? Wapi?

Right here, he says, this building is on fire! Get out! Get out!

He runs, is already halfway down the stairs before turning to look back at me. There is a glow behind him, which gives his sweat-run face a red gloss. Not only is this mall extension made of wood, the products on sale are extremely flammable. There are explosions in the distance. Hot air engulfs us. But there is no sign of a fire engine or of attempts to combat the conflagration.

Come quickly down, pleads Salim, the stairs will go soon! Tafadhali, Bwana! . . .

Smoke rises around me.

Wait! I shout at him. Here, hang on to this—go, run, I will follow you . . .

AUTHOR'S NOTE

I am greatly indebted to a number of people, who have assisted me in various ways in various places during the writing of this novel. They are, first, Sultan and Zera Somjee, Radha Upadhyaya, Shariffa and Yusuf Keshavjee, Neera and Suresh Kapila, Muzaffar Khan, Begum and Pyarali Karim, and Susan Linee of Reuters, all of Nairobi. They welcomed me warmly and gave much of their time and knowledge. Bethwell Kiplagat shared his knowledge and experience during a stimulating conversation in Nairobi; Kariuki wa Thuku volunteered many hours of candid discussions in Nairobi and Nyeri; Pheroze Nowrojee was a wealth of information and insight; and two wazees of Nyeri, who knew the freedom struggle from up close and had learned to forgive, and selectively to forget, with twinkling eyes presented me with enigmas to solve. Harish Narang and Pankaj Singh supplied me with information, checked my Punjabi, and read the manuscript; my wife Nurjehan provided her usual thorough reading; Miguna Miguna took time off from a busy schedule to clear up some language matters; Rashid Mughal shared his enthusiasm and remembrances of Nairobi; Benegal and Debbie Pereira of New Hampshire generously opened up their house and their library to me. Benegal's stories about his father Eddie's days in Nakuru and his own enthusiasm for the railways were an inspiration for which I owe an extra debt of gratitude. The Asian Heritage

Exhibition, which had just opened in Nairobi as I began my inquiries, was an inspiration and a visual aid. It was a long time coming, this acknowledgement of identity, history, and heritage, and I hope it prevails. I also wish to acknowledge here the friendly facilities of the Kenya National Archives, the basement of the Macmillan Library in Nairobi, the generous and efficient though forbiddingly hushed-tone services of the Rhodes House library in Oxford, England, and the indifferently helpful New York Public Library. Finally, it is with sorrow that I acknowledge my debt and gratitude to Jayant Ruparel, who met with a tragic death in Ethiopia soon after our last meeting; his enthusiasm and love for his native city Nairobi were inspiring, his knowledge of its history was extremely useful, and the kindness and hospitality of his family often left me speechless.

I must also thank Stella Sandahl for providing me with a refuge within the dark labyrinths of Robarts Library; my agent, Bruce Westwood, and his associates for their enthusiasm; my editor, Maya Mavjee, for her solicitous readings and many suggestions; Nick Massey-Garrison for his patient assistance with the manuscript; and Sonny Mehta for his comments and suggestions. As always, my gratitude to my wife and sons for their unflagging support and their faith that going away each February was not only to escape winter.

Finally, some explanations. My usages of Kiswahili (or Swahili), Kikuyu, Hindi, Punjabi and Gujarati should be self-explanatory in their contexts. It should be noted that the terms "Indian" and "Asian" are interchangeable in this book, being terms in use in East Africa and meaning "South Asian" in today's language, and "European" denotes "white." This is a work of fiction. Although real public figures, especially the late President Jomo Kenyatta and the late J. M. Kariuki, appear in this novel, they do so as fictional characters only.

The Eliot quote in the epigraph is from *T. S. Eliot: The Complete Poems and Plays* (Harcourt Brace, 1971); the Swahili proverb is from *Swahili Sayings 2*, by S. S. Farsi (Kenya Literature Bureau, 1998).

M. G. Vassanji was born in Kenya and raised in Tanzania. Before moving to Canada in 1978, he attended M.I.T. and later was writer in residence at the University of Iowa. Vassanji is the author of five acclaimed novels: *The Gunny Sack* (1989), which won a regional Commonwealth Prize; *No New Land* (1991); *The Book of Secrets* (1994), which won the Giller Prize and the Bressani Prize; *Amriika* (1999); and *The In-Between World of Vikram Lall*, which won the 2003 Giller Prize. He is also the author of a collection of short stories, *Uhuru Street* (1992). He was awarded the Harbourfront Festival Prize in 1994 in recognition of his achievement in and contribution to the world of letters, and was in the same year chosen as one of twelve Canadians on Maclean's Honour Roll. Vassanji lives in Toronto with his wife and two sons.

A NOTE ON THE TYPE

Pierre Simon Fournier *le jeune*, who designed the type used in this book, was both an originator and a collector of types. His services to the art of printing were his design of letters, his creation of ornaments and initials, and his standardization of type sizes. His types are old style in character and sharply cut. In 1764 and 1766 he published his *Manuel typographique*, a treatise on the history of French types and printing, on typefounding in all its details, and on what many consider his most important contribution to typography—the measurement of type by the point system.

Composed by Stratford Publishing Services,
Brattleboro, Vermont

Printed and bound by Berryville Graphics,
Berryville, Virginia